Kate El'   and
studie   vinning
auth   Wesley Peterson detective novels, as well
as the Albert Lincoln trilogy and the Joe Plantagenet
mysteries.

Kate has won the CWA Dagger in the Library Award for
her crime writing. She has also twice been shortlisted for
the CWA Short Story Dagger and been longlisted for the
Theakston's Old Peculier Crime Novel of the Year Award.

Visit Kate Ellis online:

www.kateellis.co.uk
@KateEllisAuthor

Praise for Kate Ellis:

'A beguiling author who interweaves past and present'
The Times

'Clever plotting hides a powerful story
of loss, malice and deception'
Ann Cleeves

'Haunting'
Independent

'The chilling plot will keep you spooked
and thrilled to the end'
Closer

'Ellis skilfully interweaves ancient and
crimes in an impe
Publish

KATE ELLIS

SERPENT'S POINT

PIATKUS

PIATKUS

First published in Great Britain in 2022 by Piatkus
This paperback edition published in 2023 by Piatkus

1 3 5 7 9 10 8 6 4 2

A CIP catalogue record for this book
is available from the British Library.

ISBN 978-0-349-42575-7

Typeset in New Baskerville by M Rules
Printed and bound in Great Britain by
Clays Ltd, Elcograf S.p.A

Papers used by Piatkus are from well-managed forests
and other responsible sources.

Piatkus
An imprint of
Little, Brown Book Group
Carmelite House
50 Victoria Embankment
London EC4Y 0DZ

An Hachette UK Company
www.hachette.co.uk

www.littlebrown.co.uk

1

The bridegroom had strangler's hands. Strong hands. Restless hands. Hands that could squeeze the life out of some unsuspecting victim. Susan didn't like the bridegroom.

Not being invited to her best friend's wedding hurt like a knife twisted in the stomach. Susan had known Avril since primary school. They had played together, laughed together, cried together. But not any more. Not since Avril had met him. Not since he'd set about separating her from her friends and family.

Susan had decided to stand outside the register office. If Avril saw her, at least she'd know she was there for her.

But when the moment came and they emerged from the building, her courage failed her and she darted into a shop doorway. It was just the two of them, bride and groom, Avril wearing a floral dress and her new husband in an expensive suit. No bouquet. No buttonhole. A couple of strangers Susan didn't recognise followed behind sheepishly, muttered awkward congratulations then walked off together. Witnesses dragged in off the street, perhaps? There were no family members at the wedding – and no friends either. Just Avril and Ian alone. Avril gazed adoringly at her new husband as he bent to give her a half-hearted kiss.

As Susan watched them walk off together, she was afraid for her friend. But there was nothing she could do about it. Some people were their own worst enemies.

Five years later

The story of Serpent's Point featured in all the books of local legends for sale in the tourist shops of south Devon, but Susan knew it was just a fanciful tale that had grown up over the years. A painted devil to scare foolish children. Evil came from people, not places.

It was said that many centuries ago, a huge serpent, guided by his master, Satan, stole the promontory from the sea, and that the creature still lived there beneath the ground, surfacing every now and then to make mischief. In centuries gone by, superstitious farmers claimed the land was cursed, but that had never stopped them grazing their livestock there. Economics beat the devil any day.

With the coast path so close to her new temporary home, she liked to begin each day with a walk to clear her head. That morning she followed the now familiar route, pausing every now and then, as she always did, to take in the wide vista of the sea spread out before her, its ripples sparkling like jewels as they caught the sun. Sometimes a large cargo vessel crawled lazily across the horizon, but today there were only yachts with gleaming sails. And whenever she saw one, she couldn't help wondering whether *he* was aboard.

As the day was young and the schools hadn't yet started their summer break, she found herself alone on the path with all that beauty to herself. She breathed in the sea air and closed her eyes for a few seconds, listening to the cries of the gulls wheeling overhead and the buzz of the bees in the hedgerow. With the rolling green landscape to one side and the calm sea to the other, this was the nearest thing to heaven she'd ever experienced. But she knew she mustn't forget why she was there. She was so close to finding the evidence she needed, and only when she'd accomplished her mission would she resume her normal life. Justice would roll down from the mountains eventually – but not quite yet.

The sound of approaching footsteps made her turn, bracing herself for the walkers' ritual of bidding each other good morning with a suitably friendly smile.

But a few minutes later, she was lying beside the path, her dead eyes staring up at the summer sky.

2

Olivia Stanley, known to her friends as Livy, had never imagined that her unusual Christmas present would give her so many hours of entertainment – along with the added possibility that it might one day change her life. Once her friend Sophie had bought one too, using her birthday money, they hunted as a pair. Two metal detectors were better than one because they could cover twice the area. Twice the area, double the chances of making their fortune. The other girls at school were into make-up and clothes, but it would be Livy and Sophie who'd have the best of everything one day – once they'd hit the jackpot.

Livy's dad owned the field, so they didn't need permission, although he had told her that when they found treasure, he wanted his share. She couldn't tell whether he was serious, but she'd agreed. Of course he'd get his cut.

To Sophie's relief, Livy's dad had moved the cows into another field. Unlike her friend, she hadn't been raised on a farm and didn't care for the way the big reddish-brown beasts watched her with their knowing, hostile eyes, as though they were planning something nasty. And sheep were almost as bad, with their beady-eyed, insolent stares. Livy, who was used to livestock, told her she was a wimp.

The field sloped gently towards a high hedge, beyond which lay the coast path and the wide area of scrubland leading to the clifftop. A few hundred yards away to the left, the girls could see the grey slate roof and tall chimneys of a large house, half hidden behind a row of trees. Sophie didn't know who lived there, but on the way to call for Livy she'd seen a lot of activity on the lane. Huge vans standing in front of the house and people milling about in strange clothes. She told Livy she'd heard in the village that they were making a film there, and suggested they should go and take a look. But Livy pointed out that they were on a quest that might make them rich one day, so they could do without distractions.

'Ready?'

'Ready,' Sophie replied.

They walked slowly forward, a little apart but keeping to a straight line as they swept their machines from side to side. Their faces were set in concentration, listening for any telltale bleeps in their headphones.

Sophie came to a sudden halt and Livy looked round. 'Got a signal?'

Without a word, Sophie took her trowel from her pocket and handed it to her friend. She'd borrowed the trowel from her mum's garden shed without asking, but she knew it wouldn't be missed. Her mum wasn't much of a gardener.

As Livy squatted down and started to dig, Sophie watched with growing excitement. It might be a ring pull from a can, a length of barbed wire or a rusty old nail. Or it could be long-lost treasure: gold coins or a priceless jewel. She watched her friend heaping the soil to one side of the hole, feeling like a gambler in the casino at Monte Carlo, waiting for the roulette wheel's rattling ball to land on her chosen number. Would this be the big win?

But one look at Livy's face told her they hadn't beaten the bank just yet. The object in her soil-stained hand was a large nail, coated with brown rust. But their luck was bound to change soon.

'Early days,' said Livy philosophically as she replaced the soil under the flap of turf. 'Rome wasn't built in a day,' she added. She'd heard the phrase once and it seemed an appropriate thing to say.

Half an hour later, the girls had found three rusty bolts, possibly from some ancient farm machinery, five pieces of barbed wire and a small toy car that had lost its paintwork – their best find so far.

It was coming up to midday and they were grateful to their mums for providing sandwiches, crisps and cans of fizzy drink in case they were hungry. Their school friends would probably scoff at the way they were spending their free post-exam time, so they'd made an unspoken pact never to mention it – and nobody was likely to see them there.

'Let's do a bit more before we have something to eat,' Sophie suggested when she saw Livy looking longingly at the rucksacks abandoned next to the boundary hedge.

Livy didn't argue. They began walking again, their optimism flagging along with their energy levels. They could hear voices drifting over on the breeze, possibly coming from the big house with the huge vans outside. When they'd finished in the field, they might sneak over there to see what was going on. But in the meantime, they needed to focus.

Sweep, sweep. They trudged on. Still nothing.

Then Livy heard an urgent screaming in her headphones. She'd got a signal. And it sounded strong. She tapped Sophie on the shoulder and pointed to a patch of ground.

Sophie watched as her friend started to dig again. She clenched her fists with excitement. Was this the big one they'd been waiting for? Or was it just another rusty nail?

After a minute or so, Livy pulled something from the clinging earth, holding it up in triumph like the Lady of the Lake wielding Excalibur.

'What is it?'

'It's a coin.'

Sophie felt a stab of disappointment. An old penny, perhaps, with Queen Victoria's head on if they were lucky. But when Livy passed her the trophy, her heart lifted. It was dull, but it could be silver, and she didn't recognise the roughly embossed face on the front.

'What do you think?' Livy asked.

'Looks really old. Could be worth a fortune.'

Livy passed the metal detector over the earth again and got another signal, even stronger this time. Her heart pounded as she enlarged the hole and saw another coin lying there against the red soil, shining and undimmed by its long burial. She knew that meant it was gold. This was it! This was what they'd dreamed of. They were going to be rich.

Sophie fell to her knees. She was wearing her oldest jeans, so a bit of dirt didn't matter, not under the circumstances.

'We should tell my dad,' Livy said. 'And maybe a museum.'

'Or we could flog 'em on eBay.'

The girls sat side by side, torn between the devil of greed whispering in one ear and the angel of the Portable Antiquities Scheme in the other.

But later on, when the police arrived, the decision was made for them.

From the journal of Dr Aldus Claye

May 1921

I have left Exeter and taken the house at Serpent's Point on a five-year lease, which should allow me sufficient time to conduct my investigations. The elderly widow who owns the property has gone to live with her sister in Axminster, and according to her solicitor, she no longer has use for the large house, which has become a burden to her in recent years. However, it is a burden I am happy to assume because of an interesting fact that has come to my attention.

I first heard of the strange discovery when I dined with Professor Fredericks, a former colleague from the British Museum. It seems the small sheet of lead was unearthed by a farmer in a south Devon field just before the war, and he gave it into the care of his local vicar because he thought it might interest him. The vicar, being familiar with Latin, had little difficulty making the translation, and when he discovered that it appeared to be a curse of some kind, he thought it a curiosity that might intrigue anybody who had a particular interest in the history of the Roman occupation of Britannia. That was when a friend put the reverend gentleman in touch with Professor Fredericks, who contacted me, knowing my passion for the subject.

There was, however, something the farmer failed to mention to the vicar, something I learned when I paid the man a visit six months ago to enquire as to the exact location of his strange find. At first he was reluctant to share the information with me, but when I assured him that my sole interest was the history of the site and promised not to alert the authorities, he confessed that the object in question wasn't his only discovery. He had also found bones, but had stayed silent about this because, in his own words, he didn't want all those policemen in their size twelve boots trampling over his field frightening his livestock. I told him I understood perfectly, and so it was that I gained his permission to investigate.

I have been made aware that the farmer has an unwritten arrangement with my new landlady to use that particular field to graze his cattle, as she has no use for it. I will consult my solicitor, but I suspect this means that, as the tenant of Serpent's Point, I am free to use the land as I wish, with or without the farmer's permission.

There is a fear at the back of my mind that the human remains the farmer found might belong to a victim of violent death – and yet the possibility that the bones might be connected with the curse excites me greatly. I must know the truth behind the strange discovery, for should my suspicions be proved correct, my standing in the world of antiquarian study will be greatly enhanced.

My wife looks pale and I tell her that she must get more fresh air. The countryside around here is most conducive to walking. Perhaps I will persuade her, although I have discovered since our marriage that she possesses an unfortunately stubborn nature.

3

DCI Gerry Heffernan stood at the entrance of the crime scene tent, newly erected beside the dusty path, and stared at the body. She was lying face up, limbs at an awkward angle as though she'd been felled by an unexpected blow and crumpled suddenly to the ground.

'Have we got an ID for her yet?'

The dead woman was probably in her mid thirties, dressed in shorts, sensible walking boots and a T-shirt apparently extolling the virtues of a brand of real ale. She was petite, and her fair hair was swept back into an untidy bun. She must have been an attractive woman in life, but now her face was contorted and her eyes bulged in amazement.

'Sorry, sir,' said the tall young CSI, who was dressed in what Gerry always referred to as a snowman suit. 'There's no bag and nothing in her pockets apart from this.' Lying in his plastic-gloved palm was a small and unremarkable Yale key. 'It was wedged inside the pocket of her shorts. House key?'

'Possibly,' said Gerry as he took the key and glanced at the man standing to his left. He'd always acknowledged that DI Wesley Peterson was the brains of the team, and now he watched as Wesley studied the body in front of them as though he was willing it to give up its secrets.

'First impressions, Wes?'

'From the marks on her neck, I'd say the cause of death was strangulation. Her clothing appears undisturbed, which suggests the motive wasn't sexual.' Wesley checked his watch. 'Colin should be here by now.'

'It's not Colin. He's on holiday.' Gerry grunted in disapproval, as though taking a holiday was a gross misdemeanour.

'We can't keep him locked up in the mortuary just in case we need him, Gerry.'

'More's the pity.'

Wesley couldn't help smiling. Over the years, Gerry had become used to Dr Colin Bowman's genial presence whenever there was a suspicious death to deal with. And Gerry didn't like change.

'So who's his replacement?'

'Me.'

The two men turned their heads and saw a young man standing a few feet outside the tent's open entrance. He was tall, with short dark hair and a pleasant freckled face, and he was already wearing his crime-scene suit in preparation for what was to come.

'Dr Cornell Stamoran at your service.' He grinned, raising a plastic-gloved hand in salute. 'Colin's on holiday. Vienna.'

'We know,' said Wesley. 'I'm DI Wesley Peterson and this is DCI Gerry Heffernan, the SIO.'

'Your name's familiar,' said Gerry accusingly.

'Cornell's a family name. I share it with a cousin who

11

lives in Lyme Regis.' The doctor paused for a moment, as though he was trying to retrieve something from his memory. 'I remember my cousin saying he had a visit from the police a few years ago, in connection with a murder case, I think. That wasn't you, was it?'

Wesley smiled. 'It was. Small world. He's a writer, isn't he?'

'That's right. The artistic side of the family.' Stamoran suddenly assumed a businesslike expression. 'Well, what have we got?'

'The dead woman was found an hour ago by a couple out walking the coast path. Tourists – retired teachers staying in a holiday cottage in Stoke Beeching. They've been interviewed and told to go home – they seemed pretty upset.'

'I'd better take a look.' The doctor picked up the bag he'd put down at his feet and Wesley lifted the crime-scene tape to admit him into the inner cordon, announcing his arrival to the sergeant whose job it was to record the comings and goings. Wesley followed him, with Gerry trailing reluctantly behind.

'Do we know who she is yet?' Stamoran asked as he squatted down beside the body.

'No ID apparently,' Wesley answered. 'I've ordered a search of the lane nearby for a vehicle she might have arrived in, but nothing's been found yet. We don't know how far she walked, so if she parked some distance away, it might take a while to find her car. Or she might be local and didn't need a car to get here.'

'Think her killer might have been walking with her?' Gerry asked.

'There are no car keys on the body, so that's as good a

theory as any. If her companion took the keys and returned to the car . . . '

'In which case, he could be anywhere by now.'

'Not like you to be so pessimistic, Gerry.'

The DCI didn't reply, and they watched in silence as the doctor conducted his examination. Unlike Colin, Cornell Stamoran didn't chat while he worked. Instead he concentrated on the task in hand, and Wesley was content to wait in the sunshine for him to finish, listening to the soft swish of the waves below and the cries of the gulls wheeling around the headland. Gerry, however, wasn't blessed with the same patience.

'Well?' the DCI said as soon as the doctor stood up.

'She hasn't been dead for long – two or three hours probably, but I might be able to tell you more once I've done the post-mortem.' He shifted to one side. 'Can you see those marks on her neck?'

'Strangulation?'

'Got it in one, Detective Inspector.'

'Call me Wesley, please.'

'Very well, Wesley, you're probably spot on – unless the post-mortem throws up some surprises. He didn't use his bare hands. She was killed with a ligature of some kind. A scarf, perhaps, or an item of clothing. Something soft that didn't leave a distinctive mark; not a rope.'

'You said he.'

'Well, Detective Chief Inspector, I wouldn't rule out a strong woman. They are capable of murder, you know.'

'Too right. The female of the species and all that. And my name's Gerry.'

Wesley looked down at the body. The T-shirt the dead woman was wearing showed a wide-eyed sheep holding a brimming pint glass. 'This T-shirt might provide a clue. Ritter's Sheep Shocker. Heard of it, Gerry?'

'Are you suggesting that I'm the authority on all things beer?'

'I know you like your real ale.'

'The name's not familiar. It could be a micro brewery limited to a few outlets – which might make our job a bit easier.'

'I'll get someone onto it,' said Wesley, thinking of his old friend from university; in his experience, archaeologists tended to know about that sort of thing. 'Neil and his colleagues might be able to help us.'

'I don't doubt it,' Gerry muttered under his breath. 'When can you do the PM, Doc?'

'How about four thirty today?'

'Perfect. We'll be there, won't we, Wes?' Gerry's eyes focused on the dead woman. 'Bet she didn't expect to end up like this when she set off for her morning walk.'

Wesley stayed silent as he watched the doctor pack up his things.

'Sir,' said a young uniformed constable who was standing outside the cordon, shifting from foot to foot like a child asking to be excused. 'Can I have a word?'

'Have as many as you like,' said Gerry wearily. 'What can I do you for?'

Wesley followed the DCI to the barrier of blue and white tape, eager to hear what the constable had to say.

'A couple of girls were metal-detecting over there.' He waved his hand vaguely towards the fields inland from the path. 'They heard the commotion and came over to see what was going on. They've been there most of the morning, so they might have seen something. Do you want a word?'

'Metal-detecting. Sounds like your department, Wes. I'd better get back and organise an incident room.'

'Right,' said Wesley to the constable. 'Let's have a word with our treasure hunters.'

4

Wesley left the shelter of the crime-scene tent and strolled over to the girls. The chances of them having anything to do with the woman's death were slim to say the least. But they might have seen something, and he knew that the best way to put them at ease was to talk about their hobby.

Sitting on the grass verge like a pair of prisoners awaiting sentencing, they looked very young: one small and slight with dark hair, the other taller and plumper with a blonde ponytail. Their youthful faces were marred by the occasional pimple, and they appeared almost puzzled, as though they'd stumbled into an unfamiliar situation and found themselves out of their depth. Their adventure had now turned serious.

'Morning,' Wesley said, trying to put them at their ease.

'Morning,' they mumbled warily, as though they were wondering what this good-looking, smartly dressed black man with the friendly smile was up to.

'I'm Detective Inspector Wesley Peterson. What are your names?'

'Olivia Stanley and Sophie Carter. We're not in trouble, are we?'

'I shouldn't think so. I see you've been metal-detecting.'

He saw the girls exchange a sly look. They were hiding something. Perhaps he'd have to revise his initial impression.

'I studied archaeology at university, so I know a bit about it. Find anything interesting?'

There was a long silence. Then Olivia delved into the pocket of her jeans and brought out a coin, holding it out like an offering.

Wesley took it from her and examined it closely. 'Where exactly did you find this?' he asked, trying not to sound too excited.

'We didn't do anything wrong,' Sophie piped up. 'It's Livy's dad's field and he said it was OK. You can ask him.'

'I'm sure you did everything properly.' He wanted their co-operation, and the best way to get it was to appear to be on their side. 'It's just that it's unusual to find this sort of thing around here, so it might be important. Find anything else?'

The girls looked at each other again, then Olivia put her hand back in her pocket and pulled out another coin. It had the telltale glint of gold, and Wesley's heart began to beat a little faster.

'I expect the constable told you there's been an incident on the coast path?' he said. Even though his inner voice was screaming at him that he might have stumbled on something of archaeological importance, murder took priority.

'She didn't say what had happened. Has someone had an accident, or—'

'They wouldn't make this much fuss for an accident,' Sophie butted in.

'You're right,' said Wesley. 'A woman's body has been

found, and we're treating her death as suspicious. Have you been metal-detecting in the field all morning?'

Both girls nodded their heads.

'Did you see or hear anything unusual?'

'We had our headphones on most of the time, and you can't see the path from where we were because of the hedgerow.' Livy glanced at her friend, who nodded in agreement.

'What time did you arrive this morning?'

It was Sophie who answered. 'I called at Livy's about ten.' She waved her hand in the vague direction of the stone-built farmhouse nestling on the hillside a few fields away. 'We asked her dad if it was OK, then we walked down here.'

'You did everything properly,' said Wesley with an approving smile. 'Where do you live, Sophie?'

'In Bereton. We finished our exams last week, so we've got time off.'

'How did the exams go?'

Livy looked surprised and rather gratified that the detective was taking an interest. 'OK.'

Wesley was about to say that it was good to see the girls out enjoying the fresh air instead of being hunched in front of screens in their bedrooms, but he stopped himself just in time. He didn't want to sound like a critical dad.

'Did you happen to see a woman? Fair-haired, dressed in shorts and a T-shirt with a picture of a sheep on the front?'

The girls shook their heads. 'We didn't see anybody. It was dead quiet until we heard someone screaming, then all the police arrived, and the helicopter.'

'What time did you hear the screams?'

'About half eleven, and then we heard the sirens soon afterwards. We thought someone had had an accident.'

Wesley nodded. The walkers had found the body around 11.30. 'You didn't hear or see anything unusual before then?'

They looked at each other again before Sophie answered. 'When I was walking to Livy's, I saw a lot of people at the big house over there.' She pointed towards a distant dark grey roof, just visible between the tall surrounding trees.

'What can you tell me about them?'

'They were wearing old-fashioned costumes, and there were big vans there.'

'I think they're making a film, or it could be TV,' said Livy.

'Maybe they'll be looking for extras,' Sophie added hopefully. 'Might be worth a try.'

Wesley smiled again. 'It won't do any harm to ask.'

He was coming to the conclusion that talking to the girls hadn't been a waste of time. If the woman had been killed before they arrived in the field at around 10.30, this fitted with Dr Stamoran's initial assessment. And he now knew there was a film set just half a mile from the murder scene. Could the woman have been associated with the filming? Even if she wasn't, somebody there might have information.

In the meantime, there was something else he wanted to know. He glanced in the direction of the crime scene. It looked as though Gerry had everything under control, and what he had in mind wouldn't take long.

'Can you show me exactly where you found the coins?'

The girls didn't hesitate, and when they reached the spot, they stood there like proud big sisters showing off a new baby. Wesley asked them to sweep over the area again, and both machines got a signal, suggesting that there was something else down there to discover. But he knew that

any further investigation ought to be carried out by someone who knew what they were doing.

He took out his phone and selected the number of
his old friend from university, Dr Neil Watson, who now
worked for the County Archaeological Unit. This was something he'd want to know about.

The two constables who walked up the weed-infested gravel
drive of Serpent's Point were greeted by a strange sight.
They were used to conducting routine house-to-house
enquiries, but this was a first.

The house was Georgian, with sash windows and a
columned portico, an entrance any heroine of a Regency
romance would be happy to emerge from. But today there
were no elegant carriages. Instead, three massive dark
green vans were parked out front, concealing the ground-
floor windows. The logo on the side of the vans said
ForberFilms, and thick black cables stretched between the
vehicles and the house like giant umbilical cords.

The officers looked at each other, wondering if this was
an appropriate moment to intrude on the filming. But even
if they'd chosen a bad time, it couldn't be helped. This was
a murder inquiry.

Twenty minutes later, they called DCI Heffernan's
number and told him they'd spoken to a few people but
they hadn't been particularly helpful. If CID paid them a
call, however, they might be inclined to be more open.

5

'Your Pam'll be interested when you tell her about this,' said Gerry as they came to a halt halfway up the drive and watched the film crew hurrying to and fro.

'Wonder what they're filming.'

'Maybe something by Jane Austen, from the look of the costumes,' said Gerry. 'My Kathy used to love her Jane Austen. Mind you, I was no Mr Darcy, even in those days.'

Wesley turned his head and saw a wistful expression on Gerry's face, the same look that always appeared whenever he mentioned his late wife, who'd been killed in a hit-and-run accident many years ago. The DCI now lived with his new partner, Joyce, who worked at Morbay Register Office, but any mention of Kathy still caused a flash of grief, there for a moment then quickly suppressed. Pain like that never went away. You just learned to live with it.

Wesley suspected that Gerry had guessed correctly. Along with the technical crew and assorted people wandering around with clipboards, there were several actors in Regency costume, some with twenty-first-century jackets and cardigans draped over their shoulders as they studied their scripts.

Nobody took any notice of the two officers as they made

for the open front door. Wesley had the key found on the dead woman, and before he entered the house, he took it out of its plastic evidence bag and tried it in the lock. To his disappointment, it wasn't a fit.

Once inside, he looked for the person in charge. The door to a stylish drawing room stood open, and when they crossed the threshold, they saw a middle-aged man with long grey hair tied back in a ponytail from his vulpine face. He was sitting on an antique chaise longue studying a clipboard, and as soon as Wesley and Gerry entered, he looked up and scowled.

'Get out. Now.'

'I don't think so, sir,' said Wesley as they produced their ID. 'DI Peterson and DCI Heffernan, Tradmouth CID. I'm afraid we need to ask you and your colleagues some questions. And you are?'

The man rolled his eyes theatrically. 'Crispin Joss. Director of this bloody fiasco.'

Wesley took his notebook from his pocket. The officers who'd called earlier to make initial enquiries had noted that Joss was uncooperative – and that they thought he might be holding something back.

'Filming not going too well, then?' said Gerry. He didn't sound sympathetic.

'We've had bloody coppers here this morning going on about some woman who's got herself killed on the cliff path. I told them I hadn't seen her, whoever she is. She's nothing to do with the shoot. Cast and crew all accounted for. They're coming back to take statements from everyone sometime this afternoon, which is all I bloody need. We're behind with shooting already because of that rain a fortnight ago. The weather in this bloody country ...'

'What are you filming?' asked Wesley.

Joss sighed. 'It's called *The Awakening of Lillith Montmorency*, an erotic coming-of-age drama set in the Regency period.' He smiled. 'Although I doubt very much if Miss Austen would have approved.'

Wesley caught Gerry's eye. 'I see. How long have you been here?'

'We started filming three weeks ago, but the way things are going, we'll be here till Doomsday.'

'So you'll be around if we need a word.' There was a threat in Gerry's statement, and Wesley saw a shadow of apprehension pass across the director's face.

'Look, I can't tell you anything, and nor can anyone else here,' Joss said impatiently. You're wasting your time and mine.'

'Where are you staying?'

Joss hesitated, as though he was reluctant to part with the information. 'The Sandview Hotel.'

Wesley knew the place. The large white building stood on the waterfront between Tradmouth and Bereton and had a reputation for luxury. 'Very nice. Is everyone staying there?'

'No. The main actors have found a B & B and the technical crew and supporting cast are at a caravan park nearby. It's a bit run-down, but they're used to that sort of thing.'

'Isn't the English class system wonderful,' Gerry murmured in Wesley's ear. Wesley hoped the director hadn't overheard.

'Are you quite sure you haven't seen anybody answering the dead woman's description around here? She was wearing a T-shirt advertising a real ale called Ritter's Sheep Shocker. Ring any bells?'

Joss shook his head.

'Who owns this property?'

'Grey Grover. He's more likely to know something than we are. We're just birds of passage. Here today, gone tomorrow.'

'Where can we find him?'

'He'll be in the library.' The director must have seen the puzzled look on Gerry's face, and expanded on his statement. 'Not the public library; he has one of his own. Out into the hall and third door on your left.' He picked up his clipboard again, a signal that the interview was over.

Even though he'd taken a dislike to the man, Wesley suspected there might be some truth in what he said. The cast and crew most likely kept themselves to themselves. And the victim hadn't looked like the type of woman who moved in the world of film production – although you never could tell. He gave Gerry a nudge. If they needed to speak to Joss again, they knew where to find him. The owner of Serpent's Point was a more promising prospect.

They found the door to the library ajar, and when they pushed it open, they saw a man lounging on a threadbare sofa in the centre of the large, elegantly proportioned room. But the proportions were the only elegant thing about it. Unlike the drawing room, there were no antiques here. Instead, the furniture was either shabby second-hand or the cheapest available modern chipboard. Bookshelves lined the walls, but the books they'd once held had been replaced by an eclectic mixture of objects, mainly what Wesley would have categorised as tourist tat: tribal masks, big-eyed donkeys wearing sombreros, a cluster of models of the Statue of Liberty and a fluorescent Eiffel Tower. If they were souvenirs of travel, their purchaser hadn't chosen wisely. Wesley wouldn't have given them house room. There was a row of books about modern art on a far shelf, along with a few paperback best-sellers. A collection of garish abstracts hung on the unoccupied walls, and some smaller canvases were propped up untidily on the shelves amongst the souvenirs.

The man looked up as they entered and stubbed out the cigarette he was smoking. He was in his early thirties and good-looking in a louche sort of way, with shoulder-length black hair and sharp, almost feline features. He had the world-weary look of a man who'd seen it all.

'I understand you're the owner of this house,' Wesley began after they'd introduced themselves.

'I've already spoken to your lot and told them I couldn't help.' The man lit another cigarette, a signal that he was bored with the whole proceedings.

'Your name is?'

'Grey Grover. Artist of this parish.' His lazy drawl suggested a privileged upbringing.

'These yours?' Gerry asked, pointing to one of the abstracts.

'Rather good, aren't they? Not that any of the gallery owners in Tradmouth appreciate my genius. I understand Van Gogh had the same trouble.'

Wesley was tempted to smile at the comparison, but one look at Grover's expression told him that he'd been deadly serious.

'You will have been told that a woman has been found dead on the coast path and we're treating her death as suspicious.'

'Look, if some old biddy's gone walking along the coast

25

path by herself and someone's decided to push her off the cliff, I don't see what that has to do with me.'

'She was wearing a T-shirt with a logo – Ritter's Sheep Shocker. Probably a real ale. Do you know it?'

'Do I look the real-ale type?'

The question was casual, but Wesley noticed a subtle change in Grover's manner. 'You recognise the name, don't you?'

'I've heard of it. It's local, so that's hardly surprising.' His words sounded defensive.

'Who sells it round here?'

He shrugged. 'I believe it's made at the pub nearby – the Seashell. It's one of those places with a small brewery attached. I suppose other places sell it too, but I'm no expert.'

'Do you know anyone fitting the dead woman's description?' Wesley hadn't wanted to use the picture he'd taken of the victim lying on the path, fearing it was in bad taste, but now he felt he had no option. He found it and held his phone in front of Grey Grover's face but the man shook his head.

A few moments later a woman floated into the room. She was wearing a long muslin dress dotted with daisies, and her thick auburn hair tumbled down to her waist. At first Wesley wondered whether she was acting in the film. But when he saw the rows of wooden beads around her neck, and realised that she was about seven months pregnant, he suspected he'd got this wrong.

'What's going on?' she said. Her manner was haughty, as though she feared the newcomers were eyeing up the family silver. 'Who are these two? Not the fucking bailiffs?'

'Police,' Gerry said, producing his ID. 'And you are?'

'Krystal. I'm staying here. What's that?'

Wesley held his phone out and she leaned over to peer at it. 'Oh God, what's happened to Susan? She looks bloody awful.'

At last Wesley felt they were getting somewhere.

6

Krystal stared at the dead woman's image as though she was trying to remember every detail.

'You're sure it's Susan?'

'Absolutely.'

'You didn't mention this to the officers who called before?' said Wesley.

Krystal shook her head. 'I didn't see them. I've been upstairs asleep.' She gave the man on the sofa a sideways look. 'I can't think why Grey didn't recognise her,' she said with wide-eyed innocence, as though she knew perfectly well and was intent on making things uncomfortable for him.

Grover squirmed against the cushions. 'I didn't look too closely. And she looks different . . . like that . . . dead.'

'Squeamish, are you?' said Gerry. 'Can't say I blame you.'

'Tell me about Susan.' Wesley leaned forward like a priest about to hear a confession. 'What's her surname?'

'Brown, I think. Or it might be Green. We're not usually that formal round here.'

Grover stood up, walked to the window and gazed out at the overgrown garden as though he was fascinated by the view of the statue at its centre: a Roman goddess stained with moss and weathered by the Devon climate. Krystal took his place on the sofa, making a great show of lowering herself down carefully. Wesley's first thought was that she was probably at the same stage of pregnancy as his colleague DS Rachel Tracey, who was back at the police station in Tradmouth, infuriated by Gerry's insistence that she confine herself to light duties until her maternity leave began later in the month.

'She's staying here,' said Krystal. 'She's house-sitting for Andrea, who rents the stables from Grey. She's gone to France for a few months.'

'The stables?' Wesley had a brief vision of the dead woman sharing her accommodation with horses.

Grover kept his back to them so they couldn't see his expression. 'My great-uncle had the stables converted before he kicked the bucket, and I rent them out. Anything for a bit of extra income. God knows we need it.'

'How long has she been here?'

Krystal rested her hands fondly on her bump. 'About a month, isn't that right, Grey?'

There was a grunt from the window, but he didn't turn round.

'Where did she live before?'

'No idea. I really only knew her to say hello to.'

'Do you know if she had any friends around here? Or family?'

Krystal shrugged. 'She sometimes helped out behind the bar at the Seashell; it's half a mile away on the road to Bereton. Other than that, she kept herself to herself, didn't she, Grey?' She twisted her head to look at Grover, but he ignored her. 'I suppose you'll have to let Andrea know what's happened.'

'Tell us about Andrea,' said Gerry.

Grover turned round. 'She's an artist too – Andrea Alladyce. She's quite well known locally,' he said, suddenly animated. 'My aim is to turn Serpent's Point into a community of artists, and Andrea moving in was a real coup. I inherited the place from my great-uncle eighteen months ago, but it's turned out to be a bloody money pit – hence Crispin Joss and his Regency romp.'

'Must be a great intrusion.' Wesley tried to sound sympathetic.

'It's been horrendous,' Grover muttered. 'They've taken over the whole bloody place – they're filming their sex scenes in my bedroom, so I've had to move to one of the others.'

'The one with the great big damp patch on the ceiling,' said Krystal. 'Mind you, the others are even worse.' She gave Grover a look that Wesley found hard to interpret.

'Money's money, so we can't complain.'

'Does anyone else live here?' Gerry asked.

'Only Marcus, but he's away,' Krystal said quickly.

'Who's Marcus?'

'Another artist,' said Grover. 'His work's incredibly ground-breaking. We're so lucky to have him here.'

Wesley looked at Krystal and saw a sly smile on her lips as Grover carried on talking.

'He's crashing in one of the old servants' rooms on the top floor and using the room next to it as a studio. There's plenty of space here, although it's hardly the Ritz.'

'Where is he at the moment?'

'This isn't a prison. I don't keep tabs on my fellow artists. I haven't seen him since yesterday. You said he left last night, didn't you, Krystal?'

She nodded earnestly. 'He said he'd be away for a few days.'

'What's his surname?'

'Pinter. Like the playwright, though he's no relation.'

Wesley knew it was time to bring the conversation back to the dead woman. 'Is there anything else you can tell us about Susan? Did she have any visitors?'

'No idea,' Grover said. 'I mind my own business. People are entitled to their privacy.'

Wesley was disappointed. Juicy gossip and observant neighbours were two things every detective dreamed of.

'Did she have a car?'

'An old Fiat. I let her put it in one of the garages off the courtyard. Didn't think it would survive for long outside in the sea air. Look, she was house-sitting for Andrea and that's all I know about her.'

'We didn't bother her and she didn't bother us,' Krystal added. When she rested both hands firmly on her bump, the gesture seemed final, a signal that they had no more to say on the subject.

It was time to investigate the stables, the temporary home of their murder victim. The two detectives took their leave, treading carefully over cables and avoiding the technical crew, who were still going about their unfathomable business while the actors sat round looking bored.

'Think I might give *The Awakening of Lillith Montmorency* a miss,' Gerry whispered as they walked across the cobbled courtyard towards the stables.

'What did you think of Grover and Krystal?' Wesley asked.

'Pretentious and self-absorbed. Seen their type before.'

'Suspicious?'

'Not sure. We'll get someone to run their names through our magic machine and see if anything comes up.'

Wesley fished the key from his pocket, and when he put it in the Yale lock, the door opened smoothly. 'Let's take a look,' he said as he pulled on his crime-scene gloves and led the way into the building. They'd leave the search team to deal with the dead woman's car.

The front door opened straight onto the living room, and at first sight, they couldn't see anything unusual or out of place. The white walls were hung with bright canvases in the impressionist style, painted by someone with considerably more talent than Grey Grover. Wesley's time in the Met's Art and Antiques Unit had left him with an appreciation of art in all its forms, and he liked what he saw. The intertwined letter A's at the bottom of each painting told him that these must be the work of Andrea Alladyce, the artist who'd gone off to France, leaving her home in the victim's care.

They walked through the house, careful to touch nothing; the crime-scene people would conduct a thorough search in due course. The single bedroom contained a double bed, neatly made and topped with a colourful Indian throw. Susan had been a tidy person in life; if she'd been entrusted with looking after someone else's house, that would be an asset.

The studio upstairs had a large north-facing window and contained the usual paraphernalia of the artist's work; canvases both finished and blank, paints, brushes and easels. At the end of a narrow passage they found another, smaller room, which appeared to serve as a study. Wesley presumed this was where Andrea dealt with the business side of her work. But he was surprised by what he saw.

The set-up was familiar. It was one they used themselves during an investigation. Gerry was standing behind him, and Wesley heard him gasp.

'It looks like a ruddy incident room, Wes. What the hell was she up to?'

From the journal of Dr Aldus Claye

May 1921

I visited my wife's room this morning. Clarabel is twenty years my junior, and we met when I taught her brother Alfred at Oxford. Alfred was an affable if pedestrian student who perished in the war, one of the sad casualties of the Somme, leaving Clarabel as her father's sole heir. Her attraction to myself, a middle-aged bachelor don whose interest in the history of the Roman Empire verges on passion, was both surprising and gratifying, but when she accepted my proposal of marriage, I confess I failed to experience the elation that many would expect me to feel in the circumstances.

Clarabel is a pretty young woman of limited wit and conversation, and the interest she once showed in my work has dwindled since our marriage. Even the antique splendours of Rome, where we spent our honeymoon, appeared to bore her. Now she spends much of her time in her room doing goodness knows what, and even the incomparable beauty of the Devon landscape fails to lure her out of doors. I sometimes wonder whether something ails her, but she denies it, saying she enjoys excellent health and merely has no desire to leave the house. She tells me she misses the company of her friends in Oxford and finds life here tedious, comparing it to a prison.

Today I wrote to a young man of my acquaintance, a friend of Professor Fredericks who shares my interest in the Roman occupation of Britannia. His name is Fidelio Phipps – I can only surmise that his parents favoured the music of Beethoven – and he is an enthusiastic and experienced archaeologist who worked with Flinders Petrie in Egypt before the war. Sadly, the conflict left him wounded, but I am told that he refuses to allow his disability to interfere with his archaeological work, for which, in my opinion, he is to be greatly admired.

I asked him if he was free to investigate the field I now think of as mine, and I await his reply with impatience. The weather conditions here are ideal to begin an excavation and I have great need of his expertise. He will, of course, stay here at Serpent's Point. It is a large house, and a guest, particularly such a distinguished one, will cause little disruption.

7

On closer examination, the incident room in the converted stables covered two separate cases. The wall was divided into distinct sections, with internet printouts, press cuttings and handwritten notes linked to each investigation.

'How do we know all this doesn't belong to Andrea Alladyce?' Gerry asked.

It was a reasonable question. They didn't know for sure that it had anything to do with the victim.

'I'll get Rachel over here to make sure the search team do a thorough job,' said Wesley, his eyes focused on the wall. 'As far as I can see, one is a missing persons case – Simone Pritchard. But this other one – Avril Willis – went missing and was found murdered a few weeks later.'

Gerry studied the photographs of the two women. 'Avril was murdered up in Yorkshire four years back and Simone went missing in Gloucestershire a couple of years ago. There doesn't appear to be any link between them, so why was our victim taking such an interest? If it *was* her and not this artist woman.'

Wesley scanned the press report pinned up next to Avril Willis's photograph. 'According to this, Avril went missing in Whitby after a row with her husband. She walked out and the husband assumed she'd gone to her mother's. She was found dead a couple of weeks later. This piece from the internet says the police made an arrest. Warren Chips killed two prostitutes in Leeds and another in Bradford, and he confessed to Avril's murder too.'

'What about the missing persons case?'

'There's only one small piece about that – police are trying to trace, et cetera. Simone Pritchard walked out on her husband, who thought she'd left him for another man and that she might be in Bath, though he wasn't sure. There's been no word from her since. Her sister, Michelle Williams, said it was out of character. Reading between the lines, the police went through the motions but weren't too worried.'

'We can leave it to Rach to check them out.'

'She's already on her way.' Wesley knew that Rachel resented being cooped up in the CID office. Gerry imagined he was being considerate, but Rachel had told Wesley that it felt like a punishment – like being in prison and told it was for your own protection. He sympathised with her frustration.

'We need to contact this artist woman, Andrea, to confirm that it was our victim who's been taking an interest in these cases. She's bound to have some information about Susan. You don't let just anybody live in your house, do you? She must have known her – or at least had references.'

'Getting in touch with her might be easier said than done. All we know is that she's somewhere in France.'

'France is a big country,' said Gerry with a sigh.

'We might find a contact number or an address for where she's staying. I'll tell the search team to keep a lookout.'

'What about Grey Grover's other lodger – Marcus Pinter?'

'I'll put him on the list of people we need to talk to.'

Gerry looked at his watch. 'I thought it'd help to have a local incident room, so I've arranged to use Bereton church hall. They should be moving all the equipment in as we speak. I'd better go and see how they're getting on.'

Wesley took out his phone and took a photograph of the study wall. They needed to follow every lead. And they needed to discover all they could about Susan. Who was she? Where did she come from? And who might want her dead?

'Think it might have been a random attack, Wes?'

'Do you?'

Gerry tilted his head to one side, considering the question. 'Not sure. But my gut instinct tells me it might have been targeted.'

Before he could say any more, Wesley's phone rang. It was Neil, so he slipped out of the room to answer the call.

'If that's your mate Neil, tell him to call back when we're less busy,' shouted Gerry to his disappearing back.

From the landing window, Wesley could see the search team arriving in the courtyard, which was now packed with police vehicles.

'I'm told there's been a murder,' were Neil's first words when Wesley answered.

'You've been told right. Have you found Sophie and Livy?'

'I'm with them now. I've a feeling they might have stumbled on something exciting.'

'Yes, I saw the coins they'd found.'

'You should come over.'

Wesley hesitated. The investigation was in hand and a quick visit to the field to see his old friend wouldn't take long. Besides, he told himself, the two young metal-detectorists might have remembered more about the events of that morning. There was a chance they'd seen something and hadn't realised its significance at the time.

He said he'd do his best, and as he put his phone away, he saw DS Rachel Tracey at the foot of the stairs. Her blonde hair was gathered back into a neat ponytail, and her ever more obvious baby bump reminded him that she'd soon be going off on maternity leave; he wasn't sure how the team would manage without her.

'I'm told the victim had some sort of incident room,' she said as she climbed the stairs slowly, holding onto the banisters. 'After our jobs, was she?'

'We don't know for sure that it was her who set it up. It might have been the artist who lives here, Andrea Alladyce. She's in France and the victim was house-sitting for her.'

Rachel raised her eyebrows. She looked well, hardly the fragile creature of Gerry's imagination. Pregnancy suited her. 'Then we need to track her down sooner rather than later. Do we have the victim's phone?'

'It wasn't on the body, but it might turn up during the search. I didn't see any sign of a laptop in the study, but if the team find one hidden away, we can get the techies to deal with it. Unless her killer stole it.'

'There's no sign of a break-in, is there?'

Wesley shook his head.

'I've just seen the search team,' said Rachel. 'Nothing out of the ordinary was found in the victim's car. Are we assuming it wasn't a random attack?'

'We'll see whether there've been any similar incidents in other isolated spots around the country, but Gerry thinks it might have been targeted.'

Rachel nodded, her face serious.

'Gerry wants to get over to the new incident room. It should be up and running by now. Are you OK supervising things here?'

She looked him in the eye. 'Being pregnant hasn't affected my brain. Of course I can manage. I'm surprised you have to ask.'

The note of amusement in her voice reassured Wesley that she hadn't taken offence. They'd worked together for so long they could almost anticipate each other's thoughts. At one time there'd been an attraction between them – although thankfully neither of them had acted on it. But this was something he'd never shared with anyone, not even Neil, his closest friend – and certainly not with his wife, Pam.

After telling Gerry he wanted to take another look at the crime scene, he walked back towards the coast path, where he saw Neil's car parked next to his own, on the lane next to the field where Livy and Sophie had made their potentially exciting discovery. When he opened the metal farm gate, he saw Neil talking earnestly to the girls, who were pointing at the ground. Neil looked round and grinned at him, while the girls greeted him warily, as though they feared they were in for more questioning.

'I haven't got long,' said Wesley. 'I need to have another look at the place where the woman's body was found.'

'Oh yes. I almost forgot about that.' For Neil, archaeology trumped murder every time. 'I've had a look at the coins and they're definitely Roman. A denarius of Vespasian and a gold aureus of Hadrian. That one's worth a bit.'

'Wasn't he the one who built the wall?' said Livy.

'That's right. The thing is, it was always assumed the Romans never took much interest in Devon, certainly

40

nowhere further south than Isca Dumnoniorum – that's Exeter,' he added when he saw a look of confusion on the girls' faces. 'More recently, evidence of Roman activity has been found at Ipplepen, but nothing this far south. That's why this is potentially so exciting.'

The girls looked puzzled, but they nodded obediently.

'Are the coins worth a lot then?' Sophie asked. 'Are we going to be rich?'

Wesley knew Neil was about to dampen their enthusiasm.

'Can't say yet. I'd like to get some colleagues over to investigate the area properly. This field belongs to your dad, does it, Livy?'

'Yeah. He bought it from the owner of the big house six months ago.'

'Do you think he'll allow us to dig?'

'He only uses this field for grazing, so it shouldn't be a problem. But the coins belong to us, don't they?'

'Any precious metal objects have to be reported to the coroner, I'm afraid. But if your dad gives us the go-ahead for an excavation, you can lend a hand if you like.'

The girls looked disappointed as their dreams of riches faded, and they didn't seem at all convinced that being part of an important archaeological discovery would make up for it.

Wesley decided it was time to ask them a question. 'I was wondering whether you've managed to remember any more about this morning. Are you sure you didn't see anyone, or hear anything?'

Livy shook her head.

'What about that man with the baseball cap?' said Sophie, looking at her friend.

Wesley held his breath and waited for her to continue.

'You can't see the path from the field because of the hedge, but I thought I saw the top of a baseball cap, bobbing like someone was walking along. At least I think it was a cap. Black or dark blue.'

'You never said,' said Livy, sounding hurt.

'I've only just remembered. When the police asked before, I was confused.'

'What else can you tell me about it?' said Wesley, hoping his self-indulgent detour to meet Neil was about to produce something useful.

Sophie screwed up her eyes, making a great effort to remember.

'I think there was something white on it. Writing maybe. Or a logo. It was a long way away and I only caught a glimpse.'

'What time was this?'

'Just after we arrived, I think. About half ten.'

'Thanks, Sophie. That might be very helpful.'

He left the girls with Neil and wandered down to the coast path. The body had been taken to the mortuary, but the CSIs were still at work there, taking samples and searching the surrounding bracken and hedgerow.

'Any sign of a weapon?' Wesley asked a young woman in a crime-scene suit, but the answer was a shake of the head. There was no weapon, no phone, and it hadn't rained for a few days so the ground was too dry for useable footprints.

He was walking back to his car when his phone rang. It was Rachel.

'We found Andrea Alladyce's contact details in the house and I've spoken to her. She denies putting the missing persons stuff up in the study. Says it must have been Susan, the house-sitter.'

'Did she tell you anything else?'

'She said she'd heard about Susan from a friend who drinks in the local pub. He recommended her because she'd done house-sitting before. She thought she used to be with an agency, although hers was a private arrangement.'

'Is the pub the Seashell?'

'That's right.'

'We've been told that Susan sometimes helped out behind the bar there. I wonder if they sell Ritter's Sheep Shocker.'

'It's never been one of my haunts, but I think a few places round here sell Ritter's. It's getting quite a following, according to my brothers, who are real-ale enthusiasts.'

'Has Andrea's friend from the pub got a name?'

'Darren. Andrea doesn't know his surname, and when I asked for a description, she just said long grey hair, average height, average everything . . . and he's an electrician.'

'This means some lucky person is going to have to conduct enquiries at the Seashell.'

'I'd imagine that's one job Gerry will want to keep for himself.'

'With me driving, so I'll be on the alcohol-free beer. What about house-sitting agencies?'

'The only one round here is called Edenwood Homes; it's in Neston. I've tried ringing, but there was no reply, so they might have closed early. We can pay them a visit tomorrow.'

Wesley thanked her and rang off. At least he now knew that the incident room in the stables was the work of the dead woman. As he drove to Bereton church hall, he kept seeing the victim's contorted face – and wondering who would want to end someone's life like that in such a lovely spot.

8

The incident room was running smoothly. Wesley always felt a little guilty about taking over church halls used by the community for toddler groups, WI meetings, jumble sales and amateur dramatics. For the time being, the place was commandeered by the murder investigation, so the local play group's colourful toys would be pushed to one side.

Wesley and Gerry set off at four o'clock to drive to Tradmouth Hospital. Wesley knew he'd be late home that evening, but he didn't feel inclined to break the news to Pam until the post-mortem was over.

'I always miss Colin when he's not here,' Gerry grumbled as he pushed open the swing doors of the mortuary entrance.

'You miss his tea and biscuits ... and the gossip.'

'Guilty as charged.'

'Dr Stamoran seems to know what he's doing.'

Gerry grunted. Any pathologist who didn't happen to be Colin Bowman was questionable in his eyes. As they passed Colin's empty office, he gave it a longing glance. After the grim business of the autopsy was over, the pathologist always provided refreshments: leaf tea, and biscuits baked on the royal estates. The sweet after the bitter.

Stamoran was waiting for them in the post-mortem room in his surgical gown. The mask he wore made it impossible to tell whether there was a smile of greeting.

'Are we ready to start?' He looked from one to the other, as though assessing how likely they were to cause a disturbance by fainting. It was something Wesley had done when he'd witnessed his first post-mortem as a young detective constable, something he'd felt embarrassed about at the time because the rest of his immediate family were doctors and therefore used to that sort of thing. These days he looked away at the most gruesome moments, but on the whole, he had become hardened to the procedure over the years. The best way to deal with it, he'd found, was to banish the thought that the person on the slab had once been a living, breathing human being who'd laughed, cried, loved and hated. But he never managed to forget completely.

After making his initial observations, Dr Stamoran recorded them into the microphone dangling above the table. He was a man of few words, unlike Colin, who always kept up an inappropriately cheerful running commentary as he worked. It was only when the doctor finished that he finally seemed to relax. 'I suppose you want to know my findings,' he said once he'd discarded his gloves, plastic apron and mask and headed out into the corridor.

'Would be useful,' said Gerry.

Stamoran led them into his office and invited them to sit. 'Tea or coffee?' he said as he flicked on the kettle standing on top of a filing cabinet. 'Won't be up to Colin's standard, I'm afraid, but one does one's best.' He treated them to a wide smile, as if they'd passed some sort of test.

Once they had their drinks in front of them, he sat back

in his swivel chair. 'Well, as you could probably see, the cause of death was strangulation, and I've no reason to change my initial impression that the ligature was something soft, like a scarf. We'll have to wait for the samples I've taken to be processed, but hopefully, whatever the killer used will have left some tiny fibres on the skin. I spotted something reddish brown, but the lab will tell us more. Her last meal was breakfast – bran flakes, a banana and herbal tea. She believed in healthy living.'

'Didn't do her much good, did it,' Gerry muttered.

Stamoran smiled. 'If you're unlucky enough to meet a crazed strangler on an isolated path, all the fresh fruit and veg in the world won't keep you this side of the pearly gates, I'm afraid. I'd say she died within an hour of eating her last meal, so at a guess, the time of death was probably between nine and ten o'clock, maybe a little before. She had breakfast, went out for her morning walk and—'

'Goodnight, Vienna,' said Gerry.

The pathologist raised his eyebrows. 'If you want to put it like that. I've taken samples from her fingernails, of course, but again, we'll have to wait for the lab. I think she was probably facing her killer when he strangled her, and her neck was scratched as though she'd tried to grab at the ligature.'

'Anything else?' Wesley asked.

'Not really. She was in pretty good health.'

'So it's just a matter of tracing her relatives and finding out more about her,' said Gerry.

'And who might want her dead,' said Wesley.

'You don't think it was a random attack?' said Stamoran, tilting his head to one side.

'We're seeing whether there have been any cases with

a similar MO in other parts of the country, but if we find this is a one-off, we'll work on the assumption that she was killed by someone she knew.'

'Not a serial killer, then.' The doctor sounded almost disappointed.

'Early days,' said Gerry, draining his cup. 'Well, time and crime wait for no man – or woman – so we'd better get back. Thanks, Doctor.'

'You'll have my full report in due course,' Stamoran said. 'Nice to be working with you. Colin's always sung your praises,' he added, looking directly at Wesley.

'Thanks,' said Wesley, his cheeks burning at the compliment.

When they left the hospital, they drove back to the incident room in Bereton, where they found most of the team busy at their desks, making calls and tapping away on computer keyboards. Gerry called for attention, and the low buzz of conversation ceased.

'Right,' he said after he'd climbed onto the stage at the far end of the room, standing in front of the dusty velvet curtains. 'The post-mortem hasn't thrown up much that we didn't already know, and as usual, we'll have to wait for the lab to get their fingers out before we find out more. Thanks to the digestion of a breakfast healthy enough to make any doctor proud, the pathologist has pinned down the time of death to around nine thirty, give or take an hour or so, of course – you know what these pathologists are like about committing themselves. This means she was probably dead before those lasses started metal-detecting in the field nearby at ten thirty. What is interesting is that one of them said she thought she saw someone wearing a baseball cap on the path soon after they arrived in the field.'

'If she could see his hat over that hedge, he must have been tall,' said Wesley.

'True. And if it was just someone walking along the path, we have to ask ourselves why they didn't report finding the body.'

Wesley saw Rob Carter's hand shoot up. Rob was nothing if not keen.

'Either it was someone who didn't want to get involved, or it was the killer.' The DC sounded proud of his reasoning.

'My thoughts exactly, Rob.' The overconfident young man didn't always bring out Gerry's avuncular side, but this time his smile was almost benevolent. 'Which means we need to find this character. Perhaps a TV appeal ... ' He glanced at Wesley, who suspected that if there was to be an appeal, it would be up to him to make it. In the chief super's opinion, using an officer from an ethnic minority in front of the media did wonders for the force's reputation for diversity. Although Wesley was more than happy to leave any public performance to Gerry, who enjoyed that sort of thing.

'Anybody got anything to report?' Gerry scanned the room hopefully.

It was DC Trish Walton who spoke this time. Dark-haired, sensible Trish was a reliable officer, even though flashes of inspiration rarely came her way. 'I've searched the database for similar murders or attacks in all police authorities throughout the UK, but I haven't found any unsolved cases.'

'So the killer might have targeted our victim for personal reasons rather than an urge to visit a beauty spot and do away with the next unfortunate person who happened to pass by. What have we found out about her? Any next of kin to be informed?' Gerry looked round expectantly, as though hoping to learn her entire life story, along with the identity of her killer.

But his question was greeted by silence. Then a young woman who'd just been transferred from uniform put up a nervous hand. She had mousy hair and didn't look much older than the two metal-detecting schoolgirls. 'I've been trying, but the trouble is, there are a lot of Susan Browns and so far none of them seems to be ours. There are so many women with that name that it's going to take ages to account for them all. And if she's divorced or widowed and using her maiden name, that'll complicate things.' She sounded quite upset about her failure.

'Well, keep looking.' Wesley felt sorry for the girl. Sometimes Gerry could seem rather intimidating to those who didn't know his little ways. 'Good work, er . . . '

'Ellie, sir.'

'Good work, Ellie. Keep at it.'

Gerry climbed down from the stage and Wesley hurried over to join him. 'What if Susan Brown wasn't her real name?'

'Why would she change it?'

'Perhaps she was running away from someone – or something – and she didn't want to be found.'

'And where better to hide away than the stables at Serpent's Point?'

9

At seven o'clock, Gerry announced that he was going to visit the Seashell and he wanted Wesley to go with him. A couple of uniforms had already been sent there to take statements, but Gerry wanted to have an informal chat with the regulars and staff, especially the Darren that Andrea Alladyce had told them about. They needn't be long, he said. Once they'd had a quick drink, Wesley could get off home. They had to make an early start in the morning.

But as they were preparing to leave the incident room, Rachel came over to Wesley's desk. She looked fed up and tired, so he fetched her a chair and told her to sit down. For once, she didn't point out that he was being patronising. Instead she looked grateful and placed her hand in the small of her back as she lowered herself down.

'What's up?'

'I'm just a bit tired, that's all. And don't you dare tell me to take it easy. I'm sick of people trying to run my life for me.'

'I wouldn't dream of it,' said Wesley. He knew it would be safer to stick to the subject of work. 'Gerry and I are off to the Seashell to talk to some of the people who knew the victim, so why don't you go home? There's nothing much more to be done tonight.'

He'd expected her to argue, but instead she gave him a grateful look. He knew there'd be a lot for her to do once she got home, but she always protested that she was a farmer's daughter, so being a farmer's wife was little different. Wesley was reluctant to point out that her mother, Stella, hadn't held down a demanding job in CID at the same time as being heavily pregnant and helping her husband run the farm.

Gerry seemed keen to be off. The prospect of a visit to licensed premises often had that effect on him. Wesley drove, as usual. Since his arrival in Tradmouth all those years ago, he had never known Gerry to get behind the wheel. He often wondered whether it was Kathy's accident that had caused his aversion to driving. It was something he'd never liked to ask.

The Seashell stood on the edge of a sandy cove, well within walking distance of Serpent's Point along a winding lane. It was the beginning of July, and the summer visitors – those without children, who weren't tied by school terms – had started to flood into the county. There were plenty of cars outside the low whitewashed building, and most of the wooden picnic tables outside were occupied. The weather was fair and the place was busy.

As they walked up to the bar, Wesley nudged Gerry's elbow and nodded at one of the hand pumps. Ritter's Sheep Shocker. And sure enough, the bar staff were wearing T-shirts identical to the victim's. One was displayed behind the bar – available in small, medium and large, priced £10.99.

The two officers displayed their ID and asked the

barman if they could speak to the landlord, who duly arrived from the far end of the bar and introduced himself as Harry Ritter.

'How can I help you, gentlemen?' he asked. He was a well-built man with a beard and a worn checked shirt. His manner was genial, but Wesley could sense a wariness behind his cheerful greeting. 'I take it this is about poor Sue. I can't believe it, I really can't. She was such a lovely woman. Why would anyone want to harm her?'

'A pint of Sheep Shocker and an alcohol-free lager, please,' said Gerry before the eulogy could continue.

'Certainly, sir.' The landlord sounded relieved, as though he'd expected Gerry to launch into an interrogation right away. 'We've already had the police round and I told them everything I know, which isn't much. When I heard someone had been found dead on the coast path, I thought it must be some tourist. But when the constable said she might have worked here and asked if I knew anyone matching the dead woman's description, the only person I could think of was Sue.'

'We prefer not to release details of the victim's identity until the next of kin have been informed, so we'd be grateful if you'd say nothing to the press at this stage.'

'Understood.'

'We're treating her death as suspicious.'

The landlord nodded sagely. 'A couple of my regulars said there were a lot of police up there – and crime-scene people – so we wondered ...'

'How long had she worked here?'

'Only about a month – just casual bar work.'

'Cash in hand?'

The landlord nodded nervously, as though he imagined

he was being accused of something. Wesley was quick to put his mind at rest.

'Don't worry. We won't tell the tax man. She was wearing one of those.' He pointed to the T-shirt hanging behind the bar. 'You sell them here?'

'That's right, and all the staff wear them too. Shocker's very popular, being brewed on the premises.' A note of pride had crept into the man's voice.

'It's your own brew then?' said Gerry.

'And a very fine brew it is. It gets a mention in a lot of the real-ale guides, and we've started expanding our outlets. I'm trying out a new one too – Pig Startler. Bit more hoppy than the Shocker.'

He'd finished pulling Gerry's pint and handed it to him with a flourish. He looked at Wesley. 'Sure you won't try some?'

'Much as I'd like to, I'm afraid I'm driving.' Wesley tried his best to sound apologetic.

'Pity,' said the landlord absent-mindedly.

Wesley took a photograph of the dead woman from his pocket. 'Just to confirm that this is Susan.'

Harry's mouth gaped open. Gone was the genial mine host. He looked like a man who'd just received a bad shock. 'Yeah. That's Sue. I hoped there'd been a mistake, but . . . '

'How did she get the job here?'

'She came in and asked if I had any shifts. Said she was house-sitting up at Serpent's Point while Andrea was in France. I had the impression money was tight and that was why she needed the work.'

'What else can you tell me about her?'

He frowned. 'Not much, to be honest. I reckon she was lonely up there on her own in the old stables. I hear the people from the main house are a bit odd – not that they come in here very often. Sue liked to chat to people – just small talk really; she didn't give away much about herself. Bit of an enigma, she was.'

'We've been told she had a friend here called Darren.'

Harry gestured towards the inglenook fireplace, where a man in his forties with long grey hair was nursing a pint. He wore beads round his neck and a cheesecloth shirt, and he had the look of a man who'd been there for a while. A fixture. 'He lost his wife last year and he comes in here most days after work. Reckon this place is a life-line for him.'

'Pubs provide a valuable social service,' said Gerry with sincerity.

'Got it in one, Chief Inspector.'

'By the way, where were you this morning? Before ten thirty?'

'From eight this morning till opening time, I was here taking deliveries and getting everything ready. Never left the premises. Joe was here too.' Harry nodded towards the barman. 'He'll tell you.'

'Thanks for your help,' said Wesley. 'And can we ask you not to talk to anyone about what we've discussed. As we said, we want to inform the next of kin before we release the victim's name to the press. I don't suppose you know anything about her family?'

Harry shook his head. 'She never mentioned them to me. But don't worry, I'll keep shtum. In my job, you get used to keeping confidences – I tell my staff that anyone who works behind a bar has to be like a priest, bound by the secrets of the confessional.'

Wesley had to smile. After some initial misgivings, he

found himself liking Harry Ritter, who'd undoubtedly found his calling in life.

Darren was staring into the empty fireplace as though he was in shock, and Wesley guessed that he'd heard the news. He looked up as the two officers pulled up a couple of stools and sat down next to him.

'Darren, is it?'

'Who wants to know?'

They produced their ID, and the man put his half-empty pint down on the table.

'You got a surname, Darren?'

'Bailey. I suppose you want to talk about Sue. I just can't believe it. She was a lovely person. I hope you bloody catch whoever did it.'

Gerry leaned forward. 'We understand you knew her.'

'Yeah. We passed the time of day. Like I said, she was a lovely woman.'

Wesley assumed a sympathetic expression. 'Sorry we have to ask all these questions. It must be difficult for you.' Gerry often said he'd inherited a good bedside manner from his doctor parents. 'You weren't here earlier when the police came in?'

'No, but Harry told me what had happened. I heard the helicopter and I thought it was a rescue. I never imagined ... ' Darren stared at his drink. 'How was she ...? Did he ...?'

'We believe she was strangled.'

He shook his head wearily, as though this was just one more tragedy he'd had to endure in his life.

'What do you know about her?'

'Not much, to tell the truth. Whenever I asked her anything personal, she changed the subject.'

'Did she ever say anything about an ex-partner?'

'She said she was divorced, but that's all.'

'Was she from round here?'

'She told me she was from Yorkshire, but like I said, she never discussed her private life.' He sighed. 'Mind you, that might have been my fault. I'd lost my wife, and Sue was a really good listener, if you know what I mean.'

Gerry nodded. He knew all right. When he'd lost Kathy, he would have been glad of a sympathetic ear. Instead he'd bottled up his grief and focused his energies on work and restoring his yacht, the *Rosie May*.

Darren lowered his voice and glanced at the bar. 'I reckon Harry fancied her.'

'Was anything going on between them?'

He looked wary, as though he was afraid he'd said too much. 'Oh no. I don't think it was anything serious. I saw him chatting her up once or twice – and he said she looked good in the T-shirt.'

Wesley and Gerry exchanged a look. Someone would be double checking Ritter's alibi in due course.

'I believe you recommended her to Andrea Alladyce.'

'That's right. I met Sue while she was house-sitting for this bloke in Neston. He had to work abroad for a while, so he wanted someone to look after his house and his cat. She told me she'd got that job through an agency – Edenwood Homes, it's called. I've done some work for the boss there.'

'What's the name of the man she was house-sitting for?'

'Harrod – like that posh shop in London. Matt Harrod. I'm an electrician and I put in some lights for him while he was away. Sue was there and we got chatting, and that's why she always used to talk to me whenever I came in here.

She knew I was no threat, if you know what I mean – and it kept Harry at bay.'

'Tell us about Andrea Alladyce.'

'I've known her for a while. She's a regular here when she's not in France, and I've done some work for her too. She wanted someone to look after her place 'cos she wasn't too happy about those film people hanging about, and I thought of Sue. The agency charge a fee, so it saved Andrea a lot of money. Though Sue made me promise never to tell anyone where she was, in case the agency got to hear.'

'Do you know what she did before she started house-sitting for Mr Harrod?'

Darren thought for a moment. 'She said she'd been in Chipping Campden before she came to Devon – that's in the Cotswolds.'

'Thanks, that's helpful,' said Wesley. 'Do you know of any relatives, or any other friends?'

Darren shook his head. 'I think Sue was one of those people who keep their lives in compartments. She never talked about anyone else.'

Wesley asked him if he recognised the names of the two women who featured in Susan's incident room, or whether she'd said anything about being interested in missing persons cases, but the answer to both questions was no.

'Where were you this morning?' he added. 'Sorry, but we have to ask.'

'I had a job in Dukesbridge. Arrived about eight thirty and I was there till three. I can give you the address if you like,' Darren said confidently.

They made a note of the address. Someone could check it out as a matter of routine the next day. They asked for

Matt Harrod's address too, and Darren obliged before returning to his pint.

'What do you think?' Wesley asked once they'd left the building.

'I don't see Darren as our man – or the landlord. Mind you, stranger things have happened.'

'But it sounds like Harry Ritter was keen on Susan. If she rejected him . . .'

'He seems to have a good alibi, but we need to get it confirmed. We also need to speak to Matt Harrod in Neston. And I'd like to know what she was up to in Chipping Campden.' Gerry checked the time. 'You'd better get home, Wes. And don't tell Pam you've been to the pub, or she might get the wrong idea.'

Wesley didn't need telling twice. After dropping Gerry off at his house on Tradmouth's waterfront, he drove up the hill to the top of the town.

Pam greeted him with the news that his dinner was in the microwave. She seemed preoccupied, and he was soon to find out that it wasn't his lateness that was bothering her. His daughter Amelia came to the top of the stairs to say hello, but Michael, her elder brother, stayed in his room – as any self-respecting teenager would. He knew Amelia would be reaching that age soon and he wasn't particularly looking forward to it.

As he sat down to eat at the kitchen table, Pam pulled out the chair opposite and made herself comfortable.

'I heard about the body on the coast path on the local radio,' she began. 'Won't do the local tourist industry much good. Was it murder?'

'Afraid so,' Wesley said, tucking in. He hadn't realised he was so hungry.

'Your sister rang.'

Wesley's sister, Maritia, was a part-time GP in nearby Neston and lived in Belsham vicarage with her husband, the Reverend Mark Fitzgerald.

'She said your mum and dad made it safely back to London. It was nice to see them.'

Wesley's parents had been in Devon for the past week, staying with Maritia and Mark. Luckily Wesley had been able to take time off work to see them, and the selfish thought flashed through his mind that he was glad Susan Brown hadn't been murdered a week earlier.

Pam abruptly changed the subject. 'I nearly forgot. Neil rang. He said he didn't want to call while you were still at work.'

'He doesn't usually bother with such niceties. I saw him earlier. Some girls found a couple of Roman coins in a field near the murder scene.'

'He sounded very excited. Kept going on about the Romans not making it this far south. I listened politely,' she added with an indulgent grin.

As soon as Wesley had finished eating, the family cat, Moriarty – named after Sherlock Holmes's arch-nemesis – came rubbing up against his legs as though she hadn't been fed for days. Few suspects he'd ever come across in the course of his career were as good at lying as Moriarty. Wesley, always a soft touch, sorted out some cat treats and threw them into her bowl before selecting Neil's number on speed dial.

'I'm getting a team over to that field tomorrow with some geophysics equipment,' Neil said as soon as he answered. 'It won't get in the way of your crime scene, will it?'

'Shouldn't think so.'

'I've been asking around, but nobody knows anything about the site, so I'll see whether I can find something in the archives. If you're in Bereton tomorrow, why don't you drop in and have a look at the field. There are all sorts of lumps and bumps in it. If there are foundations underneath, it could be really exciting.'

Before Wesley could point out that he'd be far too busy investigating the murder of Susan Brown, Neil rang off.

From the journal of Dr Aldus Claye

May 1921

Today marked the arrival of Fidelio Phipps at Serpent's Point. He is a young man whose knowledge and modesty endear him to me. From his reaction when I showed him what had been discovered, I suspect his enthusiasm matches my own, and he is eager to get to work.

At dinner this evening, we talked much about the excavations he has undertaken, and I was intrigued to learn more about the work of Flinders Petrie. I thought as he spoke how fortunate I am to obtain the aid of a man with such experience, and I hope the work I have to offer him will not disappoint. But if, as I suspect, we are about to discover something of phenomenal importance, I think he will be glad that he made the long journey to Devon. I am so optimistic about the farmer's find that it would be remiss of me not to investigate further.

As soon as Phipps arrived, I took him to the field and he observed that the land was uneven, something he has seen many times before when the foundations of a building lie beneath the ground. He wishes to walk through the field tomorrow to make further observations and to see whether anything can be found on the surface. I said I will go with him, as I am eager to hear his opinion. Although I am well versed in the history of the Roman conquest, my knowledge of archaeology is scant.

Phipps is a good-looking man with dark curls and a mouth that smiles easily. He walks with a pronounced limp, but the injuries he sustained in the war seem not to be sufficiently serious to hamper him in his work. Perhaps I will ask him about his time in France, although some, I have heard, are reluctant to talk about their experiences.

Clarabel came down to dinner, something I was not expecting. She said little, but I saw her stealing glances at our guest, who was politeness itself.

Tomorrow we will discuss our plans for the field. How I look forward to it.

10

Six thirty seemed far too early to start the working day, Wesley thought as he reached the incident room.

Gerry hadn't yet arrived, so he seized the opportunity to tackle the mound of paperwork that had built up on his desk. But he soon found himself contemplating the two missing persons cases in Susan's incident room. He knew many people were fascinated by true crime and fancied themselves as detectives, but he wondered whether she'd had some personal reason to concentrate on those two cases in particular.

Gerry trudged in at 7.30, yawning as he took his place at his desk at the front of the hall, nearest the stage and next to the door to the kitchen. From there he could keep an eye on everyone, he said. And it was handy to be near where the tea was brewed. Wesley had the desk next to his and Rachel was only a few feet away.

'Right, Wes,' said Gerry once he'd sifted through the messages that had come in in his absence. 'Why don't you and Rach go to that agency in Neston and see what you can find out about our house-sitter.'

'Shouldn't we visit the man she was house-sitting for in Neston first?'

'All in good time. Someone must have provided our victim with a reference. You wouldn't trust your house and possessions to just anyone who walked in off the street, would you?'

Wesley couldn't fault the boss's logic.

By the time he left the church hall with Rachel by his side, the incident room was buzzing with purposeful activity. At this stage in the investigation every moment counted as they tried to discover all they could about the victim. Wesley was a believer in the old detective's mantra: to discover how someone died, it helped to know how they lived.

'She might have been a barmaid at the Seashell, and quite sociable by all accounts, but she didn't give away much about herself, so at the moment she's an enigma,' he said as they were driving along the main road to Neston.

'Not like you to sound so despondent, Wes,' Rachel said, putting her hand lightly on his sleeve then swiftly withdrawing it as though she'd realised the gesture might be inappropriate.

Wesley pretended he hadn't noticed and continued to navigate his way down the narrow back streets of the pretty Elizabethan town, now popular with those of a New Age inclination. He found a space in the car park at the rear of the modern council offices, a relic of the 1960s that jarred with its picturesque neighbours. The offices of Edenwood Homes lay down a narrow side street, and at first they took it for a small private terraced house with office-style vertical blinds at the single front window. But the stainless-steel plaque bearing the name beside the door told them they'd come to the right place.

Wesley rang the bell and the door was opened by a

middle-aged woman with a thin, pinched face and a severe haircut. Once they'd introduced themselves, she led the way into a front office lined with steel filing cabinets. The only decoration in the room was a large black-and-white photograph of Neston's high street hanging over the boarded-up fireplace.

'What can I do for you?' she asked as she sat down. Her manner was cool, with none of the curiosity most people displayed when they received a visit from detectives.

'A woman was found dead on the coast path near Bereton yesterday,' Rachel began. 'We're treating her death as suspicious.'

'I heard about it on the radio, but I don't see how I can help you.'

'We believe the victim was on your books as a house-sitter.' Wesley took out his notebook. 'Her name was Susan Brown and she looked after the house of a Matt Harrod while he was abroad.'

'I'll need to find the file.' It was hard to read the woman's expression as she stood and walked to one of the cabinets, returning a few moments later with a cardboard folder.

'We're particularly interested in any references Ms Brown might have provided for you. Or any personal details: bank account, National Insurance number, anything like that.'

Wesley could have sworn he saw the woman's face turn red beneath her thick layer of make-up. 'We don't actually pay our house-sitters. It's up to our clients to make those arrangements. We merely put them in touch – with a fee to cover our expenses, of course.'

'Of course,' said Wesley. 'May I see her file?'

She hesitated as though she was reluctant to hand it over. But eventually she pushed it slowly across the desk. Wesley opened it and Rachel leaned over until she was almost touching his shoulder.

The file contained one reference, from a Neville Grasmere at an address in Chipping Campden, saying that Ms Brown used to work for him and was a completely trustworthy employee. She'd also stayed in his house and he'd found her pleasant and honest, so he wouldn't hesitate to recommend her as a house-sitter. There was no indication of what Mr Grasmere's line of business might be, or what Susan's duties had been while she'd been in his employ. There was a telephone number but no email address.

The only other papers in the file were connected to Matt Harrod. Wesley noticed that Edenwood Homes charged a hefty fee for their services. He wondered how the woman would have reacted if she'd known about the private arrangement Susan had had with Andrea Alladyce. No wonder Susan had asked Darren to keep quiet about it.

'Business good?' he asked as casually as he could.

'There are a lot of second homes round here and people are only too pleased to know that someone's looking after their property.'

He took that as a yes. 'What can you tell me about Ms Brown?'

'Not much. She turned up at the office one day asking whether she could work for us as a house-sitter. She was staying in a B & B nearby and was keen on getting something in Tradmouth or Neston. She told me she'd just moved here from the Cotswolds and she provided a reference, so everything seemed to be in order.'

'You checked the reference, of course?'

There was another hesitation. 'Of course. I rang the

gentleman and there was nothing to make me think that anything was amiss.'

'There's nothing else you can tell us about her?' said Rachel.

'She seemed a pleasant woman and Mr Harrod had no complaints. In fact, he contacted us soon after she left him to see whether we had an address for her because he wanted to engage her again, but unfortunately we hadn't, and the mobile number we had for her was unavailable. That's really all I can tell you. You'll appreciate we have a lot of people on our books and she wasn't one of our regulars.'

'Mind if I take the file?'

She looked as though she was about to object, but before she could say anything, Rachel had whipped it from under her nose.

Their next port of call was Matt Harrod. Wesley wasn't sure what he did for a living, but as so many people worked from home these days, he hoped there was a chance of finding him in. His address was in the centre of Neston, a large white stucco semi probably dating from the Regency period – the same era Crispin Joss and his cast and crew were attempting to recreate back at Serpent's Point. There were Roman blinds at the sash windows and a glossy front door in a tasteful shade of sage green, no doubt described on the paint chart as a heritage colour. A pair of healthy-looking bay trees flanked the entrance. If this had been Susan Brown's home for a while, the converted stables at Serpent's Point must have seemed like a disappointment.

They were in luck. Matt Harrod himself opened the door. He was medium height, athletic and in his late thirties, with pale red hair and a small, neat beard. He was wearing an open-necked shirt and well-pressed chinos and he had the quietly prosperous look of a successful professional man. When the detectives showed their ID, he looked mildly curious.

'How can I help you?' he asked.

'We'd like to talk to you about the woman who house-sat for you a while ago. Her name was Susan Brown.'

'Why? What's happened?'

'You'll have heard that a body was found on the coast path near Bereton?'

'I heard something on the news.' He sounded wary, as though he was afraid of what Wesley was about to say.

It was Rachel who spoke next. 'The deceased was Susan Brown, who house-sat for you while you were abroad. I'm afraid we're treating her death as suspicious.'

He stood in stunned silence for a few moments before stepping aside. 'That's terrible. You'd better come in.'

He led them into an elegant drawing room, tastefully furnished, with china-blue walls dotted with paintings. Wesley immediately recognised that some were by Andrea Alladyce.

'You like Andrea Alladyce's work?' he said.

'I love it. You're familiar with her paintings.'

'Yes. They're very . . . atmospheric.' Having established a rapport with the man, Wesley seized the chance to ask his first question. 'Did you know that Susan Brown was house-sitting for Ms Alladyce when she was killed?'

There was a long silence. Harrod's face was a neutral mask and it was hard to guess his thoughts. 'I didn't know that. She left without leaving a forwarding address.'

'I understand it was your electrician, Darren Bailey, who put her in touch with Ms Alladyce.'

'Really.' He paused. 'Darren did some work for me here

while I was away, so presumably that's how Susan met him.' He bowed his head. 'If she found herself in the wrong place at the wrong time, I can't help feeling a little responsible for setting off the chain of events that put her there.'

'You can't blame yourself, sir,' said Rachel.

It was the first time she'd spoken, and Harrod looked up at her curiously. 'Please sit down, Sergeant,' he said anxiously, as though he'd only just noticed she was pregnant. 'And you, Inspector. Would you like tea? Coffee?'

'Coffee for me,' said Wesley. Creating an atmosphere of cosy confidence usually helped.

Rachel asked for tea and Harrod hurried from the room.

'Nice place,' she whispered.

Wesley didn't answer. He was considering the questions they needed to ask.

'What were you doing abroad, sir?' he asked when Harrod returned.

'I'm an architect and my work took me to Spain. I was supervising the construction of a villa for a client.'

'You found Ms Brown through Edenwood Homes?'

'That's right. We met up here to discuss her duties and we got on very well, so I had no qualms about leaving her in charge while I was away. I called her every day, of course, to make sure Tacitus was all right. That's my cat,' he said fondly. 'He seemed very happy with her, which was the main thing.'

'Where was she staying before she came here?'

'A B & B in Tradmouth. I suggested that she came to stay here in the spare room until I left. There was a lot I needed to explain about looking after Tacitus. This was a week before I was due to travel, so she didn't have to put up with me for very long.'

'If she was living here in your house, you must have come to know her quite well.'

'Yes, and I liked her very much.' The ghost of a smile appeared on Harrod's lips. 'She was a ... warm person. She rarely talked about herself. She was more interested in other people and I appreciated that about her.'

'Was she interested in anyone in particular?'

He considered Wesley's question for a few seconds. 'Not that I remember. I told her I used to do a bit of sailing before ...' His face suddenly clouded, as though the subject had revived a bad memory. 'She asked a lot of questions about boats and the sort of people who owned them, but apart from that ...' He paused, a faraway look in his eyes as though he had fond recollections of the dead woman. 'I asked her if she'd been married, and she told me she was divorced and her ex worked in Dubai. She said she hadn't seen him for years and he had a new family. She also mentioned that she'd lost a close friend a few years ago. A childhood friend, she said. Susan was very sensitive and I think that loss affected her badly.' Wesley noticed that Harrod's eyes were glassy with unshed tears.

'Did she tell you what the friend's name was, and how she died? Or was the friend a he?'

'I don't know the name, but I think it was a woman. When I asked her for more details, she said the subject was too painful. I know all about grief, so I understood.'

This caught Wesley's attention. He glanced at Rachel and saw that she too was listening intently.

'I'm really sorry, but that's all I know. She'd been staying in the Cotswolds before she came here, but she was from Yorkshire originally.'

'Was Brown her maiden name?'

'I don't know. Sorry, I'm not being much help, am I?'

'I wouldn't say that, sir,' said Wesley with a smile. 'She took a part-time job at a pub called the Seashell not far from where she died.'

'I didn't know that.'

'Your electrician, Darren Bailey, is a regular there.'

'Darren's not a suspect, is he?'

'Why? Is there anything about him that made you suspicious?'

'No. Not at all. He seems like a decent man.'

'Do you live here alone, sir?' Rachel asked.

A cloud of sadness passed over Harrod's face. 'My partner, Rory, passed away a couple of years ago, before I moved here. A boating accident in Portugal. I've been alone ever since.'

'I'm sorry to hear that,' said Wesley with sincerity. 'Darren lost his wife, I believe. Did it help to talk to someone in the same situation?'

'Some things are personal and painful – too painful to share with your electrician.'

'But you shared them with Susan?'

'She was a very sympathetic person. Easy to talk to. To be honest, it was nice having her about the place for that week. I enjoyed her company. Do you know when her funeral will be? I'd like to pay my respects.'

'We're still trying to trace her next of kin. I don't suppose you can help with that?'

Harrod shook his head. It seemed strange to Wesley that Susan still remained such an enigmatic figure, and he was becoming increasingly convinced that she'd been running away from something bad. Something that had eventually caught up with her on that coast path.

The shrill sound of the doorbell shattered the silence,

and Harrod looked at the detectives as though he was waiting for permission to answer.

'Don't you want to see who that is?' Wesley said.

Harrod hurried out of the room and Wesley heard voices in the hall. Curious, he poked his head round the door and saw their host talking to a middle-aged woman with long dark hair. He retreated into the drawing room, not wanting to be caught eavesdropping.

A photograph on the mantelpiece caught his attention. Matt Harrod with another man around his own age, maybe slightly older. They were in a sun-drenched bar with their arms around each other's shoulders. Presumably this was Rory. They looked happy, but sadly, that happiness hadn't lasted.

He heard the front door close and stepped away from the fireplace.

'That was my neighbour,' said Harrod on his return. 'She's expecting a parcel – asked if I can take it in.'

'The perils of working from home, I suppose. Mind you, it's always reassuring to know your neighbours,' said Wesley, making conversation.

'I suppose so.' Harrod didn't sound convinced. 'I find it rather intrusive, to tell the truth, but I heard there was a break-in at one of the flats in that new warehouse conversion by the river while I was away, so I suppose it's useful to have people around. Especially as the police don't seem to come out for that sort of thing these days.'

Wesley saw Rachel raise her eyebrows at the implied criticism.

'Can you tell us where you were yesterday morning between eight thirty and ten o'clock?'

'Certainly, Inspector. I was here working. A client's

having a house built on the outskirts of town and he wanted some alterations to the plans.'

'Where do you work?'

'My studio's at the back of the house.'

'Any witnesses?'

'Only Tacitus, I'm afraid.'

'May I see your office?' Wesley asked politely.

A momentary look of irritation appeared on Harrod's face. 'Of course.'

He led them through to a spacious room overlooking the small, neat back garden. The studio was south-facing and filled with light, and Wesley saw that it was equipped with a state-of-the-art computer. A drawing board took pride of place. On it were detailed plans for the front elevation of a large detached house. Other designs lay on a long table at the far end of the room.

'I prefer to do my initial designs on paper rather than straight onto the computer,' Harrod said when he saw Wesley looking at the plans. 'I get more of a feel for the finished project that way.'

'Was Susan interested in your work?'

'She did show an interest.' He smiled. 'Although it might just have been out of politeness.'

'We understand you were trying to get in touch with her through the agency.'

'That's right. Another trip abroad is on the cards, so I wondered if she'd like to stay here again. But the agency didn't have a current address for her and I couldn't get through on her mobile number.'

They thanked him and left, staying silent until they were back in the car.

'What did you think?' Rachel asked.

'I think he's lonely, which is understandable if he lost his partner recently.'

'Did you believe what he told us about Susan?'

'Didn't you?'

'He wasn't too pleased when that neighbour arrived to ask a favour, and I don't think he liked the idea of his electrician being a mate of that artist while he has to buy her work from expensive galleries.'

'Understandable, I suppose.'

'You know what your trouble is, Wes? You tend to think the best of everyone.'

Wesley began to laugh. 'In this job? You must be joking. We have no reason to disbelieve what he told us, have we?'

'You're right.'

'And he's gay, so he's unlikely to have taken a sexual interest in the victim. Although she might have stumbled on some dark secret of his while she was staying at his house.'

'It's not like you to let your imagination run away with you. But I'll keep an open mind and check whether his name came up in connection with either of those missing persons cases. Just for you.'

'Everything OK?' Wesley asked. 'Nigel all right? The farm?'

'I've never known a time when a farmer says everything's fine. My dad always has some gripe or other. If it isn't the weather, it's the price of feed.'

'How's Nigel looking forward to being a dad?'

She glanced down. 'I think he's so used to births amongst the livestock that he's treating this one the same.' She laid a protective hand on her bump. 'I wouldn't put it past him to call out the vet.'

Wesley laughed and she joined in. Then the laughter suddenly stopped.

'It'll change my life, Wes. And I don't know whether I want my life changed yet. I like it how it is. I like my job.'

'I know you do.' He suspected that whatever he said would probably be the wrong thing, so he changed the subject. 'Let's get back to the incident room and see if there's anything new.'

His phone rang, but when he saw the call was from Neil, he didn't answer. He had too much to do and he didn't need distractions.

They were halfway back to Bereton when it rang again. It was Gerry this time, so Wesley pulled over.

'Bit of good news, Wes. The search team found a laptop at the victim's house, hidden away at the back of a cupboard. We've found her mobile phone too. We've given them to the techies, so we should have something soon.'

Wesley's first thought was that if the laptop was hidden away, it might belong to Andrea Alladyce and have nothing to do with Susan. But when they reached the church hall, they found Gerry waiting, beaming all over his face.

'We've had some luck with that laptop and phone, Wes.' The DCI sounded like a child who'd woken on Christmas morning to find his sack bulging with toys. 'There's not much on either of them. Tom from Scientific Support says they were both bought recently. The browsing history on the laptop shows she had a fondness for old cases: missing women all over the country, not just those two on her wall. So either she fancied herself as an amateur detective ... '

'Or she had a personal reason for taking an interest.'

11

According to Scientific Support, Susan must have purchased the laptop and phone after she arrived in Devon, because nothing on them pre-dated the time she began house-sitting for Matt Harrod. And she clearly hadn't been someone who lived her life on her phone; apart from a few calls to the pub where she worked, the only person she called and texted was someone called Drusilla Kramer. Drusilla had sent her numerous emails with links to reports of missing persons cases and unidentified corpses that had turned up in various parts of the country, even as far away as Scotland and Northern Ireland. One case was in Chipping Campden, and Wesley wondered whether this was relevant. Had she been travelling the country examining these cases? Had she been trying to solve them when the police had failed?

Some of the texts concerned arrangements to meet in 'the usual place at the usual time', so it looked as though Drusilla, whoever she was, might have been Susan's partner in detection. Which meant they needed to find her as soon as possible. If she knew what Susan knew, she too might be in danger.

'Tom's doing his best to get an address for this Drusilla,'

said Gerry, as though he'd read Wesley's mind. 'He said it won't be a problem.'

'Good. And we need to speak to the man who provided Susan with her reference for the house-sitting agency. His name's Neville Grasmere and he lives in Chipping Campden. I've got his number. I'll call him now.'

Wesley went to his desk to make the call, but there was no reply. As the number was obviously a landline, its owner might not be at home, so he left a message asking Grasmere to call him back. He was growing increasingly curious about Neville Grasmere. He'd provided Susan with a glowing reference, saying he'd employed her and found her trustworthy, but they had no information about him or his exact relationship with the dead woman. It seemed rather brutal to break the news over the phone, but at that moment Wesley had no choice. He'd either have to be patient and wait for the man to return his call or get Grasmere's local station to contact him.

He decided on the second option and asked an officer from his nearest station to pay Mr Grasmere a visit. He told them to break the news gently, hoping they'd show some sensitivity.

While he was waiting to hear back, he trawled through the reports that had piled up on his desk and found the statements from Grey Grover and Krystal Saverigg of Serpent's Point. Grover had seemed reluctant to identify the photograph of Susan he'd shown him, and Wesley wondered why. Had he been cagey because he didn't want to get involved, or was there a more sinister reason? He needed to speak to the pair again.

As for the film people, their statements were all remarkably similar. Each one of them, including the director,

Crispin Joss, claimed they didn't know the woman who'd been staying in the converted stables; they'd seen her around but nobody had spoken to her. They knew nothing about her death and they'd been tied up in the filming so they'd noticed little else. Wesley supposed this was possible, and yet he couldn't help wondering whether one or two of them knew more than they were admitting. Again, it might be worth asking more questions, even if it meant disrupting the filming of *The Awakening of Lillith Montmorency*.

It was coming up to lunchtime when Gerry received the phone call. Wesley heard the DCI calling his name and saw that he was beckoning him over frantically, with his other hand placed over the telephone receiver. He joined him, eager to hear the news – and hoping it was good.

'Tom's come up trumps,' Gerry said. 'He's got an address for Drusilla Kramer from her email. Don't ask me how he does these things. It's a mystery to me.' He regarded Tom's computer skills with the awe his ancestors would once have reserved for some famed alchemist – Elizabeth I's Dr John Dee, perhaps. He handed Wesley the address, his eyes glowing with excitement. 'It's in Morbay. Let's pay her a visit.'

As he stood up, the legs of his chair scraped loudly on the wooden floor, and Rachel looked up from her computer.

'Where are you off to?' There was a note of disappointment in her voice, as though she feared she was missing out on something important.

Wesley explained what was happening.

'You sure the boss is the best person to break that sort of news?' she asked.

He caught her meaning at once. Rachel was experienced in family liaison, so she'd tackle the situation with tact and sensitivity. But he knew the DCI's mind was made up, so he told Rachel they'd call her if they needed her. She didn't look too happy about it.

Drusilla's flat was in a small 1960s block on the outskirts of the resort. It was a pleasant area boasting an abundance of trees, and there was a small park opposite. The plaque outside the block declared that it was called Park View Court – not particularly original, but Wesley guessed it sounded classy enough to add a couple of grand to the asking price of any flats that came up for sale. It was Friday, so Drusilla might be at work, but with any luck, the neighbours would be able to tell them where to find her.

The label against the bell for Flat 3 said *D. Kramer*, and Wesley pressed the buzzer. When a disembodied female voice answered, his heart lifted. They'd found her at home. The barking in the background suggested she had a dog.

The woman who opened the front door was in her late thirties, tall, athletic and tanned, with shoulder-length black hair and strong features. She wore leggings, a pale blue T-shirt and the sort of trainers you don't buy for the purposes of fashion. She looked slightly dishevelled, as though she'd just been out for a run, and she was holding the collar of a medium-sized brown dog of indeterminate breed. It was wagging its tail and looked keen to greet the newcomers.

'Drusilla Kramer?'

'That's right. Sorry, I was just about to have a shower. What's this about?' she asked, a note of anxiety in her voice, as though in her world, the police didn't come calling unless it was to bring bad news.

They were standing at the entrance to the flats and Wesley asked if they could come in. It wasn't an interview he fancied conducting in a public space. She hesitated for a moment before leading them up to the first floor, with the dog following, tail still wagging as though it was hoping the newcomers might throw a ball or take it for a walk.

The flat was bright, with large windows, light wooden floors and pale Scandinavian furnishings. When Drusilla invited them to sit, Gerry made himself comfortable in an armchair upholstered in oatmeal linen, while Wesley perched on the edge of the matching sofa. The dog, spotting a soft touch, made for him, and Wesley fondled its soft head while it looked up at him with hope in its large eyes.

Drusilla remained standing, fidgeting nervously with the hem of her T-shirt. It was time they told her why they were there.

'Do you know a woman called Susan Brown?'

'Sue? Yes. Why?'

Wesley caught Gerry's eye. 'I'm very sorry to have to tell you that she was found dead yesterday near Bereton and we're treating her death as suspicious.'

She shook her head, clearly stunned by the news

'I'm sorry you've had to hear it like this, love,' said Gerry. 'Mind if we ask you some questions? If Susan was a friend of yours, you might be able to help us.'

'Yes. Anything. I can't believe it, I really can't.'

Gerry gave a small nod, a signal that he wanted Wesley to ask the questions while he listened.

'How long had you known Susan?' Wesley asked gently.

'Only a couple of months. She was house-sitting for some guy in Neston. I was in a vegan café there and we got talking.'

'I understand she was divorced?'

'We both are ... were, but she never said much about her ex. Mine went off with a woman from his work – well, a girl really. She was only eighteen and he was twenty years older.' She pressed her lips together, angry at the memory of the betrayal. 'She's welcome to him.'

But Wesley wasn't interested in Drusilla's marital difficulties. 'What about Susan? What was her story?'

'She came from Yorkshire, somewhere on the coast, and then moved to the Cotswolds.'

'Did she mention any boyfriends?'

She thought for a moment. 'I said I had an ex who'd kept hanging around once I'd finished with him, and she told me there'd been a bloke up in Yorkshire who'd done the same. I got the impression this was a few years ago, but ... ' She paused, as though she was trying to retrieve an elusive memory. 'She did say once that there was someone she was trying to avoid.'

'Around here?'

'I don't know. She only mentioned it the one time. I think she might have been a bit embarrassed about it.'

'Was it the man from Yorkshire?'

'Like I said, I don't know. I did ask her, but she said she didn't want to talk about it and changed the subject. I suppose if the man from Yorkshire wouldn't take no for an answer and found her down here ... ' Her eyes widened as though she suddenly realised the implications of what she'd just told them.

'Did she tell you his name or anything about him?'

She shook her head. 'Sorry, no.'

Now that he'd found out a little more about Susan's past, there was an important subject he had to raise. 'We've seen the emails you exchanged with Susan. She was very interested in old missing persons cases.' He watched Drusilla's reaction carefully.

'Yes, she was quite ... obsessive about it, to be honest. She said a friend of hers had gone missing once, someone she'd known from when she was little, so that probably explains it. I'm into true crime myself, and whenever I came across a case on the internet, I sent her the link.'

Gerry caught Wesley's eye, then broke his silence. 'The case of this missing friend – was she following it up down here?'

'She seemed to be interested in all sorts of cases, not just that one. Although I think there was a lot she didn't tell me. Perhaps given time ... ' She bowed her head. 'But she's run out of that, hasn't she?' She took a tissue from her pocket to wipe her eyes.

'Did you ever visit her at Serpent's Point?' Wesley asked, wondering if she'd seen Susan's incident room.

'No. We always met in cafés and sometimes for lunch in my local pub.'

'Have you ever been to the Seashell near Bereton? Susan worked there.'

'She said she'd taken part-time bar work to bring in a bit of money. I meant to go there, but I never got round to it. It's not always possible to find time in my job.'

'What do you do?'

'I'm a nurse – it's not easy when you have to work shifts. Sue liked the Seashell. She mentioned someone she knew there called Darren, but I don't think there was any romantic involvement.' Drusilla hesitated. 'I can't say I really knew her, even though we were friends.'

Wesley took his notebook from his pocket. 'Have you heard the name Avril Willis?'

'I don't think so.'

'What about Simone Pritchard?'

She shook her head. 'Doesn't ring a bell.'

'They're both women who disappeared. Avril was later found murdered, but Simone is still missing. Susan was taking a particular interest in them. Were they among the missing persons cases you sent her links to?'

'Sorry, I can't remember. Whenever I saw an appeal for information on social media, I sent her the link, that's all. There were such a lot of them.'

'We have reason to believe Ms Brown changed her phone recently. Do you know anything about that?'

'She told me she lost her old one.'

'She changed her number.'

Drusilla shrugged. 'She said the old one was a pay-as-you-go and she took the chance to upgrade. The change of number didn't bother her because she said there wasn't anyone from her old life she wanted to keep in touch with. She wanted to make a fresh start.'

Wesley looked at Gerry. That explained why Matt Harrod and the agency hadn't been able to contact her.

Wesley stood up and Gerry struggled out of the armchair where he'd made himself a little too comfortable.

'Thank you for your time, Ms Kramer. And if you remember anything else, don't hesitate to get in touch,' said Wesley as he handed her his card.

'I will, Inspector.'

'Sorry to be the bearers of such bad news, love,' said Gerry.

Wesley hesitated at the door. 'What's the dog called?'

Drusilla looked down at the animal. 'Sherlock. He belonged to a neighbour who liked detective stories.'

'Good name,' Wesley said, thinking of his cat, Moriarty.

'She asked me to look after him while she was in hospital, and nobody else in the flats would take him so I felt I couldn't refuse. She was only meant to be in for two days, but she died unexpectedly, so I've been landed with him. I really don't have the time to look after him properly, so I'm thinking of contacting one of the rescue charities.'

It was hard to tell whether this was said with regret. Wesley stroked the dog's head and was rewarded by a wagging tail in response. 'He's a nice dog,' he said.

Drusilla nodded, but she didn't seem particularly interested.

She saw them to the entrance to her flat, and when Wesley glanced back, he thought she looked worried, as though there was something else she wanted to say. But instead she shut the door. It had probably been his imagination.

12

On their return to the incident room, Wesley and Gerry were greeted with the news that nobody from Neville Grasmere's local station had managed to contact him and his neighbours thought he might be away. Wesley couldn't help wondering whether Mr Grasmere was unavailable because he was down in Devon murdering the woman he'd provided with a reference. Perhaps his years in the police had given him a suspicious mind.

Paul Johnson and Trish Walton had been given the job of finding out all they could about the two women who featured in Susan Brown's incident room: Avril Willis and Simone Pritchard. They'd both been reported as missing persons, but only Avril had been found. She'd been murdered; strangled just like Susan.

Gerry found a message waiting for him on his desk. The team who were still searching the converted stables had found something interesting; would the SIO like to come over and have a look?

'Why can't they just say what it is?' he muttered to nobody in particular. Then he turned to Wesley. 'Come on, Wes, let's go back to Serpent's Point. Odd name for a house if you ask me. Would you call your house after a nasty slithery creature?'

Wesley shook his head. As a child, he'd attended Sunday school every week, and he automatically associated the word 'serpent' with evil. Satan himself had appeared in the form of a serpent. Gerry was right: it wasn't a name you'd choose to give your home.

Serpent's Point was five minutes away by car, and Wesley parked in front of the stables, squeezing the vehicle past the production company's huge vans. Grey Grover, he thought, must resent the intrusion, but filming meant money, and from the look of the place, money was badly needed.

Rob Carter greeted them at the entrance to Susan Brown's temporary home. As usual, he had the keen, hungry look of an ambitious man, and Wesley suspected he was hoping Gerry would appoint him acting sergeant when Rachel took her maternity leave. Wesley himself preferred the more plodding DC Paul Johnson, or possibly Rachel's former housemate and Paul's partner, DC Trish Walton. In his opinion, Rob tended to be impulsive and cut corners.

'You should see this, sir. I reckon Little Miss House-Sitter wasn't as innocent as she made out,' said Rob loudly, his eyes glowing with excitement.

'Let's get inside,' said Gerry as he spotted a young man in Regency costume wandering across the cobbled yard with his head in a script. 'Have all the film lot been interviewed now?' he asked once they'd shut the door.

'Yes, sir, they've all given statements. Cast and crew. Mind you, every one of them did a good imitation of those three wise monkeys – saw nothing, heard nothing, saying nothing. And that director bloke says he's going to complain to the person in charge about the disruption to his schedule.'

'Going to give me grief, is he?' said Gerry.

'I pointed out that this is a murder inquiry so he didn't have much say in the matter. That shut him up.'

Wesley resisted the temptation to comment. Sometimes Rob tended to rub people up the wrong way. Tact, in his experience, was often a more potent weapon than aggression.

Rob led the way into the living room, which the search team had gone through like a swarm of locusts. Everything had been opened, examined, turned upside down. Pictures had been removed from the walls, rugs and loose floorboards taken up. The previously tidy house looked like a tip.

'We found them hidden in the bedroom, taped to the back of a drawer,' said Rob as he climbed the stairs ahead of them.

They came to the main bedroom. Lying on the dressing table was a plastic evidence bag. Inside, Wesley could see a passport and driving licence lying beside some other official-looking documents.

'We've got a former address for her in Whitby.' Rob's voice was triumphant, as though he was taking the credit for the discovery.

Wesley put on his crime-scene gloves and picked up the bag.

'Aren't you going to open it?' Gerry sounded impatient, like a child faced with presents on Christmas morning.

Wesley took the contents out carefully, one by one. There was a passport in the name of Susan Gilda Brown; the photograph was definitely that of the dead woman. The driving licence was in the same name, with an address in Whitby.

'Avril Willis came from Whitby,' he said. 'Susan told Drusilla Kramer that a childhood friend of hers had gone missing, so my money's on that friend being Avril.'

Gerry turned to Rob, who was hovering behind them, eager to be in on the discussion. 'Tell you what, Rob, get on to Whitby nick, will you. Ask them to let us have everything they've got on Susan Brown and find out whether her name came up in connection with the Avril Willis case. Give them the address on these documents and ask them to send someone round there pronto.'

'Right you are, sir,' said Rob, with the eagerness of a sheep dog who'd just been given the task of rounding up a flock.

'Anything else?'

Rob shook his head, looking disappointed that he couldn't produce the killer, duly cautioned and hand-cuffed, for them. They left him to it, hoping his enquiries would produce something useful.

'I'd like to take another look at the murder scene now the circus has left town,' said Gerry.

'I'll come with you.' Wesley had spotted Neil's car on the lane on the way in, although he hadn't mentioned this to Gerry. 'I'd like to see if those two girls are still around with their metal detectors. I want to find out whether they've remembered anything else.'

'Your mate Neil's there, isn't he? I saw that car of his.'

'He's doing some field walking – said he was going to ask the girls to help out.'

'I didn't come in on the last boat, Wes. You want to see if he's found anything, don't you?' The twinkle in Gerry's eyes belied the scolding words.

'I won't tell a lie. But I promise I won't be long.'

'Let's have another look at where the victim died first, then I'll come with you. I could do with some inspiration – and a break.'

The two men walked down to the coast path, where the crime-scene tape still fluttered sadly, marking the location of the tragedy. They stood in silence for a while, staring at it, until Gerry spoke.

'What exactly was Susan up to, I wonder. Did she fancy herself as a private eye? A one-woman missing persons bureau? And was she being stalked by this bloke in Yorkshire Drusilla Kramer mentioned? Had he tracked her down and still wouldn't take no for an answer? Or maybe it was the ex-husband.'

'If we knew that, we'd be halfway to solving her murder.'

Gerry gave a solemn nod. 'I reckon a visit to Whitby's on the cards. If that's where she's from, that's where we'll find out more about her. And we need to know what prompted the move to Devon.'

'Presumably with a stop at Chipping Campden on the way down – hence the reference from Neville Grasmere. Was she on some sort of road trip with the aim of finding missing people? Or was she was running away from something – or someone?'

'She was hardly keeping a low profile down here,' Gerry pointed out. 'House-sitting and working in a pub.'

'All that means is that she didn't regard those particular people as a danger. Although she might have been wrong about that.' Wesley stared at the spot where Susan's body had been found. 'Someone either followed her here or was lying in wait.'

'Or she'd arranged to meet them here.'

'The girls saw someone in a baseball cap. If they could see the hat over the hedge, he must have been very tall.'

'Who's to say it was a he? Dr Stamoran didn't rule out a strong woman.'

'But the girls didn't arrive in the field until ten thirty, and Dr Stamoran thought Susan was dead before that.'

'The killer might have come back to check that he hadn't left anything incriminating behind.' Gerry thought for a moment. 'Or it might have been someone who stumbled on the body and didn't want to get involved. Whichever it was, we need to speak to him. Or her.'

'Pity they don't have CCTV around here.' Wesley shook his head. The thought of such a beautiful spot being blighted by modern cameras spying on walkers enjoying the wonders of nature seemed abhorrent ... and yet he couldn't deny it would have been useful in this case.

He led the way to the field, hoping Neil's activities would take his mind off violent death. Sometimes a distraction helped you see things more clearly. He hadn't expected to see quite so many archaeologists there, spaced out and walking slowly and purposefully in straight lines, their eyes fixed on the ground. Every so often one would bend down to pick something up and put it in a plastic tray. Sophie and Livy were with them, engrossed in what they were doing.

'They're field walking,' he explained to his companion.

'Thought one of them had lost a contact lens,' was Gerry's quick reply.

An awning had been set up in the far corner of the field, and Wesley saw Neil emerging from its shadows. He walked over to meet them, grinning widely.

'Wes. I was about to ring you. You're missing all the excitement.'

'A woman's been murdered,' said Gerry. 'We've got all the excitement we need.'

Wesley's gaze strayed to the two girls picking their way

across the field with the others. 'You've got them working, I see.'

'They seem to be enjoying themselves. I contacted our old department at the university and asked for volunteers. As you see, there was a good response.'

'Found anything?'

'Some shards of Samian ware. A few tesserae.'

Wesley raised his eyebrows. 'Tesserae? You mean there could be a mosaic?'

'I'll leave you to draw your own conclusions. We've already geophysed the lower section of the field.'

'And?'

'Come with me.' Neil rubbed his soil-stained hands together with glee. 'Have I got something to show you!'

'What's he so excited about?' said Gerry as they followed Neil to the awning, where three trestle tables had been set up in a rough triangle. Wesley didn't answer. The mention of tesserae, those tiny squares of stone that made up a mosaic, had set his imagination working, even though his thoughts went against everything he knew about the history of this particular part of Devon.

The printout from the geophysics survey Neil had organised lay on one of the tables, weighted down by two plastic trays containing pieces of stone and pottery. A couple of these stones looked to Wesley like tesserae, small and square, but there was a chance he could be wrong; that he was seeing what he wanted to see.

'We'll have to do the rest of the field, but from what we've got already . . . What do you think, Wes?'

Wesley studied the printout. 'The Romans never took any interest in this part of the county, surely.'

'If I can prove otherwise, it won't do my standing in the

archaeological community any harm.' Neil tapped the side of his nose.

Wesley caught his meaning right away. 'It certainly won't. The geophysics survey suggests that there are building foundations under there. But it might not be what you're hoping for.'

Neil's smile vanished. 'I'm well aware of that, Wes. It might be old farm buildings. But I've had a word with the farmer, Livy's dad, and he doesn't think there was ever anything like that round here, so I'm staying optimistic.'

'Could still be old. Medieval?'

Neil grinned. 'Pessimist.'

'What was all that about?' Gerry asked as they walked back to the car.

'Archaeology talk,' said Wesley. It wasn't something he felt like sharing before Neil knew more. But he knew that, in the unlikely case of his friend being right, it would cause a sensation.

They reached the courtyard in front of the stables that had been Susan Brown's temporary home. But as they climbed into the car, they were unaware that they were being watched.

From the journal of Dr Aldus Claye

May 1921

Phipps asked the farmer if some of his labourers could be spared to help with the excavation, but the man claimed that their work on the farm would keep them occupied most of the day. However, he promised to ask them if they were willing to help during their leisure hours, emphasising that they would expect to be paid well for their trouble.

While we await the verdict, Phipps has insisted that we make a start. First we walked up and down the field in the manner of ploughmen trudging to and fro. On Phipps's insistence, we kept our eyes fixed upon the ground, looking for any object that might have been thrown up from the depths over the years. Inexperienced as I was, I found three sherds of pottery, which Phipps rejected as late medieval. He was searching for something earlier.

The farmer had shown us the exact spot where the curse was found, and Phipps decided to begin digging there. When I reminded him of the bones the man claimed to have seen, it didn't bother him one jot. They'd be ancient, he said, so there'd be no reason to trouble the authorities. It was a mere curiosity. A murder mystery from the mists of antiquity. I wish I could share his confidence.

So it was that our dig began. I was surprised when Clarabel arrived in the field, saying she wished to watch the proceedings. I had never known her to take an interest in such things before, and I observed that Phipps was remarkably patient with her, explaining what he intended to do. We sank a trench, with Phipps, the expert, giving orders while I assumed the role of labourer, hauling buckets of soil to the edge of the field.

Phipps excavated the area quickly, and I knew he was searching for the bones. Romans, he said, were often buried with grave goods, so it was imperative that we locate them. His eyes glowed, hungry for some dramatic find. For the first time, I began to wonder whether I had been wise to invite him, but I had been dazzled by his scholarship and reputation.

I observed my wife's behaviour in his presence. Even when he uncovered a skull, she showed no horror. Only excitement.

13

Neil decided to have another word with Livy's dad, Nick Stanley, while the geophysics survey continued. He found him in the cowshed, where Nick greeted him like an old friend, saying he hoped his daughter and her friend weren't getting in the way. Neil assured him they weren't, relieved that the man didn't seem at all bothered about the invasion of his land by an army of archaeologists and their equipment.

'When our Livy asked if they could use their metal detectors down there, I thought why not,' Nick said. 'I told them if they dug up any treasure to let me know,' he added with a grin. 'Never expected they'd find anything but a few rusty old nails, but you never know, do you.' He looked Neil in the eye. 'Those coins they found – are they going to make me a rich man, then?'

'Can't promise anything, Nick, but I'll keep you posted.'

Nick went on to explain how he'd recently bought the field from Grey Grover up at Serpent's Point. For years his family had had permission to graze cattle there, but six months ago, Grover had offered to sell him the land at a knock-down price, and Nick had accepted the offer before the man had a chance to change his mind. Grover would be kicking himself if it turned out there was treasure there.

Neil noticed that the farmer rolled his eyes, as though he didn't have a high opinion of the man who owned Serpent's Point. Nick Stanley reckoned Grover had money worries. Serpent's Point must cost a fortune to maintain, he said, which was probably why he was letting those film people crawl all over the place.

Neil asked him what information he had about the field, but all Nick knew was that the soil was unsuitable for crops so it had always been used for grazing. When Neil asked whether Grey Grover might have more information, Nick said he doubted it; Grover had never taken much interest in things like that.

The farmer seemed in no hurry to get away. He was a friendly sort of man with an open manner, used to taking social interactions at a leisurely pace.

'Do you think you've found some sort of building, then?' he asked.

'Too early to say yet.'

'I can lend you a small digger, if that's any use to you.'

Neil thanked him profusely. A mechanical digger would certainly help when it came to removing the top layers of earth.

'If you're going to talk to Grover, I wish you luck,' said Nick once that was settled. 'Artist, he calls himself. Piss artist more like. He's not well thought of round here. Not like his great-uncle, who owned the place before him. He passed away a couple of years ago and Grover inherited. According to my dad, the great-uncle was a gentleman. He bought Serpent's Point in the 1920s after the previous owner was involved in some sort of tragedy.'

'What happened?'

'Don't know. All I heard was that he started digging in

that field and there are those who say he woke up the serpent and it took its revenge.'

This caught Neil's attention. 'What serpent?'

'There's an old story that Serpent's Point is named after a giant snake that lives under the ground. All rubbish, of course, but you know how folks like a good tale.'

'You say he started digging. What did he find?' There was no record of any excavation in the immediate area, but Neil had to consider the possibility that an enthusiastic amateur had once decided to dig up the field to see what he could discover. There'd certainly been a craze for that sort of thing at one time. There was even a rumour that Henry VIII himself had tried to dig at Sutton Hoo, although history didn't record how his diggers got on. Perhaps, having more kingly things to do, he'd lost interest before he could do too much damage.

'Don't know, but a story started that disturbing that field was bad luck.'

Neil took his leave, trying to decide whether to call at Serpent's Point. In the end, his curiosity got the better of him. He'd heard there was filming going on at the house, with actors and directors crawling all over the place. He'd never seen a film shoot before, and besides, the geophysics survey was progressing perfectly well without him.

He walked to the house, inhaling the fresh sea air and listening to the gulls wheeling overhead. It was a lovely spot and he wondered how the old story of the serpent had started. Perhaps someone had found adders there once and the tale had become embellished over the centuries. Or perhaps it had been invented to keep the peasants off the lord's land.

He was considering the possibilities when he came to a

faded sign beside a pair of crumbling gateposts. *Serpent's Point. Private Property. Keep Out.* He ignored it and walked up the uneven drive until he came to the house.

The bottom storey was half obscured by the film company's vans, but, undeterred, he headed for the open front door and wandered in. The first person he encountered was a young woman in Regency costume, busily scrolling through her mobile phone. After she'd directed him towards the back of the house, he hung back in the hope of seeing something exciting – an actor he recognised, perhaps, or the shooting of a dramatic scene. He had no idea what it was they were filming, but it seemed like a glamorous and alien world to a humble archaeologist.

In the absence of any action, he followed the young woman's directions and found Grey Grover alone, slouched on the sofa watching an antiques programme on daytime TV. He was staring at the screen as though he was taking a special interest. Perhaps he was trying to work out the value of some of the house's contents, Neil thought, remembering what Nick Stanley had said about his financial position.

'Who are you?' Grover said as he straightened up. His tone was hostile. Not a good start.

When Neil explained the reason for his visit, Grover's expression softened a little and he greeted the news of the planned excavation with a shrug. Neil didn't mention the coins; it seemed tactless to inform the man that he'd sold the chance of possible riches at a knock-down price.

'Can't help you. I got rid of that field at the beginning of this year, so you don't need my permission to dig. You'll have to ask Nick Stanley – land's his now.'

'I realise that, but I wondered whether you had any old estate documents or records mentioning that particular field. Mr Stanley said that someone who once lived here might have carried out an excavation there.'

'I don't know anything about that.' Grover looked away, a signal for Neil to leave. 'I'm an artist, and all this disruption is ruining my concentration. I'm taking a break to clear my head. As I said, I can't help you. Those bloody film people have taken over – crawling all over the place like bloody cockroaches. I never imagined it would be this bad, I can tell you. Then we've had the police round because some woman who was staying in the old stables got herself strangled.'

'Can't be easy,' said Neil with as much sympathy as he could muster. But he didn't feel inclined to give up. 'In a house this size, old documents often get left in attics or cupboards, so I wondered—'

'You wondered? Don't you understand what I've had to put up with? Now you want to start ferreting about as well.'

'All I want to know is whether there are any old papers. If you point me in the right direction, I promise you won't even know I'm here.'

Grover flung his head back as though he was about to let out a howl of frustration. 'Do what you bloody well like. It's Liberty Hall here ... obviously.'

Neil sensed a glimmer of hope. 'Where would I find—'

'There's stuff in the attic from my great-uncle's time and before.' Grover waved his hand dismissively. 'Help yourself, but don't fall through the bloody ceiling, will you. That would be the icing on the cake.'

Half an hour later, Neil was picking his way slowly across an attic filled with the detritus of Serpent Point's history. Cracked mirrors, broken chairs, unwanted dressing tables, skeletal iron bedsteads without mattresses. He spotted a dark chest of drawers with several missing handles. The drawers were stiff; he managed to pull them out one by one, but found nothing.

He continued his search, treading carefully in case Grover's warning about falling through the floor hadn't been made in jest. He noticed that in some places, the layer of dust had been disturbed, as though someone had been up there moving things about. Eventually he spotted a promising-looking old trunk in a dark corner, and when he opened it, his heart began to beat a little faster. It wasn't exactly Tutankhamun's treasure, but it felt like it at that moment. A trunk full of old documents and ancient books with marbled covers – exactly what he'd been hoping for.

But just as he was about to make a start, he was interrupted by a call from Dave, his second in command. Could he come back to the dig? They'd found an intriguing feature and they needed his opinion.

He shut the lid of the trunk reluctantly. Duty called.

Drusilla Kramer had a lot on her mind as she got ready to go out with the dog, who was waiting patiently for her to put his lead on.

Things had been going so well, and Susan's murder was the last thing she needed.

There was only one person she could ask for advice. He'd know what to do.

14

Rachel hauled herself out of her seat as soon as Wesley and Gerry crossed the threshold of the church hall.

'I've spoken to Neville Grasmere,' she called out.

Wesley hurried over to her desk. 'What did he say?'

'He wants to speak to the person in charge of the inquiry. Not on the phone, he said. Face to face. Apparently he doesn't like telephones and he doesn't want some snotty-nosed young constable from the local station either – his words. He made it clear that he's expecting you or the DCI to make the trip.' She tilted her head to one side. 'I believe the Cotswolds is lovely this time of year.'

'Lovely it might be, but the journey up there will take time we don't have.'

'He was very insistent; says he's in possession of some important information.'

Wesley wondered whether this was true, or whether Grasmere was a lonely man yearning for company and a bit of excitement. On the other hand, they could hardly ignore his request if what he had to say could hold the key to the investigation. There was only one thing for it, and that was to seek Gerry's opinion.

Gerry, as it turned out, was keen to go up to Chipping

Campden. 'We'd be neglecting our duty if we didn't follow it up,' he said cheerfully. 'We'll set off first thing tomorrow and leave things in Rachel's capable hands here.'

Wesley suspected he was looking forward to a day out, and he had to admit that he craved a change of scene himself. It would give them both space to think.

The team were working hard, gathering all the available information on Avril Willis and Simone Pritchard, but so far nobody had found any record of Susan Brown's name coming up in either investigation. They suspected that Susan had known Avril, but she had no apparent link to Simone. Wesley couldn't forget that Drusilla Kramer had mentioned an unwanted admirer up in Yorkshire. This was a line of enquiry he wanted to follow up as a matter of urgency. Stalkers could turn into killers.

The old clock on the church hall wall told him it was 6.30 already, and he felt a heavy hand on his shoulder. 'Go home, Wes. We'll make an early start for Chipping Campden tomorrow. You're driving.'

Pam wasn't expecting him so early, and she was pleased to see him, greeting him with a kiss and accepting his offer to cook one of his chilli con carnes.

'Is Michael all right?' he asked as he was chopping the onions. Michael had contracted glandular fever back in May and was still recovering, only attending school when he felt up to it. Wesley's sister had assured him that a slow recovery was perfectly normal, but it still worried him to see the formerly lively thirteen-year-old boy so subdued.

'He's OK. He went to his room as soon as he got in, claiming he had homework, but I suspect he's chatting to his friends.'

Wesley smiled, glad to hear his son was getting back to normal.

'My mother rang earlier.'

Pam's mother, Della, was a child of the sixties who'd never really managed to leave that decade behind. Sometimes Wesley found her fecklessness amusing. But more often he thought her irritating – especially when her behaviour worried Pam, her more self-controlled daughter. Often Pam seemed like the parent and Della the wayward child.

'How is she?' he asked warily.

'Her usual self. She went on about all the men she's meeting online. Honestly, Wes, she's like a teenager. Though I'm sure I was more sensible in my teenage years.'

'I don't doubt it,' he said, throwing the chopped onion into the pan.

They were interrupted when Amelia came downstairs for a drink of milk and popped her head round the living room door.

'Dad, can we get a dog?'

Wesley looked at Pam, who shook her head.

'Why do you want a dog? We've got Moriarty,' he said, looking at the imperious black cat curled up on the sofa beside him.

'My friend Fenella's just got a puppy. She takes it for walks.'

Fenella had featured a lot in Amelia's conversation recently. The new best friend.

'I've done well in my first year at high school. I've worked really hard and I came top in English. Please, Dad.'

Wesley tried hard not to smile. 'It's up to your mum.' Pam taught three days a week at the local primary school, and he suspected, with his long hours during a major inquiry, that she'd be the one to shoulder most of the responsibility for feeding, training and walkies.

'We'll see,' said Pam. Mother-speak for 'no'.

This appeared to satisfy Amelia for the moment, but Wesley had a feeling it was a temporary pause in the battle. His daughter had inherited his determination – or as Pam called it, his stubborn streak.

Wesley and Gerry set off for the Cotswolds at seven the next morning as planned. Wesley calculated that the journey would take more than three hours each way, but at least he'd be home that evening, which wouldn't be the case if they needed to go to Whitby. That would involve an overnight stay – something that wouldn't please Pam.

When he'd arrived in Exeter all those years ago to study archaeology, he had fallen in love with the Devon countryside. But the Cotswolds had a beauty all of their own, with their villages of golden stone and their gently rolling sheep-covered hills.

Chipping Campden was a small, pretty town with a long main street. Tourists wandered to and fro in the same slow, meandering way they ambled through the narrow streets of Tradmouth.

Neville Grasmere had told Rachel that he'd been away for a few days on what he described as a 'buying trip'. He had added that if he wasn't at his home address, he'd be in his antique shop off the main street. It was called Neville's Bygones and they couldn't miss it. Whenever anybody said that about a place, in Wesley's experience, it was invariably hard to find.

Having called at the little cottage on the road leading to the ancient golden stone church and found nobody at home, he parked the car and they walked to the high street. It wasn't long before Gerry spotted a sign directing them to Neville's Bygones, which they found tucked away down a small lane behind the main thoroughfare.

When they arrived, they saw that Grasmere was doing a roaring trade with a coachload of American visitors, who were admiring the goods on offer. The shop bell jangled as the two detectives walked in, but the man behind the counter was talking to a lady with stiffly set hair who was interrogating him about the provenance of a silver hand mirror.

Wesley waited patiently, but Gerry, more restless as usual, began to look around the shop, picking up an antique police truncheon and waving it in Wesley's direction with a grin. Eventually the customer parted with her money and the man they assumed was Neville Grasmere bade her farewell with an obsequious smile. The object she'd bought had been expensive, Wesley guessed. She'd been a dream customer.

'Mr Grasmere?' Wesley asked as he produced his ID.

'Ah, you must be the officers from Devon.' Grasmere shook his head. 'I was told the news over the telephone. Terrible business. Terrible business.'

Neville Grasmere looked like an antique dealer from central casting, with his tweed jacket, bow tie and carefully arranged bright silk handkerchief protruding from his top pocket. He wore half-moon glasses, and his luxuriant grey hair touched his shoulders. He gave off a slight whiff of pipe tobacco. It was hard to guess his age, but Wesley thought he was possibly in his seventies. He got the impression that Grasmere had deliberately created an image for himself, one that went down well with his customers.

'Of course I'm happy to help in any way I can,' the man continued. 'But I really didn't want to conduct the interview over the telephone. I don't mind using the instrument for routine matters, but for something so sensitive . . . '

'I quite understand,' said Wesley.

'I'm so glad, Inspector. Many people don't these days.' He gave Gerry a sidelong look, as though he suspected he might number among the unsympathetic. But he was wrong: Gerry Heffernan was no lover of technology in any of its forms.

The Americans had all departed, leaving the shop empty. Grasmere turned the sign on the door to *Closed* and flicked down the lock before leading them into the back of the shop. They found themselves in a neat office with shelves along one wall to hold stock that had yet to be displayed. There was something businesslike about the room that belied its owner's vague and scholarly manner.

They asked him where he'd been for the past few days, and he told them that he'd been at an antiques fair in Suffolk. He provided details of his accommodation before offering tea, which was accepted gratefully. It had been a long journey.

'Well, gentlemen,' he began when they were settled. 'You want to know about poor Susan?'

'You gave her a reference for her house-sitting job.'

'That's right. I always found her pleasant and reliable.'

'She worked for you here?'

'Indeed. She was only here for a few weeks, but I never had any reason to regret taking her on. I was sorry when she decided to leave.'

'How did she get the job?'

'Ah, now I must confess that was a little unconventional.

She was helping out on a fabric stall in the weekly market – just casual work, you understand – and she came into the shop to have a look around. We started chatting, and it turned out she knew a bit about antiques. Her uncle had been a dealer and she was genuinely interested.'

'What about the stall owner. How did he come to employ her?'

'She'd come down from Yorkshire and was planning to get a job in a hotel or restaurant. But as soon as she arrived, she asked the stallholder if he needed anyone and he took her on. Then a week later, she started here. It worked out very well, as I said.'

'Where was she staying?'

'In a B & B at first, then I said she could move in with me until she found somewhere suitable. The poor girl was struggling for money and happy to take on any work avail-able – not like some these days.' He paused. 'It was nice to have a young person around the house. I lost my wife some years ago, and my daughter's up in Scotland. I confess I was glad of the company.'

Wesley was struck by the similarity to Matt Harrod's story; a lonely, bereaved man welcoming Susan into his home. It suggested that she'd been a sympathetic pres-ence – and yet his experience of the worst of human nature made him wonder whether her motives hadn't been as straightforward as they appeared.

'If she stayed in your house, you must have got to know her well,' said Gerry.

'Oh, there was no hanky-panky if that's what you're getting at.' The man obviously wanted to make this clear before they made assumptions.

'Of course not, sir,' said Wesley with a glance at Gerry,

who was listening intently. 'Did she tell you why she left Yorkshire?'

'When I say she lived in my house, Inspector, that didn't mean she confided all her secrets. She was a very private person.'

To a detective, those words were almost as bad as 'she kept herself to herself'. Wesley tried again.

'Did you get the impression she was running away from someone or something?'

'No. I don't think so.'

'She didn't mention a man who'd been bothering her?'

'No. Nothing like that.'

Wesley caught Gerry's eye again. Grasmere hadn't said anything he couldn't have told them over the phone, and he felt annoyed that he'd brought them all this way for so little.

'Is there anything else you can tell us about her?'

'She did have a tendency to be rather mysterious.'

'What do you mean?'

'Sometimes she disappeared in that little Fiat of hers without saying where she was going. Not that it was any of my business where she went, of course. And she always asked if she wanted to take time off from the shop.'

'Is there anything else you remember? Anything at all?'

Grasmere thought for a moment. 'She took a particular interest in a girl who'd gone missing locally, about six months before she arrived. In fact, while Susan was here, the girl was found. She'd run off to London with her fancy man and came back home with her tail between her legs.'

'Did Susan say why she was so interested in the case?'

'No, but she asked an awful lot of questions. She even asked where she could find the girl's relatives, but I told her

I had no idea. The girl turned up safe and well soon after that, so I assume she never made any effort to contact the family. I really don't know what she found so fascinating about the case – it was a rather sordid little incident, if you ask me.'

Grasmere's face reddened, as though he'd just recalled something embarrassing. 'There is something else, but I don't know whether it's important. I never went into her bedroom, you understand. That would have been a terrible invasion of her privacy. But once I happened to be passing when the door was open and I saw that she'd pinned pieces of paper up on the wall. I didn't like to ask her about it, but when she left, I found holes made by drawing pins and I had to have the room redecorated. But apart from that, she was a very considerate lodger.'

Wesley nodded. It seemed Susan had brought her incident room with her to Devon. 'Did she ever mention any other missing persons cases apart from the local girl?' He held his breath, waiting for the answer.

'Now you come to mention it, Inspector, she did mention once that a friend of hers had gone missing and was later found murdered. When I tried to ask her about it, she wouldn't say any more, and she was very quiet for a few days afterwards, as though she was angry with herself for giving too much away.' He hesitated. 'Do you think her death might have something to do with this friend's murder?'

Possibilities were whirling around Wesley's mind, but he didn't yet have the answer to that particular question. Instead he asked whether Susan had left anything behind.

To his surprise, Grasmere opened the drawer of his desk and took out an envelope. On the front was Susan Brown's name and a Whitby address.

'It had fallen down behind the radiator in her room. As I mentioned, I had it decorated after she'd left, and the decorators found this. I wondered whether to try and send it to the agency who asked for her reference, but I'm afraid I never got round to it. I thought you might like to see it.'

'Thank you, sir. It might be useful to our inquiry,' said Wesley, taking the envelope from Grasmere's outstretched hand.

'Of course, Inspector. And if you need to talk to me again, you know where I am.'

Wesley could hear the eagerness in his voice. The man was lonely, and that was why he'd been so ready to welcome Susan into his home – Susan who was a good listener; a sympathetic presence.

He smiled and thanked Grasmere again, and as they said their goodbyes, he thought of the envelope he'd put in his pocket for safe keeping. As soon as they were in the car, Gerry leaned over, his eyes shining with anticipation.

'Come on, Wes, open it. Let the dog see the rabbit.'

Wesley did as he was asked.

15

The letter was handwritten – a rarity in these days of emails and other electronic communication. It was dated five years ago and signed *Avril*, with three kisses beneath the name. From the warmth of the words, the sender was a close friend.

'Avril Willis, the lass in her incident room – the one who was found murdered,' said Gerry as he took it from Wesley to read.

> *My dear Sue,*
>
> *I just had to write to tell you how wonderful Ian is and how happy I am. He took me to this fantastic hotel after we got married and we had champagne and the works. It's the first time I've tried oysters and I didn't like them much, but Ian said they were an aphrodisiac so I ate them anyway. I've no regrets about marrying him in spite of what you said. And I'm sorry about not inviting you to the wedding. Ian insisted on a quiet do. He said he wanted it to be spontaneous, and we dragged two witnesses off the street like you see in the films. Ian said a wedding like that would be romantic, and it was – although part of me still wishes I could have had you as my bridesmaid like we promised when we were kids. But honestly, once you get to know him better, I know you'll love him.*

*Have you heard any more from that guy from work? When
I saw him in the pub staring at you that time, he gave me the
creeps. If you like, I can get Ian to have a word, but like you
said, it might be best not to poke the hornets' nest.*

The rest of the letter was about Avril's mum and her
operation and how the sainted Ian had given her a lift to
a medical appointment, although he hadn't gone in with
her because he didn't like hospitals. Wesley read it through
again, thinking that Avril Willis sounded like an ordinary
young woman who'd had the misfortune to cross paths with
a killer. Like so many other innocent victims, she'd been
in the wrong place at the wrong time. He felt sorry for her
husband. How could anybody live with such a tragedy?

'Someone spoke to the inspector from North Yorkshire.
He said that the man who was convicted of her murder had
raped and strangled three other women, and when he was
interviewed about Avril, he held his hand up for her and
all. Full confession.'

'So if it was an open-and-shut case, why was her name on
Susan's wall?' Wesley had already read the letter through
twice, but he started to read again, just in case there was
anything he'd missed.

'Well, at least we've now got a definite connection to one
of those names,' said Gerry. 'Looks like Avril was our victim's best mate and she kept her old letter for sentimental
reasons. This guy from work she mentions; could he be
the one she told Drusilla about? Sounds like he might have
been stalking her.'

'If he was, maybe North Yorkshire will have something on him.'

'Unless she never made an official complaint.'

112

'You mean she tried to deal with it herself, but it back-fired when he tracked her down all these years later? It's possible.'

'We won't know if we don't ask, Wes.' Gerry looked at his watch. 'We'll get someone to check out Grasmere's buying trip. And after we've done that, there's a nice pub over there. I'm in need of something to eat. I'm a growing lad.'

'Growing in the wrong direction,' said Wesley, glancing at Gerry's stomach.

Gerry started to laugh. 'Hell, Wes, you're getting as bad as Joyce.'

Wesley felt hungry himself, and the open pub door looked inviting, so he didn't take much persuading. After calling the incident room to ask someone to confirm Grasmere's alibi, they left the car and made for the pub, where they enjoyed a ploughman's lunch in the courtyard. As they ate, they discussed the case, getting things straight in their minds, and when they'd finished, they drove to the nearest police station to ask whether Susan had con-tacted the family of the local missing girl who'd turned up unharmed. She hadn't, but it didn't feel like time wasted.

The return journey to Devon was uneventful, and they were back in the incident room at quarter to five. Rachel waved Wesley over and he sat down by her desk.

He had Avril Willis's letter to Susan in a plastic evidence bag, and he placed it in front of her. 'This was found at the place Susan was staying in Chipping Campden. It had fallen behind a radiator in her room.' He waited until she'd read it. 'What do you think?'

'Maybe the guy from work Avril mentions – the one who gave her the creeps – followed Susan down here.'

'But the letter's dated almost five years ago.'

'Stalkers can make people's lives a misery for years.' She looked up. 'If Susan kept rejecting him, perhaps something snapped.'

'"Yet each man kills the thing he loves."'

Rachel tilted her head enquiringly. 'Where have I heard that before?'

'Oscar Wilde. *The Ballad of Reading Gaol.*'

'Trust you to know that. What did you make of Neville Grasmere?'

'I'd say he was trustworthy. Someone's just called the hotel he was staying at in Suffolk to check his alibi. He was definitely there at the time of the murder.' He paused. 'He said Susan took a great interest in a local missing persons case in Chipping Campden, but the woman involved turned up safe and well while she was there. If she fancied herself as some sort of private eye tracking down missing people, why include her friend, Avril? They found Avril's killer and he was sent to prison.'

'My money's on the man who gave Avril the creeps, whoever he is. What if he was still obsessed with Susan and she left Whitby to escape him? He has to be our prime suspect.'

'There's no evidence for that, but we'll check all the local tourist accommodation to see whether they had any men staying on their own at the relevant time,' said Wesley.

Rachel nodded solemnly. 'I'll ask Paul to arrange it. The house-to-house enquiries have been completed, so ... '

His eyes were drawn to the file open on Rachel's desk. 'Can I have a look at that?'

It was the file on the missing woman from Gloucestershire. Simone Pritchard. They needed to find out why Susan had taken such an interest in her case.

*

114

Archaeology looked really exciting when you saw it on TV. Then there were the films – the Indiana Jones movies and *Tomb Raider*. But for Sophie and Livy, the reality didn't match up to the hype, even though Dr Watson, the man in charge, seemed thrilled by every tiny soil-caked object that came out of the ground.

Once Livy's dad's digger had carefully removed the top layer of soil, the archaeologists had dug three trenches, but only one more coin had been found. Livy and Sophie had been given the job of sweeping the heaps of soil next to the trenches with their machines, and they'd found one piece of shapeless metal that one of the archaeology students had told them was part of a brooch. It hadn't looked much like a brooch to the girls.

Dr Watson – Neil, as the students called him – had promised that they'd soon be allowed to do some digging. They'd had visions of using their machines to look for more treasure, until one of the students told them in a rather patronising way that it didn't quite work like that – not in the scholarly world they aspired to inhabit.

Neil was busy examining a tray full of finds, and it looked as though keeping Sophie and Livy occupied was the last thing on his mind.

Livy gave her friend a nudge. 'Fancy going over to the house to watch the filming?'

Sophie nodded. 'We can leave the machines here. Don't reckon anyone's going to nick them.'

Without another word, the girls propped their precious metal detectors against the hedgerow and sneaked out of the gate. Watching archaeology without taking part was like watching paint dry. Observing a film crew was bound to be more exciting.

It took them ten minutes to walk to Serpent's Point. To their delight, the vans were still there, and the buzz of generators told them something was going on. Even better was the fact that three young women in long but revealing muslin dresses were sprawled on the grass studying scripts. The girls hadn't realised it was possible to be that bored when something as thrilling as filming was going on around you, but the actresses looked as if they'd rather be elsewhere.

Neither of them dared to approach the glamorous creatures on the weed-infested lawn. They watched out of sight, tucked behind a large rhododendron.

'Better get back,' Livy said after a while. 'The dig's more exciting than this.'

As soon as the words left her lips, a tall man with a clipboard appeared and the three young women rose to their feet and followed him into the house. They'd clearly been summoned.

'That's that then.' Livy turned to go.

But Sophie didn't move. She was staring after the disappearing women with her mouth open. 'Did you see that?'

'What?'

'The guy with the clipboard. Did you see what he was wearing?'

'T-shirt, shorts? Baseball cap?' A look of realisation spread across Livy's face. 'A black baseball cap with a white logo. But there must be loads of them around.'

'He was very tall. Tall enough for us to be able to see his head over that hedge.'

'So who's going to ring the cops and tell them we've seen a tall man in a baseball cap?'

16

In the end, Sophie and Livy decided to leave the job to someone else. Neil Watson was alone in the shade of the awning, examining some printouts, so they reckoned he was just the man – especially as he had a friend in the force: the rather dishy black cop who'd seemed several cuts above your average plod.

It was shortly after five o'clock when Neil made the call. Once he'd finished speaking, he looked up. 'My mate's coming over and he'd like to talk to you. We'll be packing up for the day soon, so maybe you can help put the tarpaulins over the trenches while you're waiting. It's not forecast to rain, but I don't believe in taking chances.'

Neil's mate, Wesley, turned up twenty minutes later with another plain-clothes detective, a tall, athletic-looking man with an open face whom he introduced as Paul – DC Johnson. Once the girls had repeated their story, the two policemen asked them to go with them to Serpent's Point and point out the man they'd seen.

This was the most exciting thing that had happened all day. They'd found themselves involved in a manhunt.

*

Wesley didn't have time to waste. If Crispin Joss, the director, wasn't pleased about his filming being disturbed, that was too bad. A murder investigation took priority over everything.

He marched to the front door with Paul beside him. The DC had been his school's cross-country champion at one time, and he was still a keen runner, so Wesley didn't fancy their man's chances if he tried to flee. Livy and Sophie held back, trying to conceal their excitement but failing. They'd wanted to watch the filming and now they'd be getting closer to the action than they'd ever hoped.

'OK. Cut,' a man's voice drawled from the direction of the drawing room. As soon as Wesley opened the door, he was dazzled by spotlights. He screwed up his eyes and saw a couple lying half naked on the chaise longue. When they spotted Wesley and Paul, the pair grabbed the clothing they'd discarded on the floor in an attempt to cover their modesty.

'What the hell are you doing here? Get out!' Crispin Joss shouted, his face so red with fury that Wesley feared for his blood pressure. 'You heard me. Piss off. Now.'

Wesley and Paul held up their ID. 'Sorry to disturb you, sir,' Wesley said with studied politeness. 'We're looking for one of your crew. A tall man wearing a baseball cap. Is he around?'

'How should I bloody know? I'm trying to make a film here. I've no idea who you're talking about, and if you don't leave now, I'll complain to your superiors.'

Wesley recognised an empty threat when he heard one. He looked round the room, and once he was satisfied the man they wanted wasn't there amongst the lighting and camera crew, he turned to go, almost having to drag out the girls, who were staring at the half-naked couple in fascination. He had to smile to himself. They'd certainly got their bit of excitement.

'There he is,' said Livy as they emerged into the sunshine. She was pointing at a group of people chatting next to one of the vans.

'Excuse me, sir. Police. Can we have a word?' said Wesley as he and Paul began to walk towards the group.

The man's eyes widened in alarm, then he took to his heels across the lawn. Paul set off after him at a sprint. Wesley thanked the girls and said they could go, then followed the DC. Ahead of him, their quarry vanished into the tangle of rhododendrons fringing the expanse of grass. Paul plunged after him into the undergrowth, but Wesley found it hard to keep up. He could hear crashing footsteps somewhere ahead, and although he couldn't see anything through the thick foliage, he pressed on, trying to follow the sounds. But when he reached a small clearing, he found Paul standing alone and breathless, looking round frantically.

'Sorry, sir, I lost him,' he panted.

'He can't have gone far.'

'I think he's heading towards Bereton. I'll get on to the incident room – ask them to keep a lookout.'

'Hopefully he'll run straight into the long arm of the law,' said Wesley. He knew Paul had done his best, and the last thing he wanted was to make him feel bad about his failure. 'In the meantime, let's have a word with his colleagues. See what they can tell us about him.'

17

Wesley's optimism turned out to be justified. Their man was picked up half an hour later by a patrol near the Seashell. They discovered that his name was Calvin Brunning – Vinny to his friends – a loner nobody knew particularly well. And when they looked him up on the system, they found that he had a record for violent offences.

On Gerry's orders, the suspect was taken by patrol car to Tradmouth police station for questioning. Wesley drove Gerry over there, passing the long stretch of beach where US soldiers had rehearsed the D-Day landings. The results of the rehearsal back in April 1944 had been tragic, with the loss of almost eight hundred lives, and now a tank recovered from the sea stood next to the car park as a memorial to the dead. The sight moved Wesley every time he passed. So much death. And here he was, over seventy-five years later, dealing with more.

Brunning was waiting for them in one of the interview rooms, the one with a window that actually let in some daylight. He'd been given tea in a plastic cup and he didn't look pleased.

'You've got no right to hold me,' he said in a nasal whine as Wesley and Gerry sat down opposite him. He was over six feet five, with gangly limbs and a long face, and Wesley noted that his accent was northern, possibly Yorkshire.

'We just want a little chat,' said Gerry with a dangerous smile. 'First of all, why did you run away?'

'Wouldn't you run if someone started chasing you?'

'We did identify ourselves and ask nicely first,' said Wesley. 'You knew we were police.'

'Didn't hear you,' Brunning said. He sounded like a sulky child.

'Let's get down to why you've been brought here,' said Wesley, suddenly businesslike. 'You were seen near the scene of the murder on the coast path the day before yesterday. This was on Thursday, about ten thirty in the morning. What were you doing there?'

'I wasn't there. Who says I was?'

'Two reliable witnesses.' Wesley couldn't think of any reason why the two young metal-detectorists would lie, but it was still possible they'd made a genuine mistake and he'd got the wrong man.

'Like I said, I wasn't there.'

Gerry consulted a file he'd brought in with him. 'According to some people, computers are wonderful things. You can get access to anybody's criminal record at the touch of a button. Yours makes interesting reading. GBH, burglary, drug dealing. How did you get the job with the film company?'

Brunning shrugged. 'I'm casual, aren't I? A mate from the pub told me someone had had to drop out. They needed a replacement quickly, so they took me on. I do the lifting and carrying. Lowest in the pecking order.'

Wesley guessed that Crispin Joss wasn't too fussy about

who he hired to carry out the menial roles that kept the wheels of production turning.

'Do you like the work?'

Another shrug. 'Thought it'd be glamorous, but Joss treats everyone like shit. I've learned to keep out of his way.'

'Judging by your accent, I'd say you're not from round here. When did you come to Devon?'

'About six months ago.'

'Jobs?'

'I did some washing-up in the Excelsior Hotel in Morbay, and had a stint at the arcade on the prom. Casual work.'

'Where were you before that?'

'London. Why?'

'Not the Cotswolds? Or North Yorkshire?'

'I worked in Sheffield a couple of years ago. Fairground. Where's the Cotswolds?'

'The dead woman's name was Susan Brown. Did you come across her on your travels?'

'Course not. Never even heard of her.' He sounded affronted at the suggestion.

'Where were you before Sheffield?'

'Leeds.' He said it with some reluctance.

'What about Whitby?'

'No.'

'Did you meet Susan Brown while you were up in Yorkshire?'

'No.'

'Did you kill her?'

Wesley's words obviously took Brunning by surprise. 'I might have been a bad lad in my time, but I'm no murderer.' He sounded indignant, as though he regarded the question as a personal slur.

'Let's put this another way. Why were you on the coast path that morning?'

Wesley had expected a denial, but instead Brunning bowed his head. 'OK, I was there. But I didn't kill nobody, I swear.'

'Did you take anything from the scene?'

He shook his head.

'Can you tell us what happened?'

There was a long silence before he answered. Wesley hoped he wasn't using the pause to think up a good story. They needed the truth.

'I thought the filming'd be exciting, but most of the time you're just sitting around doing nothing. Anyway, I went for a walk and had a smoke to clear my head. The house is near the path, so I sort of ... wandered down there.'

'What did you do when you got there?'

Brunning looked sheepish. 'Well, I, er ... rolled a joint and ...' He took a deep breath. 'I was walking along minding my own business when I saw this woman lying there. I thought, "Bloody hell, has she had a heart attack or something?" Then I saw her face was all twisted. There were marks on her neck and her eyes were sort of bulging.'

'Why didn't you call for help?' said Gerry.

'I could tell she was dead, so why would I get involved? I know what you lot are like.'

Gerry studied the file in front of him. 'You beat up a girl in a nightclub in Morbay four months ago. You have a history of violence against women, so why should we believe you?'

''Cos it's God's honest truth, that's why.'

'Susan Brown lived in the converted stable block at Serpent's Point. You must have seen her there.'

'Might have done. Can't remember.'

'Did you try it on with her? Did she tell you to get lost so you strangled her?'

Wesley watched Gerry. He was doing well – getting under the suspect's skin.

'I never. I swear.'

'But you did recognise her when you found her on the path?' said Wesley.

'She looked a bit familiar, so I must have seen her around. But I never spoke to her. Not once. Honest.'

Gerry leaned forward so that his face was almost touching Brunning's. 'Fancied your chances, did you?'

'She wasn't my type. Too old.'

The thought flashed through Wesley's mind that Calvin Brunning was no oil painting and Susan Brown had been an attractive woman in life. However, Brunning had recently spent a lot of time on the film shoot ogling the untouchable young actresses, so he might have assumed the more mature Susan would be grateful for his attention. If he took her rejection badly, how would he have reacted? He certainly wasn't out of the frame.

'She used to work behind the bar at the Seashell. Did you ever meet her there?'

Brunning gave a dismissive grunt. 'Wouldn't go near that place if you paid me. It's full of tourists and those so-called actors. I have enough of them during the day without drinking with them and all.'

'So where *do* you drink?' Wesley asked.

'The Bell in Bereton. Ask anyone.'

'We will,' said Gerry. 'We've heard the victim had some trouble with a man up in Yorkshire. Was that you?' He sat back with his arms folded and waited for the answer.

Brunning rose to his feet, sending his chair clattering to the floor. He pointed at Gerry, jabbing his finger at his face. 'You're a bloody liar. I never saw her before I got here. If you've heard I have, you've heard wrong.'

Gerry caught Wesley's eye. Brunning's reaction suggested he had something to hide. 'Sit down, Mr Brunning,' said Wesley, trying to calm the situation. 'Where are you staying?'

'I'm not staying anywhere. I've got my camper van, but I won't be going nowhere, not till the filming's over.'

Wesley checked the time. 'I think we're finished for now. We'll continue in the morning.' He announced to the recording machine that the interview was suspended. 'We'd like to offer you our hospitality overnight.'

'No way. I haven't done nothing.'

The two officers ignored his protests. He was the best suspect they had so far, and they weren't going to let him drive off in that camper van of his.

'What do you make of him?' Gerry asked once they were outside in the corridor.

'He's got a temper. If he was stoned and he tried it on with the victim when he met her on the path ... ' Wesley didn't have to finish his sentence. He and Gerry were thinking along the same lines.

'Could he be the man in Avril's letter? He might have ventured further north than Leeds and Sheffield – maybe as far north as Whitby. What if he followed her down here and took a job near where she was staying?'

Wesley shook his head. He couldn't see it somehow, but he agreed that it was worth bearing in mind when they questioned Brunning again in the morning.

'In the meantime, we need to find out more about

him – if he's ever lived in or near Whitby, he could have crossed paths with our victim.' Gerry consulted his watch. 'It's eight thirty. Why don't we knock off for the day.'

When Wesley arrived home, he saw a strange car parked outside. And as he let himself into the house, he wondered who'd come calling.

From the journal of Dr Aldus Claye

May 1921

We concluded that this was the skeleton the farmer had spoken of, because Phipps said there was evidence that the soil had been disturbed by previous digging. From what I have read on the subject of Roman burial practices, I thought it unlikely that we would find a cemetery in such a place. However, Phipps wanted to expand the area of our investigation, just to make sure.

The skull and few surviving bones were in poor condition, but Phipps sent over to the house for a box to place them in, saying the museum in Exeter would be interested in our finds. The skull appeared to be female, he announced with confidence, and with it was a row of amber beads, although the string that had once held them together had long since rotted into the ground. I recognised the brooch lying near the shoulder blade as typically Roman in style, and there was an object beside the ribs that Phipps said might be the handle of a knife. On closer examination of the remains, he thought there might be a small nick on one of the remaining ribs near where the heart had once beaten, but it was hard to tell as the bones were so fragile. This didn't stop him announcing *enthusiastically that she was probably the victim of a murder, although her killer would be long dead and beyond any justice save that of the Almighty.*

He wanted Clarabel to examine the bones with him, but I insisted that it would be too distressing for her. So, with a roll of his eyes and a quick glance in her direction, he packed the remains carefully into the old wooden tea chest my manservant had found in the attic and nothing more was said about our gruesome find.

To our relief, a couple of the farmer's men turned up in the late afternoon. They had been muck-spreading and they smelled somewhat unpleasant; even so, we were glad of their help. Phipps ordered them to start work on the far side of the field, and they worked swiftly with the spades they'd brought with them, digging down until one of them called out that he'd found a wall. In spite of his injury, Phipps almost skipped over to them to take a look, and the expression of rapture on his face told me that they'd discovered something remarkable.

He didn't summon me immediately. Rather he called to Clarabel, who tripped daintily across the field, her parasol held high to shade her delicate complexion.

It looked like a wall all right, and when Phipps took out his trowel and scraped the soil away, there was evidence that it had once been decorated with plaster painted in muted reds and greens.

18

Wesley had been looking forward to a relaxing evening, preferably slumped in front of the TV with a glass of wine in his hand. He sometimes wondered whether he was becoming middle-aged and boring, but so far, Pam hadn't complained.

He heard voices coming from the living room; women's voices, low and confiding. He opened the door and saw Pam sitting on the sofa beside a dark-haired woman with a pleasant, round face. He recognised her colleague, Jan, at once.

'Hi, Jan.' He looked at Pam. 'Sorry I'm late, love.'

Pam shrugged. She was used to the hours he worked.

'I'm just off,' said Jan, rising to her feet. 'Nice to see you again, Wesley.' She gave him a dazzling smile. Wesley had noticed before that Jan's smile lit up her face and turned her from unremarkable to attractive. Jan and Pam had become friends as soon as they'd begun working together, and Wesley had first met her in a local restaurant when the school staff had an evening out with their partners.

Jan was a pleasant woman who'd been widowed tragically in her thirties when her firefighter husband had been killed on duty in Newton Abbot. She'd had no family in the town, so she'd moved south to Tradmouth to escape bad memories and make a new start. At the restaurant he'd felt sorry for her on her own, so he'd made a special effort to talk to her, finding her friendly, if a little shy. Later that evening, he'd joked to Pam about introducing her to Neil now that Lucy seemed to be off the scene in Orkney. But Pam had been quick to point out that Jan was hardly Neil's type.

When he'd met Jan before, he'd sensed a sadness about her, probably because of her tragic loss. But now he felt that the sadness had lifted. Pam showed her out, and when she returned, she sat down beside him.

'Jan's got a new man. She called in because she's going away with him for the weekend, and I offered to lend her my travel hairdryer.'

'Have you met him?'

'Not yet, but I caught a brief glimpse of him when he picked her up after work. He's quite attractive and he's got a nice car. A Merc.'

'Good for her. After all the tragedy she's had in her life, she deserves some luck.'

'How's your latest murder? I saw Gerry on the local news making an appeal for witnesses.'

'We're working on it. You know Neil's digging in a field near where it happened?'

'He rang and told me. He seems very excited about this dig – or should I say even more excited than usual.'

'I've been too busy to take a look at what's going on,' Wesley said with some regret.

Both exhausted from their day's work, they had an early night. Even so, when the alarm clock went off at six the next morning, Wesley didn't feel much better. But he had to get to the incident room. Calvin Brunning had spent the night in the cells, and they were running out of time before they had to either charge or release him.

Before they resumed the interview, they called the incident room to find out whether the team had managed to dig up any old addresses for their suspect. It would help if they could establish a connection between him and the victim, and if they'd once lived in the same part of the world, that would be a good start.

As it turned out, the news was promising. Brunning had been born in Leeds but had moved out of his childhood home after a series of rows with his mother's new boyfriend. He'd moved around the country, taking any casual work he could find, in fairgrounds, amusement arcades and hotel kitchens. He was known to various police forces for low-level drug dealing, but he also had a few convictions for violence, usually when drunk. Since his arrival in the south-west, his only arrest had been for the assault on the girl in the Morbay nightclub. They'd had a drunken fight and she'd come off worse, with a black eye and a cracked rib. He'd claimed self-defence, but the police report was sceptical. Since then there had been no more incidents, so perhaps working in the film industry was helping him to stay on the straight and narrow. Or maybe he just hadn't been caught.

'We'd better get on with it,' said Wesley. 'We haven't got much more time.'

'The fact that he's worked all over the country opens up all sorts of possibilities,' said Gerry. 'We need to know whether he was ever in Whitby. I keep thinking about that letter.'

Wesley thought for a moment before he replied. 'It was a long time ago, and Avril clearly says that Susan met the man at work.' He took out his notebook and began to read. '"Have you heard any more from that guy from work? When I saw him in the pub staring at you that time, he gave me the creeps."'

'Maybe Brunning took a job in Whitby for a while and they worked in the same place.'

Wesley suspected that Gerry was trying to twist the facts to fit his theory. It wasn't like him not to keep an open mind. But they couldn't know anything for sure until they received more information from Whitby. Someone from the local station had promised to get back to them about Susan's last known address, but as yet, they'd heard nothing. Neither had they been able to trace her ex-husband, but if he was indeed in Dubai, that might not be an easy task.

'I'd like to speak to someone from Whitby before we go into that interview room all guns blazing,' he said. 'We need to confirm that Brunning was on their patch. He's the slippery type. We need to be one step ahead of him. And I want that camper van of his searched.'

Gerry didn't argue. He sat on the corner of Wesley's desk as he made the call to the search team, and then another call to Whitby, picking up a stapler and playing with it absent-mindedly as he listened impatiently.

Wesley tried to ignore his boss's fidgeting and concentrate on asking his questions. Gerry watched his face, hoping to see some excitement, anything to suggest he was learning something helpful. But Wesley displayed no emotion and Gerry feared he'd hit another dead end.

'They sent someone round to the address on that

envelope as we asked,' said Wesley once he'd put the receiver down. 'It's a flat, and the current residents didn't recognise Susan's name. Nobody at the station there knew anything about Calvin Brunning, so your theory's looking a bit shaky, Gerry.'

'All that means is that if he was working in Whitby, he kept his nose clean.'

'If she never made an official complaint, Susan can't have been too bothered about the man Avril mentioned in her letter.'

'Some people just don't like the police.'

'But normally those are people who have a good reason not to include us on their Christmas card list – such as criminals. Nothing came up when Susan's prints and DNA were run through the system.'

Gerry gave a long sigh. He'd been hoping for something juicy from Whitby and he found it hard to hide his disappointment. 'Better have another word with Brunning. Can't put it off much longer.'

When they walked into the interview room, the suspect looked as though he'd lost some of his defiance, which meant his night in the cells might have produced the desired effect.

'How long are you going to keep me here?' was his first question.

'Until we get the truth,' said Gerry. 'Tell us again what you did on Thursday morning.'

Brunning recited the story again. It hadn't changed. 'Look, I never killed that woman. Why would I?'

'Because you used to know her when you lived up in Yorkshire.' It was a gamble, and one Wesley didn't feel particularly confident about winning.

'I swear to God I never saw her before in my life.'

'You didn't come across her in the place where she used to work?'

'I don't even know where that was.'

'We've learned that someone she'd met through work was paying her unwanted attention.' Wesley was beginning to wonder whether they were reading too much into Avril's words.

'Well, that wasn't me.'

Brunning looked desperate, and Wesley believed he was telling the truth. 'We're making enquiries up in Yorkshire, so sooner or later we'll find out if you've been lying to us.'

'I'm not.'

'Have you ever been to the Cotswolds?'

'You asked me that before and the answer's still the same. Like I said, I don't even know where the Cotswolds are.' He looked from one man to the other. 'But I'll tell you something for nothing. I saw the dead woman talking to Joss, the director. I couldn't hear what they were saying, but they weren't just passing the time of day.'

Wesley and Gerry looked at each other. This was something Joss had failed to mention.

'When was this?'

'Wednesday – the day before she was found dead.'

'Why didn't you tell us this before?'

'I forgot. Had a lot on my mind, didn't I. It's him you should be questioning, not me,' Brunning continued. 'I never did nothing.'

'You found the body and didn't report it, so you can see why we're treating you as a suspect.' Wesley's words sounded so reasonable that the man didn't bother to argue.

It was clear they were getting nowhere, so they released

Brunning pending further enquiries, telling him not to leave the area.

'Well? Did he do it?' Gerry asked as they left Tradmouth to drive back to the incident room.

'I'm not sure. His claim that he didn't report the body because he didn't want to get involved seems feasible to me, given his past run-ins with the police. But we can't forget that woman he beat up in the nightclub in Morbay. I'd like someone to have a word with her and get her side of the story.'

'Too right. He's six foot five, so I don't see how giving a woman a black eye and a cracked rib could have been self-defence,' said Gerry with a roll of the eyes. 'There's nothing I'd like better than to put him behind bars, but nothing was found in his camper van apart from a quantity of cannabis, which I imagine he'll claim was for his own use.'

'Pity. No reddish-brown scarf?'

'Nothing like that. Let's face it, unless we get something from Yorkshire, we've no real reason to hold him for Susan Brown's murder.'

It was Sunday, although it didn't seem like that to Wesley. As they pulled up outside the incident room, he saw a few locals talking by the church gate, casting surreptitious glances in their direction, doing their best to pretend that they weren't interested in the goings-on at their church hall.

'Morning, ladies,' Gerry called out with a friendly wave, doing his bit for public relations. One of the women raised her hand in nervous acknowledgement. The others scurried away down the path between the gravestones as if they'd been caught doing something shameful.

The church bells began to ring as they walked into the

135

incident room. Rachel stood up as soon as she saw them, placing her hand in the small of her back.

'How did you get on with Calvin Brunning?' she said.

'Didn't have enough to hold him, I'm afraid,' said Wesley. 'Anything new?'

'I called the police station in Tewkesbury, where Simone Pritchard, the other woman from Susan's incident room, lived. Apparently she walked out on her husband, taking their savings with her. The husband told them he suspected she had another man – there had been rumours where she worked, apparently. They reckoned she might have changed her name so he couldn't track her down. Her sister, Michelle Williams, reported her missing, but once they'd spoken to the husband, they put the investigation on the back burner. There was no reason to believe she'd come to any harm, they said.'

'Perhaps we should speak to the husband ourselves.'

'He left the area, saying the memories of the relationship were too painful and he wanted to start a new life. They don't have an address for him.'

'So it's case closed as far as they're concerned.'

Rachel nodded. 'Although they said the sister kicked up a bit of a stink. She said it wasn't like Simone and she didn't know of any affair. The sergeant I spoke to reckoned she just didn't want to believe it, and she didn't particularly get on with her brother-in-law either.'

'What about the rumours of an affair?'

'The husband said she was friendly with a man at work who'd recently moved to another town.'

'Did they follow it up?'

'I don't think so. The sergeant said they were fully stretched at the time.'

'I'd like to speak to the sister.'

'The sergeant tried to call her, but she's away at the moment, visiting relatives in New Zealand. They said they'll let us know when she's back. And we got the number of Susan's old phone from Edenwood Homes and looked at her call log. One of the numbers she called while she was in Chipping Campden was Michelle Williams's – a call lasting ten minutes. As for the rest of her calls, she received a lot from Matt Harrod's number, probably checking up on his cat while he was away, and we're going through the others, although there doesn't seem to be anything out of the ordinary.'

Wesley thanked her, careful to hide his disappointment. It seemed they'd just have to be patient.

19

It was Sunday, but this didn't matter to Neil and his enthusiastic team of excavators. The dig was progressing well. The team in trench three had turned up an interesting semicircular feature with some painted plaster. Since then, everyone had been in a state of suppressed excitement, wondering whether this could be the big one; the discovery that might change their assumptions about the history of Devon.

With the finds proving so intriguing, Neil accepted reluctantly that searching through the trunk full of documents in the attic at Serpent's Point would have to be put on the back burner for the moment. But his gut instinct told him that it might contain something interesting – especially as he was convinced that he wasn't the first person to excavate in that particular field.

Wesley studied his computer screen. There was so much information, it was hard to take it in: Susan's bank account details, as well as her more recent phone records. He'd get one of the DCs to sift out anything of interest, but he liked to see everything for himself first. Pam had once accused him of being a control freak, but he didn't think that was fair. He was thorough and there was nothing wrong with that – not during a murder investigation.

'Anything interesting?' Rachel asked.

'According to her bank details, the victim was just about solvent. She had her bar work, and she was house-sitting, so her accommodation was free. And she lived frugally by the look of it. I don't think there are any clues there.'

Feeling restless, he walked over to the little kitchen at the side of the church hall stage, where he found Gerry dipping a tea bag into a mug of boiling water. 'I can stretch this to two cups. Want one?'

'Thanks,' said Wesley. 'I've learned never to refuse a cup of tea.'

A figure appeared in the doorway. DC Rob Carter was bursting with untold news.

'Sorry, sir, Joss isn't at Serpent's Point, but he'll be back at half past if you want me to go back.'

Gerry made a noise that sounded like a growl.

'But my visit wasn't wasted,' Rob continued. 'I've been talking to one of the actresses.'

'As long as you don't let your love life interfere with your work.'

Rob took the boss's words seriously. 'No, sir, I wasn't ... She said Joss is a bastard and she wouldn't put anything past him, even murder. He treats the actors like dirt and he's even worse with the crew. He's staying at a posh hotel while the rest of them have to slum it in short-term lets and caravans.'

'Even the stars?'

He nodded. 'Mind you, I've never heard of any of them, so they can't be famous or anything. It's a low-budget film. *Very* low-budget, according to my ... friend. She said Joss is paying the owner of Serpent's Point for the use of the house but nowhere near the going rate most production companies pay. She reckons the owner's broke so he's glad of the cash.'

Wesley had already concluded that *The Awakening of Lillith Montmorency* was probably little more than an excuse for some serious bodice-ripping and the cast most likely consisted of unemployed actors desperate for any work they could get. Everyone associated with the filming had been interviewed and nothing of note had turned up. But according to Brunning, who may or may not have been lying, Joss had had words with the victim shortly before her death, so they needed to speak to him again urgently. He wouldn't be pleased about it, but he had no choice.

'It's Sunday. Are the film people still working?'

'Oh yes, sir. Time is money and all that.'

Gerry checked his watch. 'Joss should be back by the time we get there. Let's go and rattle his cage.'

'Do you need me, sir?' said Rob hopefully.

'We can manage.'

Wesley suspected the young DC had been hoping for another encounter with his actress informant, and Gerry had just scuppered his plans. He almost felt sorry for him, but he knew that Joss would be less willing to argue if it was the two officers in charge of the investigation who were responsible for disturbing his filming schedule.

They found the director outside Serpent's Point's front entrance, berating a crestfallen young actor in shabby Regency dress while a skinny girl with a clipboard looked on. They heard the words 'not good enough'. The lad was in trouble.

'Mr Joss. Can we have a word in private?' Gerry bellowed as they walked towards the little group.

Joss swung round, his face red. He looked as though he was about to swing a punch in Gerry's direction. Fortunately he stopped himself in time.

'This is harassment. I'll complain to your superiors.'

Wesley wondered which TV cop show he'd learned that particular threat from. He half expected his next words to be that he was a good friend of the chief constable and they played golf together – but perhaps that was a lie too far, even for Joss.

After a few moments, the director realised that he had no choice. He led them to a quiet corner of the gardens, away from the humming of the generators inside the vans. There was a stone bench overlooking a decapitated statue of some Roman god – Bacchus probably, judging from the grapes he was holding. Wesley thought the statue looked genuine but he guessed that it was more likely to be a copy placed there by some former owner of the house who'd been on the Grand Tour.

'Last time we spoke, you said you'd never met the woman who was found murdered on the coast path nearby,' said Gerry.

'That business has nothing to do with me. I'm just here to make a film.'

'You were seen talking to the victim. A witness has come forward to say you were having words with her the day before she was found dead. What was your relationship to Susan Brown?'

Wesley saw the man's eyes flicker to one side, as though he was trying to find an escape route. The colour had drained from his cheeks and he looked like a cornered animal.

'There was no relationship. I didn't know the woman.'

'Then what were you talking to her about?'

'I can't remember, so it couldn't have been important.' After a short silence, his eyes lit up. 'Some woman cornered me once to complain about the disruption. She said the vans were blocking her garage and the crew were leaving a mess in the courtyard – food wrappings, she said. I told her we were making a film and she'd have to accept it.' He began to fidget with the artfully tied scarf around his neck. 'I might have said something about people like her not understanding the effort we put in to create something worthwhile. The last thing I need is interfering curtain-twitchers with their petty complaints.'

'Can you remember anything else about the conversation?'

'It wasn't important. *She* wasn't important. She was just jealous of those who lead more exciting lives.'

'Well, she hasn't got a life now, exciting or otherwise,' said Gerry. 'You had an argument with a murder victim shortly before her death, then you lied about it. That makes you a person of interest.'

Crispin Joss looked horrified. 'I didn't lie. I forgot.'

'Someone will be round to take a fresh statement from you. And we want the truth this time – filming or no filming.' Gerry made it sound like a threat. Wesley was impressed.

'What do you think?' Gerry asked in a whisper as Joss began to walk back towards the house.

'I'm not sure. Failing to mention it because he didn't consider the woman important enough seems to fit in with what we know about him, but ...' Wesley hesitated. 'Did you see that pretentious scarf around his neck? I'd call that reddish brown, wouldn't you?'

'I would, Wes. We're still waiting for the report on those fibres, but let's get it off him and get forensics to examine it.'

'Excellent idea.' Wesley raised his voice. 'Excuse me, Mr Joss.'

Joss turned, his expression wary, anticipating more trouble. When Wesley made his request, he looked as though he was about to refuse. Then he thought better of it and took off the scarf, dropping it obediently into the evidence bag Wesley was holding.

As they began to walk back to the incident room, Wesley glanced at the headless statue, wondering if Neil would be interested. Perhaps he'd mention it next time they met.

'We haven't heard anything about Grey Grover's lodger,' said Gerry as they were about to leave the grounds of Serpent's Point. 'Marcus Pinter. He's supposed to be away, but the timing sounds a bit vague to me. I don't like vague.'

'Nor do I. Let's send someone round to follow it up.'

As soon as the words had left Wesley's lips, he noticed movement in the rhododendrons lining the drive and caught a glimpse of a pale muslin dress. At first he assumed it was one of the actors in Regency costume. But when the woman emerged from the shelter of the shrubs, he realised he was mistaken. It was Krystal Saverigg. And he feared she'd overheard everything they'd said.

20

Sherlock greeted Drusilla Kramer eagerly when she arrived home at six on Sunday evening. She'd made so many excuses for not taking him in, insisting that the life she led wasn't ideal for pets. But old Mrs Carpenter from the neighbouring flat had hated the thought of putting her beloved pet in kennels, and she'd promised that it would only be for a couple of days while she was in hospital. In the end, Drusilla felt she could hardly refuse.

But Mrs Carpenter had never come out of hospital, so Drusilla found herself stuck with the dog, the other neighbours having dreamed up cast-iron excuses as to why they couldn't help out. Sooner or later she'd have to find a permanent solution to her canine problem, but for the moment she had other things to think about.

She'd felt restless since that visit from the police. The late Mrs Carpenter, a great fan of detective series on TV, would have loved the drama. But Drusilla knew that the reality of crime was quite different; full of risk and violence. The two officers who'd called had asked her about Susan and she'd told them very little. She wondered if they'd be back, hoping for more information, but she knew she couldn't give them any.

She was pouring her third glass of wine when she heard a knock on her flat door. Sherlock looked up from his chosen place on the rug, then immediately went back to sleep; he wasn't much of a guard dog. Suddenly cautious, Drusilla shouted through the door, asking who it was. Her neighbours were always leaving the downstairs door on the latch, so anybody could walk in.

Her visitor answered and she told them to hang on before shutting the door between the living room and the hall. Then she fixed a smile to her face and opened the front door.

'Did you see that Krystal, Wes?' said Gerry when they set off back to the incident room. 'Think she was earwigging?'

'Perhaps she was just curious. People are.'

'True,' said Gerry, although Wesley couldn't help feeling uneasy that someone might have overheard their private conversation.

'Have you told your Pam we're off to Whitby first thing tomorrow morning?' Gerry asked.

'I called her earlier,' Wesley said, looking round the hall, where officers were still busy making calls and tapping into computers.

As he made his way home, he felt a nag of guilt about his impending absence. Pam had once told him that she felt like a single parent when he was dealing with a major case, and the memory of her words echoed in his mind at times like this. And it wasn't only Pam he felt he was letting down. He'd had several missed calls from Neil. Tempted by friendship and archaeology though he was, he'd felt obliged to ignore them.

When he arrived home, Pam greeted him with the news

that she'd been over to Belsham with the children to have Sunday dinner with Maritia and Mark. Wesley felt a pang of regret that he hadn't been able to take part in the family gathering. When he told Pam about Whitby, she seemed to take the news philosophically.

'Jan rang me this morning before we set off for your sister's,' she said as he sat down to eat. 'She was really excited; she said she needed to tell someone. This morning her new man took her to see the house he's having built before they went on to the hotel where they're staying.' She smiled. 'She's like a lovesick teenager. It's Callum this, Callum that.'

'Lucky Jan. Where's the house?'

'On the outskirts of Neston. It's a building site at the moment, but she says it's going to be beautiful – four bedrooms, all en suite.'

The mention of the house revived a memory of plans he'd seen on a drawing board, and he wondered whether this was the same one Matt Harrod had been working on.

'Where does Callum live at the moment?

'He's renting a flat in a new warehouse conversion by the river in Neston while the house is being built. He's got a boat too, so he can't be short of cash.'

'She's seen the boat?'

'Oh yes. Why do you ask?'

'No reason.'

'You don't suspect he's a bank robber or a drugs baron, do you?'

Wesley laughed. 'With a Merc, a posh house under construction and a boat, it's a possibility. Either that or Jan's just hit the jackpot.'

*

The following morning, Neil Watson arrived at the dig site with a feeling of excited anticipation. The trenches they'd opened had produced a lot already: sections of wall, painted plaster, pottery, even a couple of brooches and some beads. He was planning to expand the excavation that day in the hope of revealing the whole outline of the building. And from the finds so far, it looked as though he might be about to make the discovery of his career.

There was a lot of speculation amongst his colleagues, of course, but nobody had dared to say conclusively that they were digging up something of great importance. The champagne was on ice but the cork wasn't yet out of the bottle.

He was the first to get to the field and he expected to see the tarpaulins still stretched over the open trenches. A couple of them were lying beside the holes in a crumpled heap.

He hadn't seen any vehicles in the lane, but he called out in case one of the others had arrived early. But the only reply came from the gulls wheeling overhead. They sounded as though they were laughing, but to Neil, any unexpected disturbance to his site was no cause for amusement.

As he approached the trenches to take a closer look, his worst fears were realised. Somebody with no archaeological experience had been digging, making a mess in the carefully excavated soil.

The nighthawks had paid a visit.

21

Wesley was about to set off for Whitby when he received a call from Neil. With Gerry sitting beside him in the passenger seat, he was tempted not to answer, but Neil didn't usually call this early in the morning, so there was a chance it was urgent.

He cast an apologetic glance in the boss's direction, but Gerry was serenely munching a bacon roll he'd brought from home and didn't seem bothered.

'Hi, Neil, what is it?'

'We've had nighthawks. God knows what they've taken from the site. They must have had metal detectors. They've made a bloody mess.'

'You don't think the girls had anything to do with it?' The mention of metal detectors seemed to make Sophie and Livy prime suspects.

'I'm sure it wasn't them. They seem as horrified as the rest of us. And before you ask, they've no idea who it could be.'

'Have you called the police?'

'I thought you *were* the police.'

'I mean the local patrol. Murder's more my thing, and as you know, we're rather busy at the moment.'

His words would have silenced most people, but Neil was undeterred. 'Aren't you going to come over and have a look?'

'Sorry. I'm going up to Yorkshire for a couple of days.' Wesley hesitated, fearing he'd sounded a little harsh. He knew how devastating a visit from nighthawks could be to an archaeologist. 'I'll call the station for you and make sure they treat it seriously. OK?'

'It'll have to be. You do realise how important this site could be?'

'So you keep telling me. I'll ring them now.'

Gerry had almost finished his roll, scattering crumbs all over the pool car's pristine carpet. Wesley hadn't much time, so when he called the station, he kept it short and to the point.

'What was all that about?' Gerry asked, rousing himself from his bacon-fuelled stupor.

'Neil's had nighthawks.'

'Has he seen a doctor?'

Wesley knew that some people took the DCI's Liverpudlian wit the wrong way. But they'd worked together for so long now, he was used to it. Sometimes he even found it funny.

'OK, Wes. I know what nighthawks are. Did they get away with much?'

'Neil's not sure. I've told the station to send someone round. Laid it on thick and said the thieves might have stolen some valuable antiquities. Hopefully uniform'll take it seriously.'

His phone rang again, and after a short conversation he ended the call and turned to Gerry. 'That was Tom. He's found some deleted emails on Susan Brown's computer.

It looks as though our victim spent some time on dating websites.'

'She was probably looking for love like the rest of us.'

'She concentrated on sites dealing with Gloucestershire and North Yorkshire, so I suspect her interest wasn't personal. I think it could be connected with her investigations.'

'I know it's mostly done online, but there must be people we can phone and offices we can raid,' said Gerry with an irritated grunt. 'This is a murder inquiry and I like to speak to human beings.'

Wesley couldn't help agreeing. Now that so much was done online, everything seemed nebulous and fragile. It took someone with the talents of Tom from Scientific Support to pin anything down. But hopefully their visit to Whitby would throw up some new leads.

The journey up to Yorkshire was long but uneventful, and they arrived at the guest house near the harbour in Whitby in the late afternoon. The landlady greeted them, looking them up and down warily. But Wesley gave her his most charming smile and, sensing she was the curious type, told her that they were from Devon and Cornwall Police and pursuing an investigation. Her expression softened as though her worst fears had been allayed, and she became quite chatty as she showed them to their rooms – although her recital of the house rules suggested that they'd be under strict surveillance.

'She reminds me of the fearsome seaside landladies we had in Llandudno when I was a kid,' Gerry whispered once she was out of earshot.

'Well, we're not staying long. I told Pam two nights at the most.'

They'd already learned from the local police that Susan Brown's parents had both passed away and that she'd had no brothers and sisters. Wesley didn't know whether to be relieved that they'd been spared the pain of hearing their daughter was dead or sorry that Susan had suffered such loss in her lifetime. He couldn't help feeling sad at the thought of her being alone, pursuing some self-appointed mission she'd never managed to complete.

The local station had called Avril Willis's mother, Mrs Marley, to warn her that they wanted to talk to her. The sergeant they'd spoken to said she'd sounded pleased, as though she rarely had visitors and was looking forward to the company. They'd arranged to go round that evening, and at 6.30 they drove to her address, a small red-brick semi on the road out of town.

Mrs Marley was a solidly built woman with tight grey curls and a no-nonsense manner. She offered them tea as soon as they set foot in the house and asked them how their journey had been. She seemed cheerful, but Wesley couldn't forget that her daughter had been murdered, which was something nobody would ever get over. She must still be grieving – although she was hiding it well.

'I hope talking about Avril won't be too painful for you,' he began.

'Painful? I don't mind talking about her at all. Folk avoid mentioning her like she never existed, and to my mind, that's far worse.'

'You've got a point there, love,' said Gerry as he took his first sip of the strong tea in front of him. 'Do you remember a girl called Susan Brown? We're told she was a friend of your daughter's.'

Mrs Marley nodded slowly and when Gerry caught Wesley's eye he knew it would be up to him to break the news.

'I'm afraid Susan was found dead last Thursday in south Devon. We're treating her death as suspicious.'

Mrs Marley froze as though the news had revived dreadful memories. Then she took a deep breath. 'If there's anything I can do to help ... '

'Can you tell us about Avril and Sue.'

The woman gave a sad smile. 'They were always close, from when they met at infant school. Sue was a nice girl and the pair of them were thick as thieves. Avril was Sue's bridesmaid when she got married. Mind you, that didn't last long. He were up and off abroad before the ink was dry on the marriage certificate. Itchy feet, I reckon.'

'We haven't managed to contact Susan's ex-husband yet.'

'Chris Selby, his name was. I heard he's somewhere in the Middle East now, with a new family. Sue went back to using her maiden name and put it all behind her. I remember our Avril saying she was better off without him.'

'What about when Avril got married?'

'Sue warned Avril not to marry that Ian, but she took no notice. Said just because Sue's marriage hadn't worked out she thought all men were the same. Our Avril knew her own mind, you see.'

'How did you get on with your son-in-law?'

'I didn't. I weren't even invited to the wedding – nor was Sue, and they'd always been such good friends. I never saw much of Avril after that. Only a couple of times when I had to go to hospital – she persuaded him to give me a lift, but I reckon he wasn't too pleased about it.' Wesley heard the pain of rejection in her voice. 'Ian was ... ' she searched for the right word, 'possessive. He didn't like Avril seeing me or going out with her mates; always insisted on knowing where she was and who she was with.' She pursed her lips in disapproval.

'You mean he was controlling?' said Wesley, glancing at Gerry.

'Avril took it as a sign that he loved her. I tried to set her right, but she wouldn't listen ... until it was too late.'

'The inquest said she ran away from home and then had the bad luck to meet her killer.'

'That inquest didn't know nowt. My Avril would never have done owt like that if she hadn't been driven to it. And I reckon it was Ian who did the driving. He said he thought she was on her way to see me, but she never made it, more's the pity. I'd never have let her go back to him. Never. Bloody Ian Willis. I wish to God she'd never clapped eyes on him. I told her she were daft, but would she listen? Would she 'eck. That man had her exactly where he wanted her. He might have been good-looking, with a good job, but handsome is as handsome does in my opinion.'

'Mine too, love,' said Gerry. 'Where can we find this Ian? We'd like a word with him.'

'Oh, he's long gone. No idea where he is now.'

'You said he had a good job.'

'That's what Avril told me.'

'What did he do for a living?'

'He was some kind of salesman. Or it could have been marketing. Always well dressed, he was. The sort who could charm the birds from the trees,' she added as if it was an insult.

'Can we see a photo of him?'

'Haven't got one. Avril took all the photos when she moved out. I've got a lot of her, mind.' She pointed to the row of framed pictures on the mantelpiece: Avril in various stages of development, but none of her in her wedding dress and no sign of her bridegroom.

'What did he look like?'

'Short fair hair. Glasses.'

'Any tattoos? Distinguishing marks?'

Mrs Marley shook her head. 'Nothing like that, as far as I know.'

'We've seen a letter Avril wrote to Susan. It mentions that Susan was being bothered by a man she'd met at work; someone who gave Avril the creeps. Do you know anything about that?' Wesley sat forward and waited for the answer.

'Now that you mention it, I do remember something. Susan worked in an estate agent's in town – Pottinger and Clare – and she showed a man round a house. This was a few weeks before our Avril got married. Back then she used to meet Sue from time to time without telling Ian – what sort of a relationship was that?'

Wesley waited for her to continue the story.

'Anyway, this man asked Sue out but she turned him down. After that, he kept popping up everywhere she went and buying her flowers. She thought it was a bit weird.'

'Was that why she left Whitby?'

'Oh no, this was years ago. She didn't go off until early this year and before that she used to come round to see me quite regular. She never mentioned any man bothering her, so I presume he must have been long gone.' She thought for a few moments. 'I don't think Sue ever got over our Avril, you know. I reckon she took it worse than when her mum passed away. I think that's why she kept in touch.' There was a long pause before she spoke again. 'It was when she was last here in February that I told her about the letter.'

Wesley leaned forward. 'What letter?'

'It came in late January.' She took a tissue from her sleeve and crumpled it in her hand. 'It were from him – the man who killed our Avril. He said he didn't do it. Said he'd confessed because the police were piling the pressure on and that he was dying now and he wanted to put the record straight. I showed it to Sue and she went all quiet. I only saw her the once after that, just before she quit her job and left Whitby.'

She walked to the bureau in the corner of the room, took out an envelope and handed it to Gerry. In simple, almost childlike terms, the writer of the letter swore he was innocent of Avril's murder. He ended with the strangely formal 'Yours faithfully, Warren Chips'.

'So Susan left town shortly after seeing this?' Wesley asked.

'Aye. She came to see me to say goodbye. She said she didn't know when she'd be back.'

'What else did she say?'

'Something like she had to go away for a while because there was something she had to do. That's all I remember.'

'Do you think she was trying to discover the truth about Avril's murder?'

'She didn't say – and I don't know how she could have done that. Besides, when I showed the letter to the police, they said Chips was lying. Murderers often do, they said. "Playing mind games" was how they put it. I don't know how anyone could be so cruel.' She turned her head away.

'Nor do I,' said Wesley quietly.

'How did Avril and Ian meet?' Gerry asked, changing the subject.

'I think it was through some agency or website. For the

discerning, she said. She tried to persuade Susan to give it a go, but Sue wasn't having any of it. Said she'd had enough of men after what happened with Chris Selby.'

'What was the name of the agency?'

Mrs Marley frowned, trying to remember, before shaking her head. 'Sorry, I don't recall the name, but Avril said it was only for those who wanted serious relationships.' She sniffed. 'Bit like saying no time-wasters. I think it was quite local and that's why she chose it. She didn't want to be matched up with a bloke from the other side of the country, did she.'

'Was this Ian the only man she went out with?'

'Oh yes. First and last. She was smitten. Whirlwind romance.'

'So he was from this area?'

'No. He'd just come to live round here and he didn't know anyone, he said. That's why he used the agency.' She dabbed her nose with the tissue in her hand. 'I reckon she'd still be with us now if she hadn't met that man. I blame him.'

'Not the man who was convicted of her murder?'

She looked at the letter. 'I've spent years hating Chips for what he did. If they still had hanging, I'd happily have put the noose round his neck myself, but since that letter arrived . . . What if the police got it wrong and he's telling the truth? She was missing for over a fortnight before they found her in the river. Ian told the police she was on her way to see me on the night she was killed. According to him, they'd had a row and she walked out. If that man hadn't driven her out of her own home with his controlling ways, she'd never have been on the streets at night . . . and what if he tried to stop her leaving and killed her during their row? Avril had money put by from when her dad passed away. What happened to that, that's what I want to know.' She pressed her lips together as though she'd said all she was going to say on the matter.

Wesley caught Gerry's eye. 'We'll leave you in peace, Mrs Marley. You're sure you have no idea where we can find Ian Willis?'

'He's vanished off the face of the earth, and good riddance. He'll have moved on to another poor girl. Men like that always do.'

As they thanked her, Wesley found himself wishing that Rachel was there with him. She always seemed to know the right thing to say to bereaved relatives, while he was terrified of coming out with something clumsy that would add to their grief. But Avril Willis's mother had channelled her mourning into anger. And once she'd received the letter from Warren Chips, that anger had switched from the convicted killer to Avril's absent husband.

Wesley imagined the letter had been a catalyst; that she'd always resented Ian Willis and that was why she'd been so ready to believe Chips's denial. But he and Gerry weren't so emotionally involved. They just wanted to discover the truth.

Once they were back in the car, he rang the local police station to ask whether anybody knew the whereabouts of Ian Willis. The answer was no.

From the journal of Dr Aldus Claye

May 1921

Phipps was in a state of high excitement at dinner this evening. He talked non-stop about what we had found. The farmer's men, a taciturn trio, had expanded the excavation further and revealed the outline of a room. Phipps himself had investigated more closely the place where the bones had been dug up, and discovered a spring nearby, some way from the walls and in the approximate location the curse was found. It was common to put curses near sacred water sources, I believe. Many have been found at Aquae Sulis, the place we now call Bath. The gods, people believed, dwelled in such places.

Phipps said the spring might have served as the water supply for the people who lived in the villa – he is sure that is what we have found. He said he would send a telegram to Professor Fredericks, because it is an important find and Fredericks might want to bring more diggers down to excavate the rest of the field and the surrounding land. His excitement was palpable and it seemed to transmit itself to my wife. I saw her watching him, her eyes bright where once they were dull and apathetic. I do not know whether to welcome her

new interest in archaeology or to be concerned that the excite-
ment might have a detrimental effect on her delicate nervous
condition.

Clarabel insisted that she sleep alone, saying she was
exhausted by the excitement of the day's activities. Phipps
and I spent the rest of the evening enjoying my best port and
discussing plans for the excavation.

When I consider the potentially momentous nature of our
find, I feel somewhat overwhelmed.

22

The following morning brought a generous Yorkshire breakfast, the sort Gerry claimed he always dreamed of. The DCI tucked in heartily, claiming it would set them up for that day's visits.

As arranged, they arrived at the local police station first thing. Gerry wanted to know whether there was anything concerning Avril Willis's murder that hadn't appeared in the official reports. He reckoned there was always something the locals knew that hadn't necessarily been written down when the case was presented to the CPS. And as luck would have it, the officer who'd been in charge of the case, DCI Norman Clough, was still there.

'How do?' said Clough. 'You've come a long way to see us. We're honoured.' There was a question in his statement.

'We're here about the Avril Willis murder,' Gerry said.

'Aye. So you said on the phone yesterday. Open-and-shut case, it was. The bastard held his hand up for it. He murdered two women in Leeds and one in Bradford – attacked them when they were walking home at night. Raped and strangled, they were.' He shook his head with distaste. 'I was glad when he was put away, I can tell you. When he was

160

interviewed about Avril, he put his hand up for her and all, which was bloody good for my clear-up rate.'

'He sent a letter to Avril's mum claiming that he was innocent.'

'If you believe that, you'll believe anything. The bastard's playing games. Bloody cruel, if you ask me.'

'So you think he was lying?'

There was a short hesitation before Clough answered. 'Course he was. There was a lot of evidence against him. Even the best defence barrister couldn't have argued with it.'

'DNA?'

'There was plenty for the others, but he'd dumped poor Avril in the river and she was there a couple of weeks, so it was destroyed in her case. But there was no doubt about it. His van was seen in Whitby the evening she disappeared, and she was strangled like the others. Besides, he confessed – asked for it to be taken into consideration.'

'Even so, we'd like to have a word with him if he's still in the land of the living.'

'He is as far as I know.'

'In that case can you contact the prison for us and speak to the governor?'

Clough looked sceptical. 'If you insist. But I can't see it'll do you much good.'

'Was Avril's husband ever in the frame?' Wesley asked. 'Ian Willis. We spoke to her mother last night and she wasn't too complimentary about him.'

It was the first time he had opened his mouth, and Clough gave him a wary look. There had been no hint of hostility when they'd first been introduced, and Wesley wondered whether the well-bred accent he'd acquired at his expensive London school caused more suspicion in certain people than the colour of his skin.

'We interviewed him when her body was found, and he told us that they'd had a row and she'd walked out. He assumed she'd gone back to her mother's and said he thought it best to leave her to cool off. But when he called her mother a few days later, he found out she hadn't seen her. That was when he notified us.'

'What did you make of him?' Wesley asked.

'Smooth.' The word sounded damning, like the worst insult the man could think of. 'I didn't like him, but he had a solid alibi for the night she disappeared. He'd gone drinking at the golf club after the row. He spilled a drink and there was a bit of a kerfuffle. Everyone remembered it.'

'Do you think there's a chance Avril could have disappeared earlier than Willis claimed? The previous evening, maybe?'

'Oh no. A witness saw her earlier that day. A woman who called at the house – something to do with mortgages. She didn't stay long because she sensed some tension between Avril and her husband – sharp remarks and all that, which isn't surprising if she walked out on him that night.'

'Was this woman interviewed?'

'She was.' Clough looked in the file. 'A Mrs Pollard. Nice woman.'

'Know where we can find her?'

'When we got round to interviewing her, she said she was about to give up her job and move abroad. Portugal, I think. Look, Chips confessed and we had no reason to disbelieve him.'

'Do you know where Ian Willis is now?'

'No idea. He upped and left soon after the arrest and

162

didn't attend the trial. Told one of my officers he'd find it too distressing.'

'Did that strike you as strange?'

Clough shrugged his broad shoulders. 'There's no accounting for folk, is there?'

'Just one more thing. In the course of the investigation, did you come across Avril's friend Susan Brown?'

'Oh aye. She reckoned we should be looking at Ian Willis, but she didn't have any evidence to back that up. She claimed he was guilty of what we'd call today coercive control.'

'Was that ever followed up?' Gerry asked.

'We had her killer, so there didn't seem much point. It was only hearsay. Even if Willis was guilty of controlling behaviour, it would be Susan Brown's word against his, and I reckon she had a grudge against him.' Clough swept a hand towards his pile of paperwork, as if to indicate that he had enough on his plate without pursuing claims that could never be proved. 'You said you were here because Susan's been murdered. Are you thinking there's a connection?'

'Two friends found dead at opposite ends of the country. Both strangled. Seems too much of a coincidence to me,' said Gerry.

Clough considered this for a moment and his expression softened. 'Aye. I reckon I might be thinking the same – if Avril's killer wasn't safely behind bars.'

'Did Susan Brown ever make a complaint about being stalked?'

Clough shook his head. 'Not to us.'

'Ever heard the name Calvin Brunning? Has a record for GBH and drug dealing.'

'Can't say I've come across him. Look, if you gentlemen

are staying tonight, why don't we meet up for a pint? I can show you some proper Yorkshire hospitality.' He beamed at them. It was a hard invitation to turn down.

'That'd be grand,' said Gerry, beaming back.

'Right,' Gerry said eagerly as they left the station after making the arrangements. 'Next stop the estate agent's where Susan used to work. Then, with any luck, we might have time to do a spot of sightseeing. It's years since I've been to Whitby. Nice place. Associations with Dracula.'

'It's not a vampire we're after,' said Wesley with a smile. He thought for a moment. 'Although I confess I wouldn't mind taking a look at the abbey. And St Mary's church. Very interesting box pews, I believe.'

Gerry gave him an indulgent look and they began to walk towards the town centre. The sound of gulls crying overhead and the scent of seaweed reminded Wesley of Tradmouth. But here there was a chill in the breeze blowing in from the North Sea.

Pottinger and Clare, estate agents, stood in a prominent position in the centre of the main street, and the array of desirable properties in the two wide windows flanking the entrance suggested that business was good. Wesley pushed the door open, and a plump young woman in a business-like black suit looked him up and down suspiciously. Her expression remained guarded when the two of them produced their ID and asked to see the person in charge. She vanished into the back office and returned a few moments later. They were to come through.

The man who greeted them with a hearty handshake was completely bald and almost dwarfed by his huge pale-wood desk. He introduced himself as Peter Clare and invited them to take a seat.

'What can I do for you, gentlemen?' he said, rubbing his hands together obsequiously, every inch the good citizen doing all he could to help the forces of law and order.

'Susan Brown used to work here, is that right?' Wesley began.

'Yes. Susan was a valued part of our team here at Pottinger and Clare. She worked here for six years and we were very sorry to lose her when she left for pastures new. Why are you asking? Has something happened?'

Wesley hesitated before breaking the news. 'I'm afraid Susan was found dead in south Devon last Thursday. She was murdered.'

The man looked stunned. 'That's terrible. Poor Susan. Have you any idea . . . ?'

'We're still pursuing enquiries. Did she say where she was going?'

'Sorry. She was a little vague about her plans.'

'She didn't mention why she was leaving?' Gerry asked.

'She said it was for personal reasons, and I didn't like to enquire further.'

'While she was working here, there was an incident.'

Clare looked alarmed. 'I don't think so.'

'She met someone who began bothering her. This might have been around five years ago. Did she ever say anything to you or her colleagues?' Wesley tilted his head to one side enquiringly and watched the man's reaction.

At first Clare looked as though he was about to deny all knowledge. Then he thought better of it. He lowered his eyes and stared at his hands. 'Now that you mention it, I do remember something, but I assure you it wasn't serious. One of our clients took rather a shine to her. She showed him round some properties and he started sending her flowers – and once or twice I saw him outside in the street when the office closed for the day. She never said anything to me, so I assumed he didn't mean any harm.'

'We'll need the name of this client, Mr Clare.' Wesley smiled reassuringly. 'Just to eliminate him from our enquiries. I promise he won't know that it was you who provided his details. You do have records going back that far, I take it?'

Clare rose and opened the filing cabinet behind his chair. After a lengthy search, he pulled out a thin file and passed it to Wesley.

'I think this is the man. Ebenezer Smith. He was looking for a two-bed terrace near the middle of town and always insisted on Susan showing him round. He viewed several properties, but none turned out to be quite what he had in mind.'

'So he didn't buy a property from you?'

'As I say, he had a few viewings, but we heard nothing from him after that.'

'But Susan did?'

'I did suspect that she was the reason he kept coming back.' There was a pause, as though Clare was making a decision. 'This was a long time ago, and I didn't see him again for years.' He hesitated. 'Until a couple of weeks before Sue left us, when I spotted him in the street near the harbour.'

'Did Susan mention that he'd contacted her again?'

'No, nothing like that. Do you think he might have something to do with . . . ?'

'You wouldn't happen to know where we can find Mr Smith now?' said Gerry, flicking through the sparse file.

'The address he gave us originally is in the file: somewhere in Scarborough, as I remember. But if he was genuinely interested in acquiring another property, of course he might well have moved since then.'

'Can you describe him?'

'In his thirties – around Susan's age. Medium height. Brown hair, thinning a bit on top. Ordinary, really.'

Gerry made a note of the address in the file and stood up. 'Well, thanks for your time, Mr Clare. And by the way, where were you last Thursday?'

The man suddenly looked flustered. 'Er ... I was away. On a walking holiday.'

'Alone?'

'Yes. I do it once a year. My wife goes away with her sister and I take the opportunity to get some fresh air into my lungs and enjoy the countryside.'

'Which particular part of the countryside were you enjoying this time?' Gerry's question sounded casual, but Wesley knew what he was thinking.

'Er ... your part of the world, actually. North Devon. Around Ilfracombe. Fortunately the weather was kind.' He smiled nervously.

'You didn't see Susan while you were down there?'

'Of course not. I didn't even know she was in Devon.'

Wesley caught Gerry's eye.

'If we could have the address where you stayed ...'

'Of course. It was a pleasant little B & B on the edge of Ilfracombe.' Clare scribbled down the details and handed them to Wesley, who noticed that his hand was shaking slightly.

They thanked him, and as soon as they'd left, Wesley was on the phone to the incident room. There was something he wanted them to check out.

*

Wesley hadn't really expected to find the mysterious Mr Smith at the Scarborough address he'd given to Pottinger and Clare all those years ago, but it turned out he was wrong. The house was in the middle of a dingy Victorian terrace near the town centre, a few streets back from the beach and its attractions. Several of the other houses in the terrace had B&B signs outside, but Smith's address had been converted into flats. The names beside the bells were illegible because they'd faded in the sun, so Wesley tried Flat 1 and hoped for the best.

When there was no answer, he began to try the others, aware of Gerry shifting from foot to foot on the step behind him. At last there was a reply, and Gerry leaned forward to speak over Wesley's shoulder. 'Delivery for Flat 1, mate. Can you sign for it?'

Wesley thought such subterfuge was going a bit far, even for Gerry, but he said nothing. The DCI had obviously read his mind. 'Some people don't seem to like us, Wes. I can't think why. And nothing beats the element of surprise.'

Wesley heard footsteps on the stairs, and when their owner opened the door, the man standing there matched the description Peter Clare had given. He was wearing jeans and a short-sleeved checked shirt.

They produced their ID. 'Mr Smith, I presume.'

As soon as the words left Gerry's lips, the man took a step back. He looked terrified, as though he'd just come face to face with a pair of man-eating tigers. And when he opened his mouth to speak, his first words were 'I didn't do it. I swear.'

23

.

At the local police station, the duty solicitor, a young woman with a thin face, was poised on the edge of her seat like a nervous animal. Wesley suspected she was new to the job.

'Right then,' Gerry began. 'We'd better have your full name.'

'Smith. Ebenezer Smith.'

'You must have come in for some stick at school with a name like Ebenezer – especially at Christmas.' Wesley detected a note of sympathy in Gerry's voice.

Gerry gave him a nod. It was up to him to open the questioning.

'You said you didn't do it. What were you talking about?'

Smith bowed his head. 'Can you promise my mother won't find out?'

'What don't you want her to find out?'

'I didn't do it. Honestly. The shop made a mistake.'

'Why don't you tell us all about it, Ebenezer.'

'Ben. I prefer Ben.'

Wesley assumed his most sympathetic expression. If the suspect thought he was on his side, he'd be more likely to open up. 'Right, Ben, tell us exactly what happened.'

'The man in the model shop said I hadn't paid, but I had. I paid with my credit card and they found out later I was in the right. I never thought they'd call the police.'

Wesley saw Gerry raise his eyebrows. It seemed they'd got their wires crossed. 'We're not here about that, Ben,' he said gently. 'We're from Devon and we're conducting a murder inquiry.'

'Murder?' The man's eyes widened in astonishment. 'What's that got to do with me?'

'We understand you knew a woman called Susan Brown, who used to work for Pottinger and Clare, the estate agent in Whitby. A few years ago you sent her flowers and waited outside for her after work.'

'Is that a crime?'

'You were seen in Whitby earlier this year.'

Smith nodded. 'I had a job interview. I'd been working down south for a few years, but I had to come back just after Christmas because Mother wasn't well.'

'Did you see Susan while you were in Whitby?'

His face turned red. 'I passed her office, but I didn't see her.'

'Did you start stalking her again?'

Smith looked affronted. 'I never stalked her, I swear. I'd never do anything like that.'

'Ms Brown moved away, first to the Cotswolds and then to south Devon. Was that to get away from you?'

'Of course not. Why don't you ask her?'

'We can't ask her anything,' said Gerry. 'She was murdered last week. Found strangled on a coast path.'

It was as though a bombshell had been dropped into the gloomy room. Smith stared at him, opening and closing his mouth in shock. 'I don't believe you.'

He took a used tissue from the pocket of his jeans and blew his nose.

'I'm afraid it's true,' said Wesley. 'Susan was living in Devon when she died. Did you know where she was?'

'No.' Smith looked crestfallen, and Wesley found himself feeling sorry for him.

'Tell me about Susan.'

A fond smile appeared on Smith's lips, as though he was reliving a happy memory. 'I met her when she showed me round some properties four or five years ago. She was really nice – very kind. I asked her out, but she had other things on, so . . . Sometimes I visited the pub she went to with her colleagues, hoping I'd get a chance to talk to her. I sent her flowers, and I used to try and bump into her . . . by accident, like. She was always nice to me and I'm sure she liked me. If it hadn't been for Mother . . . '

There was a long silence before he spoke again. 'I had to move away because of work, so I didn't see Susan for years. But like I told you, when I moved back in February, I walked past her office to see if she was still there.'

'And was she?'

'No. I'd hoped she'd be there, but . . . '

'Where were you last Thursday?'

Smith looked confused, as though Gerry had posed an impossible question. Eventually he gave his solicitor a side-ways glance and said, 'No comment.'

'Do you live alone, Ben?' By unspoken agreement, Wesley was playing the role of good cop.

'I live with Mother,' Smith muttered, as though he was embarrassed. 'But I was looking for a place of my own until work moved me down south. That's why I went to the estate agent's in the first place. But now Mother's health has got worse. There was a neighbour she relied on, but she moved into a home before Christmas, so … Mother can't cope on her own, you see.'

'And she wanted you back?'

He nodded sadly.

'What's the matter with her?'

'The doctors can't find anything wrong, but she says she feels weak all the time. She hated me being away down south. She says she likes me there … just in case.'

The job down south must have been a blow to his mother, and Wesley couldn't help wondering if her illness had begun when she'd decided to put a stop to her son's attempt to strike out on his own. Perhaps he was being uncharitable. In his job, he was used to thinking the worst of people's motives.

'So your mum will confirm that you were at home at the time in question? Or would she lie for you?' Gerry leaned forward and glowered at Smith, who squirmed in his seat.

There was a long silence before he answered. 'I was away.'

'I'd advise you not to say any more,' the solicitor piped up.

Smith turned to her. 'They'll find out. Mother always tells the truth.' He paused for a moment, then looked Wesley in the eye. 'I went to Birmingham. There was an exhibition on at the NEC – fantasy figures. I went on Wednesday and stayed a couple of nights at a TravelStop. Mother wasn't feeling well on Wednesday morning and she didn't want me to go, but I called her sister and she came to stay with her.'

Wesley couldn't help feeling glad that the man had called his controlling mother's bluff.

'Were you at the hotel alone?'

'No comment.'

The solicitor gave a satisfied nod, as if to congratulate her client for following her advice.

'We can check.'

Smith's face reddened. He was a useless liar.

'Is there anyone who can vouch for you? Don't worry, we're known for our discretion, aren't we, Inspector Peterson?'

'I, er . . . was with a lady.'

'What's her name?'

'Jacky. But I don't want Mother to find out. She doesn't like me having girlfriends, and she certainly wouldn't approve of me carrying on with a married woman.'

Wesley saw real fear in the man's eyes. There was someone in his life who was far more terrifying than the police.

'Did your mother know that you were stalking Susan Brown?'

'I told you, I wasn't stalking her. I liked her, that's all.'

'And now she's dead.'

Smith bowed his head.

'Were you lying when you said you didn't see her when you went back to Whitby?' said Gerry. 'Did she reject you? Tell you to get lost? Because if she did, that's a good motive for murder in my book. She was strangled. Was it a crime of passion?'

'No. I'd never have harmed a hair on her head. Honestly. I'm not like that.'

'Let's get back to this married woman you were with in Birmingham,' said Wesley. 'Tell us about her.'

There was an embarrassed silence while Smith looked pleadingly at his solicitor. When she didn't come to his rescue, he spoke almost in a whisper. 'I'm sorry. I wasn't telling the whole truth. She was a . . . I mean, she does it for a living.'

'A sex worker?' said Wesley, wanting to get things clear. If this was true, then Smith's alibi might be hard to track down.

The tears started to roll down Smith's pale cheeks, and Wesley wasn't sure whether they were tears of grief or remorse.

'Where do you work?'

'Car showroom. But I was made redundant. It's got branches all over the country and they wanted me to stay down south, but I had to come back here for Mother.'

Wesley found himself feeling even more sorry for Ebenezer Smith. But he couldn't allow his sympathy to get in the way of the investigation. The man still had to be a suspect.

Once they had details of Smith's Birmingham hotel, they wound up the interview. He'd denied any involvement in Susan's murder and Wesley doubted whether he'd have had the ability to track her down. But obsessive love could make people determined, and if he'd glimpsed Susan on his return to Whitby, perhaps his long-dormant obsession had been rekindled. Wesley suspected that life at his mother's beck and call would have given him a lot of time to research Susan's whereabouts.

Gerry rang the TravelStop and found that Smith had indeed stayed there at the time of Susan's murder. He sounded disappointed when he broke the news to Wesley. But he admitted that the person on the other end of the line had no reason to lie. They also checked out Smith's place of work down south, and discovered that he'd kept asking one of the female customers out. No official complaint had ever been made and everyone there, including the customer, assumed he was harmless. But it showed a pattern of behaviour nonetheless.

'What did you think of Ebenezer Smith?' Gerry asked as they drove back to Whitby. 'Are we treating him as a suspect? These chain hotels like TravelStop are pretty anonymous. He might have checked in, but that doesn't mean he actually spent the night there. And this sex worker he said he was with will be hard to find.'

Wesley considered the question for a few moments. 'Smith was keen on Susan and made a slight nuisance of himself, but I think that's as far as it went – same with the customer down south. There's no evidence at the moment that there's a more sinister side to his character, although I could be wrong. It looks like he considered Susan to be the love of his life at one time – until his mother put the kibosh on his dreams. He could have tracked her down to Devon.'

'So we keep him on the suspect list?'

'I think we have to, Gerry. But if he was on our patch, he would have had to stay somewhere, so I'll ask the team to check all the local accommodation.'

'We'll set off for home first thing tomorrow,' said Wesley. 'Wonder whether the lab's got a result back on Crispin Joss's scarf yet.'

'Would he still be wearing the murder weapon around his neck if he was guilty?'

'I think it's exactly the sort of thing he'd do.'

Gerry nodded slowly. 'Hidden in plain sight. You're right, Wes. He's the type who thinks he's too clever for us.'

Gerry's phone rang and he muttered something under his breath before answering. It was DCI Clough, and Wesley fell silent, hoping he had something new to tell them – and that whatever it was would be good. Gerry put the call on speaker. It would save repeating the information later.

'You wanted to see Warren Chips to ask about that letter

he sent to Mrs Marley. I've spoken to the governor of the jail where he's serving his sentence, and he confirms Chips has a terminal illness and only has a couple more weeks to live. Wish I could say I was sorry, but after what he did to those women ... '

Wesley willed Clough to come to the point.

'The governor told me Chips got religion when he was diagnosed and started claiming that he gave a false confession to one of the murders – said he wanted to put the record straight before he goes to meet his maker.'

'Avril Willis?' said Wesley.

'The governor's sceptical, but ... '

'Are you still up for that drink tonight?' said Gerry.

Clough answered in the affirmative.

24

The more the excavation progressed, the more excited Neil was feeling. He'd abandoned the idea of returning home to his flat in Exeter each evening, deciding instead to stay on site, and had borrowed a tent from one of his fellow diggers, along with a Primus stove and a sleeping bag. A Portaloo had been moved onto the site so he could make himself at home.

The weather was fine, and as a student, he would have considered the accommodation to be the height of luxury. Only he wasn't a student any more, and after a day's digging, he was longing for a warm bath to ease his aches and pains. And he knew there was one place he could find it: Wesley and Pam's.

He arrived on Pam's doorstep at seven that evening with a hopeful expression on his face.

'Wasn't expecting you,' said Pam before inviting him in. 'We've just eaten or I'd ...'

'Don't worry, I had something in the pub. Wes in?'

'Didn't he tell you? He's up in Yorkshire. Won't be back till tomorrow evening.'

'He probably mentioned it, but I've had other things on my mind. Any chance of a bath? I'm camping out on our site. We've had nighthawks.'

'Oh dear,' Pam said. 'Did they take much?'

'Can't really tell. The bath . . . ?'

'Of course. Help yourself. The kids are in their rooms. Perhaps you could look in on Michael.' She sounded a little worried. 'He really enjoyed visiting that last dig you were on, and he spends far too much time in his room, on his phone.'

'That's normal at his age, isn't it?'

'Perhaps, but I think some fresh air would do him good.'

'Well, our present dig might interest him.' Neil lowered his voice, as though he was afraid of being overheard. 'I think we might have found a Roman villa. A lot of people would say that's impossible round here, but with every day that passes . . .' He took a deep breath. 'If I'm right, this could be mega – the sort of thing that'll take the archaeological world by storm. Nobody thought the Romans got this far south in Devon, but . . .'

'You've found proof that they did?' Pam was used to Neil's excitement. When she'd met him and Wesley at university, they'd both been fired up with passion for their subject. She'd gone out with Neil for a while before choosing Wesley, and she'd never had cause to regret her decision. Neil lived and breathed archaeology, but at least Wesley left his work behind once he was home. If she'd opted for Neil, she'd have taken permanent second place to a hole in the ground.

'It's looking increasingly likely. Wesley's been to the site, but he was distracted by some woman getting murdered.'

'How thoughtless of her. You know where the bathroom is.'

Neil was halfway up the stairs when he turned round. 'You grew up round here. Have you any idea why that place we're digging at is called Serpent's Point?'

Pam shook her head and disappeared into the living room.

Later, when Neil came downstairs rubbing his long hair with a towel, Pam offered him a cup of tea, which he accepted gratefully. As he sipped it, he noticed a small statue standing on the mantelpiece.

'That's Mercury, messenger of the gods. Where did you get it?'

'An antique shop in Tradmouth. I bought it this lunchtime. I couldn't resist it and it wasn't that expensive. I knew Wes would approve. Do you like it?'

Neil made for the object and picked it up carefully, turning it over in his hands to examine it. 'It's bronze.'

'I doubt it. It's some cheap metal made to look like bronze. It's a fake. They probably churn them out in the Far East and ship them over here by the container load.'

Neil sank down into the nearest armchair, still clutching Mercury with his winged helmet, unable to take his eyes off the small figure.

'I don't think this is a fake, Pam. Which shop did you say you got it from?'

The following morning, after another huge breakfast, Wesley and Gerry's first port of call was the prison in South Yorkshire, where the governor greeted them with a hearty handshake. He was a tall man with a small beard, and Wesley thought he didn't look the type to fall for a sob story.

'The doctors don't think Chips has long,' he said solemnly. 'Since his diagnosis, he's become rather ... devout. He's been spending a lot of time with the padre reading the Bible. He's made it known that he's anxious to repent of his sins.'

'Any chance of him being released on compassionate grounds?' said Gerry. 'In other words, could this miraculous conversion be an act to con the authorities into thinking he's a reformed character?'

The governor shook his head. 'I don't think even Chips could fool the entire medical team at the local hospital. His illness is terminal – no doubt about it. And as for him finding God, I suppose knowing you're shortly going to die focuses the mind. Even for the likes of Warren Chips.'

The governor invited the two detectives to sit before carrying on. 'The man's definitely changed since his diagnosis. He was a cocky character, in denial about what he'd done. He knew he had a whole-life tariff because of the nature of his crimes, but it didn't seem to bother him. If any porn slipped through the system, he'd be the first to partake. It might be unprofessional of me to say, but he was a nasty piece of work with a complete contempt for women. One psychiatrist who assessed him reported that he didn't think he'd done anything wrong when he raped and killed his victims. They were sex workers, so he regarded them as prey – fair game.'

Wesley thought he saw the governor shudder. 'You'd say he's a psychopath?'

'That's the opinion of some professionals who've seen him. Others disagree, but I certainly think he has those tendencies. That's why I've been sceptical about his conversion to the path of righteousness. Is he taking advantage of the padre's good nature? It's the man's job to think well of everybody, after all.'

Wesley nodded. His own brother-in-law, Mark, was a vicar, and he tended to give everyone the benefit of the doubt. As the governor said, it went with the job. And from what he knew about Warren Chips, he feared the padre's trust might have been misplaced.

'We've heard he's denying responsibility for one of the murders he was sent down for.'

'According to him, the police added it to the charge sheet at the last minute to help their clear-up rate.' The governor took a deep breath. 'I know it's beyond my remit, but I had a look at the details myself, and that particular victim, Avril Willis, had a very different profile to the others. They were sex workers, but Avril ...'

'Was just in the wrong place at the wrong time,' said Gerry. 'But she was strangled like the others. There was no evidence of rape, but after the body had been in the water all that time, it was hard to tell.'

'Precisely. But I'm wondering why he should change his story now. He's still happily admitting to the others, so why is this one different?'

Wesley considered the question for a few moments. 'Unless he doesn't want to be remembered as someone who killed a woman he thinks of as innocent.'

'You could have a point, Inspector. In which case he might be lying through his teeth. He's in the infirmary, receiving end-of-life care. He had another visitor back in February. A young woman.'

'Was her name Susan Brown?'

'That's right. She spoke to him for a while.'

'Can we talk to him?'

'If the medical staff agree, that's OK with me.' The governor stood up. 'I'll take you.'

Walking through the prison corridors made Wesley uneasy. There was a smell about the place that he couldn't quite pinpoint; a combination of disinfectant, lavatories, stale cooking and sweat. He'd smelled it before, in other prisons. When they reached the infirmary, they found it brightly lit and similar to any other hospital ward. Warren Chips was in a room of his own.

Wesley's first impression was that the shrunken man in the bed looked harmless. His head was completely bald and his parchment skin was blotchy. He appeared just like any other dangerously ill middle-aged man, and Wesley had to remind himself of the evil he had wrought during his life.

Sitting by the bed was a large, muscular man in a short-sleeved shirt and a dog collar. He had an array of tattoos up his bare arms and a Bible in his hands, and he was reading to the prisoner, whose eyes were shut. The padre looked round and fell silent.

'Warren's asleep,' he said quietly once the governor had explained who the visitors were. 'He's really not up to questioning, but he's told me everything, so if I can help . . . '

'No seal of the confessional, padre?'

'Not my denomination. Besides, Warren has been asking to see the police. He's anxious to set the record straight before he passes away.'

'I understand that a woman visited him – Susan Brown. She was a friend of Avril Willis.'

'Yes. He told me. He wrote to Avril's mother, and I think Ms Brown came on her behalf. He never said what they talked about, I'm afraid.'

'Do you believe he's telling the truth about Avril's murder?'

The padre smiled. 'I've only recently taken holy orders. Before that, I ran boxing clubs in run-down areas and I became a residential social worker. I've come up against some rum characters in my time, so people can't pull the wool over my eyes that easily. I know the appalling things

Warren did and I think coming face to face with death has made him realise the effect it had on his victims' families. When he tells me he didn't kill Avril Willis, I believe him. At this stage in his life, why would he lie about it?'

Wesley put forward the same argument he'd made to the governor earlier, but as soon as he'd spoken, a faint, cracked voice, like the rustle of dry leaves, came from the bed. Chips had woken up.

'I never did that Avril. I was nowhere near, I swear. I just want forgiveness for those others. I had no right to take their lives. Only God has that right. I see that now.'

The padre took the man's hand. 'If you're truly sorry, there is forgiveness, Warren.'

'Why did you confess to Avril Willis's murder?' said Wesley, leaning forward so he could hear the man's reply.

'It's like I told that lass – that mate of hers who came. The cops said that if I confessed to it, the judge'd go easier on me. Only he never did.' Every word seemed like an effort, and he paused for breath. 'I didn't kill Avril. As God's my witness, I did the others but not her.' He closed his eyes again and sank back on his pillow as though the effort had been too much for him.

The padre turned to face Wesley. 'Well, Inspector, I think you've got a problem.'

They'd been away two nights and Wesley was eager to head home. They had a long journey ahead of them, but before they set off, Gerry phoned Clough to fill him in on their visit to Chips. Wesley detected a slight change in the DCI's manner as he spoke to his Whitby counterpart. If Chips was telling the truth, Clough's investigation had taken the lazy way out. And that wasn't something Gerry approved of.

'What did he say?' Wesley asked once the DCI had finished the call.

'Nothing much,' said Gerry. 'If what Chips said is true, Clough got it badly wrong four years ago. And there might still be a killer at large on his patch.'

'I can't think why Chips would lie – not when he's dying.'

'Some prisoners get a kick at the thought of causing trouble for the police from beyond the grave.'

'I know,' said Wesley quietly. 'But I believed him.' He put his key in the car ignition. It was time to head home to Devon.

'Which leaves us with the million-dollar question. If Chips didn't kill Avril and dump her body in that river, who did?'

'The husband?'

'He had a solid alibi.'

'Even so, we need to find him – and sooner rather than later.'

From the journal of Dr Aldus Claye

May 1921

Phipps supervises our amateur diggers very strictly, making
sure that their rough attentions do no harm to the remains
that lie beneath the soil. Once the foundations are exposed,
he and I take over with our trowels, and now the outline
of a set of rooms is quite visible. Low walls tell of chambers
and corridors with a central courtyard in the typical style.
Phipps speculates that we have found the country retreat
of some wealthy official from the legionary fortress of Isca
Dumnoniorum, attracted by the beauty of the rich agri-
cultural land around and its stunning position so near
to the sea.

We have discovered roof tiles and much pottery and glass,
as well as an abundance of painted plaster in a remarkable
state of preservation. Then there are the tesserae we've dug
from the soil, which Phipps claims indicate the presence of
elaborate mosaics. Even more exciting was the statue we
found in such good condition that it might have been created
yesterday. I heard Phipps scold one of the farmer's men for dig-
ging down too deeply with his spade, and the man muttered
something I could not make out. I don't think he has made

friends of our native diggers, but if we are to reveal the floor undamaged, we must proceed carefully.

In the morning of the following day, Phipps and I were alone in the field, and I was surprised when Clarabel joined us, wearing an old shirt and a pair of my trousers. The sight shocked me, but Phipps seemed pleased to see her, handing her a trowel and instructing her in the skill of digging. He stood close to her, teaching her how best to scrape away at the soil so that nothing delicate is missed. I saw her rapt attention to his words. I have never seen her paying me such heed.

She joined us for dinner that evening. It appeared that the exertions of the day had not tired her.

25

The antique shop stood on the narrow street leading down to Baynard's Quay, about twenty yards from Gerry Heffernan's house, which overlooked the water on the quay itself. It occurred to Neil that Gerry would pass the shop every day on his way to the police station. It had been there for as long as he could remember. He'd even bought something there once – a little silver box for his partner Lucy's birthday, when their romance was new and fresh. Sometimes he wondered how their relationship survived so much separation, but with both of them equally dedicated to archaeology, they plodded on, reuniting from time to time before going to their separate digs at opposite ends of the British Isles.

Today Neil's mind wasn't on buying. He hovered in the doorway for a while before plucking up enough courage to push the door open. The situation was delicate and he knew he'd have to choose his words carefully if he wasn't going to put the shop owner on the defensive.

When he entered the shop, he found himself alone, so he seized the opportunity to take a look around. A tall glass cabinet to his left caught his eye, and he focused on one particular object standing at the front of the middle shelf. It was a small glass vessel about four inches high, blue-tinged and obviously ancient. Neil recognised Roman glass when he saw it, and this was a fine example.

He was still staring at the object when a voice made him swing round.

'Can I help you?' It was a woman who'd asked the question. She was, Neil guessed, in her sixties, and her grey hair fell in a single long plait down her back. She wore a colourful ankle-length skirt and she was regarding him with the suspicion usually reserved for potential shoplifters.

'Er, yeah. A friend of mine bought a statue of Mercury from you the other day. I was just wondering where you got it from.'

The woman's expression hardened. 'I can't give out information like that.'

Neil explained about his dig and the fact that there had been thefts from the site, but her hostility only increased. 'What exactly are you accusing me of?'

The question sounded like a challenge, and he felt he had to back off before she threw him out. 'Nothing. I just wondered if—'

'The statue came from a reliable source.'

'And that Roman glass in the cabinet?'

'I don't have to answer your questions and I resent being accused of theft. Now if you don't leave . . . '

Neil hurried out of the shop. It hadn't gone as well as he'd hoped, and if those objects had come from his dig, he wondered how he was going to prove it.

It was eight o'clock when Wesley reached the outskirts of Tradmouth. The sight of the sign welcoming visitors, set above a rowing boat filled with a display of bright flowers, raised his spirits. They were home at last.

'If you drop me at the station, I'll walk,' said Gerry. 'Mind you, we ought to make a detour to the incident room first to see whether anything new has come in.'

'Duty before pleasure.' Wesley was anxious to get home, but he knew the boss was right.

In the incident room, they found a few detectives on the late shift still at their desks. 'Anything new we should know about?' Gerry boomed as he crossed the threshold.

Ellie, one of the new officers assigned to the team, stood up. Wesley was pleased to see that she was gaining in confidence now that she'd discovered that Gerry wasn't as fearsome as first impressions would suggest.

'Sir, something's come in about Drusilla Kramer, who was interviewed in connection with the Susan Brown inquiry. Her dog was found yesterday wandering by itself in Smeaton's Park, opposite her flat, and none of her neighbours have seen her. The woman who found the dog went to the address on its collar but got no answer. She took the animal to her local police station; they haven't been able to contact Drusilla either.'

'Hopefully the dog ran off and Drusilla'll turn up,' said Gerry, glancing at Wesley. 'Let's get home, Wes. Early start in the morning. Team'll need briefing about our trip to Yorkshire.'

Wesley hoped the DCI was right. But a niggling voice in the back of his mind reminded him that Drusilla had been Susan's friend. Friends confided in each other. And knowledge could be dangerous.

*

Wesley lay awake half the night thinking about the case, and about the small bronze statue Pam had shown him so proudly when he'd arrived home. She'd bought it because she liked it; a bit of decorative fun for the mantelpiece. Neil was convinced it was genuine, which she insisted was nonsense; it had to be a mass-produced fake. Wesley said nothing to contradict her assumption, but if it was a forgery, it was a remarkably good one.

Pam had said that Neil wanted him to call as soon as he got home, but he'd replied that it would have to wait until tomorrow. He was tired after all the driving and he had other things to worry about. He'd even forgotten to give her the present he'd bought for her. This was something else that would have to wait until the morning.

As the night wore on and sleep wouldn't come, the statue kept replacing the case in his thoughts. Before transferring to Tradmouth, he'd worked in the Art and Antiques Unit at the Met, and he'd seen stolen Roman antiquities before. In the end, he climbed out of bed and crept downstairs to examine the statue more closely. He agreed with Neil that it did look genuine. He needed to find out more about its provenance – especially as Neil's site had been robbed just a couple of nights before.

The next morning at breakfast, Pam looked mildly amused when he finally gave her the present he'd bought in Whitby – a pair of small jet earrings he'd seen in a shop window and bought on impulse with Gerry's encouragement. 'What's this in aid of? You're not having an affair, are you?'

It was a reaction he hadn't expected, and a sudden image of Rachel in a Manchester hotel room when they'd been up there a few years ago working on a case together flashed into his head. Nothing had come of the encounter, but he still felt an uncomfortable pang of guilt every time he remembered it. 'Of course not. Just a little present to say sorry for being away so long, that's all.'

When she took the present out of its bag, she looked pleased. 'Thanks. They're lovely,' she said, giving him a swift kiss of thanks before hurrying off to get ready for work.

When Wesley arrived at the incident room, he found Gerry pacing up and down looking agitated.

'There's still no sign of Drusilla Kramer. I've sent someone over to her flat.'

'What about her dog?'

'The animal shelter in Morbay's taking care of him.'

'He's called Sherlock.'

'Good name. Apparently his lead was still attached to his collar. So either he slipped out of her grasp somehow, or she was forced to let him go.'

'So he didn't just escape from the flat? That is worrying.'

'Are you thinking the same as me? That whoever killed Susan abducted her because she knows something? Something she didn't think to share with us.'

Wesley couldn't imagine why she wouldn't have told them everything she knew when she was interviewed. Unless she was protecting someone – or her relationship with Susan hadn't been as friendly and supportive as she'd described.

'I think we should treat this as a potential abduction.' Gerry gave a heavy sigh. 'I've asked Morbay to conduct a search of the park.'

All they could do was wait for news. It would soon be time for the DCI's briefing – or his morning sermon, as he liked to call it – but in the meantime, Wesley took a seat beside Gerry's desk.

'Fancy going over what we've got?' he asked.

The DCI had a sheet of paper in front of him, something about the budget for the investigation. He picked up a pen and began to doodle: a figure in uniform that bore a vague resemblance to their chief superintendent. But when Wesley started to speak, he made notes on the back in his characteristic scruffy handwriting.

'Susan Brown was strangled by person or persons unknown. It's possible that she came down here to get away from Ebenezer Smith, but I don't see it somehow. All that happened a long time ago, and he denies knowing her whereabouts.'

'She mentioned a man who'd been bothering her to Drusilla Kramer, so Smith could have been lying. What did you make of him?'

'There's no evidence that he's ever gone beyond sending flowers and asking women out. Mind you, I could be wrong. Minor harassment has been known to escalate. Anything else come in?'

'The B & B in Ilfracombe where Peter Clare, Susan's former boss, stayed has been checked, and he was there all right. However, the landlady said he was out all day walking.'

'So he could have slipped down here in his car and murdered Susan.'

'I don't have him down as a serious suspect, but anything's possible.'

Wesley took a deep breath. 'Then there's Susan's incident wall. Two women, one missing and one murdered by a man who's since denied he was responsible. Susan was Avril Willis's friend, so her interest in her is understandable, but what was her connection with Simone Pritchard? Drusilla said she was obsessed with missing persons cases. And

Neville Grasmere in Chipping Campden said she was asking questions about a woman who went missing there, and left soon after the woman in question turned up alive and well.'

'So far we've neglected Simone, haven't we? I wonder if her sister's back from New Zealand yet.'

'Her local station's been asked to let us know when she gets back. Are we going to leave it to them to ask the necessary questions, or are you up for another trip out?'

'I don't like getting information second-hand, and Gloucestershire isn't as far as Yorkshire. It's just a drive up the M5, and I'd like to speak to the sister myself. We need to find out what links Avril and Simone.'

'Well, we know that Avril met her husband through a dating site, though that's common to a lot of people nowadays, so it might not be the connection we're looking for.'

Wesley thought for a moment. 'Do you think Drusilla's disappearance is linked to Susan's murder?'

'It could be a coincidence. According to Morbay, there've been reports of a man behaving suspiciously in that park. Lurking around behind bushes when lone women walk through. One said he flashed at her. She reported it, but by the time the patrol got there, he'd gone. The local station intended to keep a better eye on the park, but they never got round to it. And now that a woman's vanished, they'll flood the place with uniforms but it'll be too late. Our flasher will have gone elsewhere to get his kicks. What do you make of those film people at Serpent's Point?' Gerry asked, turning his pen over and over in his fingers.

'Crispin Joss was seen arguing with Susan, but his explanation seems feasible to me. Just because he's an unpleasant bastard doesn't necessarily mean he's a murderer. I'd like to know where he was when Drusilla went missing.'

Gerry nodded earnestly. 'Too right, Wes. I didn't like that man.'

'He won't be pleased if we go back to ask him. Probably accuse us of harassment.'

A sudden grin lit up Gerry's chubby face. 'Let him. We need to know.'

26

Neil had decided to camp out at the site again. He was still furious about the activities of the nighthawks, every archaeologist's nightmare, and irritated that he had no proof that Pam's statue and the Roman glass he'd seen in the antique shop had come from his excavation. Mere suspicion wasn't enough. He needed to be sure and, as it had been Wesley's job at the Met to deal with the theft of antiquities, he was putting his faith in his friend to do something about it. Once upon a time, when they were at university together, it had taken a lot to distract Neil and Wesley from the thrill of archaeological discovery. Nowadays, in Wesley's case, inconvenient crimes tended to get in the way.

The site team had packed up at 6.30, pulling the blue tarpaulins over the open trenches. A section of the building foundations was now clearly visible in the field, and so far Neil had found nothing to contradict his hope that their discovery would rewrite the history books. It was a question now of painstaking excavation. If they rushed, they might miss something vital.

The two girls, Sophie and Livy, had gone home to their families. They'd turned up every day so far to help, bearing their metal detectors as proudly as soldiers carrying their rifles on parade. Neil had let them go over the spoil heaps and they'd turned up several more coins, all bearing the heads of Roman emperors.

Earlier that evening, he'd joined his colleagues at the Seashell. The place served a decent pint, and everyone felt the need to relax after a day's digging. The rest of his team, students and professionals alike, were staying in a youth hostel nearby, and if it wasn't for the nighthawks, Neil would have joined them in relative comfort. But he was reluctant to leave the site unguarded in the hours of darkness – and because he was in charge, he felt it was his responsibility to stay behind.

He left the Seashell just before sunset and set up his tent. He had a lamp, a good book about the Roman invasion of Britain and a bottle of beer he'd brought back from the pub, and as he crawled into his sleeping bag, he went over the day's events in his mind. There had been further interesting finds: more painted plaster and a lot of roof tiles, one embossed with a cat's pawprint. The excitement was mounting, and that afternoon he'd contemplated walking up to Serpent's Point again to ask the owner if he could have another look in the attic, but he'd run out of time. He'd thought about that trunk on and off since he'd found it a few days before, wondering whether there would be any reference to a previous excavation amongst the documents inside.

He settled in his sleeping bag and started to read, but soon the combined effects of the beer and a day's hard physical exercise took effect. He put the book aside, turned off the lamp and drifted effortlessly off to sleep. There was just the thin material of the tent between him and the heavy darkness outside, but, being summer, the night was warm and he was sleeping too deeply to be disturbed by the sounds of the night: the hoot of an owl; the scream of a fox, which sounded like a terrified woman; the rustle of small creatures as they went about their nocturnal business.

The noise that woke him owed nothing to nature: the unmistakable bleep of a metal detector followed by the thud of a mattock on soil. Whoever it was cared nothing for the delicate site. They were after something of value and they didn't care what damage they caused.

Neil struggled out of his sleeping bag, adrenaline coursing through his body. He was wearing shorts and a T-shirt, but even if he'd been naked he wouldn't have cared. Someone was intruding on his precious site, potentially one of the most important ones he'd ever worked on, and they had to be stopped.

As he emerged from the tent on his hands and knees, he began shouting loudly. He wanted to frighten them off and make them think twice about coming back. But as soon as he straightened himself up to challenge the intruders, something hit him with immense force and he collapsed to the ground.

Wesley received the call just as he was finishing breakfast. Livy's dad had been ushering his cows into the adjacent field after the morning milking when he'd peeped over the gate to see what was going on at the dig and spotted Neil sprawled on the ground semi-conscious. He'd helped him back to the farmhouse, where his wife had insisted on calling an ambulance. Neil had been taken to A&E in Tradmouth to be checked over.

Wesley sat for a moment staring at his half-eaten slice of toast, taking in the news. He'd been aware of Neil's problem with nighthawks, but the investigation into the murder of Susan Brown had obviously taken priority. With this latest development, however, he wondered whether there might be some connection between the two cases.

He shared the news with Gerry as soon as he arrived at the incident room.

'You say these so-called nighthawks are an occupational hazard?' said Gerry.

'It has been known. But there hasn't been much publicity about this dig. Neil's been trying to keep everything low-key until he's absolutely certain what they're dealing with. The trouble is, they used violence.'

'That's worrying.' Gerry checked his watch. 'Why don't you go to the hospital to have a word with him? If someone's attacked near a murder scene, we can hardly ignore it.'

When Wesley arrived at Tradmouth Hospital, he found Neil emerging with a large white dressing on his head. He still looked dazed. But more than anything, he looked angry. 'Thanks for coming, Wes,' he said. 'I need to get back to the dig to assess the damage.'

'The others can deal with that. You're going nowhere.' Wesley tried to sound firm. He felt Neil grip his arm to steady himself and glanced back at the A&E waiting room. 'Are you sure you should be leaving?'

'The doc told me I could go if I took it easy. He told me to go to bed. Fat chance.'

Wesley didn't hesitate. 'I'm taking you home. Pam'll be there. It's her day off today. You can stay in our spare room until you're feeling better. No arguments. You're in no state to go back to the dig. And as for camping out ... '

Neil's acquiescence to the suggestion told Wesley how bad he must be feeling. He took his friend home, and Pam, firmer than her husband, reiterated what he'd said. Neil was staying in the spare room and that was that.

But Neil's mind was still on work and he persuaded Wesley to give him a lift to the dig, just to see what was going on. He promised not to stay there long, and one of the others could bring him back afterwards. In view of his determination, Wesley didn't argue.

As they drove out to Bereton, Wesley asked Neil to describe what had happened, but his account was too vague to be of any help. But in view of the violence used, Wesley promised that they'd be keeping a closer eye on the dig from now on.

Because of Drusilla Kramer's friendship with Susan Brown, Gerry was treating her disappearance as a priority.

Officers from Morbay were searching the park and dragging the small lake at its centre. CCTV footage of the area was being gathered too. And the message Gerry found waiting on his desk when he returned from a meeting with the chief superintendent filled him with new hope. Calvin Brunning's camper van had been caught on traffic cameras in Morbay at around the time Drusilla had disappeared.

He ordered Brunning to be brought to Tradmouth again for questioning. Last time they'd interviewed him, they'd had no proof of his involvement in Susan's murder so they'd had to release him, but this time he was hoping for better luck.

He decided to use Tradmouth Police Station's most intimidating interview room, the one with furniture fixed to the floor and no windows. Both he and Wesley hated the gloomy, oppressive room. Hopefully their suspect would hate it even more. The uniforms who'd brought Brunning in had disturbed the filming at Serpent's Point, and Crispin Joss had been furious. Gerry wondered whether the man would have a job to go back to if and when they released him.

Wesley met him in the corridor outside, and after a brief discussion about tactics, they opened the interview room door. Brunning was sitting beside his solicitor, and Wesley thought he looked more worried this time.

'Where's Drusilla Kramer?' Gerry began.

'Who?'

'She's a friend of the woman you found on the path, and she's missing.'

'She's probably the one who killed her and now she's gone on the run.' Brunning looked pleased with himself and sat back, arms folded. 'There. I've solved your murder for you. You should be thanking me.'

'Don't push it, Brunning,' Gerry said in a low growl. 'What were your movements yesterday evening?'

'Went for a drink in Morbay. Stayed till I was chucked out. Lots of witnesses.'

'Did you go anywhere near Smeaton's Park?'

Brunning looked wary. 'No. Just the pub on the seafront. The Morbay Arms.'

Gerry knew the pub and its reputation. Its regulars weren't generally the sort of law-abiding citizens who co-operated with the police.

'Why did you go to Morbay?'

'I hoped to see a mate, but he wasn't there.'

'Does this mate have a name?'

'Like I said, he wasn't there. Can I go now? You've nothing on me. This is wrongful arrest.'

'This is helping the police with their enquiries,' said Gerry.

Wesley tried a gamble, something that he hoped would catch the suspect off guard. 'Archaeologists are digging in the field near your shoot and one of them was attacked last night. Do you know anything about it?' He thought Brunning looked alarmed, although it could have been his imagination. Or even wishful thinking.

'No. Why should I?'

'What about the thefts from the site? Someone's been going over it with metal detectors once the archaeologists have left, and we think they've been stealing valuable artefacts.'

'Don't look at me. I haven't got a metal detector.'

Wesley had to acknowledge that no metal detector had been found in Brunning's camper van. But the man was definitely looking guilty about something.

When the interview was over, Gerry decided reluctantly that they had no real evidence to hold him. He arranged for the pub's CCTV to be examined, but they weren't optimistic about catching him out in a lie.

'What do you reckon, Wes? Is he our man?'

'Apart from the fact that he came across her body and failed to report it, we have no connection between him and Susan. And there's even less evidence to link him to Drusilla Kramer.' He thought for a moment. 'There's still no sign of her, I take it.'

Gerry shook his head. 'I've told Morbay to let us know as soon as there's anything.'

His phone rang and Wesley watched as he answered, hoping this was the news they'd been waiting for: that Drusilla Kramer had been found safe and well.

But the call was about something else entirely, and when Gerry had finished talking, he looked at Wesley with a hopeful look on his face.

'That was Rob Carter. He says Grey Grover's absent lodger is back at Serpent's Point. Name of Marcus Pinter.'

'But according to Grover, he wasn't there when Susan was killed.'

'He was a bit vague about that, though – and Pinter does live there, so he might know something. The victim might have confided in him, for all we know. If we don't ask, we won't find out.'

'In that case, let's get over there and have a word.'

The Marina Boatyard stood across the river from Tradmouth in Queenswear. It was approaching the height of the season, so it was a busy time. Boats that had lain idle all winter were being pressed into service when their owners visited their holiday homes, and there were vital repairs to be carried out.

One boat in particular was giving Les Perkins a headache. An incomer from London had purchased a thirty-foot yacht on a whim, in spite of the fact that his only sailing experience had been a day's course he'd attended a couple of years ago. He'd bought the boat via the internet and it was a floating wreck that would take a few weeks to put right. However, it seemed that money was no object, so Les didn't ask too many questions. He'd do what had to be done and present the bill later.

Then there was the other project: the yacht bought by a doctor, a keen sailor who'd just transferred from Tradmouth Hospital to a post in Exeter. Les had been working on this particular vessel for a few days, and now that the hull was in seaworthy condition, the next job was to strip out and renovate the interior of the cabin. He knew he had his work cut out, because the cabin was in a bit of a state and there was an unpleasant smell; so unpleasant that he'd left the doors wide open.

The lad who'd just started working with him that week stood at the cabin entrance watching him, as though some invisible force was stopping him from crossing the threshold.

'Come on,' said Les, irritated by the lad's reluctance. 'We haven't got all day. What's the matter?'

The boy shuffled in, his round face sulky, as though Les was asking him to take on some Herculean task. Without another word, Les took a crowbar and began to tear out the seating, the lad joining in half-heartedly.

But when the second bench seat had been removed, the lad tapped Les on the back. 'What's that?' He pointed at the floor.

Les could see a dark patch on the wooden planks. A stain the colour of faded rust from a liquid that must have seeped beneath the seating, trapped there long after whatever it was had been cleared up. He stared at it in silence for a while. 'Know what it looks like to me?'

'What?'

'Blood,' said Les, and the lad took a step back.

From the journal of Dr Aldus Claye

June 1921

It is almost a week since Phipps sent his telegram to Professor Fredericks, and there has still been no reply. Phipps says the professor intended to go abroad as soon as term ended, to Provence to see the new excavations at Glanum. If only he'd been aware that an exciting discovery might lie closer to home.

The box containing the bones has been placed in the attic for safe keeping, along with some of our finds. I had expected Clarabel to be nervous at having human remains in the house, but instead she seems fascinated, hanging upon Phipps's every word when we discuss our finds over dinner.

Phipps thinks it might be a clandestine burial, perhaps a murder victim interred in the grounds of the villa, although without evidence we cannot be sure. My wife mentioned the curse, wondering whether this might be connected in some way with our grim discovery. I am pleased to say that the professor returned the thing to me before he left, and it now resides in the sideboard drawer. I have, of course, shown it to Phipps, who says it is typical of its kind.

The translation reads: May he who carried off my wife, Beria Vilbia, be cursed in life and mind and his words, thoughts and memory, and may Charon and Hecate drag him down to the depths of Hades. May he not live to enjoy the fruits of his wickedness.

Phipps asked to see it again and I watched as he showed it to Clarabel, translating the Latin for her, their heads close together like a pair of children fascinated by a new toy. I felt a sudden aching in my heart. I think it was jealousy, something I'd never experienced before. I'd paid Clarabel little attention during our marriage, but now I wanted her.

That night I made love to her for the first time, and she lay beneath me, limbs tense and eyes closed. I knew I was hurting her but I did not care. I was staking my claim. She was mine. Afterwards, I heard her sobbing.

I lay awake composing my own curse: May he who would carry off my wife, Clarabel, be cursed in life and mind and his words, thoughts and memory, and may Charon and Hecate drag him down to the depths of Hades. May he not live to enjoy the fruits of his wickedness.

And yet I need Fidelio Phipps. He is the only one who is able to provide the material for the book I intend to write. I am going to change the history of Devonshire. And Phipps is going to help me.

27

News had come in that Susan Brown's ex-husband had been traced in Dubai, but he had the perfect alibi as he hadn't left that country for the past six months and hadn't seen Susan for several years. Their impulsive marriage was a distant memory, he said, although of course he was sorry to hear about her death. At least this was one potential suspect they could safely eliminate from their enquiries.

Also nobody answering Ebenezer Smith's description had stayed at any local accommodation recently. However, Gerry said he wasn't out of the frame altogether; he could have been sleeping rough, although Wesley thought this unlikely.

Wesley and Gerry were about to set off for Serpent's Point when Gerry's phone rang. He looked at the caller ID. Les from the boatyard was an old friend, but he thought it strange he should call just at that moment. The DCI's beloved yacht *Rosie May*, bought after Kathy's death to provide a distraction from his grief, had already been in for repairs and was now totally seaworthy.

He was tempted not to answer, but he told himself Les might be calling to report a problem with the repairs – or possibly that one of his workers had failed to notice something important, in which case it was a question of safety that shouldn't be ignored. He told himself it needn't take long and answered the call.

'Gerry,' said Les with a note of anxiety in his voice. 'I didn't know who else to call, but you're in the police so I thought . . . '

'What is it, Les? Something the matter?'

'It's probably nothing.'

Whenever anybody said that, Gerry always paid attention. 'Go on, you might as well tell me.'

There was a moment of hesitation before Les spoke. 'Well, me and the lad were asked to renovate this yacht. Nice thirty-footer that's been neglected for a while. A doctor bought it to do up as a project, but then he got a new job so didn't have the time any more and asked us to take care of it. He's just transferred from Tradmouth to a hospital in Exeter. Nice bloke. Been sailing since he was a kid.'

Gerry gave Wesley an apologetic look. It was always hard to get a word in with Les once he started on one of his long narratives. 'So what's worrying you, Les?' he asked before the man could launch into the entire life story of the boat's new owner.

'Well, me and the lad were ripping out the seating in the cabin when we spotted this stain on the floor. The seating's fixed and it looks as if something's seeped underneath.'

Gerry understood. The storage lockers, which doubled as bench seating around the sides of the cabin, weren't something you could move to mop underneath. 'Tell me about the stain.' He already had his suspicions. Les would hardly be contacting him if somebody had spilled oil or sticky orange juice.

'I could be wrong, Gerry, but it looks like blood. Smells like it and all. I tried to wipe it and there was this metallic smell – like meat that's gone off a bit.'

'Someone might have had an accident,' Gerry suggested.

'That's what the lad said, but there must have been a lot of it to get underneath the seating like that.'

'Have you asked the owner about it?'

'He only bought the yacht three months ago and he's as puzzled as I am. He popped down to have a look and said it was blood all right but it's been there a good while. He's a doctor, so he should know, I suppose. He seemed a bit put out, to tell you the truth. I mean, it's not very nice, is it, to—'

'What do you want me to do about it, Les?' Gerry glanced at Wesley, who was shifting from foot to foot, eager to get to Serpent's Point before Grey Grover's newly returned lodger decided to make himself scarce again.

'If you could come and take a look, Gerry. I mean, I had to report it, didn't I?'

'Of course you did. Can you do me a favour and find out who owned the yacht before the doctor?' The boat's previous owners would be registered, but Tradmouth boat owners tended to all know each other, so he might be able to find out something via the maritime grapevine. 'Sorry, Les, I've got to go. Work and woe.'

'You're investigating that murder, aren't you?'

'That's right. Let me know what you find out, won't you. Thanks, Les.' He ended the call and turned to Wesley. 'He's a nice bloke, but he'll talk the hind legs off a horse unless you're firm.'

'I know the sort,' said Wesley as they started to walk towards Serpent's Point.

This time it was his phone that rang. When he saw it was Neil, he wondered whether he should ignore it and call him back later when he had more time. But he yielded to temptation and answered.

Before he could speak, he heard Neil's voice. 'You should get over here, Wes. We've found human remains on the site. They'd been partly uncovered by the nighthawks and they're certainly not Roman. I've called the coroner and I think you should come and take a look.'

Neil's discovery was something they couldn't ignore. If the bones weren't contemporary with the site, Marcus Pinter would have to wait until they found out what they were dealing with.

They were surprised to see Cornell Stamoran amongst the small group gathered on the far side of the field. Neil knew Colin Bowman well and sometimes summoned him to look at bones he'd found. Now it seemed he had the pathologist's temporary replacement at his beck and call too.

Stamoran spotted the new arrivals and beckoned them over. 'Neil thought it might be suspicious, so he gave me a call,' he said.

'And is it?' Gerry asked.

'Oh yes. It's suspicious all right. From the shape of the wound, I'd say something like a pickaxe or a mattock was used. Someone bashed his head in.' He smiled. 'That's not a medical term, by the way.'

'Any idea how old the bones are?' said Wesley, looking at Neil, who was sitting on a folding canvas chair, his only concession to his recent ordeal.

'There are buttons and a silver pocket watch,' Neil said, 'but no zips, so at a guess, I'd say he dates from the late nineteenth or the first part of the twentieth century. After all, who uses a pocket watch these days?'

'So nothing for us to worry about?' said Gerry hopefully.

It was the doctor who answered. 'I've seen nothing to contradict what Neil said. If someone killed this man and buried him in this field over seventy years ago, it's not your problem, Gerry. But we have to be sure.' He looked at Neil enquiringly.

'I've seen nothing to suggest it's a recent burial. No modern dental work, and what remains of the clothing indicates that it's probably around a hundred years old.'

'That's a relief,' said Gerry, making a move to leave.

But Wesley was in no hurry. 'What can you tell us about the skeleton?'

'Adult male,' said the doctor. 'Around five feet eight. All his own teeth. And he met a violent end.'

Neil frowned. 'Archaeologists use mattocks. And I'm as sure as I can be that someone excavated this field before, although it's not in any archaeological record.'

'Amateurs? Treasure hunters?' said Wesley.

'Or someone who committed murder and wanted to cover it up. Any news on our nighthawks?'

Wesley glanced at Gerry, who was finding it hard to conceal his impatience. 'Sorry, we've had other things to deal with.'

'I've been thinking about that statue and the glass. They looked remarkably clean, so I don't think they could have been dug up over the last few days.'

Intrigued though Wesley was, he didn't have time to speculate.

'I think I scared the nighthawks off before they could uncover the bones properly – they probably got a signal from the pocket watch, started to dig, then I disturbed them.' Neil thought for a moment. 'Or maybe it wasn't treasure they were after. Maybe they were looking for something else. And they found it.'

28

News came through from Morbay that Calvin Brunning had been in the Morbay Arms just as he'd said, his where-abouts proved by the pub's CCTV. The timings didn't fit with Drusilla's possible abduction, and Gerry found it difficult to hide his disappointment.

When he and Wesley finally arrived at Serpent's Point, they saw a group of actors standing around looking bored. It had started to drizzle, and three thin girls were wearing waterproof coats over their muslin dresses, the hoods pulled up to protect their hairstyles. A bored-looking Regency buck sipped coffee from a cardboard cup, while the crew bustled to and fro with equipment, ignoring the actors.

'Wonder how much longer they're going to be filming,' said Gerry.

'The longer the better as far as Grey Grover's concerned, I expect. The more days they use the place, the more he'll be paid.'

Gerry laughed. 'Easy money. Pity my place is too small for this sort of thing. Mind you, I wouldn't fancy the likes of Crispin Joss calling the shots in my house. Now where's this Marcus?'

They entered by the open front door, but there was no sign of Joss, much to Wesley's relief.

'Let's find Grover,' said Gerry. 'He can point us in the right direction.'

As they passed the foot of the sweeping staircase, they heard a voice shouting, 'You're supposed to be making love to the woman, Freddie, not helping her with the washing. Get her clothes off with some passion, will you.' Joss didn't sound pleased. 'I want lust.'

'Don't we all,' Gerry muttered with a chuckle.

Wesley had to smile, enjoying one of those rare light moments when the shadow of murder lifted for a second.

They found Grover in the library again, sitting on the same sofa, as though he hadn't moved from the spot since their last visit. This time there was no sign of Krystal Saverigg.

'Mr Grover,' Gerry began. 'We've been told that Marcus Pinter is back. We'd like a word with him.'

Grover looked up, a bored expression on his face. 'He's upstairs in the servants' quarters, but I wouldn't advise you to go anywhere near the filming. Joss is in a foul mood today. Fouler than usual, if that's possible.'

They followed Grover's directions, and when they reached the landing, they heard Joss berating some hapless camera person for not getting in close enough to the action on the bed. Not for the first time, Wesley wondered exactly what kind of film he was making.

On the top floor of the house, Gerry knocked on the nearest door and they heard a grunted 'What is it?' When they opened the door, they found themselves in a plain room with apple-green walls that looked as though they hadn't been repainted since the departure of the last housemaid. It was furnished with a modern chipboard wardrobe and matching chest of drawers, and the double divan bed was occupied by a recumbent figure. A man in his thirties with a shaved head and earrings. His tight black T-shirt showed off a muscular torso and his arms were blue with examples of the tattooist's art.

'Who the hell are you?' he demanded.

'Police,' said Wesley, displaying his ID. 'DI Peterson and DCI Heffernan, Tradmouth CID.'

'Didn't expect the pigs. What do you want?'

'Just rooting around trying to find a murderer, Mr Pinter,' said Gerry. 'I believe you were away when Susan Brown was killed.'

The man hauled himself into a sitting position. 'Grey told me about it when I got back.'

'When was that?'

He hesitated for a moment. 'Yesterday. Around seven.'

'You hadn't already heard the news? It's been on the TV and radio.'

'I'm an artist. I avoid distractions.'

'Can you tell us where you've been for the past few days?'

'London. Staying with a mate.'

'When did you go?'

'A week last Wednesday. Why?'

'So you were in London the morning Susan Brown's body was found?'

'Must have been, mustn't I.' There was something evasive about his answer – and a note of defiance.

'How well did you know Susan?'

'Spoke to her a couple of times, that's all.'

Wesley looked around the room. The walls were bare. 'You haven't cheered this place up with any of your paintings.'

'My paintings aren't cheerful. They're real. Visceral. They tell the truth about life and death.'

'That's exactly what we're trying to find out – the truth. A woman is dead and another's missing, so we'd appreciate your co-operation.'

Pinter shot Wesley a look of pure hostility. 'And if I don't co-operate, is it down to the cells for a beating?'

'All we're trying to do is find out who killed Susan Brown.'

'Well, it wasn't me.'

'Nobody's accusing you of anything,' said Wesley, trying to smooth the waters. 'We're just trying to build a picture of the victim, so we're talking to people who knew her.' His words sounded so reasonable that even the most ardent enemy of the police surely couldn't take offence.

'Like I said, I hardly knew her.' Pinter paused. 'I saw her in the Seashell once or twice. She worked behind the bar.'

'When you saw her in the pub, was she talking to any-body in particular?'

'I saw her talking to Darren once – don't know his second name, but he's one of the regulars. And Harry, the land-lord. But she worked there, so . . . '

'We've already spoken to them. Do you work here in the house or do you have a studio somewhere else?'

Pinter looked surprised at the sudden change of subject. 'My studio's next door.'

'I'd be interested to see it.'

'Well, well. A pig who's interested in art. That's got to be a first.'

Wesley was about to explain that he used to serve in the Art and Antiques Unit at the Met, but thought better of it. Something about this man intrigued him. He had a strong impression that his hostility to the police was an act; something he imagined was expected of an anti-establishment artist. He'd check him out when they got back to the incident room, but it wouldn't surprise him if he had no criminal record whatsoever. People wore masks to fit in with their chosen tribe.

Pinter sprang off the bed, and Wesley and Gerry followed him into the room next door. Some past owner of the house had converted it into a studio, with the benefit of a skylight, and Wesley looked around, curious to know what kind of art this man produced. He wasn't prepared for what he saw.

The paintings hung and propped up around the wall weren't the usual tourist fare – seascapes and depictions of the Devon landscape; nor were they experimental abstracts like Grey Grover's efforts. These were graphic images of violence, dark and impressionistic, with the subjects' faces either turned from the artist or an unrecognisable blur. On an easel to the side of the room sat a large canvas covered with a sheet. Before Pinter could object, Wesley walked over to it and flicked the sheet aside to reveal the image of a woman lying in a litter-strewn alley. She was sprawled on the filthy cobbles, her legs splayed and her clothing askew. The only hint of brightness in the picture was the red of the blood streaming from her throat. Like the other pictures, it wasn't possible to see the model's face, but Wesley could almost feel her suffering.

'Like it?' The question sounded nervous.

Wesley was lost for words, the only thought flooding through his head being a deep regret that they hadn't thought to obtain a search warrant for the house. But hindsight was a wonderful thing.

Gerry was standing behind him, unusually silent. As far

as art was concerned, the DCI was one of those people who knew what they liked, and Wesley couldn't imagine Marcus Pinter's work would be to his taste.

'Murder's a strange subject for a painting,' Wesley said once he'd recovered from the initial shock.

'Walter Sickert did it. Like me, he was fascinated by the reality of life and death.'

'I'm familiar with Sickert's work, but I've also seen the aftermath of murder first-hand, and it's not pretty – certainly not something I'd want on my wall at home.'

'More a Constable and Monet man, are you?' the artist sneered.

Gerry had edged nearer the painting to examine it. 'Who was your model?' he said. 'You can't see her face.'

For the first time, Marcus Pinter looked unsure of himself, and Wesley repeated Gerry's question.

'Just someone I knew,' the artist said after a lengthy silence.

'Name?' Gerry barked, looking him in the eye.

There was a long silence. Wesley could almost see Pinter squirming. In the end, he bowed his head and answered the question. 'OK, it was Sue. I asked her and she volunteered.'

Wesley caught Gerry's eye. 'Sue Brown? She actually volunteered to pose as a murder victim?'

'Yeah. Spooky, isn't it,' Pinter said with a nervous laugh. 'But it didn't have anything to do with what happened to her, I swear.'

'So you were lying when you said you hardly spoke to her.' There was a challenge in Gerry's statement.

'It wasn't a lie. I don't talk to the model while I'm painting. Once I put my music on and start work, I can't deal with distractions.'

'What kind of music?'

Wesley wondered whether Gerry's question was relevant, but he listened carefully to the answer.

'Death metal. Loud on my headphones. It shuts out the world. The model's just a body to me – might as well be a dummy for all I care.' Pinter paused. 'I tried to use one of those shop dummies once, but it didn't work. I need to see the anatomy beneath the flesh.'

'Did Susan tell you anything about herself?' Wesley asked. 'Anything that surprised you?'

Pinter thought for a few moments. 'When I asked her to pose, she said she'd had a friend who was murdered, so the subject fascinated her.'

'Was the friend's name Avril?'

He shrugged. 'I wasn't taking much notice. It didn't seem important.'

'You weren't curious?'

'Not really.'

'We need to know where you were at the time of her murder.'

'An alibi,' Pinter said with relish. 'Am I a suspect, then?' He signalled that he needed something to write on, so Wesley passed him his notebook. Once Pinter had scribbled down the details, Wesley gave a curt nod of acknowledgement and told him that someone would be in touch.

He'd seen enough. The image on the easel had made him feel queasy. And he was surprised that Marcus Pinter wasn't more shocked that the woman who'd pretended to be a murder victim for him had actually met that very fate. He found the man's insensitivity distasteful. And possibly suspicious.

He was relieved that the job of checking out the artist's

alibi would fall to one of the DCs in the incident room. There was something repellent about Marcus Pinter, and he wondered whether Gerry felt the same. On the way downstairs, he asked him.

'I thought he was a jumped-up pretentious little prick, if you really want to know, Wes. But we're not allowed to be prejudiced, are we.'

'Think he's in the frame?'

'I'll tell you that once we've checked out his alibi, but I reckon he could be the sort of weirdo who'd kill just for the experience – to see what it's like.'

Wesley thought Gerry might have a point. If the alibi didn't stand up, they had themselves a new suspect.

He glanced back and saw a girl in a yellow Regency costume hurrying across the landing towards the attic staircase. He wondered whether Pinter had found a new model – a replacement for Susan, perhaps.

They were walking back to the incident room when Gerry's phone rang. Wesley stopped and listened, frustrated that he could only hear half the conversation.

'That was Rob Carter,' Gerry said once he'd ended the call. 'Calvin Brunning's vanished. He's done a runner, Wes. And we have to ask ourselves why.'

29

There was no sign of Calvin Brunning or his camper van, and the two DCs Gerry had sent to the shoot reported back that nobody had seen him that morning. They'd added that Crispin Joss wasn't pleased and that he'd shouted words to the effect that if Brunning didn't turn up within the next half-hour, he wouldn't have a job to come back to. The director didn't tolerate people who wasted his time.

All patrols were now on the lookout for the van. The young metal-detectorists in the field had seen Brunning an hour or two after the estimated time of Susan Brown's death. Had he killed her on her lonely early-morning walk, left the scene in panic then returned later to cover his tracks? They'd had to let him go due to lack of evidence, but when they picked him up again, Gerry was determined not to repeat the mistake. But they needed to find him first.

With the news about Brunning, Gerry had relegated Marcus Pinter to a lower place in the pecking order of likely suspects. But Wesley wasn't so certain.

The two detectives sat at their respective desks in the incident room, going over what they'd got, both feeling increasingly puzzled and frustrated. Ebenezer Smith's alibi had been checked and he'd certainly been at the Birmingham hotel as he'd claimed on the night before the murder. Wesley had asked for any sightings of his car on local traffic cameras. If he'd driven through the night, he could have made it to Devon in time to kill the object of his affection, but nothing had come in yet.

There were so many leads, particularly concerning the victim's interest in missing persons cases, that it was hard to know where to begin, especially when none of those leads seemed particularly strong. And frustratingly, Simone Pritchard's sister, Michelle Williams, was still away. At least the discovery of the bones at Neil's dig was one puzzle they wouldn't be obliged to solve if they turned out to be more than seventy years old.

Gerry reckoned they needed more manpower – or womanpower, as Rachel called it. Wesley glanced over in the direction of her desk and saw her fidgeting, trying to get comfortable.

She saw him looking, stood up slowly and walked over. 'I've heard about Brunning.'

'Gerry's convinced that letting him go was a big mistake.'

'Rules are rules. We had no solid evidence against him so we couldn't hold him any longer,' she said. 'And nothing in his criminal record suggested he was going to start strangling random women. Mind you, he has legged it, so—'

'Excuse me.'

Wesley looked up and saw that the hesitant voice belonged to a beautiful young woman in Regency costume. Her shiny auburn hair was arranged in a topknot, with flattering tendrils framing her heart-shaped face. She had large eyes and the face of a Renaissance Madonna, and she looked entirely out of place in the utilitarian surroundings of the church hall. Wesley was sure it was the girl he'd seen hurrying across the landing towards Marcus Pinter's studio.

Rachel approached her to see what she wanted while Wesley watched.

'I need to talk to someone,' the girl said, giving a fine performance as a maiden in distress. She threw Wesley a pleading look, ignoring Rachel, as though she imagined she'd get more sympathy from a man than a pregnant woman.

But Wesley decided that this was one for Rachel. He knew she'd been feeling restless, and whatever the girl wanted to say might provide something to occupy her mind.

'Detective Sergeant Tracey's the best person to deal with your problem,' he said, before disappearing in the direction of Gerry's desk.

The girl gazed after her preferred officer for a few seconds, then yielded to the inevitable. It was Rachel or nobody.

'How can I help you?' said Rachel sweetly.

'My name's Georgina Unwin. I'm in the film that's being shot at Serpent's Point.'

Rachel was about to say that she didn't think she usually dressed like that, but she stopped herself, suspecting that that sort of flippancy might not go down well. 'Some of our officers have been up there looking for witnesses to the suspicious death on the coast path. I suppose you've given a statement?'

Georgina nodded. 'I told the constable I didn't know anything, and that was the truth.'

'I'm sure it was,' said Rachel with a reassuring smile. The girl looked nervous and she invited her to take the seat by her desk.

'I'm playing Lillith. It's my first starring role,' Georgina said with a modest smile.

Rachel had never met a film star before and she was finding the experience slightly disappointing. 'Congratulations,' she said, unable to think of anything more fitting. 'So what's worrying you?'

Georgina studied her beautifully manicured hands. Rachel was an attractive woman, but this girl made her feel plain and clumsy. Her own hands were rough; she was a farmer's wife as well as a police officer, so she had no time to pamper herself. And once the baby arrived, her workload would become even heavier.

'The constable asked me if I'd seen the victim that morning, and I hadn't, but ...' Georgina fell silent, as though she was having second thoughts.

'But what?' Rachel prompted.

'The day before the murder, I heard him arguing with someone, saying they should keep their nose out of his affairs or they'd regret it. He's always shouting at someone so I didn't take much notice. Nobody likes him.'

'Who are you talking about?'

'The director, Crispin Joss. He's a complete bastard.' Georgina's face flushed, and Rachel wondered whether she had a personal reason for making that particular allegation. She'd heard about the casting couch.

'Who was he arguing with?'

Georgina shook her head. 'It was when I was walking through the stable yard. Some of the trucks had parked there and ...' She hesitated. 'I think it was the woman who was murdered.'

'Someone's already told us about this. Mr Joss said she'd made complaints about parking and litter.'

'It didn't sound like that to me. It sounded personal. I heard him say "Keep your nose out or I'll kill you." Where did he tell you he was the morning the body was found? Because shooting didn't start until ten, and he was there when we all turned up.'

'In the statement he gave, Mr Joss said he was at his hotel at the time Susan Brown was killed.'

Georgina looked smug, as though she was about to solve their case for them. 'The hotel's only half a mile from the shoot, so he could easily have walked it. And nobody else is staying there. We've had to make do with B & Bs and caravans while he's living it up in luxury. Talk about class distinction.'

This arrangement had clearly caused bitterness amongst those involved in making *The Awakening of Lillith Montmorency*. And Rachel wondered whether it was that simmering resentment that lay behind Georgina's veiled accusation.

'Why didn't you tell us about this before?' she asked with a sympathetic smile.

'I didn't think it was important.'

'And you didn't want to get on the wrong side of the director?'

'Too late for that. The creep invited me to his hotel room last night and I turned him down, so I'm being made to suffer for it. He's been absolutely beastly to me today. We've been filming my final seduction scene, and he made me go over it five times. It's quite ... intimate and I think he was getting off on it.' Her voice was peevish. The extra effort had clearly rankled. 'Then he said he was rewriting the script so a lot of my scenes were being cut.'

'Tough,' said Rachel, who hadn't heard the word *beastly*

used by a witness before. It sounded rather quaint, a relic from a bygone age.

There was a long pause. 'He threatened to strangle me, you know. He needs to get what's coming to him.'

This caught Rachel's attention. 'Tell me exactly what he said.'

'This morning he said "That woman's already been strangled and I'll do the same to you if you keep moaning." He meant it. Freddie will back me up. He heard.' Georgina began to sob, taking a tissue from the reticule she was carrying to dab her eyes. But somehow her make-up remained pristine.

Rachel passed her another tissue from the box on her desk. 'Who's Freddie?'

'My co-star. We were doing the scene together.'

'Thanks for coming in, Georgina. We'll have another word with Crispin Joss, I promise.'

Georgina stood up, flinging her head back as though she was about to make a dramatic exit. 'He needs more than a word. He needs locking up.'

Once she'd flounced out, Wesley walked over to Rachel's desk. He'd been watching the conversation from a distance and he wanted to know what had been said.

Rachel looked up at him and smiled. 'She's only gone and accused Crispin Joss of murdering Susan Brown. She said she overheard a row between them.'

'We already know about the row.'

'Yes. But she told us that Joss actually threatened to kill Susan.'

'Why didn't she say this when her statement was taken?'

Rachel gave him a knowing smile. 'She claims she didn't think it was important, but I suspect she didn't want to get on the wrong side of the director and damage her career. Her miraculous change of heart happened after she had a big bust-up with Joss. She says he threatened to strangle her like Susan was strangled.'

'Believe her?'

'I get the impression she's bent on revenge. And when she started crying, her mascara stayed remarkably intact.'

Wesley knew Rachel well enough to recognise a healthy dose of scepticism behind her last statement.

'In that case, we need to get Joss's side of the story.'

Georgina felt pleased with herself. With any luck, she'd just succeeded in making life awkward for the director – although she didn't want to disrupt the filming too much, because this was her big chance. Her intention was to teach him a lesson. She'd put her heart and soul into her role, and Crispin Joss hadn't appreciated her efforts.

She'd kept quiet about Freddie's interesting snippet of information because she hadn't wanted to distract DS Tracey's attention away from Joss. Besides, she'd told Freddie it probably wasn't important. It was best to forget it and get on with the filming.

The last thing she wanted was the police to start paying too much attention to the cast – not when she had plans of her own. How did the old saying go? Knowledge is power.

Marcus Pinter wanted to get away from his studio after all that police questioning. The black detective seemed au fait with the workings of the art world, which made him feel exposed. Raw and naked – like the image of Susan Brown on his canvas.

The Seashell called like a beacon of light in stormy

darkness. The film people had only just departed, leaving the paraphernalia of their trade lying around everywhere – cameras, sound booms, lighting and trolleys – and when Marcus left Serpent's Point at nine o'clock, he almost tripped over a coiled length of cable left lying in the hall.

Grey Grover must have been desperate for money to let them invade his property like that, and Marcus hoped it wouldn't mean he'd be expected to start paying rent. For the past three months, he'd enjoyed free accommodation because Grey liked to think he was helping out a fellow struggling artist. If he discovered the truth, his generosity was bound to dry up.

It was still light and the Seashell was busy. Marcus recognised the film crew and a few of the actors drinking at the picnic tables outside in the beer garden. They seemed to be talking shop, engrossed in their own narrow world, so they took no notice of him as he passed – which was hardly surprising, as he'd done his best to avoid them since they took over the house, especially the individual who was trying to cause trouble for him.

He'd abandoned the half-finished painting of Susan for the moment. After the police interest, it seemed the wisest thing to do. But one day he might finish it and display it in all its visceral glory. It was his masterpiece. One day the entire art world would talk about it.

The landlord, Harry, was busy serving customers, and Darren Bailey was sitting in the corner near the fireplace as usual. Marcus sidled up to him. 'All right?'

'Yeah. You?'

'I've had the police round. About Sue.'

'Me too. Tell them anything?'

Marcus shook his head.

'She told me she posed for you once, but I never said nothing to the cops.'

'Thanks.'

Marcus offered to buy Darren a drink and Darren accepted gratefully. Marcus was usually broke, but after his trip to London, his luck had changed considerably.

When he left the pub at 10.30, the lane between the Seashell and Serpent's Point was in darkness. The high hedges rearing up either side like solid walls seemed to close in on him, and he had a sudden feeling of foreboding. It felt as though some unspeakable faceless creature might be lying in wait for him, hidden and hungry. He quickened his pace, and as he rounded the next bend, he saw a movement in the shadows.

When a figure stepped out, blocking his way, his heart beat faster. Were the many sins he'd committed over his lifetime about to catch up with him?

When he realised who it was, he felt a wave of relief.

'I think we have a problem,' he said in a whisper.

'Problems are there to be solved,' came the reply.

30

From the cobbled quayside, Gerry could see lights in the boatyard across the river. It was nine o'clock and Les Perkins was still hard at work.

When he reached his front door, he saw that Joyce had lowered the front-room blind early. All the visitors strolling past and the drinkers spilling from the nearby Tradmouth Arms on the corner to sit on the benches overlooking the water made her feel as though her every move was being watched by curious eyes. She claimed this was the worst thing about living in a tourist hot spot, but Gerry had become used to it over the years and hardly gave it a second thought.

It was high tide and the gulls were still crying, attracted by the food the visitors were eating; some tourists took little heed of the notices attached to the lamp posts telling them not to feed the birds. Gerry could smell his own chips, picked up on the way home, and his stomach rumbled. They were wrapped in paper, warm in his hand, and he hesitated before opening the front door. If he was half an hour late, Joyce wouldn't mind, he told himself. And the sustenance he was carrying could be eaten any time – even on the ferry as it crossed the river.

One glance to his left told him the car ferry was just docking, so he trotted to the slipway. The ferryman knew him, so he didn't even have to show his warrant card to get a free ride, and five minutes later he was in Queenswear, walking past the little station towards the boatyard, eating his chips out of the paper just as he'd done as a kid in Liverpool. Only in those days it had been real newspaper rather than the sterile white packaging that was de rigueur in the modern day.

He finished the chips and flung the paper into a nearby bin before going in search of Les, who was standing beside a twenty-foot yacht slung from a massive hoist, doing something with the rudder. When Gerry called out, he turned with a wide smile of greeting on his face.

'Gerry. I was expecting you to turn up earlier.'

'Sorry, Les. I've been busy on that murder.'

'Found out who did it yet?'

'Give us time. We'll get there. Now, you wanted to show me this bloodstain.'

Les wiped his hands on a rag before leading Gerry to a yacht standing on the quayside. 'Here she is. *Duncountin*. She'll be a nice little vessel once we've finished with her,' he added proudly.

'You'll do a good job on her, Les, I know you will. Let's have a shufti at this stain, then.'

Les climbed the ladder up to the deck and Gerry followed, puffing slightly. He knew he should lose weight, but he always made the excuse that he was far too busy to do anything about it.

Les went ahead of him into the cabin, now stripped of all its fixtures and fittings, and shone his flashlight at a long, thin stain on the varnished wooden floor. Gerry squatted down to examine it and came to the same conclusion as Les and the boat's owner. It looked like dried blood all right. There must have been a slick of it, and whoever had cleaned it up wouldn't have realised that some had seeped beneath the lockers, impossible to get at without dismantling the boat's interior.

'Sorry, Les, but I'd like our CSIs to have a look at this. Do some tests.'

Les looked positively keen at the prospect. A bit of excitement to tell his mates about in the pub.

'No problem, Gerry. And I've got that list of the previous owners you wanted,' he added helpfully. 'The doctor I told you about bought her from a retired accountant from Derenham. He was the one who renamed her *Duncountin*.' He smiled. 'I remember him telling me he'd done the renaming properly. He removed all traces of the old name and held a formal ceremony.'

'To appease Neptune.'

'That's right. He made the effort because he couldn't stand the old name, but then he fell ill soon afterwards so the boat was neglected for a couple of years until he sold her to the doctor. I rang him this morning and he's baffled by the bloodstain. Swears he knows nothing about it.'

'What was the boat's former name?'

'Can't remember, but I wrote it down somewhere. The man who owned her before the accountant had an address in Gloucestershire. Name of John Pritchard.'

Something clicked in Gerry's mind and he felt a thrill of recognition. Simone Pritchard's husband was called John. Pritchard wasn't an uncommon name, but it seemed as though a piece of the jigsaw had just fitted snugly into place.

'Whereabouts in Gloucestershire?'

'Hang on, I wrote that down and all. It'll be in the office.'

Les descended the ladder, apparently in no particular hurry. Gerry followed him to the boatyard office, trying to conceal his impatience.

A few minutes later, Les came up with the details.

'His address was in Tewkesbury and the boat used to be called *Devil's Serpent*. Pity I didn't know that when a woman came round a few weeks ago asking if I knew of a boat with that name. I told her I didn't.'

Gerry's heart began to beat a little faster. 'Can you describe the woman?'

Les went on to give a detailed description that fitted Susan Brown perfectly. And as soon as Gerry had made a note of John Pritchard's address, he was on the phone to Wesley.

When Wesley ended the call, he stared at his phone for a few seconds. Gerry's discovery might be the breakthrough they'd been waiting for, the golden nugget of information that tied everything together. On the other hand, he couldn't forget Rachel's account of her conversation with Georgina Unwin, the young star of Crispin Joss's film. If Joss had made death threats to the victim, they needed to speak to him as soon as possible. Although he suspected the director wouldn't be the most co-operative of suspects.

It was high time they looked at Simone Pritchard's disappearance more closely. Wesley hoped that her sister would return from New Zealand soon. If anybody could provide the information they needed, he guessed it would be her.

He'd gone out into the hallway to take Gerry's call, but now he returned to the living room, where Neil had his feet up on the coffee table, looking completely at home. Wesley was torn between being glad of his old friend's company and resenting the intrusion into his domestic peace at a time when he was working long hours. But the former won. At least talking about Neil's dig – and it was rare for Neil's conversation to stray away from his work – gave him a break from thinking about a murder inquiry that was becoming more tangled by the minute.

'The dig's not far from your incident room, so how about meeting for lunch at the Seashell,' said Neil as Wesley sat down beside him and poured himself a glass of wine.

'Nice idea, but I'd better not arrange anything.'

'Following up new leads, as the dog walker said to the policeman.'

The mention of a dog walker reminded Wesley that Drusilla Kramer was still missing, but he felt obliged to give a weak smile at Neil's feeble joke.

'With those bones turning up, I'm wondering if there was some skulduggery going on and that's why there's no record of any previous excavation,' Neil said. 'There's a trunk in the attic at the house that looks interesting, but I haven't had a chance to examine it yet.'

'If you want access to Serpent's Point, you'll have to sweet-talk Grey Grover.'

'Already done and he doesn't give a toss. He said I can look wherever I like. It's that bloody film director you have to avoid. You should hear the way he talks to people. He's a complete bastard.'

'My thoughts exactly. I need to speak to him about something tomorrow, but at least I've got the power of the law behind me, so he can't argue too much.'

'Archaeologists don't count as part of the emergency services, more's the pity.'

Neil shifted in his seat. He was sitting close to Pam, and the sudden memory that they'd once gone out with each other flashed through Wesley's mind. But he banished the thought as rapidly as it had bubbled to the surface. Jealousy had never been his style, and he felt a little ashamed of himself.

'I'm ninety-eight per cent sure that we're dealing with a Roman villa, you know, Wes. You must come and have a look. Maybe do a bit of digging – keep your hand in,' Neil said, seemingly oblivious to the fact that Wesley had other things to occupy his time. 'Any progress on our nighthawks?'

'Sorry, nothing yet. We'll send someone to talk to the owner of the antique shop, but—'

'You mean you haven't done it yet?'

'We've been busy. A woman's been strangled and her friend's missing. The powers-that-be consider that a bit more important than a few Roman artefacts that may or may not have been pinched from your site.' Wesley saw a look of disappointment on Neil's face and realised that his words must have sounded harsh.

'More wine?' He could tell that Pam was trying to defuse the situation.

Neil held out his glass. 'Thanks, Pam. Good of you to let me stay.' The emphasis was on the word 'you'.

'How's Jan?' Wesley asked Pam, trying to change the subject.

'She's talking about getting engaged. I've asked her when we're going to meet Callum, but she says he's busy with the plans for the new restaurant he's opening. He wants their wedding to coincide with his house being ready in the late autumn. She's really excited.'

'Hope we get an invite.'

'I'm sure we will. She's going to be a partner in the restaurant so she's busy sorting out her finances at the moment, then there's the wedding to arrange, of course. I'm really happy for her. She deserves some luck.'

'Couldn't agree more.' Wesley stood up. 'I'll go up and look in on Michael,' he said, leaving his wife and Neil to share the bottle. If there was one thing he hated, it was bad feeling between friends.

When Wesley reached the incident room early the next morning, there was no sign of Gerry. Rachel, however, was already at her desk, tapping her computer keys with an expression of deep concentration on her face. Wesley walked across to her and sat on the edge of her desk.

'You're in bright and early,' he said. 'I thought Gerry ordered you to take it easy.'

'Don't you start. I had to get away from Nigel's fussing. He's brought my mum in on the act now. He wants her to come and stay when the baby's born. I've already got his parents living in the converted barn at the other end of the farmyard, and I don't need my mum policing my every move as well. I've come into work for a bit of peace.' She looked up at him and their eyes met in understanding.

'Anything new to report? Any sign of Calvin Brunning?'

She picked up her notebook. 'Not yet. His camper van hasn't been picked up on the ANPR, which means he might be keeping to the lanes. Let's face it, Wes, there are lots of places to hide a vehicle round here.'

'Anything else?'

'Not really. There's been no activity on Drusilla Kramer's phone or credit card.'

'I can't forget the dog. Surely she wouldn't abandon him in the park like that. What about her work? She said she was a nurse.'

Rachel shook her head. 'None of the local hospitals have heard of her and neither have any nursing homes or doctors' surgeries. Maybe you misunderstood. Perhaps she said she used to be a nurse?'

Wesley didn't answer. He was sure he hadn't made a mistake, but he knew he wasn't infallible.

Rachel took a deep breath as though she was about to make a dramatic revelation. 'There's one small glimmer of hope. Two uniforms in a patrol car thought they spotted someone answering Drusilla's description in Morbay, near the abbey. They called it in first thing. She was walking on her own at six o'clock this morning.'

Wesley shifted forward, giving her his full attention. 'I don't suppose they spoke to her?'

'She'd gone before they had a chance. Hurried off into the abbey grounds, they said. They thought they'd let us know, although they admit they could have been mistaken.'

'Or they might not have been, Rach. There's a chance it could have been her.'

From the journal of Dr Aldus Claye

June 1921

Clarabel was silent at breakfast, but when Phipps entered the dining room, she looked up hopefully, as though she saw him as her rescuer. Do I feel any guilt about my behaviour towards her last night? I'm not sure. I exercised my rights as a husband, rights I had not felt inclined to claim before. According to the law, I did no wrong. Although I suspect that Phipps would wrong me if he could, so I must keep him and Clarabel apart. There will be no more digging in men's clothing. From now on, she will confine herself to the house, and the field will be out of bounds.

But how was I to explain this to Phipps, who had welcomed her participation in the dig so warmly – too warmly? I decided to say she was unwell and that I'd told her to rest for the good of her health. She is of a delicate disposition, so she must not become exhausted by heavy physical work like kneeling in a trench scraping away at the soil.

I saw the scepticism in his eyes, but he was wise enough not to say anything. I know that action has to be taken, but this nagging thought spoils the thrill I ought to feel about what we are finding in that field.

Today we uncovered the border of a mosaic, perfectly pre-served by the look of it. Tomorrow we will carry on digging without Clarabel's help. When I went up to bed, she was already asleep. Or perhaps she was pretending.

31

When there was no further news about Drusilla Kramer, Wesley reached the conclusion that the patrol had made a mistake. After seeing what the killer had done to Susan Brown, he feared the missing woman was in grave danger, and that the next call from Morbay would bring the news that her body had been found.

As soon as Gerry arrived at the church hall, using his old excuse of a faulty alarm clock, he called Wesley over to his desk. The DCI seemed to be filled with fresh enthusiasm, and Wesley guessed that this had something to do with his discovery at the boatyard the previous night.

'Right, Wes. Let's look at everything we've got on Simone Pritchard. The address Les found for the John Pritchard who used to own that yacht isn't a match for the missing woman's, but it could have been an old address and he failed to notify the authorities when he moved. I think that bloodstain on the boat could be connected to Simone's disappearance. I've got a feeling in my water, and you know what that means.'

Wesley nodded. The DCI's hunches often turned out to be right. Often, but not always.

'A woman answering Susan's description was asking

about the boat, although Les didn't know *Devil's Serpent* was *Duncountin*'s former name at that time.'

'Which means she must have been following up the Simone Pritchard case.'

'I want to speak to Simone's local station in Gloucestershire – see if anyone knows where we'll find John Pritchard. And we can remind them to see whether Michelle is back from her travels while we're at it. Emphasise the urgency.'

'When are we interviewing Crispin Joss again?' Rachel asked. 'Georgina Unwin virtually accused him of Susan's murder.'

'All in good time, Rach. He probably won't be at the house yet.'

'In that case, why not catch him at his hotel,' said Wesley. 'Spoil his full English?'

'That's tempting, but I think we'll wait for him to arrive at Serpent's Point.' Gerry gave Wesley a conspiratorial grin. 'He won't like it when we bring him in for questioning, but it'll give the cast and crew a break from his charming company.'

Wesley returned to his desk, stopping to speak to Rachel on the way. She'd seemed worried about Georgina Unwin, and when he pointed out that she was an actress and might be pursuing her own agenda, she disagreed. She was sure Georgina had been telling the truth, although she did suspect she'd been holding something back.

Half an hour later, Gerry summoned him back to his desk. The DCI had never been good at concealing his emotions, and he looked frustrated.

'I've just been on to Gloucestershire and there's no John Pritchard at the address Les gave me. But as luck would have it, Michelle's just got back.'

'Good,' said Wesley.

'I had a chinwag with the sergeant who looked into the Simone Pritchard case,' Gerry continued. 'Uniform dealt with it because it was treated as a missing persons inquiry. It was assumed Simone had gone off with another man of her own accord. She took money and some of her belongings with her, so nobody was particularly worried – apart from the sister, who claimed she didn't know anything about a fancy man. Preliminary enquiries were made, but it was all a bit half-hearted. According to the husband, Simone had been threatening to leave him for a while.'

'Do they have a current address for the husband?'

'No. He moved out of the area soon after her disappearance – destination unknown.'

Wesley guessed this was the cause of Gerry's frustration. 'Sure you don't want someone from the local station to interview Michelle?' he said, looking at the paperwork piling up on the DCI's desk.

'You know me, Wes. I like to speak to people face to face so I can tell if they're lying to me.'

'Did you ask about Simone's bank account? Phone records?'

'She inherited a hundred grand from her grandmother a couple of years before she vanished, and the husband said they were going to use it for a deposit on a house. But she raided their joint account when she left and the police reckoned she opened a new account and bought a new phone because she didn't want to be found. Possibly even changed her identity.' Gerry gave Wesley a meaningful look. 'The sergeant said John Pritchard had an answer for everything. Tewkesbury's only a couple of hours away up the M5, so let's set off once we've had a word with Crispin

Joss. After what that lass told Rach last night about him actually threatening to kill the victim, he's moved right up our suspect list. Rach can hold the fort here, and Morbay have promised to keep us posted about Drusilla Kramer.'

'I'm worried about her.'

'So am I, Wes. But Morbay are pulling out all the stops to look for her, and there's nothing more we can do here.' Gerry gave a deep sigh. 'At the moment, our priority is finding out who strangled Susan Brown. I still fancy Calvin Brunning for it, but we need to find him first.'

The phone on Gerry's desk began to ring, and after a short conversation, he looked up with a grin on his face that Wesley could only describe as wicked. 'Right. Crispin Joss has been picked up and is waiting for us in the inter-view room at Tradmouth. Let's go and rattle his cage.'

Neil had had breakfast with Pam and the children, and found the experience quite different from the solitary snack he usually ate on the go in his Exeter flat. Wesley had already left for work, and it felt odd to be in that domestic situation, witnessing the chaos of a family preparing for the day. Michael still seemed quieter than his usual early-teenage self. The glandular fever had left him subdued, and Neil understood how hard it must be for a boy of his age to feel tired all the time.

He left the house at the same time as Pam and the chil-dren, saying he'd see her later. His body still ached and his head hurt, and he was grateful to her and Wesley for the reassuring comfort of being a guest in their house. He'd washed down a couple of painkillers with coffee at breakfast and, as he drove to the dig, he began to feel a little better, although he still wasn't up to a morning on his knees in a trench. But he reckoned that what he had planned would be equally useful.

He parked in his usual place near the gate to the field, where his team were already removing the tarpaulins from the trenches. He saw that Livy and Sophie had turned up again with their metal detectors and were waiting patiently for instructions. Pain shot through his body as he walked across the site, stopping every now and then to issue instructions. The beating he'd taken had brought it home to him that he wasn't as young as he used to be. He hated the idea, but the physical effort of digging tended to become more demanding as the years went on, especially on the knees and the back. Today he felt a hundred years old.

The bones they'd found had been removed to the mortuary. It was almost certain that the police weren't interested, so it would be up to him to determine whether the man was connected to the unrecorded excavation that may have been carried out there many years ago. However, for the moment he had other things on his mind. The outline of the building was becoming clear now. An outline Neil was now convinced was a Roman villa, albeit a fairly modest one.

He stopped for a chat with the two girls, explaining what he thought they'd found.

'You look bad,' said Livy. 'My dad said someone attacked you while you were camping out here. He says you're not safe anywhere these days.'

Neil suddenly had an idea. 'You don't know of any other metal-detectorists in the area? Maybe someone you told about those coins?'

The answer was a vigorous shaking of both heads. It had been a long shot. He told them to keep up the good work, adding a small pep talk about how important it was to go over the spoil heaps. A lot of valuable things were found that way.

He needed the landowner's permission to expand the dig into the next field, so a visit to the farmhouse to speak to Livy's dad was on his to-do list. But there was something he wanted to deal with first.

He walked to Serpent's Point, dreading an encounter with Crispin Joss. To his relief, there was no sign of the director when he reached the house, and the technical crew and actors were wandering around aimlessly, like sheep without a shepherd. Some stood around in small groups chatting, and Neil sensed tension in the air. A lithe young man in costume passed him with a worried look on his face, and Neil couldn't resist asking what was wrong.

The young man shook his head, but his carefully coiffed hair didn't move. 'The director's gone AWOL and someone said they saw him being driven off in a police car. This production's been a bloody shambles from the start, and now we're wondering whether the backers are going to pull the plug.'

'Can they do that?' Neil had no idea how the film industry worked, but he guessed this particular production wasn't blessed with a Hollywood budget.

'Oh yes. They can and they will,' the young dandy said before marching off.

Neil went in search of Grey Grover. When he found him, the man waved a bored hand. 'Look wherever you like. Archaeologists, film people it's all the same to me.'

He made his way upstairs to the attic where he'd seen the trunk. Before he reached the attic stairs he heard music coming from one of the top floor rooms. Heavy metal. At least Joss wasn't there to complain about the volume.

He opened the door to the attic room. It was dark in there – the previous owners hadn't thought to extend the electric lighting circuit to the barely used storeroom – so he used the torch on his phone. The lid of the trunk was heavy, and pain shot through him again as he hauled it open.

He began to remove things from its gloomy interior, laying them out carefully on the floor. The dusty books he'd noticed before turned out to be filled with neat old-fashioned handwriting: somebody's journals. They also contained drawings that he recognised at once as archaeological sketches, and it didn't take him long to realise that they depicted the ruins he was currently excavating. Whoever the journal belonged to had conducted a thorough – if unscientific, by modern standards – investigation of that field. The land had been dug and recorded after a fashion. But those records had never seen the light of day – until now.

He turned to the front page and saw a name. Dr Aldus Claye. There were several similar journals filled with notes and sketches. An account of Dr Claye's entire dig. Neil's heart was beating fast as he delved further into the trunk and found letters and old deeds, some dating back to the late eighteenth century. He could have spent all day going through them were it not for the pain caused by bending over. Besides, he didn't want to be away from the dig for too long.

He made a final attempt to dig into the trunk's musty depths and his hand came into contact with something cold and hard. A small metal object. He pulled it out and shone the bright beam of his phone on his prize.

It was a sheet of lead, deformed from lying at the bottom of the trunk for many years. He knew what it was at once, although he'd never actually found one before. He held it carefully in the palm of his hand. If he'd been superstitious, he might have shown more caution. This was a weapon meant to harm. This was a curse.

32

'Mr Joss. Thank you for coming.'

Wesley's words were scrupulously polite. He could tell the director was simmering with fury, but he didn't want to give him any grounds for complaint. He hoped Gerry would do likewise, but it was clear that the man was already getting under his skin.

'I didn't have much choice. Your goons picked me up as soon as I arrived at the shoot. They didn't even give me time to tell the cast what was going on.'

'Sorry about that, Mr Joss, but this is a murder inquiry.'

'That's got nothing to do with me.'

'Are you sure you wouldn't like a solicitor present?' Wesley was determined to do this by the book.

'I don't need a solicitor because I haven't done anything. You owe me an explanation.' Joss folded his arms and pressed his thin lips together.

'You've been brought here to be interviewed under caution in connection with the murder of Susan Brown.'

'Go on then. I've nothing to hide.'

'Sure about that, are we, sir?' Gerry leaned forward and Wesley tried to catch his eye. Techniques that worked with the lowlifes they frequently dealt with were unlikely to cut any ice with Crispin Joss.

Wesley began formally by asking Joss where he'd been at the time of Susan Brown's murder. The director repeated what he'd said in his statement. He'd been at his hotel. He'd had breakfast then gone to his room for a while. Wesley knew there was no CCTV at the hotel entrance – the proprietor hadn't got around to installing it yet – so there was no way of confirming or disproving Joss's story.

'A witness has come forward who heard you arguing with the victim the day before her murder.'

'You're going over old ground. I've already told you. She made a complaint. I might have been rude to her, but that's as far as it went.'

'This latest witness claims you threatened Susan Brown. You said you'd kill her, and a short while later she was found dead.' Wesley tilted his head to one side, an expression of polite interest in the reply.

'Whoever told you that was lying.'

'We believe the witness is reliable.' He wasn't sure whether this was true. He didn't altogether trust Georgina Unwin; she was a leading lady with a grudge and she might have embellished the truth for reasons of her own. Revenge being one of them.

'I admit I had words with the woman. It's like I told you before. She was moaning that one of our vans had nearly run her over and saying some of the crew had been smoking in the stable yard and leaving litter around. I told her she was a petty-minded prudish bitch who needed to get a life.' Joss looked pleased with himself. 'She shut up after that.'

'Not the best way to endear yourself to the neighbours,' said Gerry. 'Poor woman must have had a lot to put up with.'

'So have I, Chief Inspector. I can do without people like her carping about trivialities while I'm trying to make a film.'

'Who's funding your film?' Wesley asked. 'You must have backers.'

'I'm not at liberty to say. In other words, it's none of your business.'

'But murder is, so let's go over your story again.'

'It's not a story. It's the truth.' Joss stood up. 'I'm needed back at the shoot, so if that's all ...'

'You threatened to strangle a young woman.'

For a split second, Joss's small eyes widened in alarm. Then he gave a knowing smile. 'It was Georgina who told you that, wasn't it? The silly little cow's not the brightest light on the Christmas tree. Always getting hold of the wrong end of the stick. It was a joke.'

'Rather a tasteless one in the circumstances – when a woman had been strangled a couple of hundred yards away.'

'It was something I came out with on the spur of the moment; you know how it is.' He gave Wesley a man-to-man look, but the response was a stony-faced silence. 'Like I say, I wasn't being serious,' Joss continued with a pleading note in his voice. 'If I could replace the stupid little tart, I would, but half the film's shot now, so ...' He looked from one detective to the other as though he was expecting sympathy. He wasn't getting any. 'I've heard she hasn't even bothered to turn up today. Casting her in the leading role was a massive mistake. Luckily I can make sure that she never works in the industry again.'

The man looked smug at the prospect of wrecking a young woman's career, and Wesley tried hard to hide his distaste.

'We can interview your cast and crew again and see whether anybody backs up her story.' There was a threat behind Gerry's statement.

'You do that, Chief Inspector. You won't find anything because there's nothing to find.' The director's self-satisfied confidence suggested to Wesley that if he had killed Susan Brown, he'd been careful to make sure there were no witnesses. But that didn't mean he was innocent.

Neil asked Grey Grover's permission to take away some of the items he'd found in the trunk, but Grover didn't seem particularly interested. He told the archaeologist he could help himself to anything he liked, adding the caveat that this excluded anything of monetary value.

It was the small lead curse that excited Neil most. He wanted to examine it in better light so that he could translate the words from the Latin. In the end, he asked for help from two of his fellow diggers, and between them they managed to manoeuvre the trunk downstairs. At Grover's suggestion, they deposited it in an empty storeroom off the kitchen; a room that could be easily accessed without disturbing anybody else in the house.

After putting the lead curse and a couple of the journals into the pockets of the combat trousers he always wore for work, Neil made his way back to the dig with his colleagues. There were decisions to make about the exact location of the next trench they planned to open up.

When he arrived, he sensed excitement. Even Sophie and Livy had abandoned their machines and had joined the others crowded around the trench on the far side of the field.

Neil headed towards the point of interest. 'What's going on? What have you found?'

All heads turned towards him, like flowers towards the sun. 'It's a mosaic,' said one of the postgrad students, an earnest young woman who wore a bright red headscarf to keep her long hair away from her face while she worked.

The crowd parted to let him through, and he stared down into the trench. It was about four feet deep now, and sure enough, they'd reached the floor. And what a floor. A couple of square feet of mosaics had been uncovered: red, brown, black and cream, with a touch of blue here and there. Neil thought it looked like a decorative border running around the edge of a high-status room. Whoever the wealthy Roman was who'd left the civilised settlement of Isca Dumnoniorum for the wilds of the south, he'd lived in some style.

'Carry on in this trench,' he ordered. 'Be careful. And don't say a word to anyone yet.' He looked at Sophie and Livy. 'That means you two as well. Let's keep this quiet for the time being.'

There was an outhouse off the stable yard of Serpent's Point, a long-forgotten part of the old laundry where maid-servants with rough red hands once laboured to clean the clothing and bedlinen of their so-called betters.

There was still no sign of Crispin Joss. Word had it that he'd been arrested for the murder of the woman on the coast path, but Abigail Darley didn't believe that for one minute. Rumour and speculation were rife amongst the cast and crew because it relieved the boredom of hanging around waiting for something to happen. Any entertainment was better than none, and the local pub, the Seashell, now seemed as attractive as the bright lights of London's West End.

Abigail had had high hopes when she'd landed the role of Lillith's younger sister. It was hardly a meaty part, and her initial excitement had waned rapidly when she'd discovered how low-budget and exploitative the film was; quite against the feminist principles she'd always claimed to hold. She'd dreamed of a starring role in a period drama, but instead she'd found something her mother would have described as soft porn. But after so many months spent 'resting' since leaving drama school, it had seemed like a golden opportunity.

Word had it that Georgina, who played the title role, had fallen out with the director big-time and that her scenes were being cut. The thought kept running through Abigail's head that if the leading actress were to get the sack, someone would be needed to take her place. And that someone might be her – which would mean intimate scenes with Freddie. The thought made her smile.

Now that Abigail had time on her hands, the stable yard of the old house seemed ripe for investigation. The murdered woman had lived there, and her accommodation was still surrounded by blue and white police tape – just like in the TV crime series her mother watched so avidly. But there were other doors off the yard, old doors with flaking green paint, and Abigail had a sudden urge to see what lay behind them.

When she opened the first door, she realised that she'd found a washhouse, with shallow stone sinks and a drainage channel in the centre of the stone floor. There were washboards and dolly tubs, and a cobweb-festooned drying rack dangling from the ceiling. The room didn't look as though it had been touched since the last laundry maid abandoned it when the invention of the washing machine released her from her back-breaking labours. Abigail wandered around imagining what it would have been like to work here. Probably even worse than taking orders from Crispin Joss.

One corner was occupied by a whitewashed brick structure, a squat tower with a wooden lid. She'd seen something similar before on a school trip to a stately home many years ago, so she knew that it had once been used to heat water. She strolled over and was about to lift the lid when she saw something lying in the shadows in the corner, half hidden by a large mangle. At first she thought it was a pile of clothes. Then she saw a foot; bare, with painted toenails. She couldn't see a head, but the yellow satin dress had ridden up to reveal a pair of shapely legs.

She let out a scream, even though there was nobody around to hear her.

33

Crispin Joss was still being held, but the clock was ticking. When they mentioned Drusilla's name at the end of the interview, he made a show of looking puzzled, but Wesley wasn't altogether convinced.

They decided to take a break and return to the incident room to see whether anything new had come in. And when Wesley received a call from Neil, he left it unanswered. Dr Stamoran had agreed that the bones found at the dig had been old and therefore were not his problem. Whatever Neil had to say would have to wait.

Ten minutes after they arrived back in Bereton, they heard the sound of an ambulance siren in the distance but thought nothing of it. The main coast road was nearby, so the ambulance would probably be transporting some unfortunate soul to hospital in Tradmouth or Morbay. Wesley stood staring at the large noticeboard they'd set up at one end of the hall. Susan Brown was there, along with everyone they'd interviewed during the course of the investigation. He studied the section on the two women who'd featured in Susan's incident room, paying particular attention to the photograph of Simone Pritchard. Gerry had sent the CSIs over to the boatyard to take samples from the mysterious stain, and they were still awaiting the results.

Rachel interrupted his thoughts, and he could tell from her expression that she had news. 'That Marcus Pinter – Grey Grover's lodger. I've checked his alibi and it turns out he didn't arrive at his friend's house in London until the evening of the day Susan was murdered.'

'So he lied when he said he left Serpent's Point the night before. He might have been here when she died.'

'Want me to bring him in?'

Wesley could tell she was eager for action. On the other hand, he didn't like to think of her tackling a possible murderer alone. 'Take Rob with you.'

'Must I?'

'Two officers turning up always makes more of an impact,' said Wesley, pleased that he'd managed to think up a plausible excuse for his suggestion. 'I'd go with you, but we're going to have to return to Tradmouth to continue the Crispin Joss interview, and Rob looks as though he could do with some fresh air.'

'Do you fancy Joss for it?'

Wesley had never lied to Rachel and he didn't intend to start now. 'I don't like him, but I mustn't let that cloud my judgement.'

'Being a nasty bit of work doesn't necessarily make him a murderer,' said Rachel. She rested her hand on her bump protectively. 'And we mustn't forget that Calvin Brunning's gone on the run and Marcus Pinter misled us about his whereabouts that Thursday morning. There are too many suspects in this case, Wes.'

Wesley could see Gerry listening in to the conversation.

His desk was strewn with the paperwork he hated and he looked as frustrated as Wesley felt. He had Neil on his back as well, urging him to give equal attention to his night-hawks and the bones. Then there was the bloodstain in the yacht and their need to travel to Tewkesbury to follow up the Simone Pritchard case. He felt like a drowning man, sinking in the sea of possibilities.

The phone on Gerry's desk rang and Wesley watched him as he answered. The look on the DCI's face told him it wasn't good news.

Gerry stood up and called for attention. 'A woman's been found unconscious at Serpent's Point. She's been taken to hospital and is in a critical condition.'

Wesley strode over to him. He needed the details. 'Who is she?'

'Don't know yet, but she was found in an outbuilding near the converted stables where our murder victim was staying.'

'Was it an attack or an accident?'

Gerry shook his head. He didn't have the answer to that question yet. He called across to DC Walton. 'Trish, can you get over to Morbay Hospital and report back.'

She nodded and reached for her bag.

'Rach, when you go to the house with Rob to speak to Marcus Pinter, can you have a word with whoever found the injured woman.'

He turned to Wesley with a despondent look in his eyes. 'This is all we bloody well need. I reckon our trip to Tewkesbury might have to wait till tomorrow.' His mobile phone rang, and after a short conversation, he looked up. 'That was the lab. That stain in the boat is definitely blood. They asked if we've got any DNA samples to compare it with, but I had to say we hadn't. What we need is a breakthrough.'

Wesley couldn't agree more.

Rachel found Rob Carter annoying, but she did her best to be patient. She'd come across young officers like him before: men who thought they were clever; men who liked playing the tough cop. But she had no time for macho games.

She made for the stable yard, where the crime-scene team had taped off the entrance to one of the outhouses. A young CSI was emerging from the doorway, and Rachel asked her for the information that had been in short supply when Gerry received the initial call.

It turned out that the injured woman had been found by a fellow member of the film cast, name of Abigail Darley, who had identified the unconscious victim as the star of the film, Georgina Unwin. She had head injuries, probably the result of a deliberate attack.

It took a few moments for Rachel to take this in. 'I spoke to her yesterday. What time do you think the attack took place?' she asked.

'Someone saw her an hour before she was discovered, and the paramedics said she hadn't been there long. They also said that if she hadn't been found when she was ...' The CSI didn't have to finish the sentence. Rachel understood. Gerry and Wesley were treating the director, Crispin Joss, as a prime suspect, and he'd had a row with Georgina. But one thing was certain – he couldn't possibly have been responsible for the attack, because he was in Tradmouth being interviewed under caution at the time; the perfect alibi. She took out her phone and called the incident room while Rob looked on. Gerry would want to know.

'What now, Sarge?' Rob asked her once the call was over. Rachel could tell he was sulking.

'We speak to Marcus Pinter. He let us think he was in London when Susan Brown was killed, and we need to know why.'

They found Pinter in his studio, and he didn't look pleased to see them. 'You're wasting your bloody time. I've already told you lot everything I know.' He looked Rachel up and down. She couldn't forget what Wesley had told her about him painting Susan as a corpse, though that particular piece of artwork wasn't on show today. The paintings around the studio were equally grim, not something most people would choose to hang on their walls. The man seemed to be obsessed by death, and in Rachel's opinion, that definitely classed him as a weirdo. She could feel his eyes on her swollen body, and for once, she was glad of Rob's company.

'Different pair of pigs this time. I had a posh black one and a right porker last time.' Pinter looked pleased with himself, as though he imagined his farmyard analogy to be the height of wit.

'Pigs are intelligent creatures,' said Rachel, trying to hide her amusement at the suspect's description of the DCI. 'Bright enough to know when you're lying to them.'

A split-second flash of alarm appeared in Pinter's eyes, swiftly concealed behind his mask of arrogance.

'You weren't in London when Susan Brown died. Why did you lie to us?'

She could see him weighing up his options. Should he keep on lying or come clean? In the end, he made the decision. 'OK. I didn't leave for London until midday that Thursday, but I don't know anything. Someone said Sue was killed first thing in the morning, so I would have been fast asleep. And before you ask, there's nobody who can confirm that; you'll just have to take my word for it.' He looked smug, and Rachel could tell that Rob was itching to take him to the station for some heavy interrogation.

'Why didn't you tell the truth?'

'I didn't want to get involved. I don't need distractions.'

As soon as they'd entered the studio, he'd thrown a paint-stained sheet over the canvas on his easel. Rachel wondered whether it concealed the picture of Susan that Wesley had told her about. But when she stepped forward to flick the sheet aside, Pinter moved fast to stop her. 'That's private. None of your business. I want you to go. I've got nothing else to say.'

'A woman was found unconscious in one of the outhouses earlier. One of the actresses taking part in the filming – name of Georgina Unwin. Know anything about it?'

'I don't know any of the film people. And I've been here all day.'

'So you didn't see anything suspicious?'

He shook his head, avoiding her gaze.

What happened next took her by surprise. Rob darted forward and tugged at the sheet covering the easel. Rachel had expected another anonymous image of violence, but when the sheet fell to the floor, she was puzzled by what she saw.

The painting was half finished, but she recognised the subject as Krystal Saverigg. Yet there was something unusual about the image. When she'd seen Krystal around Serpent's Point, she'd noticed her particularly because her pregnancy was at around the same stage as her own. In this painting, however, her stomach was flat, her body lithe as an athlete's. She was lying on a shabby chaise longue, the one that stood at the end of the studio, and she looked as though she was laid out, her dead eyes staring at the ceiling. A corpse.

Pinter moved swiftly to cover up his handiwork, then picked up a cricket bat that had been thrust into a chipped china umbrella stand by the door.

'You shouldn't have done that,' he said, taking a step towards them.

'Painted from memory, was it?'

'None of your business. Get out.' He was approaching slowly, balancing the bat in his hand threateningly.

Rob rushed forward, placing himself between the artist and Rachel. Pinter retreated a little, his initial defiance waning as Rob took a pair of handcuffs from his pocket. If it came to physical violence, Rachel would back Rob any time. Pinter flung the bat away with a loud clatter, defeated.

Once he was handcuffed, Rachel looked around the studio while Rob stood next to their prisoner like a guardian angel, although she'd never have cast him in that role. She walked over to the old desk in the corner, splashed with paint and topped with a tray bearing brushes and tubes of oil paint, and began to open the drawers while Pinter watched helplessly.

The contents of the middle drawer proved the most interesting. Wads of banknotes – tens and twenties. Hundreds of pounds.

'Can you explain this?' she said, waving a wad of twenties at the artist.

'I sell my paintings, don't I?' The old defiance was returning.

She went to an alcove in the corner and pulled the

curtain aside to reveal canvases stacked up. When she flicked through them, she found they were all similar. Women as corpses, or scenes of murder where a dark figure loomed over a prone woman with his hands around her throat.

'I wouldn't buy any of those,' said Rob. Rachel shot him a look. She could do without his words of wisdom.

'Then you have no taste.' Pinter's cockiness was there again.

'Where do you sleep?'

'Next door. Why?'

Rachel gave Rob a nod, a signal to keep an eye on the prisoner while she searched further. As she left the studio, she could see the increasing alarm on Pinter's face.

'You've got no right to do this. You need a search warrant.' His words sounded confident, but Rachel knew he was starting to panic.

'Grey Grover owns the house and he's given us permission to search wherever we like.'

The room next door, in contrast to the studio, was neat. Rachel liked neatness because it was easier to search a tidy room. She began to open drawers, and in one of them she struck gold – literally.

From the journal of Dr Aldus Claye

June 1921

I caught them together, whispering on the landing. I watched them, the way their bodies moved closer, the way she looked at him as she'd never looked at me. But she is mine, and as soon as this work is done and I have alerted Fredericks and the British Museum, I will ensure that Phipps leaves my house and never sees her again.

Jealousy has wormed its way into my being, twining like a snake around my heart. I have often wondered why this place is called Serpent's Point – perhaps there is something evil here, something that killed the unfortunate Roman woman we found. Was she the Beria Vilbia mentioned in the curse? Was her husband so furious at her being carried off by another man that he killed her and cursed her lover? Is history about to repeat itself? All my life I have exercised an iron control over my emotions, but now I fear events are out of my control.

I was civil to Phipps today as we dug side by side. We were alone, as the men from the farm were engaged in their everyday tasks, and we worked in silence because what we were uncovering needed no words. I have never seen anything like the magnificent mosaic there in that Devon field – and neither has Phipps.

We have found the serpent of Serpent's Point.

34

Wesley and Gerry had just finished interviewing Crispin Joss when Rachel's call came through. Perfect timing. Joss seemed shocked when they told him about the attack on Georgina Unwin, and he was quick to point out that the timing cleared him of all suspicion. There was obviously a madman out there – and it wasn't him.

Georgina still hadn't regained consciousness in hospital, but an officer had been posted by her bed with instructions to report if there was any change in her condition.

Both Wesley and Gerry felt reluctant to let the director go, but they had no valid reason to hold him apart from Georgina's claim that he had threatened to kill Susan Brown. It wasn't enough; being an unpleasant bastard wasn't a crime. Although his treatment of the female members of the cast might be, if anything could be proved in a court of law.

They saw him off the premises and watched him walk across the car park into a waiting taxi. They could have given him a lift back to the incident room in Bereton, but Gerry decided against it. He wasn't in the mood for doing Crispin Joss any favours.

Rachel had called with the news that a quantity of

Roman coins had been found in Marcus Pinter's room, and that a state-of-the-art metal detector had been discovered in his wardrobe. At first the man denied having anything to do with the thefts from the archaeological site, but when Rachel threatened to consult Neil, he became remarkably talkative. Wesley planned to call Neil with the good news as soon as possible, certain that the items stolen by the nighthawks had been found – but whether any confession Pinter made would include the murder of Susan Brown, he wasn't sure. When Rachel also mentioned the picture of a very un-pregnant Krystal Saverigg, Gerry dismissed it as irrelevant. But Wesley still thought it odd.

Pinter was being brought over to be interviewed under caution, and Wesley and Gerry stayed where they were to wait for him, treating themselves to a cup of tea from the machine in the corridor. Wesley wasn't sure whether his was soup or tea, but he drank it anyway.

When Pinter arrived, his fingerprints were taken. He had no criminal record under the name Marcus Pinter, but Wesley suspected that this might not be his first foray into crime.

Half an hour later, he was sitting opposite them in the interview room, occupying the chair Crispin Joss had just vacated.

It didn't take him long to confess, given the weight of evidence against him. Especially when Wesley told him that the man in charge of the excavation, Dr Watson, was due to visit Serpent's Point to examine what had been found. Pinter admitted to being a nighthawk, but made light of it, saying it was a hobby – not really a serious offence. Wesley's opinion differed. Neil had been attacked when he'd challenged the thieves. But for the time being, he intended to let the man talk, hoping he'd be chatty enough to incriminate himself.

Before Pinter could say very much, however, the fingerprint results came back. There was a match to a Mark Pond, who had convictions for theft and deception. Pond had once worked in an auction house, and he specialised in the theft of antiques, mainly up north, where he worked with his partner, Karen Savory. When Wesley saw the picture on his phone, he couldn't help smiling to himself. Karen's speciality was posing as a pregnant woman, sometimes using her false baby bump to hide stolen goods. He left the room and called Rachel. Krystal Saverigg was to be brought in as well.

When Wesley told the suspect what he'd discovered, Pinter – or Pond, as they now knew him – seemed to bow to the inevitable. 'OK, I admit to the thefts. But that's all, I swear.'

'You sold a couple of items to an antique dealer in Tradmouth.'

'Those weren't from the dig. I found them in a tea chest in the attic, wrapped up in an old newspaper from the 1920s. There was some really good stuff there: gold brooches, beads, glass, a couple of small statues. I sold some pieces locally and took the rest to London.' He paused. 'I found part of a skull and a few bones at the bottom of the chest – looked really old.'

'Where are the bones now?'

'I took everything out that was worth selling and left the rest there. We ran out of things to sell, so Karen thought she'd try the dig site while I was away. She said there might be rich pickings there. She found some coins – would have fetched a good price.'

'What about the attack on the archaeologist, Dr Watson? You'd arrived back from London earlier that evening, so you were here when it happened. You went back to the site and he disturbed you, didn't he?'

'Yes, but it wasn't me who hit him. It was Karen. He went for her. It was self-defence.'

Wesley didn't believe that for a moment. 'Is this why you came to Serpent's Point?'

Pond shook his head. 'Oh no. The stuff in the attic was a bonus – like the dig. That was a gift I couldn't refuse, if you see what I mean. I was intending to go straight, honestly. I am an artist, you know, and I've always wanted a chance to develop my talents.'

He looked Gerry in the eye. 'The teacher I had last time I was inside told me I was really good and that I could make a living out of it, but it's not that easy to make ends meet, especially since Karen wants us to save up to buy a place of our own. It was all her idea – fooling Grey into thinking she was pregnant and getting his sympathy. She's good at playing the vulnerable card, and when she said she was homeless, he was only too glad to take her in. He's keen to start an artists' colony, so when she told him about me and how I was struggling, he said I could move in too. He'd already let the stables to Andrea Alladyce. She's quite well known – the jewel in Grey's crown.'

'Your work isn't exactly . . . ' Wesley searched for the right word, 'commercial.'

'My teacher said I had to be true to myself, and I need to convey the violence I came across inside. The world as it is, not how we want it to be.'

'The violence you'd like to commit. Murdering women?'

Pond shook his head vigorously. 'Not me. But I met

blokes inside who fantasised about things like that, and I took that as my inspiration.'

Wesley found it hard to believe the man's explanation for the disturbing nature of his art, but he had more questions to ask. 'How did Karen find out about Grey?'

'She saw an article about Andrea and how Grey was trying to get this colony together. She got in touch with him. It was easy. Grey's a generous guy.' He smiled.

'You mean he's a bit of a mug?' said Gerry.

'Look, why don't you just charge me – get it over with?'

He sounded confident, but Wesley hoped that when the interview came round to murder – and the attack on Georgina Unwin – he wouldn't be so sure of himself.

'Because we've only just begun to scratch the surface,' said Gerry. 'You admit you're fascinated by violence against women, so there's the small question of murder.'

Pond looked genuinely shocked. 'Look, I never killed Sue. You've got to believe me. Why would I?'

'Because she found out about your scam,' said Wesley.

'She didn't. And even if she had, I wouldn't have killed her.'

'Your paintings suggest otherwise. You must see that. And you used violence against Dr Watson.' He paused before asking the next question. 'Where's Drusilla Kramer?'

'Who?'

Gerry's phone rang, and he left the interview room to take the call. A few minutes later, he returned. 'That was the hospital. Georgina Unwin has regained consciousness. And you'll never guess what she's said.'

Wesley saw panic in the suspect's eyes. Then Pond suddenly bowed his head, as though he was acknowledging defeat. 'OK, I might as well come clean. Georgina was blackmailing us. She realised Karen wasn't pregnant and she overheard us talking about selling the stuff. She asked very sweetly for a couple of hundred quid to tide her over until Joss paid her what he owed her. She said she knew one of the police officers working at the church hall, and that she was terrible at keeping secrets. I knew it was a threat. We had to do something to shut her up.'

'So you attacked her.'

'That was Karen's idea. She said we should lure her to that outhouse with the promise of paying what she was asking for. We only wanted to scare her into keeping quiet – get her off our backs. But she fell and hit her head. You've got to believe me.'

'The attempted murder of Georgina Unwin and the attack on Dr Neil Watson. The charge sheet's getting longer. Did Susan Brown discover the truth about you as well? Why don't you confess to her murder too? A full confession always goes down well with the judge.'

'I can't confess to something I didn't do. I admit to the rest of it, but not Sue's murder.'

They ended the interview and Pond was taken to the cells.

'I think we might have found our man,' said Gerry, rubbing his hands together with glee. 'Then once we get the final piece of the jigsaw, we can all go to the pub to celebrate.'

Wesley had a strong feeling that the DCI's optimism was somewhat premature – and that they needed to get to Tewkesbury as soon as possible.

35

Neil was enjoying his stay at Wesley's house so much that he was reluctant to tell Pam he was feeling a lot better. His solitary life was gradually losing its appeal. His partner, Lucy, was in charge of a major excavation on Orkney, and she seemed reluctant to take on archaeological work in the south-west. Neil was starting to suspect that studying Orkney's prehistoric monuments was more important to her than their relationship. Perhaps they'd reached the end of the road.

Staying with Wesley and Pam had made him realise that the family life he'd always shunned had some attractions. But this was something he was reluctant to admit to himself, let alone anyone else.

He found himself alone in the house while Wesley and Pam were out and Michael and Amelia were seeing friends. Michael had confided that he'd missed his friends while he'd been ill, and Neil, used to the camaraderie of the dig, knew exactly how he felt. He planned to go back to Bereton later to find out what was happening. Taking it easy didn't necessarily mean doing nothing, and as long as he didn't do anything too strenuous, he could supervise and advise.

In the meantime, he had the journals he'd taken from

the trunk to entertain him. From what he'd had time to read so far, he was sure they referred to his site. He'd already learned that Dr Aldus Claye, a former resident of Serpent's Point, had been told that the farmer who rented the dig field in those days had found human remains and a curse that must surely be the one currently in his possession. He'd placed it carefully in a box and now he took it out to examine it again. It was hard to make out what it said, but once he found a magnifying glass, he set to work translating the incised words.

May he who carried off my wife, Beria Vilbia, be cursed in life and mind and his words, thoughts and memory, and may Charon and Hecate drag him down to the depths of Hades. May he not live to enjoy the fruits of his wickedness. It seemed a powerful curse, but Neil was also wondering about the human remains that the farmer claimed to have discovered. Surely they couldn't be the same ones his own team had found? From the pocket watch and what little remained of the clothing, the latest bones were old, but they certainly weren't as ancient as the curse. However, at least half the large site had still to be excavated.

His phone rang and he was pleased to see Wesley's name on the caller display.

'Hi, Wes. What's up?'

'Good news. Your nighthawk's in custody and he's about to be charged. We've also found the source of the stuff he was selling. He says he found a lot of antiquities in a tea chest in the attic at Serpent's Point, and he admits selling the statue and the glass to that dealer in Tradmouth. There were other things too, which he sold in London, I'm afraid. We found coins he admitted came from your dig. Like to see them?'

There was a short silence before Neil replied. 'Course I would.'

'They've been taken to the incident room – the church hall in Bereton.'

Neil set the journal he was reading to one side and stood up. 'I'm going to the dig, so I'll call in on the way.'

'Shouldn't you be taking it easy?'

He was torn between prolonging his stay with the Petersons and telling the truth. In the end, he decided on honesty. 'I'm feeling a lot better, so I'll get out of your hair later today. I'll move back to the hostel with the others.'

'There's no rush.'

'Thanks, but I need to be near the dig.'

'It's up to you, but you're welcome to stay as long as you like. I'll let the incident room know to expect you. By the way, your thief found something else in the tea chest – a human skull and some bones, very fragile and possibly centuries old. He left those where he found them and I'll get someone to pick them up so you can have a look.'

'Thanks. I found some old journals in the attic at Serpent's Point,' Neil said before Wesley could end the call. 'We're not the first people to excavate in that field.'

'Anything about the skeleton you found?'

'No, but from everything we discovered in the makeshift grave, the doc's pretty sure the bones are about a hundred years old, which fits with them being connected to the dig mentioned in the journals. And I've found something really interesting – a Roman curse. Want to see it?'

'Sorry, it'll have to wait. I'm about to resume the interview with the man who attacked you. Your nighthawk's about to be caged. Sorry. Got to go.'

Neil packed his belongings in his holdall and left the

house. During Wesley's long absences, he'd felt he was growing closer to Pam, and he felt a nag of guilt. Leaving was definitely for the best.

Krystal Saverigg, alias Karen Savory, had been picked up and was being questioned by Trish Walton in Tradmouth. In the meantime, they were holding Mark Pond, alias Marcus Pinter, on the charges he'd already confessed to. But Gerry was longing to nail him with the big one. Murder.

'There's still no sign of Calvin Brunning – or Drusilla Kramer,' said Wesley.

'You don't have to remind me, Wes. Pond says he's never heard of Drusilla and I'm inclined to believe him. There's been no activity on her phone or bank account, so it's not looking good.' Gerry looked how Wesley felt. Helpless.

'I realise that, but Simone Pritchard's sister's back, so we can't put off our trip to Tewkesbury any longer.'

Gerry raised his head and nodded. 'You're right. We'll go tomorrow, whatever happens – she'll have had time to get over her jet lag by then. Rach can deal with things here.' He paused. 'Mind you, I feel a bit guilty. Maybe she should be taking it easy at this stage. When Kathy was expecting—'

'Don't let her hear you say that. According to her, women once gave birth in the fields, strapped the baby to their back and carried on harvesting.'

Gerry looked alarmed. Then he saw that Wesley was grinning. 'You had me worried there, Wes. OK, Tewkesbury it is. Who knows, we might find a link to Mark Pond while we're there.'

It was five o'clock when the call from the team searching Pond and Savory's accommodation finally came. And from the expression on Gerry's face, Wesley suspected it wasn't the news he'd been hoping to hear.

The DCI strode over to Wesley's desk and sat down heavily on the spare chair, which creaked under his weight. 'No sign of any fabric matching the ligature that killed Susan Brown.'

'And the scarf belonging to Crispin Joss wasn't a match, more's the pity.'

'Seems we'll have to keep looking.' Gerry found it hard to hide his disappointment. 'This doesn't prove that Pond didn't do it,' he said. 'He and Karen might have chucked away the murder weapon, so they're not out of the frame yet, especially after what they did to Neil and Georgina Unwin. I want him questioned again tomorrow. We need to pile the pressure on.'

Wesley was about to return to his desk when Neil entered the church hall. He looked round nervously, and when he spotted Wesley, he raised a hand in greeting.

'I wasn't expecting to find you here. I thought you'd be interviewing the bastard who attacked me.'

'I have been. The rules say suspects are entitled to a break.'

Neil mumbled something under his breath, but Wesley couldn't quite make it out.

'I expect you want to see what we found.' Wesley led the way to a cupboard at the side of the hall; it was usually used to house flower-arranging equipment, but it had been transformed into a temporary evidence store. He took out an evidence bag containing five coins and a brooch in a typically Roman style, T-shaped and resembling a dolphin when viewed from the side. All the objects were caked in soil, but a couple of the coins were gold and untarnished by centuries spent underground.

'Wow,' was Neil's first word as Wesley handed him the bag. 'Trouble is, we don't have the context. We can't know exactly where they were found.'

'Our friendly neighbourhood nighthawks obviously don't have degrees in archaeology,' said Wesley, 'or they would have kept a proper record of their finds.'

Neil looked at his friend and saw a smile on his lips. 'I can always ask them to show me.'

'Maybe not at the moment. We'll have to keep these for the time being because they're evidence, but don't worry, you'll get them back.'

Neil began to examine the contents of the bag, shifting the objects around so he could get a better view through the clear plastic. 'There's a good collection here, Wes. Hadrian. Titus. Trajan, Nero.'

Wesley took them off him gently. 'They'll be safe enough in the evidence store at the station.'

Neil looked dubious, like a mother who'd been asked to trust her new baby to an irresponsible teenager.

'Tell you what, I'll take them there myself on the way home.'

'That's a weight off my mind.'

'And what's this about a curse?'

'I'll tell you when you're not so busy.'

Wesley watched Neil hurry out of the incident room. Perhaps the answer to his problems would lie in Tewkesbury. He needed to be more of an optimist. Like Gerry.

36

The following morning, he set off early with Gerry in the passenger seat, and after the long drive up the M5, they arrived in the town of Tewkesbury at eleven o'clock. Wesley had programmed the address the local police station had provided for Simone Pritchard's sister into his sat nav. She'd made a fuss when Simone disappeared because she'd left without letting her know. If the sisters were close, this seemed strange. But there was only one way to find out the truth.

Tewkesbury was a pleasant town, blessed with black-and-white buildings and a fine abbey. It was here that the Yorkists had won a decisive battle in 1471 during the Wars of the Roses. Wesley remembered hearing the story of how Margaret of Anjou watched the fighting from the abbey's great tower – the fighting in which her only son, Edward, Prince of Wales, the great hope of the House of Lancaster, was killed. The prince was buried in the abbey's chancel; the Duke of Clarence, Richard III's brother, who famously drowned in a butt of Malmsey wine, was buried there too. The place was crammed with tempting history, but Wesley had a job to do.

Simone Pritchard's sister, Michelle Williams, lived in a

small half-timbered cottage behind the town's main street, next door to a pretty café with pink gingham curtains. The local police had warned her of their visit, and she greeted them like long-lost friends. The house they entered seemed bigger on the inside than it had appeared on the outside, tastefully furnished with hand-painted furniture and colourful cushions and throws. It was a lovely place, although the ceilings were a little low for Wesley's taste.

There was a framed photograph on the mantelpiece – Michelle and a woman he recognised from the photograph he'd seen in Susan's incident room as Simone, her sister. Their arms were around each other's shoulders and they were drinking a smiling toast to the unseen photographer. They looked happy; the picture of sisterly bliss. He wondered what had happened to ruin it.

'When I reported Simone missing, the police told me that lots of people choose to disappear and said I shouldn't worry,' Michelle began before offering coffee. 'They made no real effort to look for her because she'd withdrawn all that cash, and her passport and driving licence had gone too, so they said she must have been planning to start a new life. I hoped they were right, but ... '

'You don't think they were?' said Wesley. 'According to her husband, there was another man.'

She thought for a moment. 'There was a man at her work. Andy. She used to talk about him a lot and I think they got on really well. Simone said they were just friends – in fact, she told me once that she thought he was gay – but you know how stories get around. The police spoke to her colleagues, who repeated the office rumours; they said Andy had just split up with a partner, and that he and Simone were having a fling. It was all rubbish, of course, but you know how people like a bit of saucy gossip. Andy got another job in Bath shortly before Simone left, so word got round that Simone had left John to go and join him. But I tracked him down, and when I asked him, he said the only contact he'd had with Simone since he moved to Bath was one text asking if she could come and see him. She didn't say why. They arranged to meet, but she never turned up, and when he tried her number, her phone was dead. Switched off. He was worried, so he agreed I should go to the police. But a fat lot of good that did.'

'You told the police the whole story?'

'Of course I did, but it made no difference. They spoke to Andy over the phone, but he said it was as if they were going through the motions. As far as they were concerned, she'd walked out on her husband and cleared out their joint bank account. They said if it wasn't Andy she was with, it must be someone else, and they cast her as the villain: a good-time girl who took poor John for everything he had. Only Simone wasn't like that, and the money was hers anyway. We inherited a hundred grand each from our grandparents.' She looked round. 'I bought this place.'

'Very nice,' said Gerry, making himself comfortable on the velvet sofa.

'Simone had every right to take that money, but I don't think she did. I think something happened to her, or she would have kept in touch. And why did that husband of hers bugger off so soon afterwards? That's what I want to know.'

'Tell me about John.'

'Simone met him through a dating site. He said he'd come out of a long-term relationship and was trying to build up his confidence again.'

'He was your brother-in-law. Did you know him well?'

278

'I can't say I did, to be honest. He didn't like her seeing me and tried his best to keep us apart. Our parents moved to New Zealand to be with my brother ten years ago. I've just been to see them. They flew back when Simone went missing, but they couldn't stay long. And do you know, John refused to see them. He said it was too upsetting for him; played the bloody victim. Can you believe it?'

Wesley couldn't help sympathising. If there was any truth in his growing suspicions, the man who'd played the victim had been putting on an impressive act.

'Did your parents come to Simone's wedding?'

'They weren't invited. Neither was I, for that matter, even though Simone and I had always been close before she met him. She told me they only wanted a quiet ceremony – dragging a couple of witnesses in off the street, that sort of thing.'

Wesley glanced at Gerry, remembering that Avril Willis's mother had told a very similar story.

'Don't think I haven't asked myself why they needed all that secrecy.'

'Anything else you can tell us about John? What did he do for a living?'

'He said he was some sort of salesman, but it was very vague.'

'Did he own a boat?'

She looked at Wesley in amazement. 'How did you know that? He had a yacht somewhere in the West Country; they used to go down there at weekends. I don't think she was that keen on sailing, but by then she went along with everything he said. He even wanted her to leave her job. He was trying to control her and he succeeded.' She sniffed. 'I've read all about men like that. Thank God my partner's a little treasure,' she added fondly. Then she looked at Wesley, her gaze travelling down to the wedding ring on his left hand. 'Bet you are and all, Inspector. I'm good at reading people.'

Wesley saw a grin on Gerry's face.

'And you, Chief Inspector. I bet your bark's worse than your bite.'

'Very true, love. But I prefer that to be a well-kept secret. Was your brother-in-law's yacht called *Devil's Serpent*, by any chance?'

She looked at Gerry as though he'd just pulled off a particularly impressive conjuring trick. 'Yes. That's it. *Devil's Serpent*. Serpent's a good word to describe him. He reminded me of a snake.'

'Did he keep the yacht in Tradmouth in Devon, where we've come from?'

She nodded. 'That's right. Simone mentioned Tradmouth a few times.'

It was Wesley who asked the next question. 'Do you have a photo of John?'

There was a long silence before she replied. 'He was funny about having his picture taken – always dodging away or turning his head. I've heard some people are like that, but . . . '

Wesley caught Gerry's eye. Again, Avril Willis's mother had said something similar. All his instincts were crying out that this was important.

'So there's no picture of him?' said Gerry. 'Didn't your sister give you any wedding photos?'

The answer was a shake of her head.

'Did John ever claim to be an artist?'

She looked puzzled. 'No. Why do you ask?'

'Ever heard the name Mark Pond – or Marcus Pinter?'

'No. Sorry.'

'Do you recognise the name Avril Willis? Or Susan Brown?'

Her eyes lit up with recognition. 'Funnily enough, I had an email from a woman called Susan Brown. She said she'd seen something I'd put online about Simone and knew of a similar case. I thought it was a scam at first, but then she started asking about John. Did I know where he was, by any chance? I thought she might have been one of his exes, so I said I didn't want to talk about that man after the way he'd treated my sister. But she said she was trying to find him because someone had treated her friend badly too. She phoned one day and asked if she could come and see me, and I agreed. She turned up and we had a chat, and I told her the whole story. I thought it wouldn't do any harm to mention his boat, too.'

'You told her the boat's name?'

'Yes. She swore she wasn't a vengeful ex, but even if she had been, I didn't owe him any loyalty, did I?'

This explained why Susan had pursued her enquiries at Les's boatyard. Had someone found out and silenced her because she was getting too close?

'Did she say anything else?'

'Only that she thought John had been married before to this friend of hers.'

It was Gerry who took it upon himself to break the news. 'I'm sorry, love, but Susan Brown was found strangled on the coast path in south Devon.'

There was a shocked silence while Michelle took it in. Then she spoke again, almost in a whisper. 'I didn't know whether to believe what she said about her friend. I wondered if she was a private detective trying to trace him for some reason.'

'No,' said Wesley. 'We think she was telling you the truth when she said that a good friend of hers had been involved with the man you knew as John Pritchard.' He didn't mention that Avril was dead. It seemed too brutal to suggest that Simone might have met the same fate. 'Have you ever heard the name Drusilla Kramer?'

'No. Sorry.'

'It'd help us if you could give us a full description of Pritchard,' said Wesley.

'That Susan asked me the same.' She leaned forward and closed her eyes, concentrating hard. 'He was around five foot ten. Dark hair worn fairly long. Quite nice-looking in a bland sort of way. But there was something about his eyes I didn't like. As though he was watching you, trying to guess your reaction to things. I had a bad feeling about him from the start, and I told Simone so.' She suddenly looked sad. 'Perhaps I shouldn't have told her. It made it easier for him to persuade her not to see me. He made me out to be the enemy – which I never was.'

Wesley could hear the frustration in her voice. 'Is there anything else you can tell us? He didn't leave a forwarding address?'

'No chance, and I certainly wouldn't have been on his Christmas card list.' There was a long pause. 'Just before she went missing, Simone said they were thinking of buying a house and they were going to see a financial adviser. I made a joke – told her to be careful he didn't run off with all her money. She didn't find it funny. In fact John told the police we'd fallen out over it and that's why she didn't tell me she was going.'

Michelle's words suddenly made Wesley uneasy, reviving a memory he'd pushed to the back of his mind.

'A couple of weeks later, I kept trying to call her, but her phone was dead. I went round to the house, and he answered the door and said she'd left him. "Gone off" was how he put it. It was me who went to the police, not him. He persuaded them that Simone had left of her own accord, but I knew he was lying.'

'I think you were right, love,' said Gerry.

'Just find her, will you. Even if she's dead, at least I can give her a proper funeral.' She looked up and snatched a tissue from the box on the side table.

'Can you give us Andy's number? You never know, he might have remembered something.'

Michelle nodded and looked up the number on her phone. Then, without warning, she began to sob, crying for the sister she'd lost.

They sat in silence until she'd composed herself. There was another question they needed to ask if they were to link the bloodstain on the boat to Michelle's missing sister. But Wesley felt nervous about broaching the subject, because the answer might rob her of any hope she had of finding her sister alive. 'I'm sorry to ask this, but do you have anything that belonged to Simone? Something like a hairbrush, or ...'

She caught on fast and dabbed her eyes with a tissue. 'I've got some of her things in a box in the loft. I picked them up when John said he was moving away. He was going to throw them out, but I thought ... over my dead body.' There was a flash of anger in her eyes. Then she took a deep breath and gave a nervous smile. 'I'll go up there and have a look.'

Wesley and Gerry waited for her in silence. Neither felt like talking. After a few minutes, Michelle returned with a hairbrush and a toothbrush, holding them carefully by the handles – she was obviously a watcher of *CSI* shows on the TV.

'Will these do?'

'Nicely, thanks, love,' said Gerry. Wesley held out the evidence bags and she dropped them in.

'You've found her, haven't you? You want to compare her DNA to an unidentified body.'

'We haven't found her yet,' said Wesley gently. 'But I promise we'll do our very best.'

Before leaving Tewkesbury, Wesley decided to look in at the abbey, promising Gerry he wouldn't be long. The DCI raised no objection, and as they stood in the nave, Wesley found himself saying a silent prayer that they'd find the killer before he claimed another victim. He was now certain that there was evil behind Susan Brown's murder – a web of deception they were only just starting to uncover.

While they were walking back to the car, Wesley called Andy's number. He sounded pleased to hear from them and told them he had something that could help them, but it might take him a while to find it. Wesley gave him his email address and Andy promised to get in touch.

37

It was coming up to 5.30 when Wesley and Gerry returned to the incident room. Gerry made his usual entrance, shouting out a greeting and asking what was new. Had Mark Pond coughed to the murder yet? Had there been any more sightings of Drusilla Kramer? The answer to both questions was a resounding no. Nothing new had come in during their absence. But the main thing on Wesley's mind was how they were going to find John Pritchard.

Rachel rose to her feet and followed them to Gerry's desk. 'Mark Pond and Karen Savory have been charged with the thefts from the archaeological site and with assaulting Neil Watson and Georgina Unwin, but you'll never guess what they're claiming now. They're saying the whole thing was performance art, and Pond swears it was Karen's idea and he just went along with it. I've heard more convincing fairy tales.'

'Theft of antiquities and assault as performance art,' said Wesley. 'I'll give him ten out of ten for bare-faced cheek.'

'He doesn't imagine that'll get him off, does he?' Gerry sounded incredulous.

'Who knows?' said Rachel. 'I keep thinking of those pictures in his studio. If he likes painting murdered women so much, what's to say he wasn't tempted to re-enact his fantasies?' She gave a small nod, as though she was convinced by her own explanation. As far as she was concerned, they'd got their man. 'How did you get on in Gloucestershire?'

'I think the partners of the two women in Susan's incident room could be the same man.' The idea had been brewing in Wesley's head for days, but this was the first time he'd voiced it, and he saw that Gerry was nodding in agreement. 'A pattern's definitely emerging. Our suspect doesn't like having his photo taken – that's something the partners of Avril Willis and Simone Pritchard had in common.'

'But the descriptions of Ian Willis and John Pritchard are different,' Gerry pointed out.

'It isn't hard to change your appearance. I think he meets his victims through dating sites, using a different name and identity each time. He chooses women who have money of their own, then goes to great lengths to control his victims and separate them from their friends and families. I've a feeling that he covers his tracks so well, there might be more than two victims. Perhaps that's why Susan was showing so much interest in missing persons cases.'

'You could be right, Wes,' said Rachel. 'If he's responsible for two, there might well be more.' She paused, taking in the implications. 'Simone Pritchard's never been found, so what's he done with her body?'

'If that bloodstain on the yacht turns out to belong to her, it wouldn't surprise me if she ended up in the sea,' said Gerry.

'Wouldn't she have been washed up by now?'

'Not if he weighed her body down.' Wesley thought for a moment. 'The murderers who are never caught are the ones whose victims are never found. Thousands of people go

missing every year – some of them must be murder victims.'
He saw Rachel shudder at the thought. 'I've sent Simone
Pritchard's hairbrush and toothbrush over to the lab, so if
we find a DNA match for the bloodstain on that boat . . .'

'We'll find a match, Wes. I can feel it in my water. I
reckon he killed Susan because she was on to him.'

'Mark Pond fits the approximate description. And he's
got a criminal record.'

Wesley said nothing. Rachel had clearly taken a dislike
to Pond, but he couldn't share her certainty.

At that moment, Gerry's phone rang. It was Morbay,
and he put it on speaker so that Wesley could hear what
was being said. Calvin Brunning's camper van had been
spotted parked near the seafront. A patrol car was keeping
it under observation.

'We need to get over there,' said Gerry.

'Want me to come?' Rachel asked hopefully.

'I'm going to say something horribly sexist now. Report
me if you want, but with the best will in the world, Rach,
I don't think you're up to legging it after suspects at the
moment. Tell you what, give your brain a bit of exercise and
go through all the evidence we've got. Make sure we're not
missing anything.'

To Wesley's surprise, she didn't raise even a token objection. She caught his eye and smiled. 'Good luck.'

It took them half an hour to drive to Morbay, where they
made straight for the promenade. Wesley parked behind
a patrol car, and Gerry climbed out and knocked on the
window, making one of the constables spill his takeaway
coffee over his uniform trousers.

'Where is he?' he growled as the window glided down
with a smooth hum.

'Over there near the shops, sir – by the one with the buckets and spades outside. Looks like he's decided to take a walk. He was on the beach for a while, but I don't think he took his shoes and socks off for a paddle.'

At that moment, the radio ordered the patrol car to attend a robbery at a petrol station. It sounded urgent, so Gerry told them to go – he and Wesley could manage.

The two of them approached the shopping arcade. Eventually they spotted their man standing near a group of teenagers, hands thrust in the pockets of his shorts. He looked as though he was waiting for something. Or killing time.

They headed towards him, feeling out of place in their working clothes. Brunning was staring out to sea and didn't see them until Gerry spoke.

'Hello, Calvin. Not been avoiding us, have you?'

As soon as the words left his lips, Brunning pushed past them and started to run towards his van.

'What are you waiting for, Wes? Get after him. Your legs are younger than mine, and he doesn't look as though he's about to win the Olympics any time soon.'

Wesley began to run. When he reached the end of the street, he saw Brunning slow down as the sea came into view. If he made it as far as the front, there were lots of places he could disappear – amusement arcades, shops and cafés – so Wesley knew he had to keep him in sight.

For a moment his quarry slipped out of his field of vision, but he soon spotted him pushing past a group of strolling pensioners on the road to the beach. Wesley followed, closing the gap. Brunning was looking breathless. In a fitness contest, Wesley would definitely win.

When he caught up, Brunning swung round to face him.

'We'd like to ask you some more questions, Calvin. Are you going to come quietly?'

He was unprepared when Brunning suddenly lunged at him with his fists flying, watched by gawping holidaymakers and day trippers who made no attempt to come to his aid. Before he knew it, he felt a sharp pain in his ribs, and collapsed onto the soft, damp sand.

It was lucky that a couple of bored-looking PCSOs happened to be on patrol. They dropped the ice creams they were enjoying and rushed towards the fracas.

People were standing round staring like curious sheep as Gerry descended on the scene.

'What are you lot gawping at?' he shouted. His Scouse accent always became stronger in times of stress. 'Anybody called an ambulance?'

'I'll be OK in a moment, Gerry. Don't fuss.'

'You stay there, Wes,' the DCI ordered. 'Don't make any sudden movements. You might have broken something.' He put a comforting hand on Wesley's shoulder. 'The paramedics'll soon be here to sort you out. Let's hope Dumb and Dumber manage to bring our man in.'

Wesley tried to laugh, but it hurt. He diagnosed a possible cracked rib; you couldn't be brought up amongst doctors without some of it rubbing off.

A couple of hours later, he found himself lying in A&E at Morbay Hospital after an X-ray had disproved his initial self-diagnosis. He hadn't cracked a rib, but he was badly bruised, so he was advised to take things easy. Gerry brought him the pleasing news that Brunning had been apprehended by a patrol car. He'd made straight for his camper van, where they were waiting for him. Not the brightest pebble on the beach.

'You should go home,' he told Wesley.

'No way. The doctor said I could carry on as normal as long as I was careful. No more chasing suspects and wrestling them to the ground was how she put it,' he added with a grin. 'I'm up to asking a few pertinent questions. Promise.'

Gerry looked dubious, but eventually he gave in. 'OK. We'll have him taken back to Tradmouth. It's about time we dealt with our friend Brunning once and for all.'

'You do realise he doesn't fit the description of the man we think Susan was looking for? He's far too tall, for a start. And I'd hardly describe him as charming.'

Gerry frowned. 'That's true, but he's behaving as though he's guilty of something.'

An hour later, they were back in the same intimidating interview room they'd used before.

'Resisting arrest and assaulting a police officer,' Gerry began. 'At least we can get you for that.'

'Piss off, Scouser.'

'You denied having anything to do with Susan Brown when she lived at Serpent's Point and worked behind the bar at the Seashell.'

'So?'

Wesley leaned forward. 'I think you knew her better than you've admitted. I think you followed her on the morning she died and tried it on with her. She said no, so you strangled her.' It was worth a try to see Brunning's reaction.

'I never. You're a bloody liar.' He bowed his head. 'OK, I admit I saw her around, and I tried it on once, but she told me to get lost.'

'So you killed her.'

'I didn't. I wasn't bothered. It was her loss.'

'What about Drusilla Kramer? She knew too much, so you had to get rid of her too.'

'Don't know what you're talking about.'

'She was Susan's friend, and now she's missing.'

'I don't even know who she is, and like I said, I wasn't bothered about Sue. There's an actress I fancy at the shoot. I've seen her with no clothes on,' he added with what sounded like pride.

Wesley and Gerry looked at each other. 'So you deny murdering Susan and abducting Drusilla Kramer?'

'Course I do. I didn't do nothing and there's no way you can prove I did.'

Wesley saw Gerry look at his watch. 'We'll leave it there for now. We'll offer you our hospitality tonight so we can carry on our little chat tomorrow.'

They left Brunning in the care of the constable on duty by the door. An hour later, the news came in. His van had been searched again on Gerry's orders, and this time they'd found a quantity of class A drugs. Cocaine mostly. Certainly enough to suggest that he was dealing.

'No wonder he was so keen to avoid us,' said Wesley.

Gerry thought for a few moments. 'But it doesn't mean he didn't kill Susan. If she found out what he was up to . . . '

'I don't think he's a killer,' said Wesley.

Gerry shrugged. 'You could be right. Let's go home. Sleep on it.'

After their earlier trip to Gloucestershire, they both needed to get away. But when Wesley arrived home, he discovered that a restful evening was the last thing on Pam's mind.

From the journal of Dr Aldus Claye

June 1921

It is magnificent, and quite undamaged. A serpent writhing along the floor of what once must have been one of the main reception rooms – perhaps the triclinium, where the villa's occupants dined. I know it is a remarkable thing to find such a mosaic so intact. Once it was exposed, Phipps stood upon the great snake's mottled belly and stared around him. I saw tears in his eyes as he gazed at the serpent's head with its flashing forked tongue. It is truly the discovery of a lifetime.

'We must show it to Clarabel,' he said, as though my wife was at the forefront of his mind.

I told him she wouldn't be interested, but he ignored my words and began to run in the direction of the house. I watched him go, my heart filled with hatred. This man will take Clarabel from me, and I have to stop him in any way I can.

I am ashamed to say that there is murder in my heart.

38

'I wasn't expecting you home so early,' Pam said as soon as Wesley opened the front door.

'I've been to A and E. A suspect resisted arrest.'

Her eyes widened in alarm. 'Are you OK?'

'Don't worry, I'm fine. Nothing broken.'

She touched his face. 'You should be more careful. I worry.'

He kissed her, but he could tell something was wrong – something unconnected to his trip to hospital.

'I'm a bit concerned about Jan,' she said as she led the way into the living room.

'What about her?' He could smell something good, the scent of cooking wafting from the direction of the kitchen. But eating would have to wait.

'I told you she was going to be a partner in her new boyfriend's restaurant,' she said as they sat down. 'Well, reading between the lines, it sounds as if she'll be bankrolling the whole thing, including the house he's having built, which he's promised to put in their joint names. I should be happy for her, but she'll be using all the compensation she got when her husband was killed ...'

Wesley experienced a sudden stab of anxiety as he took

both her hands in his. The memory of his meeting with Michelle Williams was at the forefront of his mind, but he didn't want to add to Pam's worry without proof.

She was silent for a few seconds, searching for the words to explain. 'I think she's so grateful to find someone after the dreadful time she had that she isn't thinking straight. She seems besotted, like a love-struck teenager.'

'Have you told her you're worried?'

'I told her to be careful and give it time, but I don't think she'll take any notice. He's promised to pay every penny back, but ... He sounds very ... persuasive.' She sighed. 'She's consulted an independent financial adviser, so it's probably fine and I'm imagining problems where they don't exist.' She hesitated. 'Is there any way you can check up on him at work, just to make sure he's genuine?'

'It's against the rules to look someone up on the PNC for personal reasons.'

'But it wouldn't do any harm, would it? I'm very fond of Jan.'

'You don't have any real evidence that he's not on the level, do you?'

'No, but ... '

'Well then. Look, why don't you invite them both round for dinner at the weekend, then we can judge for ourselves.'

'She says he's shy about meeting new people.'

'Especially new people who happen to be detective inspectors?'

'Oh no. She says he's like that with everyone.'

'Would you say he was trying to isolate her from her friends and family?'

Pam considered the question for a few moments. 'Now that you mention it, he's told her he doesn't like socialising because he wants to keep her all to himself. She takes it as a sign that he loves her. And apparently he's been so busy that he hasn't had time to meet her family.'

Wesley didn't like what he was hearing. 'That doesn't sound good. There are a lot of controlling men out there; men who are only too happy to make use of their partners' money. If Jan's fallen prey to one of them, we need to do everything in our power to make her see sense.'

'That might be easier said than done. Why won't you look him up on the police computer?'

Wesley could hear the accusation in her voice. 'OK, I'll have a word with Gerry. Mind you, if he's using a false name, it might not be any use.'

Pam looked worried as the full implications of Wesley's words sank in. 'You think he might be?'

He was tempted to tell her about the man they suspected Susan Brown had been searching for, but thought better of it. He didn't want Pam to panic, because there was every chance he was wrong and Jan's new boyfriend was exactly what he claimed to be. There was only one thing for it – he needed to meet the man for himself. But if his fears turned out to be justified, he had to tread carefully if he wasn't to scare the man off – or make an enemy of Jan if he was wrong.

'What's for dinner?' he asked.

Pam took his hand and led him to the kitchen. She sat down while Wesley took the lasagne she'd made out of the oven. The kids had already eaten and were in their rooms doing homework.

'Jan says he wants her to give up work and help him run the restaurant,' said Pam after she'd taken her first mouthful, unable to let the subject drop. 'Even her mother hasn't met him. She keeps coming up with more and more excuses for him.'

The warning bells that had been sounding inside Wesley's head were now almost deafening. Should he have made the connection before? But perhaps when it was close to home, it was harder to face up to something so unpleasant – and potentially dangerous.

'Wes, do you think he might be a con man?'

Wesley froze, his fork halfway to his mouth. Now that she'd asked the direct question, he felt he couldn't lie to her. 'I don't know,' he said. 'But I think it's possible.'

Neil and his team made an early start the next morning. He ignored the yawning students and pulled the tarpaulin off the trench. The corner of the mosaic had already been revealed. Today they'd work on uncovering the rest, and he found it hard to conceal his excitement. According to the farmer, there'd been no modern ploughing in that particular field, which meant there was a chance that the mosaic hadn't been damaged. After almost two millennia, this was by no means certain, but he was keeping his fingers crossed. And if his luck was in, this could be one of the most important finds of his career.

He worked quietly, aware of the expectant hush around him. There was a lot riding on this.

Wesley drove straight to the incident room first thing the next morning. Brunning was still the best suspect they had for Susan Brown's murder, his motive being that she might have stumbled upon his drug-dealing activities. Wesley, however, wasn't convinced they'd got the right man – and neither, he suspected, was Gerry.

Rachel was already at her desk, even though the boss had told her to come in a bit later if she wanted. Sometimes her stubbornness worried him, but if he told her that, he knew what her reaction would be. She looked up when he approached.

'Rach, can you do me a favour. Can you find out whether any local builders are working on a new home in Neston for a client called Callum White. I wouldn't ask if it wasn't important.'

'No problem.'

'And while you're at it, can you find out whether Callum White has applied to open a restaurant in Neston.'

'Will do. Any particular reason?'

'I'll explain later.' He left her to it and joined Gerry, who was on the phone, rolling his eyes and occasionally holding the receiver away from his ear. Wesley suspected it was the chief superintendent giving him grief about the investigation budget. He took a seat by the desk and waited for the conversation to finish.

Gerry ended the call and put his head in his hands. 'She wants to know why we haven't charged Brunning with Susan's murder. I told her that it was early days and we were pursuing other lines of enquiry, but she wants it wrapped up and presented in a neat little parcel for the CPS. I think I've managed to stop her breathing down our necks for the time being – told her we were still gathering evidence. Said if we were going to charge him, we'll have to make it stick in a court of law.'

Wesley decided that the time was right to share the suspicions that were building in his mind. 'You agree that there's definitely a pattern to the cases in Susan's incident room?'

'Looks like it.'

'I hope I'm wrong, but I think one of Pam's colleagues might be in danger.'

Gerry sat forward. Wesley had his full attention. 'Go on.'

Wesley explained his fears. The fact that Jan was a widow who'd received generous compensation and had few relatives in the area. The new partner she'd met online who seemed to be doing his best to isolate her from her social network. Now that he'd put it into words, her profile did sound remarkably like the others. Too similar for comfort.

'Is this Jan at work today? Do you think we should have a word with her?'

'Pam's tried to talk to her, and so have some of her other colleagues, but it's no use. She seems to be infatuated with this man, and at the moment he can do no wrong.'

'What's his name and where does he live?'

'His name's Callum White, and he has a flat in that new warehouse conversion overlooking the river in Neston. According to Jan, he's renting it while he has a house built on the edge of town. He's taken her to see the building site, which seems to have convinced her that he's a well-off businessman, and he's persuaded her to invest in a restaurant he's opening. He also has a boat moored in Neston near the bridge. John Pritchard had a boat.'

'So do lots of people round here, Wes. Including me. Look, let's look him up on the PNC. I think it's justified.'

Wesley did as Gerry suggested, but he couldn't find anybody of that name or age with a criminal record.

'Callum White could be an alias,' he said, voicing his fears.

'Mm,' said Gerry. 'If he is our ghost, he always chooses fairly common names.'

'Exactly what I was thinking. Which makes it harder for

us to trace him or match him with any related incidents in the past.' Wesley paused, looking Gerry in the eye. 'Do you think we're on the right track?'

'What we need is evidence. I'm waiting for the results of the DNA test on that bloodstain on the boat to come in.'

'Could Drusilla Kramer be another victim?'

'There's a chance Susan told her something about our man that she failed to share with us, so she had to be silenced.'

'Strange that she lied about her job. And when I asked Trish to check her out, she couldn't find anyone of that name who's the right age.'

'She might have changed her name because she's trying to get away from someone.'

'Like a controlling partner?'

'It's possible Drusilla was a victim of the man connected with the missing women too. And he might have caught up with her.'

'Surely she would have told us. We were hardly likely to betray her confidence. Unless she had reasons of her own not to trust us.'

Gerry looked sceptical and checked the time. They were due to speak to Calvin Brunning again. He'd been up before the magistrate that morning and had been remanded in custody, so at least they knew where he was. In the meantime, other matters had to take priority.

When Wesley returned to his desk, he found an email from Simone Pritchard's former work colleague, Andy, waiting for him.

Since we spoke yesterday, I've been going through stuff on my computer. I delete a lot of the photos I take, but I kept this one for some reason. It was taken just before I moved to Bath. I met Simone in a market and I wanted a picture of her – we'd been good friends, you see. I thought she was on her own, but a minute later, her bloke turned up and took her arm. He said they were late for something and almost dragged her away. What he didn't realise was that I'd taken the picture when he was approaching, so he's there in the background. I'm attaching it. Hope it helps.

Wesley clicked on Andy's attachment and sat staring at the image of a smiling Simone for a few seconds. Sure enough, there was a man behind her. And from his expression, he didn't look pleased about the attention his wife was getting.

He called Gerry over, barely able to keep the excitement out of his voice. He saw some of the team looking up from their keyboards as though they realised something was happening.

'Is that him?' said Gerry as he leaned over to get a good view of Wesley's screen.

'He fits the description Michelle gave us. I'll forward this to Whitby so they can send someone round to Avril's mother and ask her if this is Ian Willis.'

'Absolutely, Wes. Go for it.'

After Wesley had sent the photo to Whitby, he also forwarded it to Pam, along with a short explanation. He knew she'd be teaching so it might be a while before she saw it. But surely she'd check her messages in the morning break. Then it would be up to her.

Rachel waved to him, signalling that she had news.

'I called round all the local builders as you asked. There's only one large new house being built on the outskirts of

Neston at the moment, and the builder I spoke to thinks the client is from London; a lawyer who's retiring to the area. He told me the architect is Matt Harrod.'

'Small world. Can you call Mr Harrod and ask him the name of his client? I want to be absolutely sure we're on the right track.'

She made the call, but Harrod didn't answer, so she left a message for him to call her back as soon as possible.

'I made enquiries about the restaurant too,' she continued once she'd put the phone down. 'There's only one empty restaurant in Neston, and that's just been acquired by an Italian chef called Mr Bellini. There's no record of anyone called Callum White making any planning or licensing applications.'

'Thanks,' said Wesley, but before he could say any more, his phone rang. It was the lab.

39

Gerry received the news with a triumphant smile, although Wesley wasn't sure that a smile was appropriate. The results from the lab confirmed the alarming theory that had been forming in his mind. They were dealing with a calculating monster who preyed on the vulnerable. And once he'd heard from Pam, they'd know whether their quarry was about to strike again.

'So the blood on that boat definitely belongs to Simone Pritchard?' said the DCI.

'According to the lab, there's a match. And that boat used to belong to the man who called himself John Pritchard.'

'*Devil's Serpent*. It's an appropriate name. Can't say I blame the retired accountant for changing it. I'll get on to Les at the boatyard and tell him the yacht's needed as evidence so not to touch it.'

An hour later Wesley received more news. 'I've just heard from Whitby,' he told Gerry. 'Avril's mother has identified the picture. She says his hair's completely different, but she's sure it's Ian Willis. Which means . . . '

'He changes his identity and appearance each time he strikes, and chooses different parts of the country. Then he vanishes without trace with his victim's money. Call your Pam and ask her if she's seen the picture yet.'

Wesley consulted his watch. 'She'll be teaching at the moment – keeping a classful of ten-year-olds occupied. I just hope she has her phone switched on.'

He tried her mobile, and after a short conversation he turned to Gerry, his face serious. 'Jan's not in today. She called in sick. But Pam's seen the man pick her up from work a couple of times, and she thinks it could be him.'

'I'll send someone to Jan's address. We need to make sure she's safe. If she's not there, we'll check out his flat in Neston.'

Wesley thought for a moment. 'When Rachel and I spoke to Matt Harrod, he mentioned that there'd been a break-in at one of those flats. I looked it up and it was never reported to the police. Could Susan have broken in while she was staying at Matt's to look for evidence?'

'I wouldn't rule it out,' said Gerry. 'She was living nearby, so if she spotted the man she knew as Ian Willis, she might have tried her luck.'

'Pam says there was nothing remarkable about Jan's boyfriend's appearance. It's so easy for someone to alter their identity with a change of hair colour and style and a pair of glasses. He's not so much a ghost as a chameleon . . . and now he's using the name Callum White.'

Neil was in a state of excitement as he watched his colleagues scraping away the soil – very carefully, because they didn't want to damage what lay beneath. They worked silently, as though they knew that they were uncovering something momentous. Perhaps it was because Neil had told them earlier, rather dramatically, that they were changing history.

It was definitely a snake – a large reptile slithering across the floor of the room. The frieze around the edge of the mosaic was geometric, but now that at least half the chamber had been excavated, the serpent dominated it with its writhing body and flashing tongue; a huge creature skilfully depicted by the Roman artist who'd created it.

'Wonder if this is what gave rise to that legend about Serpent's Point,' said one of the PhD students, an earnest young woman in black-framed glasses. 'Perhaps there was some distant folk memory of what used to be in the field, and that's how it started.'

Neil suspected she could be right, and his mind wandered to the journals he'd found in the attic. The latest one he'd read hinted at a great discovery, and he resolved to continue ploughing through them tonight. Providing he wasn't distracted by an evening at the Seashell again.

The diggers worked on, revealing more of the snake's sinuous body, while Neil watched, frustrated that his injuries still prevented him from grabbing his kneeling mat and lending a hand. But at least he was able to answer his phone as soon as it rang.

The call was from a bone specialist who owed him a favour, and he felt a thrill of triumph when she confirmed that his suspicions were correct. The bones in the tea chest weren't in great condition, but she reckoned they were ancient; possibly Roman like the site. As for the cause of death, it was impossible to say. That would have to remain a mystery.

Wesley's heart sank when he heard the news that Jan's neighbour had seen her going off in a car with her boyfriend first thing that morning. The surprised neighbour was shown the photograph of the man they were after. She studied it carefully before saying that it could be the same man, although his hair was different.

Wesley and Gerry drove straight to the warehouse flats in Neston. They hadn't had time to organise a search warrant for the premises, but they had good reason to suspect that delay might result in the possible destruction of evidence – or even in someone's life being placed in danger.

Rachel had come with them, and she'd been given the job of interviewing the people in the neighbouring flats. Gerry wouldn't risk her getting closer to the action in case the man they were looking for presented a danger. He didn't want it on his conscience if she or her baby came to any harm.

It wasn't hard to find out which flat was Callum White's, but first of all they had to gain entry, which Gerry did neatly with the set of skeleton keys he claimed had been a present from a burglar he'd once arrested. Once the front door was open and the uniforms with them had ensured the place was empty, Gerry made a call ordering all patrols to be on the lookout for their man, then they began to go through the rooms looking for any clue to the occupant's whereabouts.

They began in the two bedrooms, finding a passport and driving licence in the name of Callum White. Gerry opened the wardrobe in the master bedroom, swishing hangers aside noisily, while Wesley searched the living room. He spotted a framed photograph of Jan on the sideboard and picked it up to examine it. In it, she was looking at their man adoringly, but he was turning away from her so that his face was in shadow. Wesley realised that it had been taken on a boat; you could just see a rail between the subjects and the background, which he recognised as the waterfront in Neston. He dropped the photo into an evidence bag, remembering the boat Jan had spoken of so proudly to her colleagues.

'Wes. Look what I've found.' Gerry's shout sounded more like a yell of joy.

Wesley bounded into the bedroom and found the DCI standing beside the open wardrobe. The clothes had been pushed to one side and he could see that a section had been removed from the back.

'Neat little hiding place. The goodies are on the bed.'

Wesley picked up the objects with his gloved hands. There were several passports, in various names. In each of the photographs the man looked different. In some he had a shaved head; in others his hair was long or short, fair or dark. But if you knew what you were looking for, he was still recognisable as the same man. Two of the passports were in the names of Ian Willis and John Pritchard. There were driving licences too. He must have had a source for the fake documents, but Wesley knew they weren't hard to obtain if you knew the right people. He bagged everything up carefully, proof that they had their man.

'We haven't found anything to link him with Drusilla Kramer yet.' Gerry sounded disappointed.

'It looks like Susan was on to him, though. She'd chased him round the country, looking for similar cases on the internet and following leads, and Michelle Williams's information about the boat he owned on the River Trad brought her down here. That was why she asked Les about the *Devil's Serpent*. Our man must have realised she'd tracked him down, so he had to get rid of her – and if she'd confided in Drusilla, she had to be dealt with too.' Wesley wasn't hopeful of finding Drusilla alive. But there might still be time to save Jan.

His phone rang, but when he saw the caller was Neil, he didn't answer. If he'd unearthed some amazing archaeological discovery, it would have to wait.

He heard a voice in the hallway calling his name. Rachel had just been admitted by the uniformed officer guarding the door, and she looked as though she had something important to say.

'I've spoken to the neighbour in the next-door flat. He saw Callum go out this morning too, and says he was carrying a rucksack and was dressed in what he described as sailing clothes. He confirmed that he's got a boat moored on the river, near the bridge. He also recognised a photo of Jan – said she was with him.'

Wesley and Gerry looked at each other. 'We'd better get down to the river, then.'

40

Gerry rushed from boat to boat with Wesley following closely behind, but there was no sign of Jan or the man they were after. However, when Wesley described them to a pair of middle-aged holidaymakers enjoying a gin and tonic on the deck of one of the nearby craft, they pointed to an empty mooring a couple of boats away. A boat called *Snake's Revenge* was usually moored there, they said, but she'd sailed off a couple of hours ago with a man and a dark-haired woman aboard. Wesley had the photograph from Callum White's passport on his phone, and when he showed it to them, they were sure it was the same man.

He didn't have to ask which direction the boat had sailed. The Trad was only navigable up to Neston, which meant it had to be heading downstream towards Tradmouth and the sea.

Gerry, a keen sailor, called the harbourmaster, who had responsibility for the river. Wesley listened to the two men chatting like old friends, Gerry only coming to the point once the usual pleasantries had been exchanged. When the conversation ended, he had a satisfied grin on his face.

'George is keeping a lookout, and the police launch is on standby along with the police helicopter. The slippery bugger can't get away unless he's got a miniature sub-marine, so I say we head downstream in the car and wait for him.'

The message from the river patrol came through as they were driving along a narrow lane near the village of Derenham, halfway between Neston and Tradmouth. *Snake's Revenge* had just moored up in the river on the Tradmouth side of the long pontoon used by the Derenham ferry. Did DCI Heffernan want the police launch to appre-hend those on board?

Derenham was packed with tourists enjoying the sunshine, but Wesley managed to find a parking space. Both men rushed down to the river, watched with interest by the drinkers occupying the picnic tables outside the waterfront pub. They ran down the pontoon, where small tethered boats bobbed gently in the water, the wooden boards echoing hollowly beneath their feet. Gerry spotted the police launch first and shielded his eyes to scan the river for *Snake's Revenge*. There was no sign of her, so he called the launch and it headed for the pontoon to pick them up.

'She's moored up half a mile downstream, sir,' said the young constable who helped them aboard. 'We've been keeping an eye on her from a distance like you said, but there's no activity aboard.' He passed both men a life jacket. Health and safety.

'We have reason to believe there's a woman on board whose life could be in danger, so let's not waste any more time,' said Gerry.

As the launch skimmed over the water, Wesley clung tightly to the side and took deep breaths. Although he didn't want to admit it, he was already feeling queasy.

309

'There she is,' the constable said, pointing at a scruffy craft moored ahead. *Snake's Revenge* was a converted fishing boat and badly in need of maintenance by the look of it. She was hardly an elegant vessel, but Gerry told Wesley that she was larger than *Duncountin*, and the accommodation below would be a lot more spacious.

'Do we board her, sir?' the constable asked.

Gerry glanced at Wesley before nodding in reply.

Wesley watched as officers swarmed aboard, reminded of pirate films he'd seen as a child. But on this occasion no cutlasses were clenched between teeth; there were just shouted warnings as the team went about their well-rehearsed business. He was impatient to know what was happening, but he knew that if he tried to ascend that ladder himself, he'd probably end up in the river.

It seemed an age before he saw the man who was calling himself Callum White emerging from the cabin, hand-cuffed and escorted by a burly sergeant from the river patrol. He held his breath, leaning on the rail of the police launch as he waited for Jan to appear. He expected to see her in the care of one of the officers, puzzled by what was happening and wrapped in a comforting blanket as her ordeal came to an end.

At last a woman appeared on deck, head bowed. But he was astonished to see that it wasn't Jan. He recognised Drusilla Kramer at once and when she looked up for a brief moment, he saw a flash of defiance in her eyes.

Officers from the river patrol took charge of the suspect's vessel and sailed her into Tradmouth, where they moored her well away from the town's jetties, in a secluded area near where the naval college kept their training craft. On Gerry's orders, *Snake's Revenge* was to be examined thoroughly by crime-scene investigators. They were to miss nothing.

Wesley stepped ashore, feeling unsteady after the short voyage. The first thing he did was call Rachel. He thought about contacting Pam, but he had no good news to give her, because there was no sign of Jan. Rachel told him that the search of White's Neston flat had turned up nothing of interest apart from the false documents and a few sets of keys, which didn't fit any of the locks on the premises. Wesley told her to hurry back; he wanted her to help him interview Drusilla Kramer.

He and Gerry weren't sure whether to treat Drusilla as a victim or a suspect, so they decided to err on the side of caution. The last thing they wanted was to be accused of bullying a vulnerable woman who'd just escaped a terrifying ordeal. On the other hand, her reaction when the police arrived didn't quite ring true.

She was taken to the interview room on the ground floor of Tradmouth police station, the room reserved for witnesses and victims. It had tea-making equipment and comfortable chairs, designed to put people unused to police stations at their ease. It wasn't long before Rachel and Wesley joined her. Gerry and DC Paul Johnson were dealing with White – if that was indeed his real name. The false documents were proof that he'd used many identities over the past few years.

Rachel sat down while Wesley made them all a cup of tea, in proper china mugs rather than the flimsy plastic rubbish from the machine in the corridor. There was a discreet machine in the room to record the interview, along with CCTV, which Wesley activated before putting the mugs on the coffee table.

'Do you feel up to telling us what happened, Drusilla?' Rachel said gently.

'I met Callum in a bar and we decided to spend a few days together on his boat. That's all.'

'People have been looking for you. We found your dog wandering in the park opposite your flat.'

'He ran off and I couldn't find him.' When she didn't ask after the animal, Wesley's unease grew. The first time he'd met this woman, she'd seemed genuine: Susan's concerned friend, shocked at her murder. But there was something different about her now, a calculating hardness, as though a mask had slipped to reveal the true woman beneath.

'You lied about your job. You're not a nurse. The hospital's never heard of you.'

'I didn't lie. I said I used to be a nurse. You must have misunderstood.' She paused. 'I'm entitled to a solicitor, aren't I?'

'We assumed you were a victim of abduction so thought you wouldn't need one. But we'll get you one if you like.'

'I would like.'

Wesley caught Rachel's eye. Drusilla wasn't behaving like a victim rescued from a ruthless abductor, and he was starting to suspect that she and Callum White were in it together – whatever it was.

'Where's Jan Bennett?' he asked.

'Who?' Drusilla sounded puzzled, but there was an almost imperceptible flash in her eyes that told Wesley it was an act.

'Let's talk about Susan Brown, the woman you claimed was your friend. Did Callum ask you to befriend her to find out how much she knew?'

'What makes you think that?'

'It was a set-up, wasn't it? Callum saw Susan, and recognised her as Avril Willis's friend. There she was, hundreds of miles from home, haunting him like an avenging angel, and he realised his past had caught up with him. I think he asked you to find out what she was up to, and through you, he knew that she'd moved out to Serpent's Point. You kept track of her for him and he decided to get rid of his problem permanently.'

Drusilla appeared to squirm in her seat. 'No comment.'

'You pretended to be Susan's friend, but you betrayed her,' said Rachel. 'Were you there when Callum killed her?'

She shook her head.

'Where's Jan Bennett?'

'I'm not saying any more till I get that solicitor.'

Wesley left her alone with Rachel and made his way upstairs to the CID office to see whether the team searching *Snake's Revenge* had any fresh information.

They hadn't found a reddish-brown scarf on board, neither had one been found in Drusilla's flat, which was disappointing, because finding the murder weapon would have clinched it. The other news they had was equally bad, but in a different way. A phone had been found aboard the boat. And that phone was registered to Jan Bennett.

From the journal of Dr Aldus Claye

June 1921

She is out there with him now and they are whispering together. I can see them from the window of my bedroom, and as I watch them, I find it impossible to take my eyes off them.

Then I see them kiss. She is shameless, and it is as though they have no fear of discovery. I must deal with this and claim her back, for I know that he will take her from me if he can.

Dark thoughts flash through my head. Do I add poison to his food at dinner? Do I arrange some accident at the dig? And what of her, my unfaithful wife, my betrayer? Do I let her live, or should she perish with her lover?

But if I kill her, it will not be a triumph for me. I will not have won. Better that she endures a long and loveless life as my companion. That will be her fitting punishment.

Tomorrow I will tell my diggers that their help is no longer needed. On my orders they will cover the site, and I will swear them to secrecy so nobody will ever know about the villa and its serpent. When they have finished, the soil will be freshly turned and thus it will be easy for one man unused to manual work to dig a grave.

How I wish that Professor Fredericks had never mentioned the name Fidelio Phipps.

41

Gerry and Paul Johnson had been interviewing their suspect in the most oppressive interview room available. He'd summoned a solicitor in an expensive suit, who sat beside his client, perched on the edge of his chair, ready to jump in if Gerry overstepped the legal mark.

The suspect had said nothing. He hadn't even given away his real name – because they were as sure as they could be that it wasn't Callum White. His fingerprints and DNA had been taken, and they hoped a match would soon be found.

The words 'no comment' were sounding to Gerry like a broken record, so he left the interview room and stood in the corridor for a while, leaning against the wall, deep in thought, wondering how Wesley and Rachel were faring with Drusilla Kramer. After a few moments, he received the news that the search team had found Jan's phone aboard *Snake's Revenge*. He needed something to nail their suspect, and this seemed like a glimmer of hope in the darkness. He went back into the interview room and sat down.

'When did you last see Jan Bennett?'

'I've already told you.' The suspect sounded exasperated at having to repeat himself. 'I gave her a lift into Neston this morning. I parked at my flat, then we went our separate ways. I arranged to meet up with her later.'

The answer sounded so convincing that Gerry almost began to believe it himself. But plausibility was the man's special talent. A talent that had proved deadly for some.

'How do you explain the fact that Jan's phone has been found on your boat?' he asked.

The man didn't flinch. 'I've never denied knowing Jan. She's been aboard my boat a few times. She must have left it there.'

'People usually panic if they lose their phone. She hasn't reported it to anyone. I wonder why.'

'Can't help you, I'm afraid.' The man looked smug, and Gerry, not normally a violent man, suddenly longed to punch his blandly good-looking face. A chameleon's face, with no particular distinguishing features.

'Where is Jan Bennett?'

'How should I know? I don't keep tabs on her. She's a free woman.'

'What's your relationship with Drusilla Kramer?'

'We're friends. She's been spending a few days on my boat, that's all.' He looked Gerry in the eye, deliberately ignoring Paul, who was sitting silently next to the DCI. 'We're all men of the world, Chief Inspector. Jan doesn't know that I see Drusilla from time to time, and I'd be grateful if you didn't mention it. Jan's a lovely lady, but she's the possessive type, if you know what I mean.'

'Ever been to Tewkesbury?'

'Where's that?' he asked innocently.

'Or Whitby?'

'What is this? A travel quiz?' he said with a smirk.

'You used to own a yacht called *Devil's Serpent*.'

'Did I? Can't remember.'

'Traces of blood were found aboard, and they're a match to the DNA of Simone Pritchard. You'll remember Simone. You were married to her.'

For the first time, the suspect showed a momentary flicker of alarm. Then he rearranged his features into an impassive mask. 'No comment. I'm not saying any more.'

Gerry bit back the words that were forming in his brain. He'd had enough, so he terminated the interview, hoping Wesley and Rachel had done better with Drusilla. They needed more.

On Wesley's suggestion, they'd requested access to Jan's bank records. They needed to know whether she'd transferred the money she'd told Pam about: the loan for the restaurant that didn't exist. An hour later, they knew the worst. Jan Bennett had transferred a hundred and fifty thousand pounds from her account. Questions had been asked by her bank, but she'd convinced the staff that it was needed to set up a restaurant. Her story was plausible, so the money had left her account. And nobody had seen her since.

It looked bad. Wesley knew their priority had to be finding her before she came to any harm – if they weren't already too late.

The results had come back for the suspect's prints and DNA. A match had been found to a Terry MacCaa, who had a criminal record for fraud and deception. The last crime he was arrested for was committed ten years ago, in the north-east; after that, he'd vanished into thin air. Now it seemed he'd reappeared.

'So we know his real name at last – Terrence John

MacCaa, known as Terry,' said Wesley. 'What about the woman?'

'You think she's involved?'

'I strongly suspect she is.'

'Then let's arrest her, then we can compare her prints and DNA with the database.' Gerry grinned. 'I think we have grounds, don't you?'

'Anything's worth a try. And I want someone to go over his flat in Neston more thoroughly. There could be something there to tell us what he's done with Jan.'

'Make the call, Wes.'

Wesley took out his phone and gave the order.

Crispin Joss was having a hissy fit, shouting so loudly that Neil felt uncomfortable as he crept along the hallway of Serpent's Point in search of Grey Grover. Whoever was on the receiving end of the tongue-lashing was to be pitied. Surely there were rules against speaking to someone like that at work. But things might be different in the film industry. It wasn't something he'd fancy finding out.

He'd been so preoccupied with the exciting discoveries they'd made during the excavation, he'd only finished reading the journals the previous night, and now he was sure he knew who the bones lying in the mortuary at Tradmouth Hospital belonged to. Dr Aldus Claye had done away with his rival in love, Fidelio Phipps, probably hitting him with one of the mattocks they'd used during the excavation. He'd watched Phipps becoming closer to his young wife, Clarabel, and disposed of the problem by burying him in the place he'd been excavating, the freshly dug soil making it easy to create a grave for his victim. Mystery solved. Of course this meant Claye was denied his moment of academic glory, because he had to keep the discovery of the Roman villa to himself. That must have been painful for him – a sort of punishment.

He opened the door to the room that had once served as a library and found it empty. He'd intended to tell Grover that he'd come to look through the trunk again to see whether the other papers in there contained any further information about the 1921 excavation. However, he knew Grover wouldn't mind, so he decided to help himself.

By the time he'd crept up the stairs, Joss had finished his tirade. When he reached the landing, he heard the drawing room door burst open and the sulky, handsome young man who'd just stormed out shout the words 'I quit!'

Neil couldn't say he blamed him.

When Wesley's phone rang, he experienced a momentary thrill of hope that Jan had been found alive and well.

But the call was from the search team he'd sent to the Neston flat. The officer on the other end of the line said he didn't know if it was important, but they'd found an Ordnance Survey map of Dartmoor. 'There's something marked on it, sir. Someone's drawn a ring round a feature called "burial chamber". I do a lot of walking, and there are several abandoned mines around that particular spot. Do you think ...?'

'It's worth looking. Do you have a map of where these mines are?'

'Some of them are very old and aren't recorded, but I've got a friend in a local potholing club who knows a lot about them. The ringed area on the map's quite small, so if it's accurate ...'

Gerry had gone off to see the chief super on the top

floor, so Wesley had to make the decision alone. It might increase the budget, but a woman's life was at stake.

'You sound as though you know the area. Can you take some officers up there as soon as possible to make a search. Take your potholing friend with you if necessary. We need to find Jan Bennett.'

Once he'd set the search in motion, he began to have doubts. What if Terry MacCaa had marked that particular spot for another reason? But when Gerry got back and they returned to the interview room, he asked MacCaa about the map and saw the colour drain from the suspect's face. He'd got it right.

Two hours later, the officer he'd spoken to called to say they'd found something in an abandoned mine. But it wasn't Jan Bennett.

42

Human remains. Almost certainly female. Shreds of clothing still clung to the bones, and the gold locket resting on the clavicle was engraved with the name 'Fiona'. A handbag had been found next to the bones; it contained a staff pass for a university up in Lancashire. The name on the pass was Fiona Crediton, and there was a photo of a plump, dark-haired woman, probably in her thirties.

The officer's potholing friend had come across the skeleton about twenty yards into a disused and isolated Dartmoor mine. Part of the iron gate at the mine's entrance had rusted away, making it possible to gain access; a potential health-and-safety nightmare if anyone wandered in there by accident. Its wild and lonely location, however, made it the ideal place to conceal a body.

Wesley's heart sank at the news. Someone would have to break the news to Fiona Crediton's family up north. In the meantime, they needed to find out her story. It wasn't long before they learned that Fiona had gone missing six years previously. Her flatmate had reported it to the police, saying that Fiona had recently become involved with a man called Paul Fletcher. It was a name Wesley recognised from one of the fake passports found in the Neston flat.

According to the flatmate, Fiona hadn't had much luck attracting boyfriends, but she'd been swept off her feet by Fletcher and mentioned going abroad with him. She'd inherited a great deal of money from her late grandfather, and often talked about travelling.

The police had recorded the flatmate's concerns but hadn't treated the matter with much urgency because of Fiona's ambitions to travel. Fiona's mother told them that she wasn't close to her daughter, but she was still hurt that she had gone off without letting her know. Half-hearted enquiries were made, but there was no real evidence that she had come to any harm. Until now.

Gerry put a hand on Wesley's shoulder. 'Now we've found those bones, he can't wriggle out of it. We've enough to charge him with murder.'

Wesley thought for a moment. 'Do you remember Simone Pritchard's sister saying that Simone had consulted a financial adviser? Pam told me that Jan had seen someone about investing in the fictitious restaurant. And what about that witness who said she'd seen Avril on the day MacCaa claimed she disappeared, giving him the perfect alibi – Mrs Pollard, the mortgage adviser? Could that have been Drusilla Kramer?'

Gerry's face lit up. 'If we find a match on the system for her prints and DNA, we might be able to nail her.'

'But we're no nearer finding Jan, and I can't help thinking . . . '

'What?'

'That she's lying at the bottom of the river somewhere. He's got his hands on her money, so she's no longer any use to him.'

'You know your trouble, Wes? You're a pessimist.'

'I'm a realist. MacCaa thinks nothing of killing.'

'True. Look what happened to Susan Brown.'

'Are we absolutely sure he killed her as well?'

'She was on to him so he had to get rid of her.' Gerry hesitated, his face suddenly solemn. 'We'd better get back to the interview room. With the map and the identification, we've got enough to charge him. And we arrest Drusilla on suspicion. Agreed?'

But before they reached their destination, Wesley received another call, this time from a member of the team carrying out a detailed search of the suspect's boat.

'I've found a key in the pocket of a coat hanging up below deck. It's got a label attached saying "Boathouse". Just thought you'd like to know.'

Neil stared at the letter and the press cutting, turning the possibilities over in his mind. Had the assumptions he'd made about the skeleton found in what they were starting to call 'the serpent chamber' been completely wrong?

He knew Wesley would be interested in this new development, so he tried his number. When Wes didn't answer, he called Dr Stamoran instead. He hoped he'd appreciate having an identity for the bones lying in his mortuary.

When Drusilla Kramer's prints and DNA were run through the system, they found she only had one conviction, and that was for drink-driving. A disappointed Gerry was about to dismiss this as irrelevant, until Wesley looked at the details more closely.

'Hang on, Gerry, check out the date of her offence – and the place.'

Gerry put on the reading glasses he'd reluctantly started

wearing and leaned over to get a better view of Wesley's computer screen.

'She was caught for being over the limit just outside Whitby the evening before Avril was reported missing. I'll send a photo up to Clough in Whitby.'

Twenty minutes later Clough emailed back. One of his officers had ID'ed Drusilla as the Mrs Pollard who gave Willis his alibi.

'She's been working with MacCaa all along,' said Wesley. 'If there's a chance she knows where Jan is, we need to pile the pressure on. Let's have another word.'

The Drusilla who was waiting for them – in the stark interview room this time – seemed harder and more calculating than the woman they had interviewed in her Morbay flat. Wesley had been worried when the dog, Sherlock, was found abandoned, but now her treatment of the animal didn't surprise him in the least. He'd been wrong about her – and he was annoyed with himself for not seeing the truth right away.

'You can't keep me here. You've no evidence against me.'

'You're being held on suspicion of conspiracy to defraud. And in relation to the murder of Susan Brown.'

She stood up, but the duty solicitor sitting beside her put a hand on her arm and told her to sit. 'I didn't have anything to do with what happened to Susan. It wasn't Callum and it certainly wasn't me.'

'His name's not Callum.'

'Of course it is,' she said with a hint of defiance.

'His real name's Terry MacCaa. How long have you known him?'

'A few months.'

'That's not true, is it? Susan Brown was on a mission to

find out what happened to her friend Avril Willis. Callum –
or should I say Terry – knew she was looking for him, and
that's why he got you to befriend her. We've seen the emails
you sent her. You bombarded her with links to missing persons cases to put her off the scent.'

She turned her head away.

'Either you killed Susan or he did.'

'He was with me on the morning Susan died.' She looked
desperate. The kind of desperation that in Wesley's experience made suspects more ready to talk. They had to make
the most of it.

There was a knock on the door and Rob Carter came in.
He whispered something in Gerry's ear and placed a sheet
of paper in front of him before leaving the room, closing
the door quietly behind him.

'You say you've only known Callum a few months?' said
Gerry, pushing the paper over to Wesley.

'That's right.'

'We've found out you were stopped for drink-driving
in the Whitby area the day before Avril Willis was
reported missing.'

'So?'

'And you've been identified by Whitby police as the
apparently impartial witness who gave MacCaa his alibi
when Avril disappeared.'

'They must have made a mistake.'

Gerry was saving the best for last. 'According to records,
you married Terrence John MacCaa eight years ago, which
means that when he married Avril Marley and Simone
Williams, he committed bigamy. Admit it, Drusilla, you've
been in on this from the start.'

He caught Wesley's eye. It was up to him to carry on.

'Terry's plausible and charming. He searched for lonely women on dating sites, and once he'd found one who had money, he moved in. He controlled these women and separated them from their families and friends.' Wesley looked at the suspect with distaste. 'Choosing his targets must have taken a lot of homework; at a guess, this was your department – am I right?' He didn't wait for her reply. 'You were given a cameo role as a financial adviser to encourage his victims to part with their money. Then when the job was done, he disposed of them, putting it round that they'd walked out on him and chosen to disappear. We've found Fiona Crediton's body in a disused mine on Dartmoor, by the way, and we're hoping it'll provide forensic evidence. We also found a map in Terry's flat marked with the exact location of Fiona's last resting place.'

Drusilla's eyes widened a little, but she soon managed to hide her shock.

'Tell us about Fiona.'

'I can't. I don't know anything.'

'Very well, we'll leave that for the moment. Let's talk about Avril. Your careful plan went wrong four years ago when her body turned up,' he continued. 'But you had a stroke of luck when a serial killer called Warren Chips got the blame.'

Her eyes flickered, and Wesley knew he'd got it right.

'It was clever of you and Terry to move around the country. But your luck changed when Avril's alleged killer wrote to her mother from prison. Unluckily for you, Warren Chips decided to come clean on his deathbed. He claimed that he knew nothing about Avril's murder and that he'd confessed after pressure was put on him by detectives who were anxious to get the case off their books.' Wesley paused, looking her in the eye. 'We know Jan Bennett is Terry's latest target. Where is she?'

Gerry had been listening carefully, and now he broke his silence. 'You realise your husband's blaming you for everything, don't you? He says it was all your idea and he just went along with it. He says you killed Susan.'

Wesley knew this wasn't quite true, but he stayed silent. If they were to find Jan, they needed to use any means at their disposal.

'That's a lie. And it wasn't him either, because he was with me like I said. We were on the boat together.'

'We already know Terry duped and killed women for money. The only thing we don't know is how many victims there were. It's no use lying, Drusilla. It's over, so you might as well tell us.'

When she pressed her lips together and stayed silent, Wesley asked a question. 'Is Jan in the boathouse? We found the key.'

The shock on her face told him he'd hit the mark.

'Where is the boathouse, Drusilla? The jury will look more kindly on you if you co-operate.'

'And Terry's landed you right in it,' Gerry reminded her.

There was a long silence. She sat there with her head bowed and her shoulders slumped as though finally acknowledging defeat. Wesley and Gerry waited. This couldn't be rushed. If they said the wrong thing, she might decide to clam up.

Eventually she looked up, her eyes dry and her gaze blank. When she spoke, it was in a whisper, and they had to lean forward to hear. 'I swear I didn't know he was going to kill them. I thought he was just going to make off with their money. When he killed Avril, he told me it had been an accident; that they'd gone for a walk by the river and she started questioning him. He thought she'd rumbled him, and when she started shouting, he put his hand over her mouth to keep her quiet. When he saw she was dead, he put her body in the river, hoping it'd be carried away.'

'What about the others? Fiona Crediton was murdered six years ago. He was killing long before Avril.'

She didn't answer.

'And you kept quiet for him. You went along with it.'

'I was frightened of him because I knew what he was capable of. I tried to warn Sue off, but she saw herself as some sort of heroine on a quest to avenge her friend. I told her to forget it – to let it go. But she wouldn't listen. She was playing with fire.'

'So Terry got rid of her.'

'I'm not lying. He really was with me.' She buried her head in her hands, and Wesley wasn't sure whether her distress was genuine or just a good performance.

He tried again. 'If what you say is true and you're afraid of him, he's in custody now so he can't harm you. Tell us where Jan Bennett is. Please.'

She took a deep, shuddering breath. 'Terry rents a boathouse on the Derenham bank, about half a mile downstream from the village.'

A vision of a smiling Jan flashed through Wesley's mind; Jan as she'd been last time he saw her. 'Is she still alive?'

'She was when we left her. Terry said he'd deal with her later. He took her to the boathouse as a treat, saying they were going to have a romantic champagne tea there to celebrate signing the contract for the restaurant.' She took a deep breath. 'He put something in her champagne to knock her out. When she started feeling the effects, he told her he'd go and get help.'

'And once he was sure she was out cold, he was going to come back and strangle her? Then he'd take her out to sea to get rid of her body.'

Drusilla bowed her head, making no attempt to contradict what Wesley had said.

That was enough. Wesley leapt to his feet and rushed from the room with Gerry following breathlessly behind. The best way to access the boathouse was by water, and the fastest way was by police launch. Gerry made the call while they were hurrying out of the building. They were to meet the launch down by the jetty.

The boat was skimming over the churning water when Wesley's phone rang.

'I've found out who those bones belong to,' Neil began as soon as he answered. 'You're not going to believe it.'

'Sorry, Neil, this isn't a good time. I'll call you back later.'

'OK.' There was no mistaking the disappointment in Neil's voice. 'But I promise you, it's worth hearing,' he added, as though he was hoping his friend would change his mind. 'And I've been in touch with the museum in Exeter. They've got something in their store that might be connected to the dig. I'm going there to see it later.'

Wesley was intrigued, but duty won out over curiosity. His only concern at that moment was saving Jan's life, but at least Neil's call had taken his mind off his seasickness, something he'd always battled with. He saw Gerry watching him with a mixture of pity and amusement.

'We'll have to get you some sea legs, Wes.' Gerry shaded

his eyes from the sun as they shot past yacht-filled creeks and thickly wooded banks.

Soon the note of the engine changed and the boat began to slow as all eyes aboard scanned the Derenham bank.

'Something there, sir. Not easy to see with all the trees, but ...' The officer handed Gerry a pair of binoculars as the boat glided to a graceful halt.

'I can see a wooden boathouse by the water's edge. Can we move in closer?'

The officer shook his head. 'Too shallow. Have to use the dinghy.'

The prospect of stepping off the launch onto the small inflatable dinghy they were towing behind them didn't bother Gerry in the least. Wearing an orange life jacket that doubled his bulk, he moved swiftly, beckoning Wesley to follow. After ordering the officers aboard to stand by, he lowered himself into the dinghy, positioning himself by the outboard motor while Wesley was helped down, gritting his teeth and trying to hide his apprehension. Gerry started the engine and the little boat shot towards the shore. Wesley hoped they had the right place.

Gerry brought them expertly to the bank and Wesley helped him tie the dinghy to one of the surrounding trees. Once it was secure, they hurried towards the wooden boathouse. At the bottom was a shadowy archway to accommodate a boat, and above it an upper storey with neat blinds at the window. The bank behind sloped upwards, and Wesley guessed the room would be accessed at the back. He was right. At the rear of the boathouse was a door, and he took out the key that had been found aboard the *Snake's Revenge*. As it turned smoothly, he felt nervous, dreading what they'd find in there. Drusilla had said Jan was still alive, but he wasn't sure whether to trust her.

Inside was a single white-painted room lit by the window at the river end. It was furnished with light wicker sofas and chairs with colourful throws, and rugs on the floor. A comfortable, holiday sort of place with a seaside theme. There was a bottle of champagne on the small coffee table, along with two glasses, one still half full, and an open picnic basket on the floor. The only sound he could hear as he began to walk slowly round the room was the lapping of the water outside.

When he neared the window, he drew level with a tall wicker chair, turned to overlook the river.

Jan was slumped against the cushions. And Wesley feared that they were too late.

43

When Wesley knelt to feel for a pulse, he could feel a weak fluttering. Jan was alive, but she needed help urgently. Gerry called the air ambulance and Wesley contacted the station. Could someone ask the suspects exactly what she had been given and let the hospital know in preparation for her arrival.

Wesley and Gerry stood on the narrow shingle beach revealed by the low tide, watching Jan being winched into the helicopter. Wesley was overwhelmed by a feeling of helplessness, but he told himself that she was now in good hands. There had to be hope.

'Let's get back and finish this,' said Gerry with cold determination in his voice, his tendency to find some humour in even the grimmest situation gone for the moment. 'I want those two locked up for a very long time.'

Wesley climbed back into the dinghy. It was time to return to Tradmouth, where their suspects were waiting for them in their respective interview rooms.

An hour later, Drusilla provided them with a full confession. Once she realised it was no use lying any more, she confirmed that they'd trawled through dating sites on the internet looking for suitable marks. Many times a promising lead turned out to be useless; if Terry met a woman without significant money of her own, or with too many friends and family who might ask awkward questions, she was discarded after the first date. Only a few cases were found to be suitable; they were the unlucky ones.

She admitted that six years ago, Fiona Crediton had been lured to Dartmoor with the promise of a luxury break in a spa hotel with her new boyfriend. Terry, using one of his aliases, had strangled her once he had his hands on her money and disposed of her body in the Dartmoor mine. Simone from Tewkesbury had travelled down to Tradmouth for a leisurely sailing weekend on the yacht Terry had owned at the time, *Devil's Serpent*. She had fought back when he'd tried to strangle her and he'd ended up using a knife from the boat's galley to kill her, severing an artery in the struggle. Once she was dead, her body had been weighted down and thrown overboard somewhere in the English Channel. There had been a terrible mess in the cabin, and when he'd returned to shore, Drusilla had helped him clear up the blood, an experience she'd never forget. They'd drugged Jan because the last thing they'd wanted was a repeat of that particular incident. It was easier to strangle an unconscious woman than one fighting for her life like a fury.

'What about Susan Brown?' Wesley asked. 'Did you know Terry was going to get rid of her?'

Drusilla shook her head. 'He didn't. I was telling the truth. He was with me all that morning. It must have been the man she mentioned – her stalker.'

'We've eliminated the man who was bothering her in Whitby from our enquiries.'

'She told me he was down here.'

'We've checked his movements, and he wasn't.'

'Perhaps she had two – one up there and one down here.' She shrugged. 'But one thing I do know – it wasn't Terry.'

Wesley wondered whether she was trying to muddy the waters. 'Do you or Terry own a red scarf?'

'No. Look, he might have killed the others, but not Sue. She must have been unlucky and met a maniac on that path. It's lonely and there are some weird people around.'

Terry MacCaa was still saying 'no comment' with monotonous regularity, but with Drusilla's confession, they had enough to charge both of them. Once they'd gathered the evidence, they could add Susan to the charge sheet at a later date. As they were leaving the interview room, Drusilla spoke again.

'The dog. Is he OK?' There was a softness in her question that hadn't been there before.

Wesley turned round. 'You abandoned him in that park. As if you care.'

'I was just asking.' She paused. 'Terry told me to get rid of him. Said the last thing we needed was a dog in tow. Er ... can you see if he's all right?'

Wesley didn't reply, but he made a mental note to call the dogs' home – just to check on Sherlock's progress. He was getting as soft as Gerry in his old age.

Neil's enthusiasm for his subject was infectious. And the assistant curator of the Roman Heritage Museum in Exeter, a young woman with a penchant for hair bands and voluminous floral dresses, was only too delighted to show him the storeroom where a number of the Roman tombstones found during various excavations in the city were held. The one that interested Neil had been found during a rescue dig back in the 1990s when some Victorian buildings had been bulldozed to make way for a new office block. When he'd mentioned Beria Vilbia to the assistant curator and told her about the curse, she'd said the name was familiar and there was a particular tombstone he might like to have a look at. As soon as he saw it, he felt like kissing her, but restrained himself. Instead he squatted down and began to translate the Latin.

I, MARCUS FLAVIUS LIVIUS, MERCHANT, DIED OF GRIEF WHEN MY BELOVED WIFE WAS CARRIED OFF BY ONE WHO COVETED HER GREATLY AND ENDED HER MORTAL LIFE WHEN HE COULD NOT POSSESS HER. BERIA VILBIA WAS A BRITON AND ONCE A SLAVE UNTIL I GRANTED HER LIBERTY AND BUILT A VILLA FOR HER IN THE LAND OF HER PEOPLE. SHE WAS A GOOD WOMAN WITH MANY DOMESTIC VIRTUES, AND HER FAITHFULNESS TO ME CAUSED HER DEATH. MAY HE WHO TOOK HER FROM ME BE CURSED OF THE GODS AND KNOW NO PEACE FOR HIS WICKEDNESS.

'Interesting, isn't it?' the assistant curator said. 'Tells quite a story. Like a melodrama or one of the more over-blown operas.' She smiled. Neil had little interest in opera, but he knew what she meant.

'I think I might have found Beria Vilbia in an old tea chest – or what was left of her.'

'A tea chest?' The young woman looked puzzled.

When he explained about his dig and the lead curse mentioning Beria Vilbia's name, he saw growing excitement in the assistant curator's eyes. 'That's amazing. What a subject for an exhibition. What do you think? Murder and passion at a newly discovered villa. Your dig could change history.'

'Or what we know about the Romans in Devon anyway. I'll bring the curse to show you.'

'Promise?'

'Promise.'

Before he set off back to Serpent's Point, Neil tried Wesley's number. But there was no answer. His loss.

Rachel felt uncharacteristically subdued. She'd been on the phone to Lancashire police about the discovery of Fiona Crediton's remains. They were going to send someone to break the news to the victim's mother.

The thought of the bereaved mother was upsetting her more than it normally would. Perhaps it was because she was about to become a mother herself, and now she could imagine what it would feel like if such a thing happened to the baby you'd loved, nurtured and watched grow to adulthood. Perhaps it was better not to think about it.

She was trying to find something to take her mind off it when Rob Carter hurried over with a triumphant look on his face.

'I've just heard from the boss. Jan Bennett's been found and we're charging Terry MacCaa and Drusilla Kramer with murder and conspiracy to defraud. Would you believe they're actually married – operated their scam together. Kramer cracked first. MacCaa is still no-commenting, but once he knows his missus has talked, it'll only be a matter of time.'

Rachel felt a little hurt that Wesley hadn't called to tell her the good news himself. She'd been waiting for Matt Harrod to return her call, but now the question she'd intended to ask him about his client seemed rather redundant.

'The only thing Kramer hasn't held her hand up to is Susan Brown's murder,' Rob continued. 'But the DCI says she's bound to tell the truth eventually.'

'She's come clean about the others?'

'Yes. But she swears they didn't kill Susan. Not that I believe her. She's lying through her teeth.'

'I wonder if Susan knew how much danger she was in. She probably thought that once she had enough evidence, she'd unmask the man she'd known as Ian Willis and that would be that.'

'She was a bit naïve, if you ask me.'

'Or single-minded. She wanted justice for her friend.'

Rob shrugged his shoulders and returned to his desk in the corner, while Rachel sat thinking. In her opinion, Susan's determination to get at the truth was admirable. She'd been like a bloodhound, tracking Avril's killer all over the country, following leads. It might have been obsessive, but sometimes obsession could be used for good. Her doggedness would have made her a good member of Gerry's team.

One of the DCs hurried up to Rachel's desk, interrupting her thoughts. Somebody wanted to speak to whoever was in charge. Said it might be important.

44

The young man was still in costume, a Regency character wandering into a church hall filled with police officers and computer equipment. But the leather jacket draped over his shoulders and the mobile phone in his hand spoiled the effect.

He had the appearance of an unnaturally beautiful schoolboy, with floppy hair framing the sort of face that wouldn't look out of place on a boy-band poster. Rachel's mother would have called him a heart-throb. But Rachel was immune to his charms. He introduced himself as Freddie Barlow, Georgina Unwin's co-star.

She asked how Georgina was and he said her condition was improving. Hopefully she'd be out of hospital in a few days' time.

'I've just finished filming my final scene, so I'm free of that bloody Crispin Joss at last,' said Freddie, self-consciously pushing back a strand of fair hair that had flopped over his face. 'I swear I'll never work with the man again. He's been an absolute nightmare.' He pressed his lips together. 'This film better kick-start my career. I don't want to have gone through all that for nothing.'

'I'm sure it'll work out fine.' Rachel knew nothing about

the film industry, but she thought she should say something reassuring. Freddie followed her to her desk and sat down as Rachel lowered herself into her chair. A kick from the baby distracted her for a second and she rested her hand on her bump. 'What can I do for you?' she asked, reaching for her notebook.

Freddie suddenly looked unsure of himself. 'I did mention it to Georgina, but she told me to forget it,' he said, as though he was trying to shift the blame.

'Why don't you tell me what it is?'

He said nothing for a while, and Rachel waited patiently.

When he eventually spoke, it was almost in a whisper, as though he was afraid Crispin Joss was hidden somewhere, eavesdropping on what he had to say. 'It's probably nothing, but it's been on my mind. On the morning that woman was killed on the coast path, I saw a man hanging round near the stables. I thought nothing of it at the time – didn't think it was important.'

At that moment, Wesley appeared in the church hall doorway and Rachel beckoned him over. Without a word, Wesley walked across and moved a chair from a nearby desk. Freddie gave him a wary look.

'Go on,' said Rachel. 'I'd like Inspector Peterson to hear this.'

As Freddie recited his story, he seemed to gain in confidence. 'I saw him there that morning around eight o'clock. I was on my way to shoot a scene, so I don't know what happened after that.'

Wesley caught Rachel's eye. 'Why didn't you mention this earlier?' he asked.

'I told Crispin, but he said to keep my mouth shut. He said they'd question me for hours and it would disrupt the whole filming schedule, so I did as I was told. To be honest, I agreed with him at the time because it didn't seem important. But now that I've finished filming my scenes, I'm not beholden to him any more, so I thought I'd come and tell you, just in case.' He suddenly frowned and looked at Wesley with pleading eyes. 'I won't get into trouble, will I?'

'What did this man look like?' Wesley said, wondering if they were about to hear a description of Terry MacCaa – or even Calvin Brunning.

He listened carefully as Freddie described the person he'd seen with remarkable accuracy. As luck would have it, the young actor was acutely observant, and Wesley couldn't help feeling a thrill of triumph.

'Would you like a cup of tea?' he asked. Freddie looked surprised by the question, but he said yes, and Wesley made for the little kitchen at the side of the church hall stage. Rachel followed. They needed to talk in private.

'It can't be him,' she said. 'Surely he would have mentioned it when we spoke to him.'

'We were distracted by Ebenezer Smith when we should have been looking closer to home. Drusilla said that Smith might not have been the only one who'd been bothering Susan, but I assumed she was trying to throw us off the scent. Maybe I was wrong.'

Wesley felt angry with himself for not carrying out checks on this individual before, but he'd misled them and they'd had no reason to suspect him at a time when they'd been pursuing far more promising leads. He asked Rachel to get someone to find out whether the man's car had been caught on any traffic cameras on the morning in question, then he filled the kettle and located the team's stash of tea bags, glad to have something to do while he waited for the information to come back.

Rachel returned after a few minutes. 'One of the DCs is taking Freddie's statement. He seems worried that he'll get into trouble for lying to us.'

'He didn't really lie – he just didn't tell us the whole story.'

'Susan certainly attracted the wrong sort of admirer,' said Rachel.

Wesley poured milk into the mugs of tea. 'She was an attractive woman. I don't mean just physically, but from what everyone who met her said, she had a sympathetic quality. If we'd had a chance to meet her, I think we would have liked her. Unfortunately, I think that might be why she died.'

Rachel gave a small nod and disappeared into the body of the incident room, leaving Wesley to finish making the tea.

Half an hour later, Gerry arrived just as Traffic came back with their answer. Their new suspect's car had been picked up on their cameras heading towards Bereton at 7.30 on the morning Susan Brown was strangled.

One patrol car followed Wesley and Gerry as they drove to Neston. Gerry didn't think it necessary to go in mob-handed, as he put it. They weren't bringing in a gang of armed robbers.

When they reached the house, Wesley knocked on the door. There was no answer, but the suspect's car was parked outside, so he probably hadn't gone far. It didn't take Gerry long to make the decision. He took his skeleton keys from his pocket and went to work. Wesley watched as he fiddled with the lock, and saw the look of satisfaction on his face when the door clicked open.

'After you, Wes.'

There was an uncharacteristic note of anxiety in the DCI's voice, and Wesley hesitated for a moment before entering the house. The silence seemed unnatural, heavy, as though somebody was watching from the shadows. He ignored the uncomfortable feeling and pressed on, opening the drawing room door first. The room was empty, and he saw that the photograph was still there; the one he'd assumed was the suspect with his late partner, Rory.

He walked over to the fireplace. When he studied the picture more closely, he noticed that even though the two men had their arms around one another's shoulders, their pose lacked the intimacy he would have expected of lovers. He saw a resemblance between the men too, and wondered if they could be brothers. There was no sign of the cat, Tacitus. But then cats tended to lead lives of their own.

The dining room was empty too, and Gerry muttered something about the bird having flown. The kitchen door was shut, and Wesley opened it and stepped into the room ahead of Gerry. When he stopped suddenly, the DCI almost cannoned into him.

The body was suspended from a hook in the ceiling that had once held a light fitting. Matt Harrod's eyes were closed, but his face was distorted with the agonies of a slow death. He had hanged himself.

'Looks like an admission of guilt, Wes. Better get Dr Stamoran over here pronto.'

Wesley turned away from the dangling body to make the call. He knew the sight would stay with him for a long time; it would be there when he woke up in the morning and it would still linger while he tried to relax into sleep. But this was something he couldn't share with Pam; she had enough worries of her own.

'Rachel rang him because she wanted the name of his client. She left a message to call her back, but he never did. Do you think he assumed we were on to him?'

Gerry sighed. 'Guilty conscience.' He looked around. 'Let's get this place searched.'

Wesley spotted an envelope lying on the worktop near the French windows leading out to the little courtyard garden. It was addressed to 'The Police' in a neat hand.

He picked it up with gloved hands. It was unsealed, so he slipped out its contents and began to read aloud while Gerry listened.

You'll be wondering what has driven me to such despair, why I've felt the need to end my life. When I lost my partner, Aurora – I always called her Rory – it felt like my life was over. She was everything to me, and we had five happy years together before she was taken from me in that terrible boating accident. I survived, along with my brother, but not a day has passed when I haven't wished I'd died with Rory.

After I lost her, I cut myself off from the world and thought I'd never find love again. Then came the job in Spain and my decision to hire someone to look after the house while I was away. This you know, of course, but I didn't tell you the whole truth. Susan stayed with me for a week before I left. I wanted her to familiarise herself with the house and Tacitus's little ways. My cat has been my only companion since I lost Rory, and he's very precious to me. Please ensure that he is well looked after.

So it was that I fell in love with Susan, but I knew she didn't share my feelings. She was on a mission, you see, although she would never tell me what that mission was – only that she was seeking justice for someone dear to her. She was single-minded and determined, but I nursed hopes that once her mysterious undertaking was complete, she'd consent to move in with me permanently. When she came here, it seemed like a miracle. She was so like Rory that she might have been her twin, and when she turned up at the house that first day, it was just as if my beloved had returned to me. Even when she left without giving me a forwarding address, and her phone number was always unavailable, I lived in hope that she might eventually return my feelings ... until the day I found out where she was and went to see her at Serpent's Point.

I told her again how I felt and begged her to come back to me, but she said she'd never thought of me in that way. I couldn't bear the thought of losing her; it would have been like losing Rory all over again. I pleaded with her, but she wouldn't be moved. She said she'd only come to Devon to get justice for her friend, and once she'd gathered enough evidence to give to the police, she would be returning to Yorkshire. I followed her on her walk in the hope that she'd change her mind, but when she saw me, she told me again that she had no feelings for me – and that if I kept stalking her, she'd tell the police.

It was when she used the word 'stalking' that something snapped inside me. She hadn't understood. It was as though Rory had rejected me, and so in a moment of madness, I destroyed the woman I loved. I found the message on my phone saying that the police wanted to speak to me again and I knew it was all over. I really can't bear the prospect of a life in prison, so it's better if I end it now.

I beg forgiveness of her family. And now death seems preferable to a life without freedom – and without Rory.

Gerry stayed silent for a few moments, trying to take it in.

'So let me get this right, Wes. Matt Harrod became obsessed with Susan because she was the spitting image of his dead partner, and when she rejected him, he lost it and killed her.'

'That's about it.' Wesley glanced up at the hanging body. 'Dr Stamoran and the team'll be here any moment. Let's take a look around.' He turned back to Gerry. 'And if I were you, I wouldn't mention to Rachel that Harrod got the wrong idea about the phone message she left.'

Gerry nodded and followed him out. The cat, Tacitus, was asleep on one of the beds upstairs, and they left him in peace. The latest of his nine lives would be disrupted soon enough. When they reached Harrod's bedroom, they found a framed photograph on the chest of drawers: Harrod with his arm around a blonde woman. Her resemblance to Susan was indeed remarkable, and Wesley saw how, in his grief, Harrod felt as though he'd found his beloved Aurora again. Susan's arrival must have seemed like a miracle. Although it was a miracle that only existed in his head.

When the pathologist and the search team arrived, Wesley and Gerry left them to it. They could no longer bear to be in that house of sorrow. Their investigation was over. But neither of them felt much like celebrating.

Extract from the
Tradmouth and District Echo

June 1921

TRAGEDY AT SERPENT'S POINT

Police have called off the search for Dr Aldus Claye, the tenant of Serpent's Point near Bereton. His wife says that he failed to return from his usual morning walk on Thursday. A shoe belonging to Dr Claye was found at the top of the cliff, where the ground showed signs of disturbance. According to the police, it is likely he ventured too near the edge and fell. The coastguard failed to find any trace of him, but they say the currents in the area are strong and it is easy for the unwary to be swept out to sea. The public are warned to exercise caution when walking in exposed locations.

45

Wesley went for a drink in the Tradmouth Arms with the team that evening. It was traditional when a case had been wrapped up. Drusilla Kramer had been telling the truth when she said she'd once been a nurse, and it was she who'd given Jan Bennett the sedative. Jan had been released from hospital after a check-up, but she was shaken by her ordeal, so her mother was coming down from up north to look after her. MacCaa and Kramer were in custody and the killer of Susan Brown had taken his own life, so the whole thing seemed to be wrapped up neatly. Although as Wesley sipped his pint, he found it hard to share his colleagues' elation.

He left the celebrations at the same time as Rachel, who'd been drinking fizzy water all evening. When he arrived home, he found Neil chatting animatedly to Pam in the living room.

Neil's greeting was enthusiastic, as though he'd barely noticed his friend's unusually subdued mood. Pam, however, saw the haunted look on her husband's face. Jan was safe and Neil's nighthawks were in custody, with most of the things they'd stolen now recovered. Things should be good. But she knew something wasn't right.

Wesley didn't feel he could tell them about finding Matt Harrod hanging from the ceiling in his kitchen, or about the man's obsessive and tragic desire for Susan to replace his lost love – a desire that had led to her death. Pam and Neil, like his colleagues at work, were in the mood to celebrate, and he knew that sharing what he'd witnessed that day would dampen everyone's spirits. He made the decision to say nothing, and he was relieved that Neil was in a talkative mood.

'I struck gold in the Roman Heritage Museum in Exeter. When I told the assistant curator about that curse tablet mentioning Beria Vilbia, it rang a bell with her, and she showed me a tombstone they've got in their storeroom. Of course the museum had no way of knowing where the Beria Vilbia named on the stone actually lived, but the curse places her in Bereton and the story on the tombstone fits perfectly with everything I've found – and those ancient bones in the tea chest.'

Pam poured Wesley a glass of wine. Neil's revelations were taking his mind off his day, and she was glad when she saw him begin to relax.

'I've made a copy of the inscription for you.' Neil took a sheet of paper from his pocket and began to read. '"I, Marcus Flavius Livius, merchant, died of grief when my beloved wife was carried off by one who coveted her greatly and ended her mortal life when he could not possess her. Beria Vilbia was a Briton and once a slave until I granted her liberty and built a villa for her in the land of her people. She was a good woman with many domestic virtues, and her faithfulness to me caused her death. May he who took her from me be cursed of the gods and know no peace for his wickedness."'

The words shook Wesley, bringing the memories of Matt Harrod's confession bubbling to the surface again. Neil carried on, oblivious to the stunned expression on his face.

'I think someone – we don't have a name, unfortunately – became obsessed with Beria Vilbia and killed her when she insisted on being faithful to her husband. Marcus Flavius Livius must have found her body and buried her near the villa, possibly so that she'd always be close to him. Then he put the curse on her murderer. At some point he must have returned to Isca Dumnoniorum and died there, because that's where his tombstone was found.'

'How's the dig progressing?' Wesley needed a distraction from murder and unrequited passion, and he suspected that a bit of archaeology talk would prove therapeutic.

'We've uncovered most of that mosaic since you last came to have a look. You haven't been far away, so I don't know why you haven't visited us more,' Neil added.

'I've been rather busy. And tomorrow we'll be moving the incident room – giving the good citizens of Bereton their church hall back – then we'll have to complete the paperwork for the CPS.'

'But you'll come to see what we've found? You as well, Pam. And the kids.'

Wesley had to smile at his friend's persistence. 'Try and stop me. I can't wait to see this mosaic of yours.'

'The Serpent. Vicious-looking thing. Wouldn't fancy that slithering across my living-room floor.' Neil looked down at Wesley's plain carpet as though he was trying to imagine it replaced with his discovery.

'It was probably the height of fashion in Roman times,' said Pam.

'Thanks for handing over the Mercury, by the way.' Neil raised a glass in Pam's direction.

'Well, we could hardly keep it, could we. Imagine the headline: "Detective inspector handles stolen goods". It belongs in a museum.'

'Too right.'

'What's going to happen to the site?' Wesley asked.

'I think it should be open to the public. But that's up to Nick Stanley, of course. It's his field. It was Nick's daughter and her mate who discovered the site in the first place, and Livy's very keen on the idea. She said she'd always wanted to be an archaeologist, until I told her there was no money in it.' A faraway look appeared in Neil's eyes. 'If Nick plays his cards right, he could charge entry and make a fortune. They say farmers have to diversify these days, don't they. But not all of them have the well-preserved foundations of a Roman villa in one of their fields.'

'Grey Grover sold that land to him, so I imagine he'll be annoyed when he finds out. Serpent's Point's a money pit, and that mosaic might have kept the likes of Crispin Joss away.'

'That's life,' said Neil. 'You win some, you lose some.'

Letter from Professor James Fredericks
to Mrs Clarabel Claye

September 1921

My dear Mrs Claye,

First allow me to express my sincere condolences on the untimely death of your husband. I always held Dr Claye in the greatest regard, and I am sorry for the delay in acknowledging the tragedy. I only returned from France yesterday, and I was distressed to be greeted with the dreadful news.

How tragic that the nature of his accident meant that his body was never recovered. That must add greatly to your grief. My thoughts and sympathies are with you at this saddest of times.

I understand from Fidelio Phipps that the high hopes your husband had of the excavation failed to come to fruition. It is often the case that the most promising sites yield nothing of interest. You will, of course, be sorry that Dr Claye's efforts will leave no lasting memorial to his work.

If there is anything I can do to aid you in the future, dear lady, please don't hesitate to contact me.

Once again, may I offer my most sincere condolences.

James Fredericks

Announcement in
The Times

July 1922

The marriage of Dr Fidelio Phipps of Oxford and
Mrs Clarabel Claye, widow of the late Dr Aldus
Claye of Devon, took place at St Cross Church,
Oxford, on Wednesday 5 July. The couple will reside
in Oxford.

46

A week later, Wesley stood beside his son, gazing down at the mosaic. The serpent had been cleaned up and the tiny tiles that formed its body stood out starkly against their creamy-white background. Its red forked tongue flicked out and its small, predatory eye stared up at them with disdain.

He could tell that Pam was still shaken by what happened to Jan, who was now recuperating under the care of her mother. Whether she would ever trust anyone again was open to question.

He himself was finding it hard to forget what had happened. He kept thinking of all the other victims of MacCaa and Kramer, who were only just coming to light in different parts of the country. He wasn't sure whether the true extent of the couple's crimes would ever be fully known, but Gerry said they should congratulate themselves on being the ones who put a stop to their deadly activities. However, when Wesley thought of the victims and their families, he found it hard to share the DCI's elation.

Fiona Crediton's mother had travelled down to Devon, insisting on viewing her daughter's remains. He'd wondered whether she realised that Fiona's body had long since rotted away in that disused mine, and that her last memory of her daughter would be a neatly laid-out set of bones. He'd left it to Rachel to say what she always said in those circumstances – that she'd see what she could do. He didn't ask her how things had gone at the mortuary. He didn't want to know.

Neil's voice distracted him from his dark thoughts.

'Looks as though Phipps and Clarabel buried Aldus Claye here with his discovery,' he said.

'Why didn't they just push him off a cliff?' Pam asked.

'There was the head wound. It would have been obvious to any competent doctor that it had been made by a mattock or a pickaxe. If they'd pushed him into the water and his body happened to be washed up somewhere, questions would have been asked. Much easier to bury him in the newly dug earth and let everyone believe the accident story.'

'No wonder they kept quiet about this site,' said Wesley, glad of the distraction.

'It must have really hurt Fidelio Phipps to keep all this to himself.' Neil looked down at the mosaic. 'The discovery would have been the pinnacle of his career. Made his reputation.'

'But he chose love instead,' said Pam. 'You say Phipps and Claye's widow got married?'

'Yes, and they went on to have three children. There are probably some descendants of theirs around who'd be interested in their story.'

Wesley turned to his friend. 'Phipps and Clarabel murdered her first husband, so maybe it's better if they don't learn the truth.'

Neil shrugged and bent down to stroke the dog on the end of the lead Michael was holding. The animal wagged its tail enthusiastically.

'How's Sherlock settling in?'

'Well,' said Wesley. 'Although Moriarty's not too pleased.'

'The kids have been nagging for a dog for ages,' said Pam. 'So when Wesley told me about that woman abandoning him in the park like that . . . ' She hesitated. 'He didn't know I went to the dogs' home to see about adopting him.'

'I admit it came as a surprise,' said Wesley, stroking the animal's head and receiving a look of adoration in return. At first he'd been afraid that taking on a dog associated in his mind with such terrible crimes might prove problematic, but then he told himself that none of it was Sherlock's fault. And the memories of what Drusilla Kramer and Terry MacCaa had done were bound to fade in time.

As they walked away, he turned his head to catch a last glimpse of the serpent. And he was sure he saw it wink.

Author's Note

Inspiration has been in rather short supply during lockdown, with research trips cancelled and opportunities for observing humanity cut to a minimum. However, the enforced isolation has given me more time to research into the past (which, luckily, is one of my favourite occupations).

For a long time I've been keen to include the discovery of Roman remains in one of Wesley Peterson's cases, but it's always been assumed that the Romans took little interest in the particular part of south-west England where my books are set. Most archaeological evidence suggests that they set up a legionary fortress in Exeter (or Isca Dumnoniorum) in the first century AD, but then, faced with the need to support military campaigning in Wales and the north, the majority of troops were withdrawn and the former fort became an administrative centre for the region.

Evidence has been found of military posts, signal stations and other Roman sites in north and east Devon, but other than that, it seems that the Romans regarded the county as a backwater. However, from time to time tantalising discoveries have been made: a fragment of a hypocaust at Exmouth, for example, and a bronze figure of Charon and Achilles at Sidmouth hint at buildings of some sophistication. A section of Roman road, along with a cemetery dating from the same period, has also been discovered at Ipplepen (heading roughly in the direction of my fictional villa), but even so, there is little evidence of a Roman presence around the South Hams. Although perhaps one day there will be a major discovery like the one I've described in this book. Archaeologists can dream!

During my research, I was excited to learn about curse tablets – typically thin sheets of lead incised with a scratched curse before being deposited in a temple, grave or other sacred place, such as a spring. Some have been found in the sacred springs at Aquae Sulis (modern-day Bath), and, being a crime writer, I couldn't resist introducing a curse into my plot. While I was planning *Serpent's Point*, I particularly enjoyed watching Mary Beard's fantastic TV series *Meet the Romans*, and I was fascinated to discover that Roman tombstones often reveal more about the people they commemorate than simple names and dates. They can include interesting information about the life of the deceased – and in some cases they even tell the story of how he or she died. The Roman Heritage Museum housing Marcus Flavius Livius's tombstone exists only in my imagination, but many Roman finds from Exeter can be viewed at the city's Royal Albert Memorial Museum and Art Gallery. I'm ashamed to say that I've forgotten much of the Latin I learned at school, but perhaps I'll give myself a refresher course so I can better understand these intriguing relics of the time when Rome ruled Britannia.

To move on to Wesley's modern-day mystery, over the years I've been writing I've been in the habit of keeping newspaper reports of interesting crimes for future reference. One case that caught my attention was that of a woman who vanished with her two children from south Devon in the 1970s. No trace of them was ever found, and at the time there was insufficient evidence to charge her husband with any crime. It wasn't until a quarter of a century later that a witness came forward with new evidence that allowed the police to re-arrest the man, who stood trial and was found guilty of murder, proving that without a body, it is very difficult for the police to obtain enough proof of foul play to obtain a conviction. Of course, although elements of this case provided the inspiration for *Serpent's Point,* the characters and details of the story are purely products of my imagination. Hundreds of people go missing every year, and the vast majority turn up safe and well. But inevitably a few might have met a tragic end, possibly at the hands of someone they trusted, just as in *Serpent's Point.*

On a more cheerful note, I'd like to thank my wonderful editor, Hannah Wann, and my agent, Euan Thorneycroft, as well as Beth Wright, my publicist, and everyone at Little, Brown who helps DI Wesley Peterson investigate all those terrible (fictional) murders in beautiful south Devon. Thanks also to the people of the South Hams, who are kind enough to tolerate their lovely landscape being used for murderous purposes. And I mustn't forget all the lovely booksellers and library staff who make sure my books are available to my readers.

Finally I'd like to say a big thank you to Cornell Stamoran for allowing his name to be used again for a very good cause (CLIC Sargent, caring for children with cancer).

**Discover Kate Ellis's next mystery in the
DI Wesley Peterson series**

November. With the tourist season well and truly over
in South Devon, DI Wesley Peterson is looking forward
to a quieter month in the CID. But when a man is shot
dead on Bonfire Night, he finds he has a disturbing
and complex murder case on his hands . . .

Read on for a sneak peek of *The Killing Place*

1

5 November

The woman in the sedan chair had been wearing a powdered wig and a fine gown of blue satin, low-necked and edged with yellowing lace. She could easily have been mistaken for the restless ghost who was said to inhabit the place. But Patrick North knew that she was no ghost. She was a corpse.

Patrick had never experienced real terror before. But this was the first time he'd ever come face to face with death.

He forced himself to keep moving, trying to ignore the sharp stitch in his side and the aching heaviness in his legs. He needed to reach safety and tell someone what he'd seen. But the woodland around him seemed endless, and as he ran, his trainers slipped on the damp brown foliage covering the ground. He could smell decay, the musty rot of dying things. An omen perhaps; a sign that his life was about to end.

He could hear explosions in the distance, loud as gunfire, and he saw faraway cascades of light brighten the sky. It was Bonfire Night, and not too far away, people were enjoying themselves, oblivious to his fear.

He stopped to catch his breath and listened. When the noise of the fireworks stopped, he could hear faint taunting laughter getting closer, as though his tormentor was confident of victory – however long it took.

Patrick took his phone from his pocket. There'd been no signal when he'd tried before, but now maybe ... But the thing was as dead as the leaves on the ground. Any chance of escape was fading fast.

He knew he was somewhere on the estate, but he wasn't sure where. All he knew was that if he didn't reach the road soon, he was a dead man. His pursuer was closing in on him, crashing through the undergrowth. Patrick flattened his body against a thick tree trunk. Perhaps if he kept very still ...

'Come out, come out, wherever you are. You can't get away. You might as well give up now.'

His tormentor's voice disturbed the crows in the tree-tops, and their raucous cries mocked him too, as though the birds were enjoying the game of cat and mouse happening below their nests. Then Patrick heard a twig snap nearby. Someone was creeping towards his chosen tree. This was it. Fight or flight. Life or death.

He broke cover, and when he twisted round, he saw his tormentor walking steadily towards him. He backed up, but found his way blocked by a thick tree trunk.

'Not much good at this, are you?' The taunting voice sounded completely calm as Patrick saw the rifle pointing straight at his chest.

Instinctively he raised both his hands, something he'd seen people do in films, but the eyes staring at him were cold and pitiless, as though this was nothing – just a game to pass the time.

Patrick had always thought himself too young to imagine how he'd face death when the time came. But to his surprise, he felt numb and detached, as though he was in the middle of a nightmare, and he'd soon wake and find everything as it should be.

He closed his eyes. A few seconds later, he was lying on the ground. Dead.

The Killing Place **is coming in August 2023.**
Available now to pre-order.